# *Shattered Vows*

## NEW CASTLE
## BOOK THREE

## LYDIA MICHAELS

**Lydia Michaels**

Romantic Suspense
SHATTERED VOWS
3rd Edition Copyright © 2023 Lydia Michaels
2nd Edition Copyright © 2018 Lydia Michaels
Cover Design copyrighted © 2023 by Lydia Michaels
Previously titled Something Borrowed

# DISCLAIMER

This romantic suspense novel contains graphic scenes of violence, which may not be suitable for sensitive audiences.

For more details, please visit

https://lydiamichaelsbooks.com/content-warnings/

Domestic violence is a real issue. The author wished to portray the truth of such circumstances as realistically as possible. Some scenes may be unsettling for sensitive readers.

In the United States, 1 in 3 adult women (35.6%) have experienced rape, severe violence and/or stalking by an intimate partner. These numbers do not take into consideration the cases that go unreported.

**If you are in an abusive situation and need a way out, the National Domestic Violence Hotline can help you develop a safety plan to escape and provide legal counsel. www.thehotline.org 1-800-799-7233**

*For Lori.*
*You are, and will always be, a part of me.*
*Thanks for all the sprinkles, root beer, and lipstick*
*kisses.*
*I love you.*

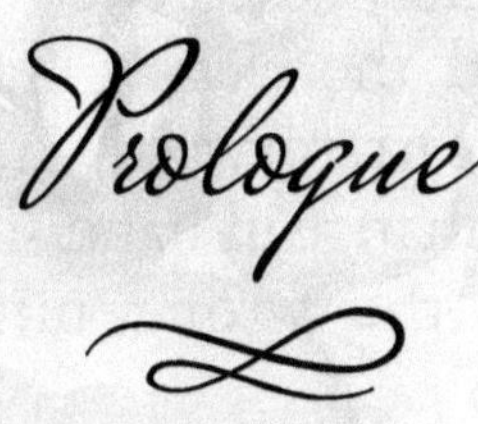

# Prologue

BALTIMORE, *Maryland*

"Mommy, can I have some candy?"

Chloe Hunt watched the last of her items roll down the belt toward the clerk at the grocery checkout, her eyes following the pricey bag of pine nuts as she distractedly wiped her youngest son's nose. "Not today, Dayton."

Her three-year-old bounced in the cart. "Please! I'll draw you a picture."

Mattie, her one-year-old, babbled and blew raspberries into the air as she moved the cart forward and opened her purse. "I'd love a picture, but no candy today. It's not on the list."

"Candy! Candy! Candy! Please, please, please..."

Mattie's glassy blue stare followed her, anxiety over justifications for the children's cold medicine already running through her mind. Over the counter was always cheaper than a prescription and trip to the pediatrician but, again, it wasn't on the list.

"That'll be ninety-seven twelve."

Chloe handed the clerk a hundred dollar bill and pushed the cart forward. According to plan, once she had the change in hand she tsked. "Oh, I'm sorry. These are the wrong nuts. Can I return them?"

Her heart hitched behind her ribs as the cash register drawer opened again.

"Wow, that's a lot of money for a little bag of nuts," the young clerk commented as she counted out the fifteen dollars and change.

*Exactly.*

She pressed the money into her palm. Chloe tucked it carefully in her pocket and folded the original receipt into her wallet and lifted the last few bags into the cart. Mattie would likely fall asleep before the car left the lot. She'd give him a dose of the cold medicine once they got to the car.

As she pulled the Volvo into their garage, her gaze flashed to the clock—just under two hours until he came home.

"Don't wake your brother, Dayton. Go to the couch and I'll put on *Thomas the Tank* as soon as I lay Mattie down."

With the boys situated and the groceries carried in, she caught her breath and got to work. She laid the receipt on the counter where Marcus always looked to review what she'd spent. To think, there was once a time when she'd lived independently, attending college, paying her own bills, organizing her own schedule... But her dreams of ever becoming a therapist and helping others were on hold until she figured out a way to help herself.

Her gaze again went to the clock as she silently pulled down the flour canister, keeping her ears open for her husband's possible early arrival. Moving to the sink, she set the canister in the basin and sifted the white powder into a large bowl. There, buried on the bottom, was her lifeline. Three hundred and sixty-two dollars, and a white-coated plastic bag of almost ten dollars in change.

Her hands trembled as she shook out the money, counting it yet again, making sure nothing was missing and adding the newest addition. Loading the bills back into the canister, she carefully scooped the flour back on top, rinsing the sink and carefully cleaning the counter. Even a speck of powder could throw her husband into a rage.

With Dayton now napping, she took the stairs quietly, rushing to the master bedroom. The room was pristine, exactly as Marcus preferred it. She walked the perimeter of the room so as not to interrupt the vacuum tracks and went to the back of the walk-in closet.

Last on the hooks was an old designer purse, seemingly empty and unused for some time. She had a plan and this time it was a good one, one even he couldn't figure out. Old injuries tightened her fingers at the thought of getting caught again. There could be no messing up or he might actually cut her fingers off this time. Her attention skated to the safe in the wall and she shivered. He had all the money a man could need sitting just four feet away. But that wasn't hers to touch. If she even tried to figure out the code an alarm would go off and he'd be home in minutes. But she knew what he kept in there. He loved opening it and taunting her, polishing his gun and loading it, taking an excruciatingly long time before removing the bullets and locking it back in the safe. She had to get out of here.

Pulling the purse off the hook, she examined the seams and stitching, testing the secret pocket she'd sewn. She should probably cash in some of her ones for some larger bills to save space. She fumbled to replace all the bags exactly as they were and tiptoed out of the room. At the foot of the stairs, she glanced out the window.

Her mind returned to the last time he'd played with his gun, flaunted it like a boy without rules or fears, a rotten brat who loved to terrorize those beneath him, watch them cower and scurry like irrelevant insects under a burning magnifying glass. Just the thought of his deranged laugh caused a cold sweat to break over her skin.

*The cold metal teased over her trembling lips. "Open your fucking mouth, Chloe."*

*"Marcus..." Tears welled in her eyes as she turned her face toward the pillows, his fingers cutting into her jaw as he smiled like a crazed lunatic above her. "Please..."*

*His grip tightened, the hard tip of the handgun grazing her temple. "This time, I want you to suck my dick like you mean it. If you can't, we'll practice with the gun."*

Her mind slammed away the memory, her hands shaking as if tuning out his remembered words took a chunk of physical strength. *Don't think about that now.*

The groceries were put away in a mad dash, leaving her only a few minutes to touch up her appearance and do one last inspection of the house. She doused a paper towel with lemon cleaner, knowing the scent gave the impression of a busy day that only just concluded. She wiped the banister and foyer tables and then went to wake her sons.

"Dayton." She gently shook her oldest. "Come on, sweetie. Time to get up. Daddy's going to be home soon. Go potty and comb your hair."

"I don't wanna." He curled back into the couch pillows.

"Come on, honey. You have to clean yourself up." She shut off the television, resetting the cable box so it wouldn't show the cartoon channel as last watched and scooped Dayton off the couch. Bending, she fluffed the pillows back into place. "Let's go wake up, Mattie."

By the time the garage rattled, dinner was ready and both boys were clean. Bracing her hands on the lip of the counter, she drew in a fortifying breath. The door opened and she stood straight, shoulders back, and smiled. "Welcome home."

He placed the mail on the counter and lifted the grocery receipt. "Good day?"

"Yes, but Mattie's getting a cold."

Her husband glanced at his son who smiled back, his grin forming around the thumb in his mouth. Marcus went to the highchair and removed his hand. "No thumb sucking." His inspecting gaze turned to Dayton. "How was your day?"

"I'm drawing a train, Daddy."

Marcus smiled, enough to appease their son, but she recognized the insincerity in his eyes. He had wanted sons so desperately, yet never showed any true interest in their little worlds. Like a spoiled child, her husband wanted her focus to solely revolve around his needs alone and there was no masking his resentment that intensified every time the boys' needs took precedence over his.

"What is this?"

Her shoulders knotted as he lifted the change from the counter—short a few dollars. "I had to pick up cold medicine for Mattie. It's on there."

He examined the receipt with a more critical eye. "What's for dinner?"

"Pasta with a light pesto sauce, fresh baked bread, and the salad you like." Normal conversation often brought unpredictable consequences.

He had the outward charm and magnetism of a favored politician but saved none of those efforts for them. At home, he was just mean Marcus, a man with wafer-thin patience and an iron fist. Polished banisters and pristine holiday cards distracted outsiders from the blemishes of reality, camouflaging the misery so plain to see if only one took the time to look beyond the well-manicured facade. But how would they? They, too, were props meant to amuse her husband, the audience that applauded his success, the voices that praised his beautiful family, and the hands that stroked his ego.

Dinner was a quiet affair laced with unspoken tension. It wouldn't be long. Her mind had only the echo of her adult thoughts to keep her sane, but even that teetering balance had been slipping. She was holding on by a thread.

The following morning started with a ritual of humiliation. "Read it. What does it say?"

Her body shook as she stared down at the scale, Marcus towering over her, ridiculing her for the weight she'd failed to lose since having Mattie almost a year ago.

"I'm trying—"

He scoffed and pivoted away in disgust. "Try harder. I want you on a vegetable diet for the next week. This has gone on long enough."

She was by no means thin, but she also wasn't fat. She was five-foot-ten with appropriate curves for a woman of her height. Initially, Marcus adored her figure—or so he pretended.

When she set the table for breakfast he removed her plate from the table. "You'll have tea."

She grit her teeth. Coffee was a necessity. He kept her on a rigorous schedule and she'd be dead on her feet by noon if she didn't have caffeine. But she didn't argue. He'd be gone soon and she'd make a fresh pot once he left.

Marcus continued to hover as she did the dishes after breakfast. Being as accommodating as possible, making him his favorite eggs and refilling his coffee so it never had a chance to cool, only curbed his chances for an outburst. He'd been angling for a fight since waking that morning.

"Why are you using that cheap, runny dish soap? It'll take you twice as long to do a simple task like washing a plate," he snapped.

"It's eco-friendly—better for the environment."

He snatched the bottle off the counter. "It's a scam. Look how much you're using. Use your head, Chloe. Or do I have to make every decision around here?" He threw the bottle into the sink, an excessive amount of liquid spilling into the basin.

The subtle snap of her tongue to the roof of her mouth was a thoughtless slip, but enough to stop him in his tracks.

"Problem?"

Her breath held as she shook her head.

He crowded closer, his voice scraping over her nerves like a rusty blade. "If you have something to say, say it."

"It's fine. You're right. I'll go back to the other brand." Her mind was split between his volatile mood and the silent presence of her sons at the table behind them.

"Pick it up."

Setting the sponge down, her trembling hand reached for the bottle of green detergent.

Marcus twisted his fingers in the back of her shirt, tightening the material and slowing her progress. "Next time I hear you snap your tongue at me, your mouth will be sore for days. Understand?"

"Yes."

"Wash the dishes."

The sponge lacked suds as she gave it a squeeze. Too afraid to drive his point home, she wiped the plate without soap. But Marcus saw what she was doing.

"Does that look clean to you? Wash it right!" His hand snapped out and green detergent spewed over the dish, spraying onto her shirt.

She gasped, her breath provoking a clipped snick against her teeth, sounding horribly familiar. The air stilled. "I didn't mean to—"

The crack of his palm across her mouth rattled her head as pain exploded through her jaw and tears stung her eyes.

"*What did I say about talking back?* You have something to say now? Huh? Say it again. I dare you."

"I'm ... sorry."

His eyes narrowed as he glared at her. She glanced at the boys. Dayton's head was down but Mattie, who didn't know what was happening, watched them.

"Marcus, please, the boys..."

He seethed and shoved away. Without saying goodbye to the boys, he thrust his arms into his coat and barked, "Clean yourself up. You look like a fat slob."

A door slammed a moment later, followed by the rumble of the garage door and the sound of his car engine speeding away from the house.

She shut off the water. "You boys finish your breakfast. I'll be back down in a few minutes."

As she pulled on a clean shirt she turned and found Dayton watching her, his big, doe eyes curious and sad.

"Hey, kiddo. Is Mattie done eating?" Her false cheer sounded incredibly transparent to her ears. Dayton wasn't immune to his father's outbursts.

His lip quivered, as he timidly stood in the doorway of her bedroom looking so small and fragile. "Why did Daddy do that?"

Unable to explain their father's behavior, she crouched to his height and deflected, "How about we go to the library today?"

But, once in the car, Chloe grew more and more angry about the way her husband treated her in front of their children. At the library, holding Mattie on her hip and distracting Dayton with a book, she used the pay phone to call the only person in the world she could trust.

"Hello?"

"Aunt Regina?"

Regina Wolfe, Marcus's estranged aunt, was one of the only friends she had left in this world. The older woman's sigh caused static on the line. "How bad, sweetie?"

She gave a quick summary of the recent incidents with Marcus, but Regina had enough experience with the men in that family to understand it was so much more than soap and a fat lip.

"If you wait until he really explodes, he'll be watching more closely. How much money have you saved?"

Regina had been married to Marcus's Uncle Maxwell on his father's side. Marcus and his uncle had more in common than their genes and portfolios. They shared a penchant for beating women. After Maxwell died, she reverted to her maiden name and cut all ties to the Hunts.

Regina was a godsend. She saw through her nephew's façade and knew he wouldn't be an easy man to mislead. Regina had been helping Chloe plan an escape since the day Marcus induced her labor with Mattie by shoving her into a dresser.

Thank God she'd been only two weeks ahead of her due date and the baby hadn't been hurt.

"You'll have to move fast, Chloe. Don't worry about clothes. Dress in layers and I'll have stuff for the boys. We'll take care of your needs when you get here." She believed her, recalling promises that Regina would not only feed and shelter her but clothe them and even offer her name—Wolfe—if it made them safer.

Her stomach rolled, thinking back to the last time she tried to run and how vicious Marcus had been when he caught her. "I can't mess this up. If he catches me..."

"Hush. You aren't alone. Not yet, anyway. You need to focus and keep moving. Do you have the address I gave you?"

"Yes."

"Don't put it in your phone. I don't understand technology enough to know what can be tracked. You get a map from the library and don't stop to ask directions along the way. Any trouble, use a pay-phone and call me. It's a straight shoot down I-95 until you reach the exit."

"Okay." It was happening. He was getting worse and the boys were no longer immune. She couldn't stand another day under his roof and Regina was right. If he had one of his worst episodes he'd be watching her like a hawk. The time to move was now. She blew out a tense breath. "I'll need an hour."

"I'll be waiting. Be safe."

The phone clattered into the receiver, shaking

with the tremor running through her arm. "Dayton, come on. We have to go."

When they reached the house she sat Mattie on the carpet and turned on the television. "Keep an eye on your brother."

"What about lunch?"

"We're going for a car ride. I'm going to pack something for along the way."

Rushing through the house, she quickly stuffed diapers into a bag for Mattie, and a few of their favorite toys and a change of clothes. Her heart jackhammered as she dumped the flour into the sink and scrambled to shake clean her money. Change slid down the drain but she caught most of it. White dust coated her hands as she rinsed the sink clean, her eyes narrowing at the sight of the soap.

She made a sandwich for Dayton and packed several snacks in a bag and then raced upstairs. She rummaged through drawers, only selecting essentials that could remain hidden in her purse. Nothing promised this would be a success, so she had to plan for any excuse, should she get caught. She folded the wad of money into the secret pocket and stitched it shut. The nearly ten dollars in loose change would have to last her until she knew she was safe.

She had no items of value aside from her wedding ring and diamond earrings. If she ran out of money, they would be a good safety net.

Dressing in layers, like Regina said, she looked as if she was only planning for inclement weather and perhaps a day at the park. It had to look like that in case this didn't work and he caught them.

"Okay, boys, TV off. Mattie, come here so I can change your diaper."

"Where are we going?" Dayton asked.

"It's a surprise." She couldn't risk telling them in case this didn't work out.

Holding her purse, the diaper bag, and Mattie on her hip, she grasped Dayton's hand and scanned the foyer one last time. Her eyes prickled with the urge to cry as fear and hope battled in her stomach. This was it. This *had to be* it.

Her chest hurt as she backed away from the house. She didn't care about leaving her home or her Williams Sonoma cookware, but it was petrifying to think she'd soon be parting from her boys. Leaving them was her only option. It was the safest way to throw Marcus off their trail, and chances were, he'd know something was up within an hour.

She had no immediate family aside from her children and Marcus. Her parents died in an automobile accident eight years ago, a vulnerable and stupid time in her life when she needed someone to tell her everything would be okay. Sometimes monsters can say the right things—nice things—and appear to be angels. But they're still monsters in the end.

They'd been happy during those early years. She'd finished her master's degree in psychology and started on her doctorate by the time they were married. Eventually, her career was pushed aside to start a family, but she didn't mind because she'd always wanted children. Life was perfect—a beautiful suburban home, two nice cars, a husband that worked hard enough to support the life they wanted, and a baby on the way. Then everything changed.

"Mom, can I have some snacks now?" Dayton called from his car seat.

Chloe took the exit to I-95, heading south toward the Carolinas. Reaching into the diaper bag, she handed Dayton a sandwich and a cup of cereal for his brother.

She was careful to follow the speed limit, but her foot weighed heavily on the gas. When she saw the first sign for North Carolina, her stomach started to cramp. They were almost out of Virginia when her phone buzzed.

*Marcus.*

He was attuned to every minute of her day and checked in often to make sure she was doing exactly what he wanted done. Some nights he'd lead her through the house, inspecting rooms and her domestic performance, an immaculate white handkerchief in hand. If she'd missed something, she'd pay. If she did a good job, more chores would be added. There was always a consequence and never a reward.

Jaw locked, she seethed behind the wheel. No. More. Consequences.

She'd lost the person she'd once been, become a woman she didn't respect or recognize. This sniveling wife wasn't who she was supposed to be. Her background in psychology was enough to diagnose her husband as a sociopath. But if she labeled him it was only fair to label herself, and she despised the idea of identifying her once independent self as a victim.

"Mom, where should I put the trash?"

"Just leave it on the seat for now."

She was done. She was never going back. This

time it had to work. She had to stop thinking she'd get caught and start visualizing her success. She'd be happy again. Free.

The car followed the exit and she rolled down the window. Her vibrating phone flashed with another missed call. No more. Hanging her arm over the edge of the door, the wind pulled at her fist gripping the phone. Her fingers let go and her eyes watched the mirror as the phone hit the asphalt and shattered. There was no turning back now.

*Born to Run* by Bruce Springsteen played on the radio the second she crossed the state line. She wasn't superstitious, but it had to be a sign. Her breath trembled in her chest as her vision blurred and she felt the first curve of a genuine smile tighten her lips. This was it. It was really happening.

Regina waited in the parking lot of a Walmart. The poor woman had taken a flight and rented a car to meet them there in time. She handed Chloe a bag and didn't waste time on formality.

"You take this somewhere with no cameras and use it before you head north again, you hear?"

Chloe nodded, her teetering fear chipping away at the euphoria that guided her this far. She'd never been apart from her boys and letting them go, even for a short while, seemed a gamble she might not survive.

"Mattie has a little bit of a cold, but there's medicine in his bag. He's due for more in an hour."

Regina opened the back door of the rental. "You have everything you need out of your car?"

Chloe nodded, holding her bag and car keys. She kissed her boys, trying not to cry in front of them. "You be good for Aunt Regina. Mommy will be right behind you."

"Why aren't you coming with us?"

"Because I have to take care of some things, baby. I'll get there a few days after you."

"Where?"

Anxious to leave, but dreading her final good-bye, she kissed Dayton's cheek again. "A magical place called Pennsylvania. Wait until you see it. They have mountains and snow and playgrounds and everything you like. You're going to love it."

"Is Daddy coming?"

"We'll see." She swallowed. "You better get moving so you don't miss the fun. I love you."

His little arms squeezed tight and she sniffled back her tears. She pressed a kiss into Mattie's pudgy cheek. "Love you, monkey."

Thank God Regina was there because she couldn't find the strength to step away. "Someone told me you boys like trains. If you peek in that bag there you'll find a surprise."

Dayton nudged open the bag and gasped. "Thomas! Mom, it's Thomas!"

Chloe stood and faced Regina. "I can't thank you enough—"

"Thank me when we know it's over. For now, you have to go. The bus will be here in a few minutes." She hugged her tight. "Don't forget the bag."

Chloe watched them pull away, a sense of isolation stealing over her so precisely, she questioned if she'd made the wrong choice. Peeking into the bag, she found a box of auburn hair dye. The woman on the package looked so happy.

Her head lifted as the rumble of a bus approached. She drew in a deep breath and tucked the dye into her purse. Looking back at the Volvo, she gave a shaky smile and dropped the keys on the pavement. She had a bus to catch.

～

This couldn't be happening. Sitting on the public restroom floor of the METRO Subway, Chloe rifled through her bag. Her fingers pierced the hole in the designer fabric, grasping nothing but air. Nausea skated through her stomach, her skin clammy. She emptied the contents of her purse. Cosmetics rolled across the filthy ground as she searched for her money. She squeezed her eyes shut as the urge to vomit swept through her. Gone, it was all gone.

In a city like Baltimore where streets, alleys, and underground railways overlapped thicker than a thatched roof, there would be no retracing her steps. And if she did, the money she'd dropped would already been stolen.

"No..." She crumpled the deflated fabric and flung the useless purse at the stall door.

Her hands slapped the wall, the flat tile surface stinging her palms. What was she going to do? She'd spent days on the road, traveling far south to throw Marcus off her trail only to serpentine her way back north to her goal. But over two hundred miles still separated her from her boys and she had nothing left.

Desperation seeped from her pores. Sifting through her scattered belongings, she found her travel sewing kit. Unable to think beyond the simple task of guiding the needle and thread along the tattered seam, she focused on mending the bag but her relentless trembling made the job almost impossible.

A distant toilet flushed, feet shuffled, and water ran, as strangers moved about the restroom, ignorant to her turmoil. The pull and clunk of paper towels dispensing from the box on the wall punctuated each person's exit. Normal—nothing like the jagged chaos living in her head.

She bit down on the thread and carefully tucked the needle back into the sewing kit. It was irrelevant how she got to this point. What mattered, the only resounding thought she had, was reaching her children.

She slowly placed her items back into her newly mended bag. Halfway there and only enough money for one phone call and maybe a vending machine dinner.

She fought the urge to cry as she forced herself off the floor. She would not give up. She would not go back. She'd do whatever was necessary to reach her boys and they were going to live the happy life they deserved. Somehow she'd make it to them. She pulled back her shoulders and went to find the nearest payphone.

~

Trenton Cole checked his watch again. What was she doing? Chloe Hunt had been in the subway bathroom for almost an hour. Had she fallen asleep? He wouldn't be surprised. After tailing her for several days, her journey had even taken a toll on him. This job would have been wrapped up if he'd known where the kids were, but she'd been traveling alone—likely making a roundabout way to the children he needed to return.

Marcus Hunt, a man he'd yet to meet in person, had contacted him soon after growing impatient with the police search for his wife and kids. He'd been hard pressed to calm his impatience, claiming his unstable wife had taken off with his two boys, Dayton and Matthew.

Trent was a man of simple means, working a myriad of jobs revolving around security. Retrieving a human paid a hefty sum and could sustain him for quite some time. Returning three missing people could tide him over for half a year and Hunt was prepared to pay him handsomely.

While playing bounty hunter was an exhausting pain in the ass, it was also financially liberating once the job was done. The astronomical sum of money Hunt offered for the return of his wife and children was impossible to turn down. Sure, Trent felt sorry for the man who worried for the safety of his sons, but he was mostly motivated by the payout.

He secured fifty-thousand up front to more than cover the job's expenses. Once the money was wired to his account, it was go time and off to the Carolinas he went. But even with such a high bounty, the pace of this specific runner was excruciating.

She'd made her way to the hilly coasts of the Carolina's—where Trent discovered her abandoned Volvo—and no traces of her or her children. After asking around, he discovered she'd taken a bus west then headed north again—without the children. It was as if they vanished into thin air or never existed at all, but she'd lead him back to the little ones. He just had to be patient.

She'd slept on buses, in fleabag motels, or standing up against walls in narrow alleyways—ripe for the pickin', but she was no good to him without the two boys. Her journey showed in her wrinkled clothes and ratty appearance. Like most runaways, she'd changed her hair from blonde to brown, but by her pictures, her face was pretty enough to pull off any color—when clean. The longer this merry chase continued the rougher she looked.

Hunt claimed his wife was unbalanced and in need of psychiatric attention. Trent's personal observations hinted this woman was not so much delusional and unstable as she was driven and scared. As much as she seemed to be running toward her children, she also appeared to be running away from something. But that wasn't his problem. A hunter that wasted time on the feelings of his prey often failed to take down the target. He never hesitated and he always finished the job. The perfect opportunity would come and he'd get the three of them back where they belonged and have himself a nice, long, *needed* vacation.

The door to the restroom opened and she finally emerged. Her face was clean of the grime from traveling and her shoulders were set. He threw his cup of coffee in the overflowing mound that was the subway's trash receptacle and pushed off the wall.

She stopped at a bank of pay phones. Her wrinkled clothing was smeared with mud and her hair was limp and lifeless, yet she'd taken the time to apply lipstick to her small, worried mouth—strange. Trembling hands reached for the receiver of the telephone, but hesitated, dropping to her side. He eased closer, wanting to catch the area code.

She took a steadying breath and reached for the phone again, this time pulling it toward her ear. Her dainty fingers with chipped, ruby nails deliberately traveled over the buttons.

*Six one zero. Pennsylvania. Bingo*

Her hand blocked the rest of the phone number, but he caught the area code. Standing by a cool stone pillar, he listened.

"Regina?"

He made a mental note to mention the name to Hunt. He said she didn't have family, but maybe this was a girlfriend from college or someone from her past.

"No, I'm okay." Her head shook wearily. "Actually, I'm not okay."

She turned to the tracks, doing a brief scan of her surroundings. It was a nervous twitch. He lowered his gaze to his phone and watched her through the reflection of a glass partition, noting the way her unsteady fingers seemed to brush a tear from her cheek.

"My money's gone. I lost it all. There was a hole in my bag. I'm using my last dollar to call you." She listened for a few seconds. "No, I won't call him. There's no going back now. If he ever finds me he'd beat me within a breath of my life. I'll just have to... I'll figure something out. How are the boys?"

Trent's shoulders tensed at her words, so belied by her expression when a smile trembled to her lips. Unstable? Or was it the mention of her sons that pushed that grin? Either way, the expression didn't hold. She had to be exhausted. Maybe he could use her desperation against her, offer her a ride and convince her—as an uninvolved outsider—that getting back to Virginia was best. How kind of him to be willing to drive her both ways.

His mind already worked over reasons why he'd be heading to Pennsylvania only to shoot back south again. Usually, when people were this rundown their logic took a hit, so he shouldn't need too solid of an explanation. He just needed to make her believe he was on her side—without his height and bulk working against him.

Just under seven feet, cut muscle defined even through his clothes, he wasn't exactly screaming, *Hey, little girl, you'll be safe with me.* The scar on his face and tattoos on his arms didn't help either. Luckily his clothes hid a good amount of his markings. And as a generally laid back guy, he'd mastered the gentle-giant thing. But even the gentlest giant could terrify a scared kitten. It wouldn't be easy getting her to trust him, so he'd have to play on her desperation.

"Make sure Dayton's taking his vitamins. If he gives you a hard time, try the pink Flintstones. He likes them best. And if Mattie's teeth are bothering him, there's some *Oragel* in the inner pocket of the diaper bag. Just rub a little on his gums every few hours. How's his cold?"

He frowned at her concern, so selfless for a

woman in her situation—out of money and far from the end of her journey. What drove her? Fear? Vengeance?

Again he chastised himself for being so curious about the irrelevant facts. This was a kidnapping case. She stole two innocent children and their father wanted to find them. No parent, no matter what the situation, had a right to flee with the children.

There were ways to legally exit a marriage and this wasn't it. She was breaking the law and he was hired to return a man's children. Just because she was the mother didn't give her the right to steal another man's kids. End of story. He couldn't waste time in the gray areas. The law was black and white and his work insisted he abide it.

This was a job. All feelings needed to take a backseat so he could get paid and get back to his own life.

Those boys were definitely with this Regina person. Finally, he was making progress. But, again, her concerns didn't seem to be the concerns of an unstable mother. As a matter of fact, her comments were rather selfless for a woman who lived on nothing but faucet water and vending machine food for several days. Something wasn't adding up and it pissed him off that he wanted all the pieces of the puzzle.

She hung up the phone and pressed her forehead to the filthy metal plate covering the wall. Her shoulders shook, as if from the force of unbearable grief. Her words replayed in his mind and he shoved his sympathy away. He had a job to do and his method had never failed him. This wasn't emotional. It was business.

Schooling his expression, he took a step toward her. She was a paycheck. That was all. Her personal problems were none of his concern. But damn it, why did she have to cry? This was why he needed to get back into security and out of the bounty hunting business. It was fucking draining.

He slowly approached, not wanting to alarm her by his size and presence, which often caught women off guard no matter how calm his mannerisms. He waited for her to notice him. When she didn't, he cleared his throat.

"Excuse me, ma'am, are you all right?"

She turned and clutched her purse tight to her chest, her back pressing into the payphone. Shit. So much for making a good first impression.

"I'm sorry. I didn't mean to startle you. It's just, you look like you could use some help. Are you stranded? I'm heading to Pennsylvania and would be more than happy to give you a lift if you're heading in that direction. My name's Trenton Cole."

He held out his hand in introduction but she didn't move to touch it. Her brown eyes formed big circles. He dropped his arm to his side.

"Do you need help, ma'am?"

Squaring her shoulders, she lifted her chin, hiding away any signs of fear with an off-putting practiced ease. "I need money." She twisted a knob of a diamond ring off her finger and held it out. "I have this I can sell you."

He frowned and she huffed, her hands moving

to her ears and plucking off two diamond studs. Opening her palm, she again held the stones out to him. "What will you give me for these? They're platinum and the diamonds are real."

Any normal person would take the jewelry, but he'd rather get paid for a job well done. "I'm sorry. I don't have that kind of money on me—"

"I'll take whatever you can spare. You surely have twenty dollars on you. I need to get to my children and I lost the last of my money."

"I can't take your jewelry, miss. I have a car. I could offer you a ride, but I won't take your jewelry."

"The last man who offered me a ride required a payment I couldn't abide. He dumped me on the side of the road when I refused to give him what he wanted in exchange. I'd rather pay for my transportation with cash."

"I don't need any payment. I just don't like seeing a woman upset and alone. I want to help you."

Her eyes narrowed. "No man expects nothing for something. There's always a cost."

"I give you my word I only want to take you where you need to go, to your children."

Skepticism danced in her untrusting eyes. "Why are you going to Pennsylvania?"

"I live there. I'm only in Maryland on business." He just needed to get her in his truck. He could figure out the rest later.

"What is it you do—Mr. Cole, was it?"

"I'm in security."

Her gazed traced down his body and remained

still for her inspection. There was no hiding his frame under his gray thermal shirt, so he opened his palms in a gesture he hoped translated to non-threatening.

"Maybe this will help." He reached for his wallet and removed a photograph. "These are my sisters and their children. I'm a good man, miss. I've never been arrested and I got a truck outside with an empty seat for anyone that needs it. I can't, in good conscience, leave you abandoned here." He held up a Pennsylvania driver's license. "That's my name and address." He smiled awkwardly, mimicking the staged smile on his ID.

Her gaze jerked to the cash in his wallet. "Then take my ring and give me some money so I can be on my way."

He considered her for a minute. "And what happens when the money runs out? I'd spend the rest of my life wondering what happened to the woman I found crying in the subway. How about this... You keep your ring, as I'm sure your husband would wonder what happened to it, and I'll give you thirty dollars plus a ride to your children."

"I don't have a husband. The ring means nothing to me."

But she didn't seem as eager to give away the earrings. Odd, since they weren't as nice. Pinching thirty dollars between his fingers, he glanced at his watch and folded his wallet, into his pocket. "No more trains are running to Pennsylvania tonight. This isn't enough for a motel in this area. Let me help you. What part of Pennsylvania are you heading to?"

She hesitated. "New Castle."

Perfect. He was familiar with the area. "I could get you to your children in a few hours."

She noticeably processed that information and he felt her resistance weakening, so he pushed his tempting offer.

"By car, you could see them tonight."

Her hands lowered, fisting the jewels in her palm. He'd strangle his sisters if they ever accepted a ride from a stranger in a subway. It was good sense to say no. But there was something else in her rejection. Something that told him this woman didn't trust *anyone.*

"I have a cell phone. You can hold it the entire way and call 911 if at any time you feel threatened."

Her mouth twisted. "Those numbers only save people who actually get through. If you wanted to hurt me that phone wouldn't be enough to stop you."

There was a sad sort of wisdom in her eyes, something that told him she knew this from experience, something that, again, complicated his job. "I just want to get you home."

The words might have registered as reassurance, but he was repeating his objective so he could remind himself what he was there to do. Get her home and get paid.

But he also wasn't a bad guy, so he added, "I have no intention of hurting you, miss."

Exhaling, she wedged the ring back on her finger and clasped the diamonds to her ears. "I'd be very grateful for your help."

"My truck's parked in the garage across the street."

She didn't walk beside him. Rather, she stuck about two paces behind, which was fine if it made her feel safer. They rode in silence. After days of traveling by bus and on foot, it seemed impossible for her to hold a rigid pose after the first ten miles. As she relaxed so did he.

He figured he should start working on the next step of his plan—building her trust. "Mind if I ask what you were doing in Maryland when your kids are all the way in Pennsylvania?"

Her answer was slow, following another long appraisal of him. "They're staying with a relative until I can reach them."

Not true. She had no living relatives according to her husband. What other lies would she tell? "You got girls or boys?"

"Boys."

A point for honesty. "Older? Boys can be a handful." He laughed. "But my sisters were no joke growing up. I guess it depends on each kid."

"Do you have children of your own?"

The more he got her to open up the more she'd let down her guard. "Nope. No kids for me. But I'm the favorite uncle. Why not travel together?"

"We needed to move quickly and I could travel faster without them."

His brow pinched as another unsettling comment joined the others he'd pushed away. He kept it light, purposefully ignoring her implication that she might be *escaping*. "Seems to me, for as fast as you say you can travel, they beat 'cha there."

She responded to his teasing with cold realism. "I didn't have a choice. I had to take a longer route."

Making light of things wasn't winning him any points. He switched up his indifference to concern. Perhaps she'd be more responsive to protectiveness. "You running from someone, ma'am?"

Again, she appraised him, her words tumbling out with a bit of force. "I'm going after the life I deserve. I prefer to think of it as running toward a happy future—for myself and my children."

Though she was guarded, Trenton was shocked how easily she gave up telling details. Although she lied about not having a husband, she seemed to offer genuinely honest answers about her situation when she didn't dodge his questions altogether. But that sort of information would make no difference in the end.

"You said you don't have a husband. Is that because you aren't married or because you don't want to be married anymore?"

When she didn't answer right away, he glanced her way. She was staring at him, eyes wide. Afraid he might've ruined their fragile rapport he quickly apologized. "I'm sorry. That's none of my business."

They sat in silence for several minutes and he cursed himself for getting too familiar too fast. He was tired. Otherwise, he would have chosen his words more carefully.

When she finally responded, her voice was small and introspective. "It must be different, being as big as you are, never having to be afraid of anything or anyone."

Surprised she broke the silence, he slowed down and responded with open an ended comment, letting her fill in the blanks. "Everyone's afraid of something."

"Maybe. But I don't think a man your size can imagine what it feels like to live every moment of your life in fear. That's what my life was like, Mr. Cole. I have no choice but to remain vigilant, unsure if the rules are going to change again. I forget what happiness feels like, but I remember enough to know life shouldn't be this miserable."

His chest tightened. She didn't seem crazy or unbalanced. Just sad. He hated thinking what sort of life might do that to a woman. He hated the idea of stealing away her hope of happiness to return her to misery.

"Your boys must make you happy."

"I can't enjoy my children without being punished. I've always wanted to be a mother, but I'm not raising my children the way I dreamed I would. I can't. Not there. I've been a wife for seven years, but as far as having a husband, a partner, a normal marriage... Well, I have no idea what that's like."

"Your husband scares you?"

"My husband's a demanding man. He had a good side at one time. I wouldn't have married him otherwise. He provided for us in a way I can't criticize but, as the years went on, it turned out he didn't need a wife as much as he needed a maid or a vessel to bear his sons." She turned to face the window, muffling her words, but he caught the almost inaudible whisper. "...and a whipping post."

Taking his eyes off the road, he gauged the sincerity of her words. The truth was there in her tired face. "Did you ever go to the police?"

"There were a lot of nice looking people in that picture you showed me. Are they all your sisters?"

Recognizing her diversion and accepting it, he nodded. "One is my sister's partner—sort of a sister-in-law—but I'm equally protective of all of them."

"What would you do if a man you trusted pushed one of them around? Some men hit women but it isn't always the punches that hurt most."

His gut twisted at her casual use of the word *punches*. He didn't want to imagine his sisters ever having to deal with that kind of treatment or any woman for that matter. "I'd probably wind up in jail myself." Because he sure as fuck would slaughter anyone who hurt those he loved.

"But revenge doesn't erase abuse. The only solution is escape. And the baggage is heavy because most disparaging remarks cut too deep to heal. Feeling worthless, hopeless, and like a failure, after you've done your best makes that sort of baggage all the more difficult to carry. It breaks a person. I'm very lucky that I've broken away. But even I know this isn't a true escape. It's just borrowed time until I figure out a better plan."

This was a bad idea. He shouldn't care about these details. She kidnapped her kids. That was against the law. Period. If he could get her to admit there was a better way to start over he could possibly get rid of the sick feeling filling his gut every time he imagined hauling her back to Virginia.

"Why not file for divorce and do things legally so you get the law on your side? I'm guessing your husband doesn't know where you are."

"Court ordered paperwork won't change who

he is. He'd never let me walk away. I had no choice but to run and I have to succeed. The last time I tried and he caught me..."

He glanced at her as she went silent, her unblinking eyes seeming to see something no one else would ever witness. She drew in a deep, slow breath and faced him.

"By now I imagine he's hired someone to find us. All I can hope is that I threw him off our trail and that I make it to my children before he does. I don't have any money and I have very little hope, but if I go back there..." Her head turned, her stark eyes reflecting on the drizzle of the passenger window. "I can never go back."

There was quiet resignation in her voice, but also determination. Why had he accepted this assignment? This woman wasn't crazy. Somehow she'd had the foresight to get her children someplace safe to protect them. Or was she feeding him a line of bullshit? Someone was lying to him and it pissed him off that his instincts said it wasn't her. Damn it.

Pushing away the unsavory wave that soured his stomach, he mentally questioned her honesty. If she was actually telling the truth, the disappointment in her eyes once he usurped her chance at freedom might haunt him forever.

They'd cross that bridge when they got to it. "Well, it looks like you will be seeing your boys soon. We're crossing over to Pennsylvania in the next mile." No need to mention she'd be getting hauled back to Virginia.

He thought it best to stop talking for a while and she didn't seem to mind the silence. As they neared the town of New Castle, she could barely keep still in her seat. She fidgeted with her bag and ran her hand over the wrinkles in her shirt.

As they approached the exit, Trent found himself slowing down to just below the speed limit, reluctant to get to the next part of his plan. "You nervous?"

"I'm something. You have no idea how much I had to go through to get here, Mr. Cole. I can't thank you enough for keeping your word and delivering me to my children."

He said nothing, guilt souring the words on the back of his tongue. They pulled in front of a medium-sized home, tucked safely away in the suburbs of New Castle.

The light on the porch flickered and she scrambled to undo her seatbelt. He had to make a move soon. Fuck. He wasn't a bad guy but at the moment he felt like Lucifer himself.

*It's just a job. Do it and go home to your family. You need this payout.*

Her breath hitched as an elderly woman opened the front door and a small child in footie pajamas burst onto the porch.

*"Mommy!"*

She sprang out of the truck and raced across the lawn, pulling the boy into her arms with surprising strength being that she appeared weaker than a tattered string. The older woman carried a toddler on her hip. Taking the youngest in her arms, she pressed kisses into his pudgy cheek.

Trent sat frozen with his hand on the door, watching the scene play out, paralyzed by crushing ethical awareness. He cursed under his breath as the older son wiped tears from Chloe's face and asked why she cried. The older woman wiped her wrinkled cheeks and smiled.

He didn't belong here. This was a private moment and one he wished he didn't have to see.

Chloe turned and smiled at him, her open hand resting over her chest. She no longer looked like the weathered, desperate woman from the subway. Happiness hid every ounce of fear he'd observed over the journey.

She said something to the woman and turned back to the truck, taking a step in his direction. His foot lifted off the brake and her smile fell, confusion knitting her brow as he eased away from the driveway. He didn't deserve her thanks because he wasn't her friend. His intentions were tarnished. Let her live with whatever memory she wanted, but he refused to accept gratitude for misleading her.

He also refused to help a man who would hurt a family like that. Hunt could find someone else to track down his wife. She could be a raving lunatic of a wife for all he cared. But he believed she was a good mother and was doing what she believed best for those two boys.

He beat himself up as he drove away, wavering between going back and letting her go. "Fuck!" So much for taking the rest of the year off. Why was the right choice always the fucking hardest?

He never did anything half ass. So he intended to see his new solution through. He'd be sure to let her husband know he lost her and the kids crossing the border to Mexico. Hunt would likely hire someone else, but Trent could at least see that she got a decent head start to a peaceful life, a happy life like she wanted. God, he hoped he made the right choice and took the right parent's side.

As he shifted lanes, something sparkled on the dashboard. Pristine and abandoned, her ring, nestled between two diamond studs, sat on the thirty-dollars he'd given her. He plucked up the cash and held it in his hand for the next ten miles. It wouldn't pay his bills, but it certainly helped him accept he'd made the right decision in the end.

# One

**NEW CASTLE,** *Pennsylvania*
**Six Years Later**


Dr. Chloe Wolfe finished her wine and went to find her coat. It was after midnight and the intimate wedding reception held at her friend slash patient's home was over. Jade Schultz was officially Mrs. Jeremy Larson and Chloe's happiness for the couple went beyond what a therapist typically feels for a client.

The coats were piled on the bed of the master bedroom. She located hers and adjusted her scarf. In the dimly lit room, she searched her bag for her keys and the floor creaked behind her. She turned, and her smile fell.

Shock jolted her veins as their gazes met, a thousand volts of electricity thawing her blood with the heat of a thousand white flames. She staggered back as her head shook, certain her mind was playing tricks on her as unforgettable blue eyes stared down at her.

The scar that scared her all those years ago now brought a level of comfort, marking him as the hero that rescued her when she'd been desperate and hopeless to reach her sons. She'd never forget him or mistake someone else for the man who saved her all those years ago.

How was he here, standing in front of her at her friends' home? Why was he here? So many questions yet her shock left her mute.

Dark hair, tied at the nape of his neck, exposed the jagged scar running from his jaw and disappearing somewhere below the collar of his shirt. The same scar she'd spent an entire car ride studying six years ago. Familiar tanned skin accented his piercing blue eyes, such an unnatural blue they seemed to glow within the shadows.

His lashes were black as a raven's wing, matching the dark sheen of his hair. But those penetrating eyes... They were too pretty for a man's face. Her attention dropped to his body.

The tailored suit teased her recollection of him, mocking the way she recalled his broken-in blue jeans and worn cotton shirt. Maybe this wasn't him. Maybe she had too much to drink and should wait another hour before driving home.

His visage wasn't what anyone would describe as pretty. Rugged, weathered, hard enough to make the slightest smile shocking—just as she remembered. It had to be him.

"Is it you?" She pressed her hand to her temple where her pulse thundered.

"I beg your pardon?" His expression one of confusion, but there was no mistaking that voice. It rattled like creaking timber, deep and strong, tinged with a slight Jersey accent.

This was not a man easily forgotten. Chloe certainly recalled him more often than she probably should. He was older now and somehow that made his appearance all the more arresting.

"The subway... You... You gave me a ride from Maryland to Pennsylvania when I was in dire straits."

The fringe of his lashes hid his eyes as his attention jerked away. "I'm sorry. You must have me confused with someone else. Excuse me." He turned to the door as if to leave the room.

He was lying. Either that, or he'd forgotten her. She reached for him, her hand wrapping around his solid wrist. "I know it's you. Your name's Trenton Cole. You have to remember. You rescued me. I had no money and was stranded. We drove for hours in your truck and you dropped me off in New Castle."

His lips firmed, drawing her attention back to the scar that crossed his jaw. He audibly swallowed, his gaze piercing her composure like a skewer to her Achilles. Her grip on his arm fell away. What was she doing touching a perfect stranger?

But he wasn't a stranger. She knew him—or had at least met him in a past life. Maybe he honestly didn't recognize her. She looked nothing like the terrified, filthy woman he saved years ago, but surely he recalled...

A smile wobbled to her lips. This was surreal.

She never expected to cross his path again. "Tell me you remember me. I haven't forgotten you."

He stiffly nodded, his posture tense. Her memory might have glorified him because she remembered a man who was relaxed and at ease. This man appeared alarmed and uncomfortable at the sight of her. Maybe he had a wife and didn't want to explain how he'd picked up a strange woman years ago.

She took a step back. "You drove away before I could thank you. You saved my life."

He glanced at the door and back to her. "I... Yes, I remember now. Are... Are you still married?"

"You *do* remember!" Her smile grew. Why was he here at her friends' house, celebrating their wedding? "I've been on my own for six years. How do you know Jade and Jeremy?"

"I was in the service with Jeremy and met Jade through him."

Her mind quickly flowed over her sessions with Jade. She thought she knew the names of everyone in her life. Oh, my God, Jade *had* mentioned a friend of Jeremy's—a giant of a man that went by Trent, but Chloe never made the connection.

His gaze tightened and his mouth remained flat. "How do you know them?"

"I'm ..." She hesitated, not wanting to betray Jade by introducing herself as her therapist. "A friend of Jade's."

He frowned as if trying to piece together his own puzzle. "How did you two meet?"

Her expression turned tender. "Through a mutual friend." As a therapist, she would always protect her client's confidentiality.

Neither one of them seemed to know what to say, so they shifted awkwardly in the dark room. He cleared his throat. "I... I never got your name."

She smiled and held out a hand. "I'm Chloe. Chloe Wolfe. It's a pleasure to finally introduce myself to you, Mr. Cole."

His head cocked as something flashed in his eyes. "Chloe *Wolfe?*"

She nodded and continued to smile. As his hand closed around hers a shaky breath filled her lungs. It wasn't a typical handshake. The gentle way he clasped her fingers, the warmth of his palm, it radiated through her entire body and stole her breath.

"The pleasure's mine. I'm glad to hear you and your boys are doing well, Chloe."

Her breath left in a whoosh as he said her name. Not only did he remember her, he remembered she had sons.

Her stomach clenched. This man changed her life and never asked for anything in return. A wave of hero worship softened her knees and she found herself staring up at him with an unbendingly smitten grin.

~

She was adorable with her fawn colored eyes and little, upturned nose. He recalled thinking she had a pretty face and trusting, under different circumstances, she'd be a bombshell. Now, even in a wool winter coat and scarf, he knew his instincts were spot on.

Tall, with enough ample curves to keep a man occupied for days, Chloe was a woman a man could hold onto. She shouldn't look at him like that. If she knew who he really was, this reunion would be going extremely differently. A small scar clipped her lip, making him wonder where it came from and reminding him of the man she'd once been married to. Her hair was still dyed auburn, no longer blonde like the picture he kept in a hidden file marked *Chloe Hunt*. Where had the name Wolfe come from? It irritated him that he couldn't ask.

She was older but appeared younger. He supposed it was her smile that gave her such a youthful glow. It was something he'd wanted to see but never had the chance.

Well, that wasn't totally true. He'd never forget her expression as she scooped up her boys the day he dropped her off in New Castle. That damn smile had cost him a hundred grand and a lot of hassle. But seeing it again reminded him it was worth it.

He was relieved to hear she never went back to her asshole husband. He'd wondered.

"You look happy."

"I am."

And sexy. It had to mean something that they were running into each other after so long when he'd always assumed there wasn't a chance in hell he'd see her again. For all he knew, New Castle was just a pit stop for her to catch her breath. He never expected her to stay here. Yet here she was.

Lust and need punched through him as she

tipped her head to the side and batted her eyes. "I just can't believe we're running into each other like this. *Here* of all places."

A soft flush tinged her cheeks. They were still holding hands and neither one of them seemed in a rush to let go. Years of wondering collided in the present as every curious thought he'd ever had about her—and there were a *lot*—rushed through him in a jolt of awareness. This woman had consumed his thoughts for months after he quit the job. She'd become an obsession he'd forced himself to quit, knowing he could never pursue his curiosity and see how she was surviving. Some days it was more than curiosity. And some days it was worry. But he'd thought of her often and it seemed impossible she was standing here now.

His fingers gently squeezed and her breasts lifted, her eyes dilating in the moonlight as she blinked up at him. Was she single? Would it be the stupidest thing he'd done this year to ask her out? Maybe he was due for a little stupid.

"Do you still live around here?" His voice came out gravelly.

"I live in my Aunt Regina's house. The house you brought me to." Her smile faltered and her hand slipped from his. "She passed away last year."

"I'm sorry."

His fingers twitched to touch her again. She shifted from foot to foot. He didn't like the idea that he might be making her uncomfortable, so he took a slight step back. "How old are your sons now?"

All signs of nervousness vanished, replaced with

evident pride. "Oh, well, Mattie, my youngest, is seven and a half, and Dayton, my oldest, is nine."

He loved the way her eyes lit up at the mention of her children. "Any other children?"

She laughed and his ears clung to the melodic sound. "There was a chunk of my life where I mastered barefoot and pregnant. Two boys are enough to keep me busy. How about you? Are you still just a favorite uncle or did you move on to being a father?"

It was a decent cover as far as answers went. Most people wouldn't detect the trauma the casual remark hid, but he saw through her words even before she deflected the reference to her past back to him. "I'm still just the favorite uncle. Never married and no kids."

He remembered how enraged Marcus Hunt had been when Trent delivered the news he wouldn't be returning his wife. The man had gone ballistic, throwing and slamming things across the room—displaying some of the traits Chloe had alluded to during their short meeting. He was grateful her boys had avoided having such a man in their lives.

He never regretted not completing the job, because that day and the despicable display of a short-tempered man vocalizing countless threats toward his runaway wife, told Trent he'd absolutely made the right choice letting her go. Seeing her now, happy amongst friends, only validated his decision, years later.

"Do your boys see their father?" He immediately regretted his question as her expression shuttered.

Her face lowered along with her voice. "No."

Fuck. He hadn't meant to upset her. If his father was the sort of scumbag Marcus Hunt was, Trent wouldn't have any relationship with him. Luckily, his dad had always been a good man and an incredibly supportive father.

"Good fathers are a gift. Unfortunately, they're rare."

She tilted her head, looking at him once more. "Yes, so I've discovered." Then she quickly turned the tables back on him. "It's a shame you never had kids of your own. You seem like one of the rare ones."

It wasn't that he disliked children. He loved his nieces and nephews, but he couldn't have children and that was always an awkward thing to explain. He could always adopt, but that was outside of bachelor territory. "Maybe if I would've married. I'm still searchin' for the right woman." He added that last part without thinking. Something in his gut wanted her to know he was single.

"Well, in my book, marriage is highly overrated. Children, however, are amazing. I hope one day you find a woman who can share that gift with you."

He hoped so, too, but it would never happen, at least not the children part. He had more than one doctor tell him kids weren't in his future. "You don't plan on marrying again?"

She laughed. "God no! Marriage and I don't suit."

Her smile enchanted him. He found himself stepping toward her again, his twitching fingers lifting to her face. She stilled and her laughter silenced. Placing his knuckle under her delicate chin he tilted her face to hold her gaze. Damn, she was pretty.

"Mr. Cole?" Her wine-scented breath teased his lips as she whispered his name. Her lashes slowly fanned upward, giving him a view of those luminous brown eyes. A dusting of cinnamon freckles sprinkled the bridge of her nose.

"Call me Trenton." He wanted to kiss her, to know if she tasted as good as she smelled. His body eased closer by mere degrees as his blood pumped heavily through his veins.

"Trenton..."

The sound of his first name on her lips sent a rush of blood to his cock. She shivered. He wasn't holding her in place, merely touching her to see into her eyes. So pretty.

The entire situation almost seemed too good to be true, so he asked, "Not married then. Dating?"

Her chin trembled as she held his stare. "I... No. I don't date."

"That, Chloe, is a shame." Yep. He was definitely thinking with the wrong head as he leaned in and brushed his mouth to hers. His lips danced, feather-light, across hers and she froze.

He eased back, still holding her chin and glanced in her wide eyes. There was an unknowing innocence staring back. "Kiss me, Chloe."

He tilted his head and teased her lips with his, his heart thundering into overdrive as he wasn't sure if this would land him in her bed—a place he'd very much like to visit—or with a Chloe shaped handprint across his cheek.

"Relax. I won't bite." *Hard...*

His tongue licked at the seam of her lips as he shifted closer, pressing his hard body against her soft front. He snaked his free hand around her back and used her sudden intake of breath to deepen the kiss and tug her closer. Fuck, she felt good in his arms.

He moaned, angling his head to taste more, but she still wasn't kissing him back. "Should I stop?"

Her hand clung to his shirt as she stared up at him. He gave her a moment to break away, but she didn't take it. So he softly traced his lips to hers again.

Her weight sank into him as she belatedly pressed her lips to his. His mouth curled into a smile as he stroked her tongue with his. His size engulfed her as she clung to his shoulders.

Her tongue shyly grazed his and he groaned, tightening his hold. Growing bolder, he lowered his hand to the curve of her ass—

There was a click and his eyes jerked open. They were no longer alone. Chloe tensed. Still tangled in his arms, she glanced around him as a man from the party stepped into the room.

Trent wanted to hold her there, but at the sight of company, she shifted away, her face flushed. He gritted his teeth, his dick heavy and pulsing behind the zipper of his slacks.

"I'm sorry. I'm looking for my wife's bag," the intruder apologized.

It was one of Jade's co-workers. Trent frowned. He'd been pretty observant of everyone there tonight and was almost certain this particular guest had arrived alone. Yet, he'd somehow missed Chloe's entrance so he obviously wasn't paying that close attention.

"Well, thank you for helping me find my coat, Trenton."

*What?* His attention jerked back to Chloe as she slipped past him and exited the room, making a fast escape down the steps and to the front door. He glared at the man who interrupted them and went after her. But by the time he made it out front into the snow she was pulling away.

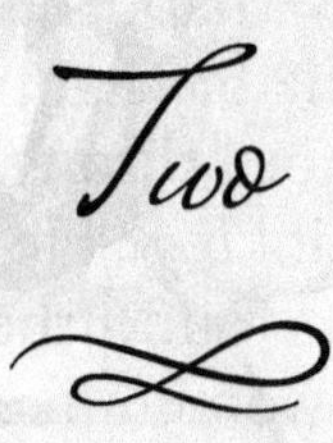

# Two

CHLOE SWERVED down the snowy street, heart racing and breath panting in the cold car. He kissed her. Trenton Cole, her hero, had kissed her. Her mind still couldn't wrap around the fact that she'd actually run into him.

By the time she was in her neighborhood, she wasn't even close to recovering from her run-in with her past. It was surreal to see *anyone* connected to that time of her life—though Trenton wasn't really connected. He'd only found her at the very end, just after she'd escaped the nightmare that was once her life.

Their kiss replayed over and over again in her head. Each time making her heart skitter out of control. She'd only meant to thank him. Never in a million years did she expect a man like that to kiss her. The fact that she'd hero-worshipped him for half a decade only made the entire situation harder to process.

As she made it into her icy driveway, she gripped

the wheel in astonished shock. "Holy crap." He kissed her.

What would have happened if they weren't interrupted? Would she have gone further with him? A resounding *no* echoed through her mind.

What was she thinking? He was obviously picky, being that he'd never found the right woman. Men like that liked what women like her weren't capable of providing—at least not anymore.

Her head fell into the seat and she squeezed her eyes shut. "He doesn't even have my number." That was a good thing, but it also felt like a lost opportunity—one she wasn't sure she had the guts to take. Yet the thought of never seeing him again... She was such a moron. Why had she bolted out of there like that?

Well, one, she shouldn't be making out with a total stranger in her client's house. That was pretty much it. She shouldn't be making out with anyone. Especially not a man she hardly knew and especially not a man his size. The voice in her head that belonged to Dr. Chloe Wolfe admonished the automatic assumption that all men were as cruel as Marcus and Chloe quickly reminded herself there were good men out there. But even good men could be risky.

Pessimism as deep as hers in regard to trust was woven into her bones. Trying to think differently when it came to her own life and safety was like trying to purposely break her arm. She might survive the snap, but why chance more pain?

Taking a deep breath, she collected her wits and put all thoughts of Trenton Cole aside to examine later. As she cut across the snowy driveway, her neighbors' porch light flipped on and the door opened, Adam's trim frame filling the entrance.

"Well, hey," he greeted, his manicured brows framing his gray eyes.

"Hey." She stomped the snow off her feet and stepped into the kitchen.

"How was the party?"

Rubbing her hands together, she worked out the chill. "It was nice."

"Honey, I hope you did a better job convincing your friends you had a good time."

She unraveled her scarf and frowned. "I did have a good time, but at the end of the night I ran into someone I wasn't expecting to see. I'm still a little frazzled."

"Who, an old friend I hope?"

"Well, not a friend, but definitely someone I was glad to see."

"Ooh, an ex *lovah*?"

"No, and that's all I'm saying. Where are my children?"

"Sleeping on the couch." He pouted. "Tell me who you saw."

Tommy, Adam's husband, breezed into the kitchen, his blond hair a perfect mess. "Was someone exciting at the party?" Although in slippers and cozy pants he still wore a stylish scarf, as if prepared for an impromptu Ralph Lauren photo shoot.

"She won't tell." Adam glared at her. "Brat."

Tommy sidled closer, nudging her with his hip. "Was it a man?"

"It was no one." Telling them would lead to too many questions and as far as answers... She had none.

"Well, whoever it was, he's got her all flustered." Adam waved his fingers as if tickling the electric air buzzing around her.

She swatted his fingers away. "Stop that. And who said it was a he?"

"Puh-lease." Tommy snapped his tongue against his teeth. "Look at you. Your cheeks are rosy, your hair's tousled, and you're not wearing a trace of lipstick." Gasping, he pressed his fingers to his lips. "You were doin' some kissing!"

A wave of heat burned her cheeks as they turned on her with greedy curiosity. "Spill! Who is he?"

"Shh. You'll wake the boys."

"Tell or my begging will only get more shrill," Tommy threatened.

Releasing a deep breath, she closed her eyes and surrendered. "The man who drove me to New Castle six years ago."

They gaped at her. "Oh-em-gee, your rescuer? Your mystery hero?"

She couldn't hide her smile. "Yes."

"How fabulous! And he kissed you?"

"That's the part I don't get, but you know what? It doesn't matter. It was a thirty-second, spur of the moment kiss, and I barely had time to kiss him back. I'll probably never see him again. Besides, I don't need any additional men in my life."

"Why? Men are the most fun," Tommy argued.

"It's complicated." And something she didn't

discuss. "I don't want to be involved and I don't think he really intended to kiss me."

"Did he trip and fall on your face?"

"No, smart ass. It was a freak thing that will never happen again, which is how I want it, so let's drop it."

Tommy snorted. "Girl, the only thing you're dropping is ten bucks on new batteries. This is some serious fantasy material. We've heard your drunken confessions about your mystery hero. That man's held the leading role in your fantasies for six long —*cough*—*lonely*—years. Throw the boy a bone and for god's sake, take one for yourself."

Adam threw his head back and laughed. "When's the last time you got boned, Chloe? I'm pretty sure you're overdue."

"You know what? Since you two are so energetic this evening, Dayton and Mattie can stay here tonight. I'm going to bed." She twisted her scarf and pushed back through the kitchen door.

"Oh, go on girl!" Tommy shouted, poking his head out the door as she trekked across the snow. "We'll give you your privacy. Whip out the nine volts! This deserves all the bells and whistles!"

Shoving her key in the lock, she held up her middle finger. "You're a pervert." She didn't have toys like that. *Maybe I should get some...*

"My perversions are only a measure of my notable intelligence. I'm loaded with wisdom regarding all things sexy and male."

But Tommy was right. She fantasized about Trenton Cole on more than one occasion and tonight would be especially vivid as she could clearly picture his face and still smell his intoxicating scent on her skin.

It had taken her years to masturbate after leaving Marcus and when she finally had, Trenton Cole was only a hazy recollection her mind sometimes stumbled across at the brink of climax. Tonight, her fantasies were so intense she could call every detail to mind. It made sleeping very difficult and no amount of playing with herself made the fantasies of Trenton Cole go away.

Each time she pictured him her body trembled. When she whispered his name, her toes curled. And every time she came she only wanted more, more, more. There was obviously something wrong with her.

The next day Chloe was exhausted and antsy. She was on her hands and knees scrubbing out the oven when the phone rang. Ignoring the call and letting it go to voicemail, she continued to scour the potent industrial cleaner into the caked on grime.

"That smells like egg farts!" Mattie groused, covering his nose.

About to pass out from the fumes, she drew back and sat on the freshly mopped floor. "Take your boots off."

Dayton tromped into the kitchen a few seconds later, drips of melting ice falling from his snow pants. "Ew! What's that smell?"

"Mom farted!"

"I did not!" She peeled the rubber gloves off her hands and let the oven slam shut. "It's the oven cleaner." It did smell like farts though. She probably did, too.

"Can we have hot chocolate?" Dayton asked.

Shifting the bandana holding back her hair, she adjusted her old sweatshirt and waited for the dizzying effects of the fumes to lessen. "Why don't you play for a while longer and I'll make some hot chocolate later?"

"I don't wanna sled anymore." Dayton's mouth pinched as he plopped into an empty kitchen chair, swinging his foot at the other one as if kicking the wood could somehow communicate his feelings.

This was her new Dayton. She was still adjusting to the unfamiliar moodiness of her first-born and frequently reminding herself not to link his irritability to his father's. But no matter how hard she tried not to make the mental comparison, her mind always landed on the same worry. Dayton looked like his father and Mattie looked like her. But she'd be damned if either of her boys turned out like him.

"Dayton, stop kicking the chair."

His foot stilled and he slouched. "There's nothing to do."

She'd hoped the snow would keep them busy, at least for a little while. "You love the snow."

"I'm too big to sled. It's only babies out there."

"Nuh-ah," Mattie piped in. "Tommy's sledding and he's way bigger than you. *You're* the one being a baby."

"Shut up, Mattie. *You're* the baby." Dayton gave his brother a slight push.

Mattie, who was smaller but more solid and rougher, pushed back, causing Dayton to knock into the table and splash her coffee.

"Hey! No hitting. Apologize to each other."

They each grumbled an insincere apology.

"Dayton, if you don't want to go sledding then do something else—"

"But then I can't go out!" Mattie cried.

"You just said Tommy was out there. As long as you stay with Tommy, you can sled. But I don't want you going off without him. When he says it's time to come in, you're not to argue. Understand?"

"Yes."

"Good. Dayton, go find something to do while I walk your brother over to the hill."

Throwing on a coat and boots, she trekked to the hill, waving when she spotted Tommy at the top of the slope with some of the neighborhood parents. He excused himself from the others and slid down the snow on a toboggan, belly first, to greet her and Mattie.

"You come to hit the slope, Chloe?"

"No, I'm cleaning. Dayton's staying in. Can you keep an eye on Mattie?"

"Of course, love." His white teeth were possibly brighter than the snow as he grinned under his designer cap.

She braved the cold a while longer to watch Mattie sled down the hill a couple times. As she was about to head back to her house, Dayton came running to where she and Tommy stood, her cellphone in his hand.

"Mom, someone's on the phone. They said it's important."

"Who is it?"

Holding her cell out, he shrugged. "Some guy named Jeremy."

She frowned and took the phone. "Hello?"

"Chloe, Thank God I got you. Can you come over?"

He was speaking really fast, not at all like the Jeremy she knew. "What's going on? Did something happen?"

"We got him. We fucking got him."

*Oh, my God...* Did he mean Jade's stalker? She had to watch what she said in front of others. "Who, Jeremy?"

"*Him.* He's dead. Last night... Jesus. So much happened after the party. I haven't slept and I'm still shaking."

Her frown etched deeper into her wind-chilled face as she pieced together his jagged words. *Him...* She knew before he clarified Jeremy was speaking of the man who had tormented Jade's world for the past year. He was dead? Still unsure who *he* was, she told herself his identity didn't matter, so long as they got him and her friend was safe. "Is Jade—"

"She's safe. But she needs you."

Her heart jerked, relief tunneling through her. "I don't understand. How did this happen? *What* happened?"

It had been months since Jade's attack and they all assumed the case was closed, leaving Jade with a trauma that might take a lifetime to forget, one she never remembered in the first place. Rape often took place in a matter of minutes, but the repercussions lasted a lifetime. Chloe knew this from first-hand experience.

But they got the guy? How? Where?

"He attacked her last night." Jeremy's words

were rough and full of pent-up emotion for his wife. "He was at the party—in our house! It was a nightmare. I thought I would never see her again. We just got back from the hospital a little bit ago. Jade's safe, but... It's not good."

After months of intensive therapy and no leads to the man who violated Jade, it took Chloe completely off guard that the perpetrator was suddenly identified—*and dead.* "Was anyone else hurt?"

Tommy quieted Mattie's exclamations to his mother about his recent sledding performance as she covered her ear to better hear what Jeremy was saying.

"She got pretty roughed up, but she's mostly shaken. Can you come to our house?"

Her heart raced as her worry for Jade became her sole concern. "I can be there in about twenty minutes. Tell her I'm on my way."

"Thank you, Chloe. Thank you for everything."

Issuing quick goodbye, she snapped the phone shut, and turned to Tommy. "It's one of my clients. There was an incident. I have to go see if she's okay. Is there any way you could—"

"Go. Take as long as you need and make sure your client's okay."

Placing a hand on his sleeve, she gave a grateful squeeze. Tommy and Adam were always there for her when she needed them. "I owe you guys."

"That's what friends are for. Now, go."

She looked at Dayton and Mattie. "You two listen to Tommy and no fighting. I don't want to hear any bad reports when I get back."

"Did someone die?" Dayton asked, a little too much interest in his eyes.

"No," she lied, quickly covering her slip on the phone. "Listen to Tommy and behave. I'll be back as soon as I can."

"Can I go to their house? I don't want to sled."

Her life sometimes seemed an unending pattern of meticulous decisions, and there was always a pileup of requests whenever she had somewhere to be. She glanced at Tommy and he nodded.

"Adam's at the house. He can go hang with him."

She didn't waste time walking Dayton inside but watched as Adam opened the door to let him in, cell phone to his ear, likely getting a quick update from Tommy.

After rushing through her house and grabbing her keys and purse, she carefully navigated her car through the recently plowed streets. As she waited at a traffic light, she rummaged through her bag for some lipstick, flipped down the visor mirror, and grimaced.

"Oh, that's not good."

A smudge of oven grease colored her wind-chapped cheek and she still wore a bandana over her hair. As she merged into traffic she licked her finger and tried smudging the grease off of her cheek, but gave up when she hit a slightly icy stretch of road. She would worry about her appearance later.

After a tense twenty minutes of piloting the slushy streets in her small yellow car, she finally reached Jade and Jeremy's neighborhood. Chloe knocked lightly on the front door and Jeremy immediately opened it. He still wore his suit pants and shirt from the evening before, but the crisp fabric was worn and wrinkled. His eyes were haunted and his hair a mess.

Chloe spotted a smudge of what looked like blood on his shoulder but tried not to focus on that. "How is she?"

"Not good." He let her in and quietly shut the door. The house looked exactly as it had the night before when she left, minus all the guests. "She's in our room. I gave her something to relax, but she's just staring at the wall. She isn't talking much. She isn't even crying."

Her mind was racing faster than her heart. She needed more information before facing Jade. "Jeremy, what happened?"

He blew out an unsteady breath. "The guy was one of our guests. He took her right from our home and drove her to a house, for fuck's sake! I don't want to think about what could have happened if my friend hadn't followed them. When he got there the son of a bitch had a gun to her head. My buddy got there just in time and the cops arrived minutes later."

Chloe placed a comforting hand on his shaking shoulder. That was enough. "If he's dead, he can't hurt her anymore, Jeremy." Jade wouldn't be the only one traumatized when this was all over.

He nodded and drew in an unsteady breath. "Will you try to talk to her? I don't want her to ... think she has to hide her pain and handle this alone. Like last time"

"She's strong, Jeremy. This is a lot, but she'll get through it. Less than twenty-four hours ago she was having the time of her life. It's difficult to process trauma. She's suffered a lot. Such abrupt closure can be a bit surreal—for everyone involved. Just give it time. Keep telling yourself it's over and remind her of the same when she needs to hear it. That's all she needs from you, time and love."

"I can't believe it's actually over. I just..."

Chloe quietly waited, as he covered his eyes and lost the fight against his tears. Once he composed himself, she repeated, "It's going to take everyone some time."

He nodded and cleared his throat, his face etched with lines of stress. "I'll take you to her."

She followed him up the stairs to the bedroom she'd been in last night. It looked completely different in the light of day.

Jade's fragile form looked like that of a child as she lay on the bed, tightly curled into herself under the covers. Her blond hair was damp, her eyes focused on something and absolutely nothing at the same time.

Jeremy placed a gentle hand on his wife's shoulder. "Jade, baby, Chloe's here."

Without moving her head, Jade's gaze traveled to Chloe's. Although she didn't blink, a tear rolled from her lashes and Chloe swallowed hard against the lump in her throat, instinctively moving to the bed.

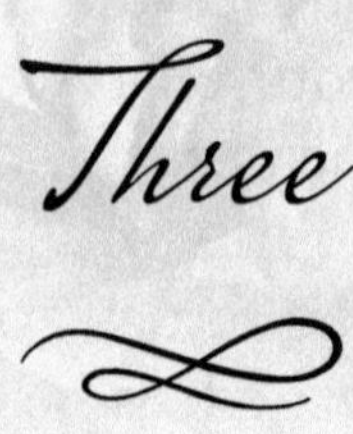

# Three

TRENT SAT at the kitchen table waiting for Jeremy to return. He'd been at his friend's home since they finished with the police. What a night—and a long morning.

He'd met Jade a few months ago and she'd quickly become someone he loved. It was like having another sister. Jade was feisty, small, and adorable. When Jeremy informed Trent he was marrying her, he couldn't blame him. A girl like that deserved to be loved. And Jeremy, a man who never showed much interest in anything more than casual sex, had fallen ass over face in love with her.

The idea that they could have lost her last night...

Trent took a deep breath and dumped his coffee, if it could even be called that. Suffice it to say they were all grateful to have Jade safe at home again.

As he washed out his coffee mug, he considered how lucky they all were and wondered what Jeremy did to make his coffee taste so terrible. The man made the worst caffeinated sludge he'd ever tasted. Doing a favor to the rest of the world, he emptied the pot and made a fresh batch. As he hit *brew*, Jeremy's heavy footsteps broke the silence.

Trent turned, resting his weight against the counter and folding his arms over his chest. "How is she?"

"Same. Her therapist just got here. I'm hoping she can at least get her talking."

Trenton returned to the table and sat. Jeremy looked like shit. The man hadn't slept in almost thirty hours. "Why don't you grab a shower? Get out of those clothes?"

"I need to be vigilant."

Trent gripped his shoulder and looked him in the eye. "I'll stay. If she needs you, I'll come get you."

His friend nodded but apparently lacked the strength to move. Then, like a stronghold made of sand, his face crumbled as he broke into tears.

Trent rushed a comforting hand to the back of his neck, gripping him securely. "Hey. It's all right. She's safe. He's dead. He can't hurt her anymore."

His friend's broad shoulders quaked with the force of too many stressful days and nights. The sudden end to such a drawn-out nightmare no doubt overwhelmed him.

Jeremy wasn't an emotional man. In most cases, he was the polar opposite. Trent had watched him haul a friend's lifeless body back from combat without even shedding a tear, but this—nearly losing his wife to a psychopath—was gutting him.

He was glad to be the shoulder his friend cried on, knowing if things were reversed, Jeremy would do the same for him. Clearing his throat, Jeremy pulled himself together and blew out a hard breath. He rose. "I'm going to shower."

Minutes later the tinkling of water rattled through the pipes in the walls.

Trent wasn't a tidy guy. He hardly emptied the cups out of his truck until they started overflowing onto the floor. Still, he needed to do something, so he paced through the house with a trash bag, collecting disposable glasses and plates left over from the party.

The quiet opening and closing of doors on the second floor vaguely registered. He didn't want to leave until he was sure everyone was okay and his friends didn't need anything else. But he also wanted to allow them some privacy.

Setting the volume on the sound system in the living room to low, an old favorite by INXS filled the silence as he filled his bag with trash. Tying off the bag he headed out back to drop it in the garbage can but paused when he heard a sniffle.

Creeping around the side of the house, he hesitated, questioning if he should just go back inside and let whoever was there have their moment in peace. His mouth went slack as he glimpsed Chloe standing stiffly at the edge of the garage, mopping away tears.

*What's she doing here?*

Clearing his throat, he stepped around the corner. "Chloe?"

She gasped and took a startled step back. "What

... what are you doing here?" Her flushed, tear-streaked cheeks reddened another degree.

Approaching slowly, he kept his expression blank. "I've been here all morning."

His fingers itched to brush a windblown tear from her cheek as his eye caught on a black smudge near her jaw. Registering her disheveled appearance he frowned.

"You're shivering." He closed the distance and pulled the lapels of her jacket together. Then his nose twitched, an unflattering odor catching in the air.

*Must be the garbage.*

Her brown eyes followed him as she scrubbed her hands over her face. "I didn't think anyone else was out here."

"Do they know you're here? Jade isn't seeing anyone right now."

"I know. I just left them."

Tipping his head curiously, he blinked in confusion. The only other person here was Jade's therapist. "What is it you do, Chloe?" When she hesitated he asked, "Or is it Dr. Wolfe?"

She visibly hesitated, her lips parting but her words chosen carefully. "I'm a therapist."

"Ah." He placed his hands in his pockets and waited for her to say more, but she didn't. "So, I suppose you're well aware of what our girl's been through."

"I talked with Jeremy." She took a steadying breath. "It's terrible. Sometimes I wonder if there are any good men left in this world."

The verbal backhand was hard to miss, but he

didn't take it personally. "I'm sure your sons disprove that theory every day."

"They're good boys, but you have no idea how much I worry over what kind of men they'll become."

She was confessing more than ordinary parental concerns, but neither of them were thinking clearly at the moment. Still, he understood how a woman who'd been married to a tyrant might fear of nature versus nurture.

"Hey." He waited for her to look at him. "They aren't their father."

She stared at him, her expression momentarily confused. Shit, had he said too much? It was difficult to remember everything she'd said in his truck six years ago, but he was certain she'd made it clear Hunt was abusing her. He quickly changed the subject. "Do you smell something?"

Her eyes jumped from questioning to mortified as she hastily took a step downwind of him. With that step, the odor lessened. "I, uh... No." Her focus darted to the street. "I have to go. Please tell Jeremy I'll be back in a few hours."

Without even returning to the house, she fled to a little, yellow car, taking the smell of rotten eggs with her. Once again she'd slipped by him. That made three times. First, the day they met. Then last night and now this. Shaking his head, he laughed and headed back to the house. She sure had a way of leaving him wanting more.

Once he had the house straightened up, he ordered some food for everyone. Tyson and Kat stopped by, which made Trent comfortable with leaving Jeremy for a while. Kat was Jade's best friend and no doubt she'd be at her friend's side for most of the day. Ty had become a good friend to Jeremy as well. The four of them, Jade, Jeremy, Tyson, and Kat formed a modern-day blended family, centered on Kat and Jeremy's biological daughter, Mia.

After returning to Jeremy's with some sandwiches from the local deli, he spotted Chloe's yellow car at the curb. It wasn't a sexy car by any means, but the sight of it got his blood pumping.

He casually hung by the counter as Ty and Jeremy talked at the table. Kat returned downstairs, rubbing her slightly pregnant stomach and looking exhausted. They were all beat.

It was selfish having ulterior motives for hanging around when he should've been thinking only of them. Still, he couldn't stop his thoughts from returning to Chloe, wanting to run into her again, maybe talk some more.

He was still digesting the fact that his little runaway had gone and become a therapist. Interesting. Six years ago she was dealing with her own traumatic situation and now she was offering others emotional advice. The irony of her success tempted an inexplicable sense of pride, making it difficult not to smile in the morose house. But he was happy for her—happy she found her happiness and somehow turned a terrible experience into a reason to help others.

"What's that goofy ass grin for?"

Trent cut off his line of thinking and scowled at Tyson, who retrieved a beer from the fridge. "What grin?"

"The one you're wearing. The one that says you're thinking about unicorns and rainbows or some such shit."

Unicorns and rainbows? Then he felt the corny grin on his face and forced his expression to blank. "I have no idea what you're talking about."

Ty rolled his eyes, tossing the beer cap in the trash. "Sure you don't." He chuckled, his words full of sarcasm.

Trent changed the subject, keeping his voice low enough so only Ty could hear him. "What does Kat have to say?"

"She said Jade's doing a little better the more they get her to talk. I should be taking my wife home and forcing her to rest, but there's no way she'll leave Jade."

This was Kat's second pregnancy. "Where's the sprout?"

Mia, Kat's first daughter, also happened to be Jeremy's daughter. The kid might be the result of a hasty decision back in high school, but the blended family thing really seemed to work in their case.

"She's with my in-laws. I don't want to bring her here with Jade still so upset. Mia wouldn't understand any of this."

At the mention of their daughter's name both Kat and Jeremy turned. "What are we going to tell her?" Jeremy asked.

Ty's brow pinched. "We don't tell her anything. She doesn't need to know any of this and we'll wait it out until things get back to normal. Maybe you'd be better off coming to our house on Wednesday instead of bringing Mia here."

"I'm not leaving Jade alone that soon."

"I can come sit with her," Kat suggested. "I can tell Mia that Jade and I are having a grown-up day. So long as she doesn't see Jade, she won't suspect anything's up."

"What about this weekend? It's my weekend with Mia," Jeremy reminded everyone.

This really wasn't Trent's business so he occupied himself with peeling back the label on his beer.

"Hey."

They all turned toward the door and Trent's heart jumped into double time. There she was. A vision of beauty compared to her earlier appearance, but he sort of liked seeing her undone as much as he enjoyed looking at her put together.

Jeremy stood. "Is she all right?"

"Sleeping." Chloe smiled, as the room collectively breathed a sigh of relief and Jeremy sat back down. "She's exhausted. I think she'll be out for a few hours. I suggest you all try to get some rest if you want to be awake for her later."

Jeremy scrubbed a hand over his face. "I'm too tired to sleep. This whole episode's made me squirrelly. Did you eat, Chloe? Trent picked up sandwiches."

She spotted him in the corner of the room and her breath noticeably hitched and held. It was no easy task being his size and going unnoticed, but funny that she almost missed him. He smiled as her face turned a lovely shade of pink.

She cut the eye contact and turned back to Jeremy. "No, I haven't, but I'm fine. Thank you."

"Don't be silly," Trent said, moving from the counter. "I got enough for everyone."

~

Trenton hacked off a humongous portion of hoagie and carried it to the table. She certainly wouldn't be eating that in front of him.

He pulled out a chair. "Sit. Eat."

Paralyzed, she stared, unable to take her eyes off of him. His size was so intimidating he somehow managed to make Tyson and Jeremy, two large men, somehow appear miniature. Thick, corded muscles bulged under the sleeves of his worn T-shirt, drawing her eyes to his broad chest and tapered waist. He was a mountain of man, chiseled to perfection, with a rugged edge that was only emphasized by the jagged scar carved across his jaw. But it was his eyes, the way they playfully danced and seemed to assess her every move, which disarmed her most.

Did the others know they knew each other? What had he told them? She made a point to leave her past in the past and she didn't want him informing anyone of that shameful time in her life— not that he had all the details. But he'd seen her at her worse and these were people she tried to only show her best. She should leave.

"I should really be go—"

He took hold of her wrists, unleashing a swarm of butterflies in her stomach, and pulled her to the table. "You have to eat, doll."

Doll? "Honestly, I'm not hungry."

The weight of his strong hands rested on her

shoulders, pressing her into the chair. Her eyes widened as he kept them there, massaging lightly and giving her no way of escape.

"I ... I can't eat all this."

"Sure you can. This deli bakes homemade rolls. They're fresh and soft. I guarantee you never tasted anything like it." His head dropped lower as he leaned just over her shoulder, wisps of his dark hair touching her cheek like some sort of tantric massage.

She glanced at the others who were all frowning at Trenton. Everyone was still and no one seemed to blink.

Trenton's warm breath teased her ear as the rich timbre of his voice dropped to a rasp. "Take a bite. Tell me it isn't one of the best things you've ever put in your mouth."

He was referencing the fresh baked roll, yet she blushed. There seemed some hidden innuendo to his words, or perhaps it was the mere sound of him whispering in her ear about putting something in her mouth.

Tearing a piece of bread so he'd stop focusing on her, she tasted it and nodded her approval. If the bread was good, she had no idea. Her tongue was too dry to taste anything at the moment.

"Melts in your mouth, doesn't it?" His large fingers kneaded her shoulder and her nipples instantly hardened. She was grateful for choosing such a concealing sweater when she went home to change and shower off that horrid fart stench.

"It's very good," she rasped.

"Atta girl, now eat up."

Chloe forced herself not to slump in her chair when his touch disappeared. The others still stared wordlessly.

"What?" he asked, dragging a chair back from the table. As he straddled the wood her gaze dropped to the shape of his thighs molded by the dark denim of his jeans.

Tyson smiled. "Unicorns and rainbows, buddy, unicorns, and rainbows."

Whatever that meant, it caused Trenton to scowl. "Bite me, Ty."

Chloe reluctantly picked at the sandwich but didn't pick it up to take a bite. The thing was cartoon sized. However, the meager tastes she allowed herself were delicious.

Eventually, Jeremy excused himself to go check on Jade. When he didn't return, Tyson suggested that he and Kat head home to pick up Mia.

Chloe should be going, too, but when the time came to actually leave she hesitated. Who knew if she'd ever see Trenton again?

He hadn't said anything to her since Tyson's odd comment, but still, being in his presence filled her with a strange sort of awareness. She wondered if he was feeling it, too.

As Trenton followed Kat and Tyson to the door, Chloe carried the plates to the sink. The house was still a mess from the party though someone had picked up most of the trash. Without wanting to snoop, she quickly peeked under the sink for something to clean the counters.

Running warm water over a soapy sponge she wiped down surfaces. By the time she heard the front door shut she was more than halfway through the kitchen.

"You don't have to do that, doll."

She jumped and gasped, her busy hands stilling as he stood directly behind her. Too close. She turned to put some space between them, but that was a mistake. Those riveting blue eyes studied her, and while he wasn't touching her, his size had a way of boxing her in.

Her breath hitched as her heart beat out of rhythm. When he looked at her like that her brains turned into mush. "I..."

"You?"

"I..." She couldn't think. "They have enough on their plate."

The scent of cold winter air clung to his now familiar scent. A shadow of dark stubble shadowed his throat, partially concealing the scar that climbed his neck to his jaw. How far did it travel below his collar?

His hair reminded her of a horsetail, so thick and dark, tied at the base of his skull. One lonely strand had escaped the knot and lay sexily over his temple. He was so imperfect, yet so stunning at the same time.

He didn't allow her much personal space, which seemed to be a thing with him. The longer that cerulean stare bored into her, the more she found it impossible to hold his gaze, so she dropped her focus to his chest.

With slow, measured movement his large fingers gently tipped up her chin and her eyes closed. She attempted to regulate her breathing so she didn't pass out.

"Look at me, doll."

Forcing her gaze to meet his she panted softly. Men didn't deserve such full eyelashes.

The corner of his mouth hooked in a lopsided grin. "You got nothin' to be afraid of with me."

He leaned closer and her breath held, but he didn't kiss her. He reached behind her and took the sponge. A mix of confusion and disappointment crept through her, throwing her more off balance. She didn't like expecting things she wasn't sure she wanted—and then being disappointed when her expectations were unfulfilled.

She stepped away, numb and mute, as he finished wiping the counters.

This was ridiculous. No one touched her, yet he'd kissed her and put his hands on her several times in the past twenty-four hours. Stranger still, she let him.

He acted as though this familiarity between them was normal. Maybe she was imagining all this electricity, which seemed to short-circuit her brain every time he was near. Or maybe he was like this with *all* women. She frowned.

Confused images of their kiss floated through her mind, multiplying, each one a little different until she couldn't decipher which one was the real memory.

"You okay?"

She stared at him blankly, but he wasn't looking back. He was wiping the table and not doing a very thorough job. She attempted to speak, but nothing came out. Clearing her throat, she tried again. "I should go."

Still not looking at her, he said, "I'll tell Jade and Jeremy to call you if they need anything."

His words pinched. Didn't he care she was leaving? Obviously not.

Disappointment flooded through her veins like ice, cold enough to sever her fantasies from her reality. She was definitely reading too much into things. His indifference was clear. Her presence was trivial to him.

"Well... Maybe we'll run into each other again sometime. It was nice seeing you." Her words, though polite, sounded clumsy and stupid. She turned and walked into the hall to retrieve her scarf, gloves, and purse.

Trenton's presence was a distraction. Her sole concern should have been Jade, but every time he looked at her or spoke to her, Chloe turned into a bumbling idiot. She resented the jolts of excitement pinging around her stomach. She didn't need his swarthy glances that hit her like distant caresses. And she certainly had no interest in bantering with him—*flirting*—if that's what it was. She wasn't sure. Her life revolved around her sons, clients, and her gay neighbors—all people who never spoke to her in a flirtatious manner.

Trenton Cole was simply too complicated and too ... *masculine* for her to be around. Even if he was interested in her, she knew better than to get involved with a man like him. The man's pores seeped testosterone and his size could annihilate a woman. She had no business even letting him into her private thoughts and didn't want to worry what he might think of her.

Once the downward spiral of her insecurities grabbed hold there was no getting back to level ground. Marcus's words resurfaced in her mind, sharp as ever and cutting through layers of hard-earned confidence.

*No one's ever going to want a woman with thighs that size.*

*You're nothing but a fat cow, past her prime, ready to be put out to pasture.*

The echo of her husband's cruel words played like fresh cuts as the record of self-doubt spun round and round in her head. Jade's home *absolutely* was not the place for her to have a vulnerable breakdown.

Though she appeared a put together, professional woman—and on most days she was—there was good reason for that. Her life wasn't complicated. It was simple and she was single by choice. Interacting with men, trusting them on any sort of personal level, seemed a daunting task she'd never be ready to take on. After trusting Marcus, suffering through his cruelty and risking her life to escape, she accepted she sucked at reading men.

Her world revolved around her boys. Her profession was her sanity, that little escape of self-made success that added additional value to her life. She preferred privacy and didn't trust easily. Of course, it got lonely, but Tommy and Adam were like family and they distracted her from everything she was missing. Trenton Cole seemed to shine a spotlight on the empty areas of her life, though she doubted he realized the effect he was having on her.

She wanted to go back in time to yesterday when Trenton Cole seemed as intangible as a guardian angel and so embedded in her past he'd never dig himself out and find his way to her present. He'd always been someone safe to fantasize about, but now that he was real every thought became more dangerous than the last.

Glancing one last time into the kitchen she saw Trent still cleaning. She left without another word.

# Four

CHLOE REACHED for Jade's file and, rather than press the intercom, went to the waiting room to greet her friend. The purple marks of exhaustion beneath Jade's eyes had faded to slight shadows, but the lingering bruises and scrapes were constant reminders of how much danger her friend had faced. They settled into the overstuffed chairs and Chloe handed her a mug of coffee.

"Thank you."

This was her favorite appointment each week, but not always the easiest. "How are you today?"

"Better." Jade took a sip of the coffee and grimaced.

"Is the coffee not okay?" Chloe thought it tasted fine.

"Nothing tastes right to me today. I think I'm getting a sinus infection or something. I feel all congested."

"I wouldn't doubt it. The last three weeks have been stressful. Your system's probably crashing.

Sometimes stress weakens immunities. Extra vitamins and rest might help. How's everything else going?"

"Okay. Mia came over this weekend. I hadn't seen her since it happened. I missed her."

"I bet. How was the visit?"

"Quiet. We stayed in most of the weekend."

"Have you heard anything back from the district attorney?"

"They told Jeremy I need to come in for another interview."

"How do you feel about that?"

Rolling her eyes, Jade huffed. "I hate it, but I know it's necessary."

They sat quietly for a moment. Jade's sessions of late held an overwhelming moroseness. Chloe knew it was circumstantial. It had only been three weeks, not nearly enough time to return to normal.

Although Chloe hadn't been back to Jade and Jeremy's home since the day after the incident, she imagined Jade was putting up a good front for others. Her office was a place Jade could let down those walls and drop the façade. It was a safe place, a place where it was okay to be a little broken.

"Have you thought any more about work?"

"Yeah. I'm bored out of my freaking mind, but I'm not ready to go back. I'm afraid they'll judge me."

It would definitely be a touchy situation since so many friends from work had also been friends with the now deceased. "Perhaps it would be better to wait until the investigation's over. If anyone's curious, it'll be on public record and they can see for themselves that you were the victim."

"I hate that word—*victim*. I wish I could change my name."

"You just did, Mrs. Larson."

Jade's laugh was halfhearted. "I know, but everywhere I go this is going to follow me."

"Are you afraid people will ask you about it?"

"Yes and no."

"Remember, Jade, our past only has as much power as we allow it. If you deal with this, come to terms with it, no one can use it against you." Some words were delivered like a memorized script, professional and comforting. But there was always that awareness that even Chloe was still partially controlled by her past and therefore a hypocrite in secret.

But this wasn't about her. It was about Jade. Chloe tipped her head empathetically. "How is your family coping?"

"My parents are a mess."

Jade's parents were unaware of the initial attack, but with the recent news coverage, they were now aware of the situation. "How much did you tell them?"

"Enough, but not all. They know about the night of the party, but nothing about the months prior. Nathan and Trent are saying it will probably be a speedy investigation and are trying to work with the police to keep things relatively quiet."

Chloe tried not to get hung up on the mention of Trenton. She was over him, or so she told herself. After replaying their brief time together to the point of analytical obsession and becoming a prisoner in her own head, she needed to verbally tell herself to stop.

He wasn't interested. She didn't know why admitting that bothered her so much when she herself had no interest in getting involved with anyone. She accepted it was simply a natural reaction to rejection, nothing specific to Trenton Cole.

She paused when she realized Jade had asked her something. Trying to recall her words, she drew a blank. Heat bloomed at the apples of her cheeks. "Jade, I'm so sorry. I spaced out there for a second. What were you saying?"

Jade laughed, a small but genuine sound. Chloe took the laughter as a good sign, a signal that her patient and friend was regaining her vitality and still able to find amusement in small things.

"I said we're having a get together this weekend at Kat's for Mia. Kind of a belated birthday party since we were away for her real birthday. We wanted you to come. Bring Dayton and Mattie. Ty's nephews will be there. They're a little older than your boys, but I'm sure between Mia, Davis, and the rest of them, they'd have a good time."

Would Trenton be there? *This isn't about him!*

She considered how blurred the boundaries were becoming between her and Jade. Could she maintain a professional demeanor if she became more involved in her personal life? "Jade, I think we have to have a talk about my position in your life."

"What do you mean?"

"I'm your therapist, but I also consider you a friend."

"Of course you're my friend—otherwise I'd never tell you half the stuff I tell you here."

"Friends don't charge a fee, Jade."

She held up a hand. "I know what you're getting at and I know this isn't the way things work with your other clients, but for right now can you just be both? If it really becomes an issue I'll start looking for a new therapist, but you were here for all the stuff that I went through and I need you to help me find closure. I don't want to start over with a new therapist and I don't want to lose you as my friend. I know I'm asking a lot, Chloe, but ... please."

She sighed, knowing there were rules in her profession. So long as Jade recognized she couldn't always be both and eventually she'd have to find a new therapist if they continued to see each other outside of the office, she supposed she could keep a professional presence in her life for a time. And maybe Dayton would hit it off with one of the other boys at the party and pull out of this funk he'd been in.

"What time's the party?"

Jade smiled. "Saturday around four. We're ordering pizza and Kat said something about an ice cream sundae station."

"Okay. Down the street from your old place, right?"

"Right. Big yellow colonial. You can't miss it."

# Five

"WHY DO we have to go to some stupid party where we don't know anyone?" Dayton griped as Chloe applied eye shadow.

Her teeth clenched, but she kept her expression serene. "Once you get there, you can make friends."

"I don't want to be friends with those people." He sat on the floor outside of her bathroom, bouncing a rubber ball against the wall, pouting.

"Dayton, please stop doing that. You'll leave marks on the wall."

"No, I won't." *Bounce.* "Why can't I stay here?" *Bounce.*

"Because you're nine and we're all going to the party—as a family."

*Bounce.* "This sucks." *Bounce.*

"Hey, watch your mouth. And stop with the ball or I'm taking it."

He grumbled something under his breath and Mattie stepped around him. "Mom, can I wear these?" Her youngest held up a pair of shorts.

"No. Where did you even find them?"

"In the closet. Please?"

"No, sweetie, it's too cold for shorts. You're wearing what you have on."

"Why?"

"Because it's winter, retard," Dayton sneered.

"Hey!" Chloe pivoted, wondering where he even heard such a word. "We do not talk to each other like that and I don't want to hear that word out of your mouth again. Apologize to your brother right now."

"Sorry, stupid."

"*Hey!*" She glared, appalled and disappointed at his defiant attitude. "Dayton, go to your room until you're ready to sincerely apologize."

The ball slammed against the wall as he scrambled to his feet, shoving Mattie as he marched down the hall. "God! I hate this family!" Ten seconds later his bedroom door slammed.

"You okay, bud?"

Her youngest shrugged.

She lovingly tousled his hair. "Dayton's just in a bad mood."

"He's always in a bad mood."

"It'll get better. Why don't you go wash your face and put on your shoes?"

"What about Day?"

"Let me worry about your brother."

A few minutes later Chloe finished getting ready and walked to Dayton's room. She knocked and entered. "Day?"

He was lying across his bed with his cheek on his arms, scowling. Dry tracks from tears marked his stoic face. She sat on the edge of the bed and laid her hand on his back. "Wanna talk about what just happened?"

"No."

"Just because you're in a bad mood doesn't give you the right to take it out on others. That's not how it works." He said nothing and kept his gaze on his bedspread. She sighed. "You owe Mattie an apology."

"Why? He's annoying."

"He did nothing to you and you called him a name and pushed him."

"He wanted to wear shorts and there's snow on the ground. That's stupid."

"That doesn't make him stupid, Dayton. That makes him a seven-year-old boy. You used to ask to do the same things."

The longer this moody preteen stuck around, the more she accepted her sweet little boy wasn't coming back. She missed that guy, missed the closeness he cut out of their relationship without warning.

Of course, her sons would grow up, but why did growing up have to mean growing apart? It killed her that he wouldn't talk to her about his feelings.

She ran her fingers through his brown hair, savoring the contact because he—for once—allowed it. "You need a haircut."

"I don't wanna get a haircut. I wanna grow it out."

Her eyes closed as his perpetual anger added to her worry. This negativity was starting to fester and affect their family as a whole. Something had to give.

"I'll tell you what. You try to be a little nicer to your brother and I'll think about it. If I hear you fighting with him or calling him names, I'm taking you right to the barber. Deal?"

He took a deep breath then grumbled, "Deal."

"Good. Start by apologizing to him. Then put your shoes and coat on so we can go."

They arrived at Tyson and Kat's around four-thirty. Cars lined the quiet street and filled the drive-way. The old house was beautiful, Ty's renovations highlighted the original charm while adding plenty of modern amenities.

Kat's welcoming grin greeted them as she opened the door and offered to take their coats. Kids shouted and ran around the living room while two older boys stood in the center playing *Wii*. Chloe nudged her boys in that general direction and headed into the kitchen, where she heard other female voices.

A tall African American woman with dread-locks charged past Chloe and snapped at Jade, "Girl, get out of my way. You got no business bein' by that stove."

"How long until that's done, Gloria? I'm starving." Jade surrendered the wooden spoon and stepped back from the stove.

"Don't rush it!" The woman waved a hand of claw-like nails at Jade, shooing her from the steaming pot.

Chloe warmed at Jade's laugh. Laughter was good. "Hey." Chloe waved, announcing her arrival.

"You came!" Jade walked over and gave her a hug. "Are the boys here?"

"Yes. I sent them to play with the other kids."

"Good." She turned to the woman at the stove. "Gloria, this is my friend Chloe. Chloe, this is Tyson's sister, Gloria."

"Nice to meet you. I'd shake your hand, but I got to guard my gumbo or Jade'll eat it. *Darrel!*" the woman shouted and Chloe jumped.

"*What*, woman?" a hassled, masculine voice yelled from the other room.

"Go pick up the pizzas!"

"*You* go pick up the pizzas!"

Gloria stilled and slowly turned her head over her shoulder. Her dark eyebrow lifted like the hook of a question mark and she stared at the wall.

Surprisingly, a man in his late twenties, presumably Darrel, appeared a moment later holding a set of car keys. "I'm going."

Gloria turned back to the pot and stirred the gumbo, muttering something about useless fools thinking they could talk to her like that.

"Come on, let's go sit." Jade took Chloe's arm and led her through the house to the dining room. Tyson and Jeremy sat laughing with Kat and an older couple Chloe assumed was Tyson's parents.

"He ain't ever gonna learn." The older woman chuckled.

"He better not mess up the order or Gloria's gonna kick his ass for sure," Tyson said and the rest nodded in agreement.

The older woman noticed Chloe and smiled. "And who is this?"

Jade nudged her toward a chair. "Celia, this is

my friend Chloe. Chloe, these are Tyson's parents, Celia and Maurice Adams."

The conversation turned to how she knew everyone but quickly moved to other topics, so as not to dampen the mood. Thirty minutes later Darrel returned with a stack of steaming pizza boxes and Chloe helped the women set out plates and situate the children.

By the time it was dark everyone finished eating and Kat arranged bowls of ice cream toppings along the counter. Jade seemed to be very relaxed and enjoying her third bowl of Gloria's gumbo.

The kids continued to play video games and Chloe was glad to see Dayton had left his place on the couch, where he'd been sulking, to join the others. Once Kat had everything set up for the sundaes, she called the kids and all her well-organized hard work was destroyed. But she was a good sport about it and smiled at their excitement.

After the children had their fill, Chloe carried the messy spoons and bowls to the sink while the adults helped themselves to dessert. Tyson approached Kat from behind and tenderly kissed his wife on the neck. Chloe suffered a pang of envy for their happy marriage.

She helped herself to a small bowl of chocolate peanut butter and rejoined the others in the dining room. As they sat, enjoying their dessert, Mr. and Mrs. Adams said their goodbyes.

Chloe waited with Jade as Tyson walked his parents out. She heard him speaking to someone as he entered the room and almost choked on a chunk of peanut butter when Jeremy said, "What's up, Trent?"

Quickly dabbing any chocolate off her lips, she hoped her lipstick was still intact. Her concern for her appearance derailed as Jade bolted out of her chair, hand over her mouth, and rushed from the room.

Her sudden exit triggered immediate concern and Jeremy took off after her. Little Davis, Gloria and Darrel's son, ran into the dining room covering his mouth. "Ew, Aunt Jade just barfed in the snow!"

"What?" Kat stood and left the room.

"I'm gonna sit this one out," Tyson said, taking his seat again.

Chloe stared at her melting ice cream as Trenton took the seat next to her and examined the leftover gumbo at Jade's vacated spot.

Tyson pointed to the bowl. "That's probably what did it."

"Don't you go blaming my gumbo for her getting sick," Gloria snapped.

Trenton's low voice tickled Chloe's ear. "And how are you this lovely evening, doll?"

Her entire body tightened as his deep voice sent chills racing over her skin. Swallowing, she pretended to be unaffected. "I'm fine. How are you?"

"Good. Good." His hooded gaze scrutinized her face and her heart beat clumsily.

"Everything all right, man?" Tyson asked as Jeremy returned.

He shook his head. "She was sick in the hedges. Sorry. She must be coming down with something."

"It's fine. Between living with a five-year-old and

a pregnant wife, it doesn't bother me anymore."
Everyone froze at Tyson's words.

Jeremy suddenly looked like he might need to take a trip to the hedges himself.

"Jeremy?" Chloe said softly.

On a long, slow exhale, Jeremy dropped into a chair.

It suddenly clicked. Jade's taste buds were off, she was congested, had a hefty appetite, and her stomach was unsettled. Either she had the flu or she was pregnant.

"Could she be?" Chloe whispered.

Eyes wide, he shook his head. "I guess. I mean, we just had our honeymoon. It isn't like we've been sleeping in separate rooms."

"Do you think she realizes—"

A door slammed and Kat rushed by, shoving her arms in her coat. "Ty, I'm running to the store!"

Gloria grinned. "She realizes."

Twenty minutes later, everyone sat silently in the dining room waiting for Jade and Jeremy to come downstairs. No one seemed sure about how to react to the idea of Jade possibly being pregnant. It was an extremely touchy subject, her old wounds still tender and sensitive.

Chloe could see the worry in everyone's eyes, except for Trenton's, but only because she refused to look his way at all. Jeremy walked in and everyone held a collective breath.

His expression was unreadable. "It's positive."

Everyone exhaled, excitedly talking at once. Kat burst into tears. Jeremy was obviously overwhelmed. Tyson passed his friend a beer and he chugged it.

Trenton whacked a large hand on his friend's back. *"Mazel tov!"*

Jeremy's grin hardly penetrated his shock. His gaze turned to her. "She's asking for you, Chloe."

91

# Six

TRENT WATCHED as Chloe left the dining room. Today was apparently a day of surprises. Between Jeremy's news, his sister getting the promotion she'd been waiting for, and Chloe's lovely presence, he'd have to say it was turning into a kickass Saturday.

She looked great in her jeans and cute little plaid *Chucks*. She wasn't a tiny woman, but there was something about her that made her ultra-feminine, adorably so.

He liked the way she wore unique pieces of jewelry, a bracelet made of old typewriter keys and another made out of a silver spoon. Unlike the day they met, there wasn't a diamond on her. Now, her earrings tended to be of less expensive metals and her rings were bold with clunky stones that were pretty in a different way.

She was something else. The more he ran into her the more his intrigue grew. The only thing he disliked was the way she had trouble looking at him. She seemed to blow him off the last time they were alone in Jeremy's kitchen, so he backed off. But she wasn't a woman easily forgotten. He'd thought about her every day, anxious for the next time he might run into her. When Ty invited him to Mia's party, he accepted on the hope that Chloe might also be here and here she was.

This time he'd try not to come on too strong. But, man, he wanted to follow her into some private corner of the house and pin her to a wall. He wanted to run his hands over her body and feel her breath hitch and her pulse flutter. He wanted to steal another kiss and possibly get her to *not* run away this time. It was a little difficult to do all of that when she avoided looking at him.

He had that effect on a lot of people, especially women, but Chloe had no problem looking at Jeremy or Ty. Why should he make her any more nervous than those guys?

Maybe it had to do with her past. Chloe had experiences that would change any woman. He couldn't just charge in demanding kisses and laying on the charm. He had to be smart, which was exactly why he gave her an escape the other day. She had to be the one to come to him, otherwise, he'd take it that she wasn't ready.

The question was, did he have the patience to wait her out? Every time he saw her she seemed more nervous than the last. Maybe all he could do was pop up in her life like this, when she connected with Jade, wear down her resistance a little more each time. The trouble was, he had a healthy sexual appetite and since crossing Chloe's path, no other women had held his attention. She was becoming his secret, dirty obsession and she'd probably slap him if he knew the things he fantasized about doing with her. All those delicious curves and that mouth...

"Hey, settle down in there!" Ty yelled as the kids in the other room were getting rowdy.

Trent put his thoughts away for another time. Jeremy nursed a beer and whispered quietly with Kat. His boy was probably worried about Jade dealing with a pregnancy so soon after her recent traumas. Trent could understand that, but as a man who'd never have children of his own, he thought the news was great.

When he was a young boy he'd been in an accident that almost killed him. He didn't recall much of the accident, only being in the back of his family's station wagon without a seatbelt. It was a freak thing. A rig, barreling down the Garden State Parkway, lost a wheel. The rim soared over the highway and spliced right through the roof of his parents' car.

His father, who was driving, lost control and spun into the oncoming traffic. Trent woke up two days later with seventy-six stitches from his jaw to his chest and ice packed between his legs—a very sore crotch.

His parents hadn't told him about his situation until he was sixteen and they found a three pack of condoms in his drawer. At the time he was relieved. What sixteen-year-old wanted to be a father? But as he grew older the lost opportunity sometimes got him down.

He loved kids and thought he'd make a pretty decent dad if he had the chance. But life had dealt him a different hand and at his age, he'd come to accept the blessings he had and not worry about the things he couldn't change.

Speaking of children—Mia walked into the room and climbed onto Jeremy's lap, bringing a smile to Trent's lips. She was a cute little thing. Being a father would be an amazing privilege. He had no doubt his friend would manage just fine the second time around.

There was a loud crash in the other room followed by children shouting.

"That's it." Tyson went to go investigate the ruckus.

Trent stood to give him a hand.

As they entered the living room the shouting escalated and Ty raced into the tussle. "What the hell?" Ty grabbed for one of his nephews, who was wrestling—not play wrestling—with another boy. "Robert, get off him!"

The tear of fabric filled the room as the other boy swung wildly at the kid's face, clipping Ty in the jaw. Ty continued to break up the fight. His other nephews stood to the side, yelling. There was a smaller boy hiding behind the arm of the sofa.

Enough was enough. Trent let out a long, sharp whistle. "*Yo!*" The room silenced.

Ty tugged Robert off the floor and yelled for his sister and Darrel. Trent stepped in and stood close to the other boy in case he decided to go apeshit again.

"What the heck is going on?" Ty demanded.

"He started it!" Robert snapped.

"Did not!"

Tyson held up a hand, silencing them both. "Kat, please go in the other room with Mia and Davis. One of you better tell me what happened. The truth."

The boys shrugged their shoulders and kept quiet.

"Somebody better start explaining, quick."

"I didn't do anything, Uncle Ty," Robert grumbled. "I swear. We were playing *Wii* and all of a sudden Dayton went crazy and shoved me across the room."

Tyson looked at the other boy. "Is that what happened, Dayton?"

"No." The kid folded his arms across his chest and scowled.

He looked ready to blow again. He also looked about a foot shorter than Robert. Trent was pretty sure Ty's nephew would've handed the other kid his ass if they hadn't broken up the fight.

"Well, no one's going anywhere until I get some honest answers. There's no excuse for this behavior in my home."

Robert shrugged his uncle off and straightened his shirt. It was obvious the kid was angry. He noticed the rip and jerked his chin at Dayton. "Fool, you ripped my shirt. Lucky I don't beat your ass again."

Before Ty could react Dayton charged, but

Trent intercepted, grabbing the kid and taking a few kicks to the shin as the boy went ballistic, cursing and shouting at Robert. "I'll kill you!"

"*Enough!*" Trent pinned the kid's arms to his side, restraining him before he seriously hurt someone—or more likely hurt himself. "You need to chill, little man."

"Get off me!"

"What's going on? Put down my son, right this instant!" Chloe stormed into the den, full momma bear, and Trent immediately released her angry little cub. Shit. Of course, it would be her son...

"Chloe, doll, the boys—"

Hard brown eyes glared at him, cutting off his explanation. "*Who do you think you are, touching my son?*"

Um, okay, this was unexpected. Taking a breath he held out his hands in surrender. "The boys had a little scuffle and—"

Her red painted nail jabbed his chest. "How dare you put your hands on *my* child? I don't care what was going on. You have no right to touch him!" The finger jabbed deeper, causing him to take a step back. "If there's a problem, you call *me*! I'm his mother and we do not resolve arguments that way in our family!" She turned back to her son. "Dayton, what happened?"

Shamefully, with each jab of Chloe's finger, Trent's blood heated a little hotter. *Totally inappropriate!*

The kid shook off his mother's attention and Ty tried to reason with her. "Chloe, they were just being boys and things got a little too rough."

She ignored him. "Where's Mattie?" The younger boy ducked lower behind the couch.

Trent tried to explain in a calmer voice. "The boys were fighting. We had to break it up before someone got hurt."

As if just registering his words, her entire demeanor changed and she gaped at her eldest son. Her chin trembled as heat colored her cheeks. "Dayton, is that true?"

The boy didn't answer so Trent filled her in. "Ty took a few swats to the face and your son kicked me some in the shins. That's the only reason my hands were on him. I was trying to calm him down. I would never hurt a child."

Lips compressed, her lashes fluttered. Shit, he hated seeing girls get upset.

Turning back to her son, she repeated in a firmer voice, "Is that true, Dayton? And do *not* lie to me." Apparently, Dayton's guilty expression was enough of an answer for her. She pointed a finger to the hall. "Go get your coat and wait by the door."

The boy left the room and Chloe ignored everyone else as she went to the side of the couch where her youngest hid. She dropped to her knees, her voice softening. "It's okay, Mattie. You can come out."

Trent frowned. The boy seemed overly upset by the scuffle. They were boys. Boys wrestled sometimes.

Chloe stood, holding the kid as if he were much younger than his actual age. Carefully putting him on the ground, she kissed his head and whispered, "Go get your coat."

The little guy actually hugged the perimeter of the wall on his way out of the den. That's when it occurred to Trent. The boy wasn't so much afraid of the other boys. He was afraid of the men.

A sick feeling settled in his stomach. It was so easy to see Chloe as a single woman who shared mutual friends. How quickly he'd overlooked where she and her boys had come from. The things they might have seen and experienced.

He should've never grabbed the kid. But Dayton would've gone after Robert again if someone hadn't stopped him. It was a crappy situation all around.

He waited by the door as she made her goodbyes with the kids. Her steps faltered as she spotted him blocking her exit, but he had to make this right. "I'm sorry about what happened, Chloe."

"Boys, go wait in the car." A mix of emotion played on her face. When her sons were no longer in earshot, her words turned clipped and frazzled. "Mr. Cole, I'm sorry for my assumption—"

"Don't call me that. My name's Trent."

"Trent... Trenton, I'm sorry I jumped to conclusions."

He tried not to let the way she lowered her gaze away from his irritate him, but it did. He gently tipped her chin until she looked at him.

"I'm the one who needs to apologize. I never meant to scare you or your boys. I'm not that kind of man, Chloe. Tell me you know that."

"Beyond a car ride and a few recent run-ins, I don't know anything about the kind of man you are."

Her words enforced the gap between them, up-setting him and pissing him off at the same time. "You know I'm nothing like Marcus."

Her eyes widened and she took a step back. "Who told you my husband's name?"

He opened his mouth, but couldn't think of anything to say. *Fuck!*

She was looking at him now. Well, more scowl-ing. "Who told you my husband's name?"

*Son of a bitch.* His heart pounded as he clumsily tried to cover his tracks. "I'm sure you mentioned his name. The night we met. You told me about your old life and how you were making a new be-ginning."

"I never would have..." Her words drifted away as an unsure frown pinched her brow.

He hated making her second guess herself. It was his fuck up, not hers.

She never gave a name. She was smarter than that. And he couldn't explain how he knew the de-tails of her marriage unless the information had come straight from her, which it hadn't. His only option was to distract her from his slip up.

"Chloe, I'm not him. I remember everything you told me that day in the truck. Please, believe me. I am nothing like your ex-husband."

Her jaw trembled, her eyes glazing with emo-tion. "I'm sorry." She pulled out her keys. "I can't do this."

"Don't run away." As he reached for her she jerked her arm away. Regret swept through him. He'd seen her flustered, determined, and even desperate, but this was the first time he'd ever seen that sort of distrust in her eyes and he hated it.

"I have to go."

# Seven

WARM BREATH PUFFED against Trent's cheek as soft fingers scratched the whiskers at his jaw. He swatted the tiny fingers away and a giggle tinkled through the quiet room.

Something tickled his nose and his lips twitched as nervous laughter wheezed playfully. A silky strand of hair tickled his nose again, this time triggering the irritating prelude of a sneeze.

More giggles.

"Brielle, get away from your uncle and let him sleep," Phoenix's voice hissed from the other room.

His niece giggled.

Trent kept his eyes closed and fought a smile. The nose-tickling continued, accompanied by tiny fingers thrumming over his socked feet. That would be his nephew, Austin. Cabinets opened and closed over the gurgle of coffee percolating. A pan clattered lightly and then came the snapping sizzle of bacon frying.

"Brie, put this tiara on him," Austin whispered.

The tickling stopped and the weight of a toy crown pressed into Trent's head. Snickers escalated to smothered hilarity. "He sure is a hairy queen," his niece lisped.

"Where're your play earrings?" Austin whispered.

More youthful laughter chirped from Brie as the soft patter of her socked feet scampered across the room.

"Get the big ones with the purple diamonds."

Trent could tell Brielle found the earrings by the way her stifled laughter punched out in little breaths. Figuring he should probably save his manhood while there was still time, he waited for her to creep closer and pounced. "*Gotchya!*"

She shrieked out a burst of laughter. Grabbing her by her tiny rib cage, he tickled. Peals of hilarity screeched across the room as Austin tackled him, looping his arms around his shoulders, a brave squire prepared to slay the giant who held his sister captive.

"Who dares wake the sleeping giant?" Trent bellowed and pinned Brielle on the couch, capturing her squirming feet.

"Austin, help! The ugly queen's got me!"

Trent roared, flipping the boy off his shoulders. They wrestled and played until they were wheezing to catch their breath. Only when Phoenix announced breakfast was ready did they scamper out of the room.

Entering the kitchen, his sister handed him a mug of coffee. "You got in late last night."

He swallowed a gulp, hoping it would settle his

headache. He was too old to start his day with rubies and wrestling. "Did I wake you?"

"I heard you locking your gun in the safe."

Taking a seat next to Brielle, he pushed her glass of milk away from the edge of the table. "Sorry. I should be back at my place tonight."

Phoenix adjusted her robe and carried a plate of pancakes to the center of the table. "How'd you make out?"

"Found the girl. She was shacked up with her boyfriend as expected."

"I bet her parents were relieved."

"You could say that, but the twenty-year-old guy harboring a minor wasn't too happy." He spread a smear of butter over his cakes with the back of his fork.

"How old was the girl?"

"She'll be eighteen in a month. I'm not sure her parents can press charges."

Phoenix sat down with her coffee. His sister was one of his best friends. She was a realist, but a pleasant one. She knew how to roll with the punches and there wasn't much that could fluster her.

"Pete says you got a good chunk of change from this job."

"Could'a been his." He'd offered the job to his brother-in-law.

She rolled her eyes. "You know I don't want him in the field anymore. Now that I'm making more money, I'd rather he stick with the desk work."

Like Trent, Pete was an excellent agent. He knew how to shadow someone for days without being detected. But over the years, since the kids were born, he tended to stick with the local end of things, turning down most of the private jobs.

Trent, on the other hand, had a hard time turning down private jobs, which paid a hell of a lot more than government sanctioned bids. Jobs like the one he just finished paid enough for him to take it easy for a while.

Of course, that sort of work also put his day-to-day life on hiatus, requiring him to travel and stay the course until the job was done and his mark was secure. He'd been on the road for the past month.

Over the years they combined their various skillsets and formed a tight little business that kept them all afloat, him, Pete, and Jeremy. Jeremy could break and rewrite codes faster than most people could put together a toddler's jigsaw puzzle, so he handled computer security. Pete handled the monetary side of things, negotiating each contract to make sure they were paid accordingly for each job. And Trent did most of the legwork.

Pete stepped into the kitchen, kissed his wife, and filled a mug. "I got a message on my phone this morning. The money's been wired to your account." He settled into a chair with the morning paper.

"Good. Thanks for letting me crash here."

"Uncle Trent, are you gonna sleep over again tonight?"

He looked at his niece, her red curls tousled from sleep and her little Hello Kitty pajama shirt sprinkled with dribbles of syrup. She was getting so big. Had it really been almost five years since she was born?

"I gotta get back home, sweetheart."

She pouted and poked at her saturated pancakes with her fork. Her food looked more like round sponges than pancakes. That pout could seal the sale of a human soul.

He kissed her pudgy cheek. "Don't worry, I'll see you Saturday for the St. Paddy's Day Parade."

"You will?"

"You bet."

Mollified, she smiled and continued to eat her sponge cakes.

"Is Aunt Bristol gonna be there?" Austin asked.

Phoenix stood to refill her coffee. "Yes, but it isn't her weekend with Dallas. He's gonna be with his dad."

Austin looked disappointed. Trent could relate. Growing up with four sisters didn't leave many options for activities boys favored. Suffice it to say, this morning wasn't his first royal makeover.

He thought about Chloe's sons. The shy one, Mattie, was younger, but Dayton seemed about Austin's age. Recalling the incident at Ty's house a couple weeks ago, he debated if the kid would be a good influence or not.

Or maybe that was just an off day. Maybe there was more to the story and Robert had antagonized the kid. Maybe the kid needed a friend. The question was could he convince Chloe to join them after the way they'd left things?

A shiver of excitement trailed down his spine at the fantasy of her smiling over a mug of green beer, wearing those ridiculous shamrock headband antlers women usually wore to the parade. He bet she looked pretty in green.

It had been nearly a month since he'd last seen her and not a day went by that she didn't cross his mind. For all he knew, she never thought of him, but if that was the case he wanted to change her thinking. He wanted to be on her mind as much as she was on his.

"I have a friend who has sons close to your age, Austin. I'll ask her if she wants to come with us."

His sister paused from taking a sip of her coffee and lifted an eyebrow at him. "Her?"

He rolled his eyes. "Yes, her. She lives over in New Castle. I can swing by her place this week and see if she's free."

Phoenix gave Pete a knowing look. "He'll swing by her place..."

Trent rolled his eyes. "Settle yourself. I have to get her to agree to go before anything's certain."

Phoenix smirked into her mug. "Pete's told me about your effect on women. She'll be there."

Later that day Trent coasted through the streets of New Castle. It took him a while, but eventually, he spotted a house that resembled the one from six years ago. He knew he reached the right place when he saw her little yellow Chevy parked in the drive. Although it was March, this far up north there were still drifts of slushy snow along the curbs.

Parking his truck, he climbed out and stepped over a pile of green army action figures staged for battle along the shoveled walk. Voices and laughter echoed from inside the house. Hoping she didn't mind him stopping by unannounced, he pressed the bell and waited.

The voices quieted and a few moments later a man opened the door. Okay, not what he was expecting.

"Can I help you?" the man asked, holding the door so Trent couldn't see inside.

Was this the wrong house? "I'm looking for Chloe Wolfe."

The man made a face that didn't tell Trent if the name was familiar to him or not. "No one by that name lives here."

He frowned. "Uh, there's no Chloe Wolfe here?" Should he use her other name?

"Are you selling something?"

He glanced at the driveway, smelling bullshit. That was her car. He recognized the license plate. "No. I'm a friend of Chloe's and that's her car."

"A *friend*? And your name is..."

"Trenton Cole. Look, is she here or not?"

The man raised an eyebrow, unimpressed with his tone. He probably figured a friend would know if he was at the right house.

Not used to justifying his choices, he explained vaguely, "I didn't have her number and I haven't been here in years. I might be at the wrong house."

"Years?" Unabashedly appraising his attire, the man asked, "And what did you say your name was?"

"Trent. Trenton Cole." He shifted his feet. "Look, it's cold. I don't mean to be rude, but if she's in there, can you tell her I'm here?"

The man mouth curved like he just discovered a secret. "You must be Jeremy and Jade's friend."

*Finally.* "That's right."

Without taking his eyes off Trent, he called behind him, "Hey Chloe, you have a visitor." His amused expression grew more defined as the door opened wide.

Trent's breath sucked deep into his lungs as her startled gaze tangled with his. She glanced down at herself then back at him. In a crew neck sweatshirt, cuffed gray sweats that only reached her calves, and little white ankle socks she looked good enough to eat.

"What are you doing here, Trenton?" Her expression turned troubled—not at all welcoming. "Is everything okay? Did something happen with Jade?"

"Everything's fine. I, uh, stopped by to ask you something." The nerves trampling his gut were unexpected.

Another man appeared and the one who answered the door whispered something in his ear. The newcomer grinned broadly and looked back at Trent. "Chloe, darling, why don't you invite your friend inside? It's miserable out there."

She shot the man a punishing look and blushed. "Would you like to come in?"

He stepped inside and stomped the snow off his boots.

Sweeping his gaze around the room he noted soft, blue walls, whitewashed wooden shutters, several patchwork quilts, and ornate picture frames on every surface. Her boys sat at the table, a *Scrabble* board spread across the center.

Mattie sat low in his chair, his eyes scrutinizing.

Dayton studied him, too, but with a glint of challenge in his gaze. Trent turned and realized it wasn't just the boys appraising him.

Chloe looked at the ground and fussed with her hair. The two men stood side-by-side beaming. Apparently, his presence pleased *them*.

He cleared his throat uncomfortably.

"Are we playing or what?" Dayton asked from the table.

"Um..." Chloe seemed totally out of her comfort zone. "Why don't you guys take a little break?"

"Oh, man! It was my turn." Dayton was clearly irritated by the interruption.

Trent was about to apologize for intruding, but the man who answered the door spoke first. "Hush up, whelp. We'll give you and Mattie ten extra points and it'll still be your turn when we continue. Now, go do as your mother asked so we adults can talk for a few minutes."

The boy grumbled but did as he was told. Trent's brows rose, impressed. Mattie took a little longer getting up from the table but soon followed his brother down the hall.

Once the kids were out of earshot, the man turned back to Trent and held out a hand. "Hi, I'm Tommy and this is Adam. We're Chloe's neighbors."

He shook their hands and Tommy invited him to sit. Chloe went to the counter. "Can I get you something to drink, Mr. Cole?"

He gave her a look he hoped told her how he felt about being addressed as Mr. Cole. "No thanks, doll."

Adam sipped from a glass of iced tea. "So what brings you by our neck of the woods, Trent?"

He again glanced at Chloe who continued to distract herself at the counter. "There's a parade tomorrow by the university in Slippery Rock. I wanted to see if you and the boys would be interested in going with me."

"I have work."

Adam clucked his tongue. "You have one appointment and it's at nine." He turned to Trent. "What time's the parade?"

"Noon. We usually get there and set up camp around eleven and after the parade, there's a Celtic festival at the park. If the weather's good we stick around for that."

"Ooh, men in kilts... How fun!" Tommy nudged Chloe in the arm as she joined them at the table.

She obviously wasn't sold yet, so Trent continued, "My sisters and their kids will be there. My nephew's about Dayton's age and I have three nieces a little younger than Mattie. I asked Jeremy if he and Jade were interested, but he said Jade's still having morning sickness and isn't quite up for large crowds. I could see if Ty and Kat want to bring Mia, though. You guys are welcome to come as well."

"Sounds fun." Tommy looked pointedly at Chloe. "I love a parade."

"I suppose we could go. We'd have to meet you there though, because of work."

"That's fine. Why don't I give you my number so we can touch base in the morning?"

"Yes, get Trent's number, sweetie." Adam tapped her phone.

Her fingers flipped a *Scrabble* chip. She'd changed her nail polish from red to a dark maroon since the last time he saw her. She wasn't wearing any rings and he found a new freckle to admire on her knuckle.

"Okay."

*Mission accomplished.*

~

Chloe shut the door and leaned her weight against it. Never in a million years had she expected to see Trenton Cole in her home. She was shocked he remembered where it was.

Tommy sauntered into the living room, a wide grin on his face. "Well pat my Swayze! Girl, you got yourself a date with Paul Bunion!"

She placed her hand on her heart to settle her nerves. "I don't think he's interested in me like that."

"Well, if you're sending out no-fly zone signals... He's probably trying to read you and move at your pace."

She didn't have a pace. She only had stop and go. She'd *stopped* dating the moment she left her husband and her heart let all beliefs about romance *go*. She had no clue how to date. If this even was a date. Was it? No, it was an outing.

"I'm not sure what this is. I mean, why would he come here?"

The guys laughed. "Because he likes you."

She rolled her eyes. "What am I supposed to do with that?"

Tommy chuckled. "Honey, if you can't think of what to do with a man like that then you need this date more than I thought."

"It's not a date. It's a parade."

"Date!" He corrected then looked at his partner. "Adam?"

"Date. He likes you, Chloe."

Heat suffused her cheeks. "You guys are going. This is your doing and I'm not going alone."

"Like you could stop us."

# Eight

TRENT WAITED for Chloe by the fairground's parking lot. She'd texted twenty minutes earlier, saying they'd be there shortly. He paced, nervously, as cars pulled onto the gravel. His family set up camp a couple blocks away and Austin was excited to meet Dayton and Mattie.

As the lot filled, cars moved systematically down the line, almost reaching the grass. The doors of a red SUV opened and he breathed a sigh of relief, grinning, as Chloe stepped out of the back seat.

In jeans and a white shirt with a gray cardigan over it, she looked sporty and cute. The front door opened and Adam climbed out. He wasn't thrilled by the other man's presence, but if her friends made her more comfortable, then he supposed they were welcome guests.

Tommy stepped out of the passenger side. He waited to see if the men brought dates, hoping to get a bead on their relationship with Chloe, but only saw the kids.

Trent waved as they approached. "You made it."

Tommy smiled and waved back, but Chloe's focus was on her sweater as she maneuvered her bag over her shoulder. She took Mattie by the hand and they moved in his direction. He met them halfway.

Once she made eye contact her cheeks darkened and he smiled. Sometimes he found himself holding his breath to see if she would blush, loving when her ivory skin flushed with heat and wondering where else the color spread.

He cleared his throat and played it cool. "Hey, Mattie, Dayton. How you boys doin'?"

Mattie smiled and said a shy hello. Dayton grumbled a greeting. Trent shook the men's hands.

"We're about a block down, but we have to go around the long way because they already barricaded the road."

"You said your sisters are here?" Chloe asked as she kept her gaze straight ahead.

"Yeah, Georgia, Phoenix, and Bristol. My older sister couldn't come."

"You all have names after places."

It was his turn to blush. *Stupid tradition.* "Yeah, even my nieces and nephews. Dumb, right?"

"No, I think it's clever."

He grinned as his heart kicked up a beat and they maneuvered through the crowd. When the throng grew overly dense he protectively placed his hand on her lower back, feeling her arch as she pulled her spine tight. Could be nerves or could be revulsion, he was hoping it was the first.

"You look pretty today." He breathed in her sweet, berry fragrance.

"Th—thanks. Mattie, stay close." She didn't take the opportunity to step away from his touch when the crowd thinned so he smiled.

Once they reached his sisters, he introduced everyone. Phoenix took the liberty of introducing Mattie and Dayton to the kids. Georgia and her partner, Amanda, chatted with Tommy, Adam, while Chloe put herself at an angle that no longer allowed for him to touch her.

"So, Trent tells us this is your first Celt fest." Bristol was always good at making people relax.

Chloe smiled. "Afraid so. We don't do much for St. Paddy's Day. Are you guys Irish?"

"No, we just like to drink and wait for the wind to blow up the men's kilts."

Chloe laughed and the soft sound went right to his cock. He watched as her eyes squinted with laughter, her fingers covering her mouth. Her nails were teal today.

Unable to resist being near her, he stepped to her side. "Don't hide your smile."

The laughter faded as she glanced up at him with questioning brown eyes and slowly dropped her hand from her mouth, but only a trace of a smile remained. It became a goal to make her smile again, and next time he intended to see it.

Vendor pushcarts weaved along the open street marked as the parade route. The kids pointed and begged for treats, but Chloe didn't give in. He would have grabbed something for the little guys, but he didn't want to overstep.

"I'll be right back." He slipped over to his sister Georgia.

"She's cute, Trent."

"Won't get an argument from me. What do you think of Tommy and Adam? Can you tell if either of them is involved with her?"

Georgia laughed. "I'm not positive, but I'd be willing to bet neither of them is interested in her like that."

"How come?" They seemed to share an open affection and comfort with her, one he was envious of.

She pressed her lips together and smiled.

The sound of bagpipes bleated in the distance as Adam returned with six green balloons, one for each kid. He grimaced, now wishing he'd gone and bought the kids something.

Tommy approached, wearing an Irish scally cap and smiled in the direction of Adam passing out the balloons. "He can't help himself. Such a spoiler."

"He seems very sweet, Tommy," Georgia commented.

"He is." The man's gaze settled on Trent. "Hey, why aren't you with our girl?"

The endearment threw him. "*Our* girl?"

Tommy smiled. "I mean Chloe. Why aren't you with...?" He paused and laughed. "Oh, wait!" Placing his hand on his chest, he tipped his head back and had himself a good old chuckle. Georgia and Amanda seemed to be in on the joke as well. "Oh boy! Trent, I'm not gonna beat around the bush, because it's just not my style—no offense Georgia and Amanda—but let's get one thing straight—I'm *not*. Adam's my husband. We love Chloe, but poodle, never in that way."

Trent didn't know if he should be relieved or concerned that a man just called him poodle. He figured he'd roll with it. "Gotchya."

Tommy patted his arm. "Now you go over there and show our girl a nice time. It's been years since she's had a straight man dote on her."

~

Chloe's attention snagged on Tommy's laughter and she hoped they weren't making fun of her in front of Trenton. As he walked toward her his tanned skin was a little flushed. Dear God, what had Tommy said? It was always risky when Adam left Tommy unsupervised for a few seconds. The man didn't have a filter.

"That was nice of Adam to get the kids balloons," Bristol said.

Trenton's sister was sweet. She immediately made her feel welcome among their group. The entire family was striking, with thick black hair, olive skin, and the same piercing blue eyes.

"Adam loves to spoil children. I think that's why Tommy's perfect for him—he often acts like a spoiled child."

Bristol laughed. "They're cute together."

Chloe's neck prickled as the heat of Trenton's palm returned to her lower back. She couldn't think when he touched her, couldn't stop her body from responding.

"You having a good time?" he whispered, mouth close enough to her ear that she had no trouble hearing his rumbled words.

She tried not to noticeably shiver as a chill raced down her spine and butterflies swirled in the pit of her stomach. She'd convinced herself this was just a social outing, but this was the second time he'd touched her like that. "Yes. Thank you for inviting us." For once she wasn't stuttering in front of him.

The parade got underway and the whining of the pipes transformed into music. The kids sat in front of the roadblocks along the curb, as men in various colored tartans marched down the thoroughfare.

Floats, done up in Kelly green and orange, preceded a batch of young Irish river dancers. Flutes and fiddles played as the girls stomped a rhythm into the pavement. Their little clacking feet pounded out a fast tempo and Chloe's heart raced with the beat. She couldn't help but smile at the talent.

"I made a bet with myself," Trenton whispered into her ear, stealing her attention.

"Oh?"

His ice blue eyes watched her as he slowly nodded. "I bet your smile was going to be the prettiest thing I saw today."

A tremor of uncertainty skittered through her chest. Men didn't say things like that to her and she would hardly describe her smile as pretty.

He grinned like a well-satisfied man. "I won the bet."

She blinked at him. "The day's not over."

"I'm not worried." He turned his attention back to the performers. "It's that pretty of a smile."

She tensed as Trent's fingers laced with hers then forced herself to relax. Good grief, he smelled delicious. He gave her hand a squeeze, and a bolt of nervous energy zipped through her insides.

"They're pretty good, aren't they?"

How did he do that? He flirted with her, saying all that about her smile, and then he acted like nothing beyond watching a parade was happening. "I've never seen anything like it before."

"My older niece danced with them for thirteen years. She's in college now, but she's who got us coming here every year. Next year Brielle will start taking lessons."

She shut her eyes as his breath tickled across her neck. Her kids were only four feet away, but the way he held her gently in place by only her hand, so domineering yet temperate, she couldn't find the will to pull free.

Unused to this sort of affection, she couldn't help but fidget each time he leaned close to speak to her over the sound. With Trenton, there was something alluring, something that made her hold her breath each time she got his direct focus. She liked it even though she knew she shouldn't.

She'd fallen into the compliant trap before and learned her lesson well. The moment she sought a man's attention, craved it, she soon started to desire his approval, sometimes to a dangerous degree. She was better off single, identifying through her personal accomplishments and not relying on anyone else's opinion of her.

She was her own person and in control of her own life. She didn't need a man, let alone one who clearly enjoyed the alpha role.

Taking a deep breath she attempted to untangle

their hands, but his grip slid to her waist and pulled her closer. Anger that he'd disregarded her non-verbal request collided with the thrill his persistence brought. This wouldn't be so difficult if his touch didn't feel so good. While her scarred heart said *no*, her neglected libido screamed *yes!*

She had a thousand questions running through her mind, but one disappointing thought, the one anchor keeping her curiosity from taking flight, was that a damaged woman like her could never sustain a man like Trenton Cole.

She believed in love, more so since meeting Adam and Tommy, Jade and Jeremy, and Kat and Tyson. But Jade was adorable and Kat was sexy and Tommy had boundless charisma. Chloe was none of those things. Oh, she was bright, intelligent, and a respected therapist. But Trenton was romance novel hot. Way out of her league.

*The older you get the uglier you are.*
*Do something with yourself.*
*You disgust me!*

She shivered as Marcus's cutting words echoed through her mind. Those flashbacks were coming more often since running into Trenton Cole.

His presence in her life seemed to stir up old doubts and maybe it was best to let sleeping demons lie. She was happy with her quiet life. She was secure. Dating might disturb that hard-earned peace.

His hand tightened on her side as he shifted behind her, his fingers flexing in slow, massaging patterns. Her back was on fire where his body pressed against hers. His size should knock some sense into her, yet she loved how his body felt against hers, loved the way his broad build made her feel proportionate and feminine. But where did it end? How much was he after?

Every man wasn't Marcus. She knew that. But there was still a fragile part of her that worried the dysfunctional aspects of her marriage stemmed from something wrong with *her*.

With one final burst of sound, the music stopped and the passing dancers paraded on in a spectacular grand finale. The crowd went nuts, clapping and shouting their praise. As exciting as it was, her senses were overwhelmed to the point of short-circuiting, so she excused herself and broke all contact from Trenton.

She remained close to the children, a safe barrier between commonsense and the sensations Trenton stirred within her body. After the parade, they walked to the park for the festival and concert. Thankfully, there were enough people in their group to keep a buffer for most of the day.

~

As the band played from the amphitheater in the center of the field, Trent waited in line with Phoenix for some green beer. "She's cute, Trent."

"I think so."

"She says she from Virginia." His sister sent him a pointed look.

"That's right."

"I vaguely remember you and Pete having a client with the name Chloe—who was also from

Virginia. If I recall, that client caused some trouble for you."

He looked his sister in the eye as they moved closer to the concession tent. "It's her."

If Phoenix was shocked she hid it well. "Does she know what you do?"

"She knows I work in security and sometimes teach self-defense."

"Correct me if I'm wrong, but her husband—"

"*Ex*-husband."

"Her *ex-husband* is a bit of a loose cannon."

Guilt rode up his spine and he grimaced. "Well, he's out of the picture now."

"Perhaps your past association with him, no matter how short, is something Chloe should know before you get involved with her."

Yeah, perhaps, but any discussion regarding her husband made her run. He didn't want to risk it.

"He's been out of the picture for years. It's irrelevant." The truth was, he didn't want to tell her. He wasn't a bad guy, but doing business with her ex made him feel like one.

But his sister was right. Chloe needed to know how he came to find her that day. In the end, he'd done the right thing, so she should realize he wasn't the villain, but he wanted her to trust he was a good guy before giving her more reasons to doubt him.

"I'll tell her when the time's right."

Adam approached as they neared the tent. "Hey, you guys planning on sticking around until the end?"

Phoenix let the subject drop. "I'm planning on enjoying some green beer. I guess it depends on how the kids hold up. I sent Pete to the car for more blankets.”

Adam looked at him. “And how about you?”

“I’d like to stay a while. Is Chloe okay?”

“She’s fine. Georgia and Amanda are about ready to pack it in. The boys are still playing ball, but Mattie’s getting tired. I was thinking of asking Chloe if she wanted us to take the boys home so she could stay. She’d need a ride though. Would you be able to do that?”

A wave of excitement churned his stomach at the thought of getting Chloe to himself. “Yeah, I can definitely do that.”

Adam gave him an appraising look. Seemed the verdict was still out as to what kind of man he thought Trent was, though it seemed like a good start that he trusted him to take Chloe home.

“You know, Tommy and I have only been in our house for four years, but we know about her past. That day you offered her a ride you did a good thing. Not a lot of strangers would help a stranded woman for nothing in return. Chloe’s special. She trusted you and it worked out. *We* are trusting you, under the assumption that you’re still that kind of man. Please don’t prove us wrong.”

He respected Adam for showing his hand. It was decent of him to step in and look out for Chloe’s best interest. That’s what good men did for the women they loved when another man came sniffing around. It’s what he did with each of his sisters.

“I’d never hurt Chloe or the people she cares about.”

"Good. I'm going to start cleaning up. Do me a favor. Get Chloe a beer. She'll be stressed if we leave. That girl needs to loosen up, but *only one*. She doesn't drink a lot and, believe me, this is not the place you want to see her drunk."

When Trent and Phoenix returned to the blanket with a caddy of green beer, Georgia and Amanda were saying goodbye. Mattie was sound asleep with his shamrock painted cheek resting on Chloe's lap. It was getting too dark to play ball, so Pete packed up the game. Dayton seemed disappointed he was leaving before Austin, but he also seemed tired so he didn't argue too much.

"I'll walk you guys to the car," Chloe told Adam and the boys.

Adam scooped Mattie into his arms and carried him toward the lot with Dayton by his side. Trent wanted to walk with her but figured he better give her this moment with her sons.

~

Chloe waited until they were a safe distance from Trent and his relatives to lay into Tommy. "What's going on?"

"We're taking the boys home for you so you can enjoy some grown-up time."

She glared at both of them, mindful of her sons' presence. Once they reached the car, she shut the kids inside and turned on them. "We came together so we should leave together."

"Love, this is a good thing. Stop making it seem

like a punishment," Adam told her as he shook the dirt and grass off the folding chairs.

"I don't like having decisions made for me. You set this up without even asking."

Both men sighed, but Tommy was the one to speak first. "Chloe, what's the worst that can happen? His sisters are here, his nieces and nephews are here. You're in a public place. The man wants to spend time with you and... I think you want to spend time with him, too."

She snapped her mouth shut, unable to deny the accusation. "I don't want to give him the wrong impression."

"Which is what?" Adam asked.

"That I'm ... interested."

"Oh, but honey, you are."

"You can't know that if I don't know that."

"So stick around and find out." Adam opened the tailgate of the SUV and loaded up the chairs. "We're not far from home. You'll have maybe thirty minutes tops with him alone. Just go with the flow and see where things lead. No one's asking you to sign over your free will."

She gritted her teeth. "If anything goes wrong I'm calling one of you to come pick me up."

"Nothing's going to go wrong." Tommy kissed her cheek and she followed him to the passenger door.

Mattie was still asleep and Dayton looked like he was about to pass out. "I shouldn't be home too late."

Adam leaned over from the driver side. "Love, it's fine. Enjoy yourself. I'll send you a text once we get the boys settled. They can spend the night. This is good. You go get to know your lumberjack."

She laughed nervously. "The way he makes me feel... What if I'm reading too much into this?"

Tommy tilted his head, smiling and somehow letting her know he saw the real her. "I don't think so, sweet. I think he's into you. Those eyes, the way he watches you, you're not imagining it."

Her palms were clammy. "I don't know if I can do this."

"You can."

Sending them each a pleading look, she whispered, "I don't remember how."

"You will. It's like riding a bike. You just climb on and it all comes back. Now, enough of this worrying. No more excuses."

She watched them pull away and took a deep breath, which her nerves promptly stole. She didn't want to make a fool of herself. But mostly, she didn't want to get hurt. She'd grown accustomed to a life that didn't come with pain, and putting herself out there meant possibly letting some of those old aches back in—possibly experiencing some new ones as well.

She wandered back toward the music and slowed as a shadow caught her eye. Trenton waited under a tree on the other side of the lot, his silhouette unmistakable.

Her mouth curved into a gentle grin as she crossed the field toward the tree. By the time she was two feet away from him her heart was thundering. The sun had set and the air carried a chill.

He pushed his weight off the tree. "You okay, doll?"

She nodded. Each inch he crossed, her stomach flipped in a way that made her want to laugh and cry at the same time.

"If you want to go, you just say the word and I'll drive you home."

"I... I'm okay. Just nervous I guess."

His thumb moved slowly over her knuckles as his eyes studied her. "Nervous about what?"

Nervous about looking stupid, nervous about coming on too strong, nervous about accidentally tripping or slobbering while talking, nervous he would kiss her, nervous he wouldn't. So many possibilities, yet she failed to verbalize a single one.

He smiled. Perhaps he understood. "Hmm." He tilted his head and tucked a piece of hair behind her ear. Her breath held as his face moved closer.

"Well, let's get this out of the way so you have one less thing to be nervous about."

He slowly leaned down and pressed his lips to hers, a rush of energy spiking from her heels to her heart. Her eyes fluttered shut, as chills crested her shoulders. His hands slid from her wrists to her hands, where he entwined their fingers.

At first, he didn't so much kiss her as caress her with his mouth, leisurely dragging his soft lips over hers. She inhaled his delicious scent, pulling it into her lungs, afraid to exhale and let it go.

"You've been haunting my dreams, Chloe."

His lips tickled the corner of her mouth, traveling to her jaw. His touch was the gentlest breeze and she was a trembling leaf, one strong pass of his hand and she'd fall. Her head tilted and he nibbled the sensitive space below her ear, sending her breath out in a rush. Her nipples beaded against the lace of her bra and she feared her knees would give out.

His mouth worked in little bites, ghosting back to hers. When his hands gently squeezed hers she opened her eyes. Those piercing blue eyes stared at her with an intensity that overwhelmed every defense she had. She looked at his mouth, mere inches from hers and dropped her gaze.

The back of his knuckles feathered over her jaw, drawing her stare back to him. "Where'd you go, doll? Stay with me."

Shaken by her attraction to this man and fearful she'd built him up to unreachable standards because he'd saved her life on one of her worst days, she shyly lifted her lashes. Unhidden, yet tucked away in this little space and time where it was only the two of them, she was overwhelmed with an unfamiliar sense of intimacy.

Trent's lips closed over hers, his tongue sliding into her mouth, warm and profound, and for once she hushed her worries and gave in to her desires. His palm cupped the back of her head, angling her for deeper access. Unable to stop herself, she lifted to her toes.

Instinctively, her hand pulled from his and rested it on his shoulders. His hand curled around her waist and pulled her body flush against his. He kissed her deeply, more deeply than she ever remembered being kissed before. His mouth was insistent and strong, but not forceful. She believed if she hinted at escape he would release her. However, she had no intention of stepping away this time.

His palm rested on her side, torturously close to her breast, and drifted lower, cresting over the swell of her hip. She tilted her head and he groaned into her mouth, a sound of satisfaction.

That large, straying hand passed over her curves, landing intimately over the back pocket of her jeans. Although she was fully clothed, the heat of his touch seared through the denim. She gasped as he clutched a slice of covered flesh.

"You feel so good in my arms."

Her heart catapulted against her ribs as she pushed to deepen the kiss. His words were her undoing. How was it possible this beautiful man was kissing *her*? She threaded her fingers through his dark mane and pulled closer.

The stubble on his chin chafed her face and an erotic tingle filled her at the idea of him leaving traces of their kiss on her skin. *This is not a dream. This is real. This is real.*

"I could kiss you for hours," he rasped against her mouth.

Drugged by his wicked mouth, she whispered against his lips, "That would be great."

He moaned and gave her ass a squeeze. Groaning as if it pained him to let her go, he carefully shifted back a step.

But she didn't want to stop. The sound of Celtic folk music drummed in the distance, the cold March air forgotten. She wondered if he would think her desperate if she asked him to take her to his car, her inhibitions suddenly a vague memory. The nearby tick-tock of a car alarm, the kind produced by a key fob unlocking a vehicle, squelched all impulses to throw herself back into his arms.

"We better get back, doll."

Chloe took a few seconds to find her bearings and slow her heart. When she met his gaze he stole her breath again. Those bright irises shifted to a smoky blue as his pupils dilated, the black consuming the sea of sapphire flecks. He kissed the tip of her nose and took her hand, leading them back to the festival.

# Nine

TRENT TRIED to walk off his hard-on as he led Chloe back to the blanket. But he had a feeling this woman might keep him perpetually aroused for the rest of the evening.

She tugged gently at his hand as her steps slowed. "Wait a second." She sifted through the bag on her shoulder.

Her face was flushed and he wanted to drag her to his truck and finish what they'd started. She smiled triumphantly—*adorable*—as she plucked a thin tube of lipstick from her purse. She lined her lips in shimmering burgundy with two practiced strokes, no mirror needed.

"That's quite a trick."

"I don't like being without lipstick."

Her mouth was swollen from their kissing and he imagined how sweet those soft, painted lips would feel kissing other parts of his body. Yeah, his hard-on wasn't going away anytime soon.

She capped the lipstick and tossed it back in her

bag. "Ready?" He loved the way her hand slid naturally back into his.

Pete and his sister sat in two camp chairs watching the stage while Brielle and Austin played on the blanket. His sister looked a little deep in her green cups.

"Hey!" Phoenix clumsily waved them over. Yeah, she was drunk. "We thought we lost you guys."

"Taking the Irish role seriously, I see."

"You bet. I'm thinking of getting one of those kilts for Pete."

Trent looked at his brother-in-law. "I don't know if you got the legs to pull that off."

Pete rolled his eyes. "Trust me, I don't."

Trent laughed and pulled Chloe closer to his side. "We're gonna head over to the stage."

"We'll probably stay here until your sister starts nodding off."

"So, about five more minutes?" Trent teased. Phoenix had always been a lightweight.

"Hey, I'm in it for the long haul tonight!" his sister slurred.

"Well, if you aren't here when we get back I'll call you later. I assume Pete's driving?"

"Definitely. Have fun you two. It was nice meeting you, Chloe."

"Nice meeting you, too. Thanks for inviting us along today."

After saying goodbye to his niece and nephew, Trent led Chloe closer to the amphitheater. Remembering what Tommy and Adam said, he snagged her a beer along the way. The band was great, straight from Dublin. He and Chloe hung close to the stage but out of the way of the younger dancers.

Holding Chloe to his front he wrapped his arms around her waist and rested his chin on her shoulder as they swayed to the ethnic beat. She sipped her beer with a relaxed grin, taking it all in. The weight of her breasts fell comfortably on his forearm and he shut his eyes, memorizing the soft scent of her hair. Her body was perfectly shaped for his.

The set changed and another band took the stage. He silently reflected on the ride they shared so many years ago, how he almost sent her home to a hidden corner of hell. His gut clenched when he remembered that ethical argument he'd had with himself, ashamed he'd even considered returning her. Eternally grateful he'd done the right thing and not the monetary one, he tightened his arms around her.

She was nothing like her ex-husband claimed. Nor was she the woman he'd rescued six years ago. Perhaps it was the mystery of her, the secrets she kept, that made him want to know her better. Regardless, he was in.

As the concert ended she ran her hand over his. He wished they had more time, but it was getting late. "You about ready to go, doll?"

She looked briefly over her shoulder and then dropped her gaze and nodded, back to not looking him in the eye. He tried not to let it bother him.

When they reached the blanket, all traces of his sister and family were gone. Chloe let go of his hand to fold the quilt. He reached for the other end and helped her double the material into a manageable bundle. As the blanket shrank between them he stepped closer. When she reached for the corners, he stilled her hands.

There were those soft brown eyes he adored. Leaning in, he placed a chaste kiss on her lips. Her mouth trembled nervously but then curved into a shy smile.

Once inside his truck, he found himself stalling for more time. "Did you enjoy yourself?"

"Yes. Thank you so much for inviting us. It was such a nice day, like a little sneak peek at spring."

"You like the warmer weather?"

"I don't mind winter, but by March cabin fever usually sets in."

"I like summer. Makes it easier to travel for work."

Her brow creased. "Does your job require a lot of travel?"

He hesitated, not wanting to get into the details of what he did. "Sometimes. I work with Pete so I have to go up to their place a lot. They get harder winters. They're about two hours north of us."

"Oh, I didn't realize. Are they driving all the way back tonight?"

"Yeah, but it's fine. Pete's used to it."

"Your sisters are nice. Tommy and Adam seemed to get along well with Georgia and Amanda."

Recalling his relief that the two closest men to her life were gay, he asked, "How long have Adam and Tommy been a couple?"

"Since before I knew them. I think they're celebrating their ten-year anniversary this year, but they've only been married two. Thank you for making them feel welcome. Not everyone's as accepting."

"Makes no difference to me. With Georgia, we grew up knowing that different people have different tastes."

"Did you always know she was gay?"

"Yes and no. She was always a little more into sports and stuff than my other sisters, but I guess it wasn't until we all started dating that I realized she was more interested in my dates than any of the guys my sisters brought home." He laughed. "We never had one of those made for TV coming out moments. She just showed up one Thanksgiving with a girl and introduced her as her girlfriend. Since then it's been accepted."

"How long has she been with Amanda?"

He thought for a minute. "I guess about four or five years."

They were silent for a few miles. He enjoyed the way his cab filled with the now familiar scent of her hair. He wasn't sure what would happen when they reached her house. He wanted to kiss her some more but also didn't want to rush things.

When he pulled into her driveway behind her yellow car, he decided to play it safe. "Can I call you, Chloe? I'd like to take you out again."

She lowered her gaze to her lap and her cheeks pinked in the soft glow of the porch light. Letting out an audible breath, she whispered, "I don't understand this. Why?"

What did she mean *why*? "Because I like you."

"But you're..." She shrugged and he wasn't sure

he wanted to know the rest of that thought. She shook her head. "And I'm … just me."

He frowned. "Yes, you're you and I would like to take you out again. Why's that difficult to understand?"

She blinked a couple of times. When she looked at him, the reflection of light shone brightly in her eyes as if they were coated with tears. "Trenton, guys like you don't date women like me. They only end up disappointed in the end."

"What are you talking about, guys like me?"

"I mean... You're... Look at you."

A pinch of insecurity nipped at his chest. He thought she found him attractive. Maybe she was just being polite and having a hard time blowing him off. Sometimes he could come on a little strong.

"Is it this?" He touched the jagged scar crossing his jaw.

"What? No!" She shook her head, eyes wide. "It has nothing to do with your appearance. I mean it does, but not in a negative way. It's just... I know what I am, Trenton. I'm not little. I'm not cute. I have freckles and difficult hair and I have no recollection of what a size twelve even feels like."

His frown transcended to a scowl. "If I wanted a size twelve I'd date one, Chloe. I like my women with a little meat on their bones. And as far as being cute, I find you adorable."

Her mouth pursed as her eyes narrowed with skepticism, so he went on.

"I think you're sexy and charming. And in case you haven't noticed, I'm not exactly small myself. Tonight, when I had my arms around you, I kept thinking how great it felt to hold a woman who fit me so well. And as far as your freckles, I could spend days mapping them out with kisses, tasting each one."

Her cheeks darkened and she smiled. She unbuckled her seatbelt and lunged at him, pulling his mouth to hers as she kissed him passionately. He laughed in surprise and wrapped his arms around her, relief tunneling through his veins.

Her fingers pulled at his shirt as she stretched across the seat. Tucking her feet under her body, she kneeled and deepened the kiss. He groaned and reached for her ass. God, he loved her ass. One kiss and his cock already pressed painfully against the zipper of his jeans. They either had to slow down or move somewhere more comfortable.

"Chloe..." The windows wore a coat of steam. "Chloe, baby, we need to slow down."

As soon as the words left his mouth she stilled. Startled awareness flashed in her eyes and she tensed as if just realizing what she was doing. Lowering herself back onto the seat, she looked down and folded her hands in her lap.

Shit. That wasn't what he wanted. He touched her cheek. "Hey."

"I ... I'm sorry."

"Doll, there's nothing to be sorry for. I was just going to suggest we either take it inside or slow down a bit."

Although his words were meant to reassure her, he could tell she was embarrassed. She reached for the door. Keeping her gaze averted, she whispered,

"Thank you for a wonderful day, Trenton. If you want to call me ... I'll answer."

The door shut before he could respond. She was up her steps and inside her house within a few seconds. But she said she'd answer if he called. He smiled. Progress.

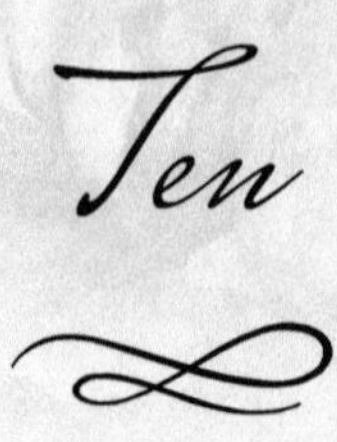

# Ten

OVER A WEEK HAD PASSED and Trenton still hadn't called. Chloe tried not to let her disappointment take over, but his disinterest stung. Why had she let herself hope that something might come from this? Her life was satisfying a few weeks ago, but now she was very aware of parts that were missing. Urges that had been in hibernation for years were suddenly wide-awake and demanding attention—attention she wasn't capable of supplying on her own.

He consumed her thoughts. She thought about him in the car, at the office, in her kitchen, in the shower, and most dangerously, in her bed. But eventually, her fantasies took a backseat to the cynical voices in her head.

Of course, she hadn't imagined him kissing her in the parking lot or in his truck, but she was sure she'd embellished the details. It seemed clear he'd changed his mind.

She supposed it was better she accepted this

now instead of later. Next time she saw Trenton she wouldn't give him the opportunity to lead her on. She was grateful it was Friday, game night with Tommy and Adam because she was running out of ways to distract herself from thinking about the man she assumed would call, but never did.

"Mom, Tommy just left for the store. He said game night's at his house tonight. He invited some other people," Dayton informed, dropping his school bag on the kitchen table.

Her nose scrunched. She didn't feel like facing outsiders. Truth be told, she wanted to get plastered, safely, in the company of her closest friends. "Did he say who?"

Her son opened the fridge. The boy never stopped eating. "No. He just said *other people* and that Adam was setting up the *Wii* for us because you guys would probably play something for grownups."

She returned to her closet—internally grumbling that she couldn't stay in her comfy clothes. She never cared about the way Tommy or Adam saw her, but other people were different.

Her boys left the moment Tommy returned from the store, excited to start gaming. She followed once she had her hair decently styled and a more presentable outfit on.

"Hey, Chloe," Adam greeted as he opened a bottle of wine. "I just ordered the pizzas."

"Hey, yourself and thanks." She stashed her purse in the corner.

Tommy's voice collided with the boys' laughter in the other room so she went to go check on them.

Mattie was hysterical on the couch, holding his stomach laughing. Dayton and Tommy stood on the carpet, where the coffee table usually resided, pointing their controllers at the television.

"What are you guys playing?"

"Nothing yet." Dayton laughed. "Tommy won't let us play until he designs his *Mii*."

She looked at the flat screen as Tommy scrolled through various eye colors and shapes.

"These options are *hideous*! They don't even let you choose a decent shirt."

She laughed. "Well, it looks like you found skinny jeans."

"Thank God for that. The lack of accessories is a crime."

"Tommy, they're girl eyes!" Dayton teased.

Continuing to scroll without pause, Tommy said, "So? As long as there's an apple there's a banana. Don't forget that, Dayton."

"What are you talking about?" her eldest asked.

Tommy pointed to his Adam's apple then his crotch. "Apple equals banana. Clothes are just a façade."

"Lovely," Chloe grumbled. "I'm going to get a glass of wine. Do me a favor and try not to corrupt my son's innocent mind."

Pouring a glass of wine, she read the instructions to the game on the counter.

There was a knock at the door and Adam called, "Chloe will you get that? I have to run upstairs."

Opening the door, she prepared to pay for the pizza, but it wasn't the deliveryman. Georgia and Amanda stood smiling on the porch.

"Hey, Chloe! How are you?"

A little taken off-guard, she tucked the money in her pocket and grinned nervously. "Uh, hey. I didn't know you guys were coming. Come in."

The girls entered the kitchen as Tommy and Adam returned. Everyone said hello and exchanged kisses and settled in at the table. Chloe took a big gulp of wine. When there was another knock at the door she handed Adam the pizza money and refilled her glass.

A bottle of wine later, she'd gotten over the aversion to hanging out with Trenton's sister and loosened up. *Loose as a goose.* By her fifth glass, she was beyond punch drunk.

"Okay, the rules..." Tommy started and Chloe giggled for no reason. "I'm with Amanda. Chloe, Adam, and Georgia will make up the other team."

"How come they get more players?" Amanda asked.

"Because Adam's terrible at games outside of the bedroom. Trust me, he's more a handicap than anything else."

"Hey!"

"You know I love you, sweetie, but it's true. Anyway, here's how it's played."

As Tommy babbled on about the rules, Chloe got comfortable. The game was like hot potato. They had to guess the word before the buzzer sounded. Rapid-fire clues led to hilarious descriptions.

Although Adam wasn't good, Chloe was worse. When the clicker came to her it didn't leave her hand until the buzzer sounded—*every* time. By her fourth turn, she finally got her team to guess a word, but only because it was "ring" and she had one on her finger to point to.

Several empty bottles of wine later, the kids were asleep on the couch and things in the kitchen had gotten wildly out of control. She was smashed.

Disco and 80's music played from the stereo and she happily bounced with the tunes. When the clicker came to her the phrase read "melon". She probably shouldn't have gestured to her breasts, but she was beyond caring what Trenton's sister might think of her. Besides, Georgia guessed the word right away and they needed the point.

"So... Have you gone out with Trent again?"

Chloe stilled. "Uh, no. I don't think he's interested in me like that."

Georgia raised an eyebrow. "I doubt that. I know my brother. He likes you."

She waved her finger at the rest of them. "Oh contraire, *mon frere*." She really should stop drinking. "A man who's interested *calls*." She pulled her cell phone out of the front pocket of her sweater and waved it at the others. "See? No calls."

"He's an idiot," Amanda commented. "I swear, men are so stupid. I'm glad I have Georgia. No offense, boys."

"None taken." Tommy laughed. "Adam and I are the exceptions to the species. We communicate and cuddle."

"Let's call him!" Georgia poured more wine. "Let's ask him why he hasn't called our lovely Chloe."

The smile left her face, panic working hard to sober her senses. "No, no, no, no, no. *Georsha*, no."

Trenton's sister plucked Chloe's phone from her hand. "Why not? I know he likes you. Let's see what his excuse is."

Chloe clumsily stretched for her phone, but Georgia held it out of her reach as she dialed. Nausea tightened her fermented belly. "Oh, God, don't call him. Really, I'm over it." Was her tongue swollen? Suddenly her words were coming out all wrong.

"Oooh, girl, is that a new phone cover?" Tommy asked as Georgia put the phone to her ear. "Bedazzlie! I like it."

"I know!" Chloe nodded and smiled, momentarily distracted. "I got it on *eBay* for fif-fif-four dollars." She laughed as her words, again, awkwardly fell out of her mouth.

"It's ringing."

*"No!"* Chloe hissed and snatched the phone from her, hanging up, and tossing it on the table. *"Georsha*! We're supposed to be a team! No calling your sexy brother."

*Bad Romance* by Lady Gaga started chirping from her phone and everyone stilled. Without touching the table Georgia leaned forward and read the screen. "Oops."

Chloe's hand flung over her mouth as her eyes went wide and she scooted away from the table. "Is it him? What do I do?"

Before anyone could offer a solution, Tommy scooped up the phone and answered. "House of Beauty—name your cutie!"

Georgia snorted and Amanda cracked up.

"Oh, Trenton!" Tommy cooed. "How lovely of you to call. How have you been, poodle?"

Chloe lunged across the table and Tommy slid his chair out of reach. Adam moved the glasses so they didn't spill.

"Oh, good. I'm actually sitting here with our girl now. Seems she's had a bit too much of the bubbly."

"Tommy, hang up the phone!" she hissed, all merriment leaving her in a whoosh.

He waved a hand for her to buzz off. "No, she's fine. She's just—"

She grabbed his sweater and tugged.

"Ahh! Honey, this is Ralph Lauren! Don't do that!"

She swatted his hand, trying to knock the phone out of his grip. "Hang up!"

"Ouch! Oh, crap! What? No everything's fine—"

She pinched his nipple.

"Ouch! Oh, poodle, I'll have to call you back. No, it's ... I gotta go, *Dancing with the Stars* is on!" He clicked off the phone. "Damn, girl! Adam, she scratched me!"

"You asked for it. Should've given her the phone."

"She never would have answered. My left nipple's going to look like a swollen udder by morning." He tsked. "Bitch."

"I'm really sorry, Chloe. I didn't think you'd get that upset," Georgia apologized.

Chloe held her head. "This is bad. Bad, bad, bad, bad."

Amanda tipped her face to the side. "Why? If he likes you and you like him, why not tell each other."

"Chloe, honey." Adam calmly pulled her hands from her face. "It's not that big of a deal. If he calls back, Georgia will answer and explain what happened. Tommy won't touch your phone and she'll tell her brother if he wants to talk to you he can call tomorrow."

She took a breath and *Bad Romance* played again. They all stared at the phone.

Georgia's eyes turned apologetic. "Do you want me to answer it?"

Chloe groaned and pushed the phone to her.

"Trent? Hey, it's Georgia. No, we're over Adam and Tommy's. Yes, she's here... She's perfectly fine... Um, I think you'd better wait until morning. What?" Her gaze shifted to the guys. "Um... Well, I guess. Okay ... bye." She ended the call. "He's coming over."

"*What?*"

Adam rested a calming hand on her arm. "Don't worry. We got this."

Thirty minutes later, after nearly hyperventilating a dozen times, Chloe still hadn't calmed down. Adam and Amanda's solution was to give her more wine while Tommy fussed over her hair and makeup. Georgia paced and apologized profusely.

Her heart pounded and she tried to convince herself no one special was stopping by. However, her stomach informed her she was a liar.

When he knocked at the door, Chloe attempted to stand but thought better of it when the room tilted. She straightened the game pieces as if they were still playing.

"Trenton, what a surprise," Adam greeted unconvincingly and let him in.

Trenton settled into the chair next to hers, his familiar scent crawling into her as his arm brushed her sleeve. She didn't look at him or say hello.

*Breathe*. She had to breathe.

"How ya doin', doll?" His husky whisper sent her ovaries into spasm.

He chuckled in her ear and sat back as Adam handed him a glass of wine. The peanut gallery watched in silence, the weight of their stares making her face hotter than it already was.

"So what are we playing?"

"Game time's over. We've moved on to stimulating conversation," Tommy said.

"Where were you tonight?" Georgia asked.

Trenton's large hand rested on Chloe's thigh, stilling her foot from its incessant tapping. He squeezed her leg affectionately and her thighs clenched together, then unclenched the instant she realized she'd trapped his fingers.

"Around. I had to check on a new set-up we did downtown. Nothing too exciting."

"What kind of set up?" Tommy asked.

"Security."

"Oh, is that what you do? Exciting!"

"Trent does all kinds of stuff," his sister added. "Tell them about that girl you found a couple weeks ago."

"You found a girl? Do tell." The men seemed

very impressed by this, but Chloe was only half listening.

"It was just a runaway. Her parents contacted our agency to help locate her. She was a minor shacked up with an overage boyfriend."

"He also catches criminals who break bail," Georgia stated proudly.

"You're like Starsky!" Tommy cooed.

Trenton's chest rumbled with laughter. "I'd prefer to think of myself as Hutch."

Georgia snorted. "There's no way you're Hutch! Jeremy's the Hutch and you're the Starsky."

"Then who's Pete?" he asked.

Georgia thought for a moment. "I don't know. Maybe he could be the *Striped Tomato.*"

Everyone burst out laughing. Chloe smiled but didn't get the joke, too distracted as Trent's hand continued to weigh heavily on her thigh.

Leaning back in his chair, he draped his arm over her shoulder and she tensed, unsure which was worse, this or the leg touching. His fingers kneaded her shoulder making it impossible to pretend he wasn't caressing her.

The conversation rolled from work and current events, but to her intoxicated brain, it all blended into nonsensical syllables and words. But damn, his hands felt good. He was slowly unknotting every twinge of tension in her neck, despite the upheaval in her mind. The next thing she knew someone was touching her cheek. She opened her eyes and the room was quiet.

Georgia and Amanda were gone. The stereo was off and the game they were playing was put away.

Tommy was washing dishes at the sink and Adam was nowhere to be found.

"Did I fall asleep?"

Blue eyes creased with amusement. "Afraid so, doll."

She cleared her throat. "Where's Adam?"

"He's moving the boys to the guest room. What do you say I walk you home?"

Chloe looked over her shoulder at Tommy who was strangely mute. "I have to check on the boys."

The boys were fine, tucked in and out cold. As she returned to the kitchen Tommy and Trenton were whispering. She couldn't hear what Adam was saying, but she did hear Trenton say, "Don't worry. I wouldn't."

"I feel like I'm forgetting something," she said, letting them know she was back in the room.

"Just your children, sweet. Don't worry, we'll return them tomorrow." Tommy kissed her goodnight.

They walked to the door and Adam called, "Make sure she locks her doors."

Her breath hitched as Trenton placed his hand on her back. "I will."

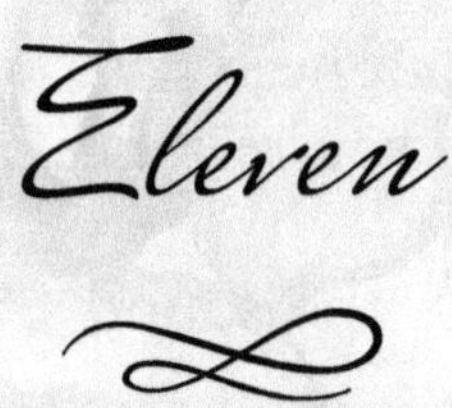

# Eleven

TRENT WAITED as Chloe struggled to unlock her door. When she stepped over the threshold she stumbled. He steadied her, pulling her close to him. "You all right?"

"Sorry. I'm not usually this clumsy." She walked on wobbly legs to the sofa.

How much had she had to drink? Her fingers fiddled with her shirt as she sat. She was doing the not looking at him thing again.

Lowering himself beside her, he sighed. "Chloe, why won't you look at me?"

Her head lowered.

"Did I do something wrong?"

She still wouldn't look at him or answer. He gently touched her cheek and her shoulders seemed to collapse in defeat. "You confuse me, Trenton."

"How's that?"

Her brow creased and she took a deep breath. "You said things to me... Things I'm not used to hearing. You kissed me and touched me and were so sweet, but then you didn't call. My head and my heart haven't been on speaking terms since we last saw each other."

"What does your head say?"

"My head says you're a nice man who's way out of my league."

He didn't like the sound of that. "And what does your heart say?"

"My heart says it would sure be easy to believe you're genuine."

"I am."

She shook her head. "But your words aren't. They're nice and you may think you mean everything you say, but you don't. If you did, this wouldn't be the first I've heard from you in since St. Patrick's Day."

So that's what this was about. He should have called. "I'm an idiot."

She looked at him. "I read too much into a few kisses—kisses you've probably forgotten by now."

"You think I've forgotten our kisses?" He thought about kissing her every hour of every day.

"Didn't you? You never called. You said you wanted to take me out again but never asked. You told me you thought I was cute and sexy and I stupidly believed you actually saw me that way."

"I do see you that way. I didn't call because I didn't want to come on too strong. I wanted to ask you out but wasted most of the week trying to think of the perfect place to take you. When I couldn't think of anywhere good enough, I started second-guessing myself. I figured, having your Ph.D. and all, you're used to dating more sophisticated men. I'm not that type, Chloe. If anyone's out of their league here, it's me."

Her mouth opened and she stared at him. God, how he wanted to kiss that mouth.

"But you never called."

"Only because I was nervous."

She actually had the balls to laugh at him. "Oh, please."

"I don't know why you think I'm without insecurities. I got as many as the next guy. And I don't know who convinced you you're not enough to make a man doubt he's good enough, but that's bullshit. You're intimidatingly beautiful." He had a pretty good idea who was responsible for her low self-esteem, but that was a conversation for another time.

Her lips pursed as she wrung her hands. "So, you weren't put off that I practically threw myself at you in the truck?"

"Hell, no! Honey, you can kiss me like that anytime."

She laughed, her head lifting a bit. "Really?"

"Yes, really. As a matter of fact, now might be a perfect time."

She flushed a pretty shade of pink. Her gaze shifted to his lips. "We have the house to ourselves."

He hesitated. "Doll, you're a little drunk."

He hated the dejected look that flashed in her eyes as she lowered her gaze again. It took everything he had not to carry her through the dark house to her bed and spend the rest of the night memorizing her every naked curve.

He supposed there was no harm in staying for a

little while, so long as they stayed out of her bedroom and kept their clothes on. Tipping her chin so her gaze returned to his, he gave her a reassuring smile. Soft brown pools looked up at him, so unsure.

"Let's get one thing straight right now, Chloe. I like you. I like you very much. I like you as more than a friend. I like you in ways that require both of us in fewer clothes than we're wearing now, but that can wait until you're sober."

"I haven't had a drink in ... what time is it?"

"A little after one and it doesn't matter. *Sober*, Chloe. I want you to remember me in the morning."

She laughed timidly and tried to lower her gaze, but he held onto her chin.

"Up here, Chloe. I'm up here."

He leaned in and her breath sucked in as she watched him carefully, lashes fluttering shut as his lips brushed hers. She was so expectant and so cautious at the same time. He loved that she allowed him to take the lead. Her mouth tasted like wine and he wanted to kiss her until *he* was drunk on all things Chloe.

~

Trenton's lips touched hers and she was done. She couldn't fight her desire any longer. Surrendering to his touch, her heart thrilled. God, he was a good kisser.

His hand gently cradled her face and she moaned, her body awakening under his gentle touch. Her arms circled his neck as he eased her back on the couch, his weight pressing her firmly into the cushions.

The stubble of his beard brushed across her cheek with the most delicious rasp.

Resting his hand on her waist, he moved over her, never breaking their kiss, as they found a more comfortable position. Her fingers ran through his dark hair, pulling it free from the tie, and he groaned.

He firmly pressed his hips into the cradle of her thighs and the evidence of his arousal was unmistakable. She matched his slow grinding rhythm, kicking off her shoes to get more comfortable. His mouth moved to her throat, nibbling a trail to her ear, sending shockwaves to the tips of her breasts. In the dark, there was only the soft whisper of clothing and their breathing. The position of their lower bodies created delicious friction as heat built between them.

His large hand cradled her breast over her shirt. She arched, pressing her chest into his gentle hold. His palm brushed over the fabric, catching exquisitely on the tip of her nipple.

He broke the kiss and kneeled between her thighs. Peeking at him from under her lashes, she grinned. His hair was tousled from her fingers, his skin flushed.

He cupped her heavy breasts in both hands. "These, I love."

"They're too big."

"No, they're perfect."

His thumbs feathered over her nipples, pressing

against the fabric of her shirt and he groaned, pulling back his touch. "Chloe, you have no idea how badly I *don't* want to leave, but we need to slow down."

"I don't want you to go yet."

Without overthinking, she ran her hand over the bulge between his legs. He shut his eyes and caught her hand, pressing himself more firmly into her palm.

"Jesus." He groaned. "I can't take anymore."

He tilted his head back and quietly counted to ten. His white t-shirt pulled tightly over his chest and shoulders. A flash of tanned, toned belly peeked out below the hem as his palms scrubbed over his face.

His rugged jeans and worn leather belt accentuated his masculinity. He was so incredibly male. Everything about him was hard and strong. It should have scared her. In a way, it did, but not enough to blind her appreciation.

"You're so beautiful." The thought whispered past her lips.

He laughed, the sound hard like thunder rumbling softly in the distance. His gaze returned to her face. "Chloe, men aren't beautiful."

"You are. Your skin's so tan and your hair's so thick, even your eyelashes are full. The contrast against your blue eyes takes my breath away. You have so many muscles, muscles in places I didn't even realize there were any."

She ran her fingertips over his shirt from his abs to the small peek-a-boo of flesh showing above his belt.

"Even your body hair's sexy. I love that, no matter how often you shave, you always have a five o'clock shadow." Her fingers tiptoed back to his midriff. "I want to see more of you."

He hissed out a curse—something about regretting this—and grasped the hem of his shirt, pulling it over his head.

*Dear God.*

His nipples were dark, the grooves and dips on his body exquisitely defined. The scar from his neck, while slightly silver by his beard, faded past his shoulder where it crested his collarbone and ended over his heart. She traced the mark with her finger. She wanted to know how he got it but didn't want to ask too much. She had scars she didn't like to discuss.

There wasn't a hint of flab on him. Dark hair followed the indent of his belly button and disappeared beneath his jeans. His hips were cut and his shoulders were broad, yet proportioned to the rest of his body.

On his left arm, he had a black tribal tattoo that wrapped his bicep. She laced her fingers with his and lifted his arm. A downy tuft of black hair peeked out, the boyish softness of it making her smile.

On his right shoulder was another tattoo. "What's that one?"

He twisted to show her. It was a beautiful inked image of Jesus Christ wearing a crown of thorns.

"You're Christian?"

"Catholic, born and raised. Thirteen years of Catholic schooling, despite several threats of expulsion."

She laughed. "I can't imagine the nuns having much control over you."

"Oh, they had their work cut out." He pulled her into a seated position and let out a sigh. "Will you let me take you out, Chloe? I'm not sure if I know of any place real fancy, but I'd like to buy you dinner."

Her nerves shivered as she searched for her courage. Would it be that terrible to go out with him? So far, he'd been the one trying to slow things down. "I'd like that, too." It had been far too long since she'd actually gone on a date.

His fingers laced with hers as they stared at their entwined hands. "I want to know you."

It was hard not to laugh. "I'm not that interesting."

"Oh, I bet you're more interesting than you think. Where were you born?"

"St. Mary's."

His eyes lit. "Here in Pennsie?"

"Yup. I lived here until after my mother and father passed away. Then I met my husband and we got married and moved to Virginia."

His voice turned pensive. "You didn't like Virginia?"

She sighed. "Sometimes I did. We lived in a quaint town with antique shops and a charming town hall. There was a lot of historic appeal. But then... Then my marriage fell apart and I began to hate it there."

"But you had your sons."

"Yes, but the more my marriage suffered, the more they saw. I left for them."

"Did you—"

"I'd rather not talk about that time. Where were you born?"

He accepted the change of topic. "I was born in Hamilton, New Jersey. My mom's from Trenton."

"I guess that's where your name came from."

"Yeah. My parents lived there for a while after they married, because that's where all her relatives were, typical big, loud, Italian family. My dad's from Bristol, that's how my sister got her name."

"And Phoenix and Georgia and..." She blushed. "What's your other sister's name?"

"Ireland. My mom always wanted to visit Ireland, but she's terrified of flying." He laughed. "We aren't sure where they got Georgia, but we think it has to do with the Ray Charles song. Phoenix was born a year after my dad returned from a business trip in Arizona. We think she was conceived on one of his visits home. How did you come up with Dayton and Mattie's names?"

"Dayton's name I heard on a soap opera and Mattie was named by Marcus, Matthew for his grandfather."

"How come you went back to your maiden name?"

Touchy topic. One, it wasn't her maiden name. It was Regina's. Two, she was technically still married. Although her name was legally Wolfe, her boys were still Hunts. They just went by Wolfe—something the schools hadn't questioned after seeing her proof of ID.

Mattie never recalled having another name. She told Dayton Wolfe was *her* maiden name, because he still recalled being Dayton Hunt. Opting for the simplest explanation, she said, "I no longer felt like a Hunt." She yawned.

"Tired?"

She was so comfortable resting against his side she could probably fall asleep, but she wasn't ready to say goodnight. "Tell me something about you. What's an ordinary day for Trenton Cole look like?"

He feathered his fingers through her hair. "When I'm not working, I'm usually doing something to keep myself busy. Sometimes I build things. Sometimes I pass the days bugging my sisters, sometimes I read."

Her eyelids turned heavy. "And when you are working?"

He took a moment to answer, either that or she was drifting in and out. "Every job's different... Some are more challenging than others... Some are more dangerous... Some you know will change you forever..."

She had questions but she was too tired to ask anything else.

His voice lowered and he pulled her close. "I'm gonna just hold you for a little longer..."

# Twelve

A KNOCK POUNDED on the door and Chloe groaned, mind still asleep, but her body uncomfortable enough to wake. Reluctantly, she opened her eyes. Trenton was gone and sunlight flooded her living room.

"Mom, open up."

Easing off the couch, she rubbed her back and shuffled to the door. The kids barreled in and Adam followed, appraising her appearance. "Those clothes look familiar."

"Shut up. Do you want some coffee?"

"Can't. We're heading down to the farmer's market. Just wanted to see how last night went."

She smiled. "I guess I should thank Tommy and Georgia for interfering."

"That good?"

She smirked, tiny butterflies skittering about her stomach. "That good."

"What's this?"

Chloe turned at the sound of her son's voice.

He was holding a piece of paper. *"Sorry to run, Sleeping Beauty. Call you tomorrow. Trent.'* Ew! Is this a love letter?"

"Give me that." She snatched the paper out of Dayton's hand.

"Is that guy Trent your boyfriend?"

"That's none of your business."

"Why not? You're my mom."

"I'm also an adult—"

"So? What about dad?"

The room silenced at the mention of their father. Adam awkwardly shifted from foot to foot, his hands firmly rooted in his pockets and his gaze on the ground. Mattie stepped into the room and watched her with an expectant expression that was neither happy nor sad, just curious.

Taken off guard, she said, "Your father doesn't live with us and we're no longer married."

"Yes, you are. This guy can't just come in and take Daddy's place."

"No one's taking anyone's place, Dayton."

His face reddened as his posture stiffened, his little hands balled into fists at his side. "This sucks! We don't get a say in anything. I don't want another dad, especially that guy. Why would you like a guy like that?" He made a sound of disgust. "You're so stupid."

"Hey! Do not talk to me like that, young man."

"Why not? You *are*. God, I can't stand it here!" He ran from the room and there was a sharp crack as he slammed his bedroom door. Mattie jumped, reminding her of his presence.

"Sweetheart, no one's going to replace your father. Trenton's just a friend."

"I don't mind if you have a boyfriend, Mommy. As long as he's nice to you."

She hugged her youngest, his words touching deep inside of her heart. "Thank you, baby."

After Adam escaped the awkward moment, she situated Mattie with a snack and a movie so she could talk to Dayton. Grabbing three extra cookies from the jar, she headed down the hall.

Lightly knocking, she entered. "Hey."

Dayton ignored her. He sat on the floor with his back against the frame of his bed, his elbows resting on his spread knees, face angrier than a storm cloud.

"We need to talk, bud." She placed the cookies on his bureau and sat on the bed.

"Why? It's not like anything I say matters."

"That's not true. We're all members of this family and we all matter." She waited for him to comment, but he didn't. "Dayton, I can't help you if you don't tell me what's actually bothering you."

"Nothing's bothering me." That was fast and unconvincing.

"Do you want to talk about your father?"

Silence.

Drawing in a steadying breath, she whispered, "It's okay to ask me about him if you have questions."

He sniffed, his face locked in a tight grimace. "I'm starting to forget what he looked like."

*Okay, you can do this...*

She took another deep breath. "Well, he had dark brown hair like yours and his eyes were hazel like Mattie's. He was tall and when he smiled his front teeth overlapped in the slightest way. He had a nice smile." When he used it.

"You talk about him like he's dead."

She stilled, realizing she could only speak of him in past tense without getting upset. "I'm sorry. I don't mean to."

"How come he never calls us?"

*Because he's a monster who can't know where we live.* "Would you want to talk to him?"

He shrugged.

She didn't want to put bad thoughts in his head, but she had no idea how much he actually remembered. Her boys had witnessed a lot of things children should never see, but at least with Mattie, his age at the time made those memories hard to recall.

"Dayton, what do you remember from living in Virginia?"

"I don't know. I remember my room was blue and our kitchen was big. I remember Mattie's highchair, but I can't remember you being pregnant, like, I remember, but only a day of it."

Chloe figured that was because by the time she was pregnant with Mattie the novelty had worn off for Marcus. He didn't care that she was pregnant. Only that she keep producing sons.

She kept her thoughts to herself. Even *her* memories of her second pregnancy were sparse and littered with bad ones. By her first ultrasound, she remembered hoping the pregnancy would go by quickly and worrying her marriage might be destroyed by the time she gave birth. Her thoughts pulled back to that day.

*"What is this slop?" Marcus's fork clattered in his bowl.*

*"It's a tuna casserole. I got the recipe from a housekeeping magazine full of slow cooker recipes." The article was for busy, cold days.*

*"It smells like cat food."*

*The evening was going to be a trying one. "I won't make it again. I had my ultrasound today and didn't have much time—"*

*"So you thought you could feed your family some sort of homeless shelter sludge?" He stood and yanked Dayton's plate away, tossing the dishes into the sink with a loud crash.*

*"He was enjoying that."*

*"Make something nutritional. I don't want my son eating this shit."*

*Standing, she went to the stove and pulled out a pan to sear what should have been tomorrow's pork chops. Rather than argue, she cooked silently.*

*Dayton fussed in his booster seat—still hungry and wondering where his dinner had gone. Marcus stormed into the living room, never once acting regretful that he'd upset his son.*

*When the pork was finished he returned and ate in silence. After dinner, she bathed Dayton and put him to bed. Marcus awaited her in the hall.*

*"Did you want to say goodnight to him?"*

*He pulled their son's door closed and nudged her toward their bedroom. When he was upset, like he so often was of late, there was very little talking during their alone time. Their bedroom door shut and his belt buckle rattled.*

*"I still have to put some things away in the kitch—"*

"*It's not my fault you're behind schedule today.*" *He shoved her to the bed and her stomach sank, knowing he was intent on making some point by flaunting his authority.*

*She slipped off her shoes and he scoffed. "This pregnancy's making you slow." Shoving her hand away, he pushed her back on the mattress and yanked off her pants.*

*"Marcus, wait—"*

*"Shut up. Those cheap dinners are making you fat. You're on salad for the rest of the week. Roll over."*

*Her heart trembled as she reached for a pillow to place under her chest, but he didn't give her time, nor did he do anything to ease his entry. At the first stab of his erection she let out a painful gasp, her eyes flooding with tears.*

*He degraded her, berated her, and as he pushed his weight into her, she worried he might hurt the baby. Maybe that was his goal.*

*There wasn't any touching or holding. He hadn't shown such tenderness in too long for her to recall, but that didn't stop him from fucking her regularly. That's what he did. He fucked her. She was supposed to be his wife, the mother of his children that he cherished and loved. But by the way he used her body, she never felt like anything more than a hole he filled and a post he kicked when he needed to scream at something.*

*Holding her stomach, she cried herself to sleep that night. She hated the feel of him on her skin but wasn't allowed to shower until morning.*

*She didn't understand why he slept with her when he only ever complained how unappealing her body was. Over time she realized he did it to punish her. What she didn't understand was how he got aroused if he found her so disgusting.*

*Part of her believed it was the punishment that turned him on. The nights he hurt her in bed, pinned her down and made her cry or beg for mercy... Those were the nights he lasted the longest and slept the soundest. Those were the nights she dreamed of suffocating him in his sleep.*

"I remember Daddy had a red car," Dayton said, pulling her back to the present.

Her skin itched as if spiders crawled under her clothes. She wanted to wash the memories away and do everything in her power to avoid discussing him, but Dayton obviously needed to get something off his chest.

Brushing her hand over his mop of hair, trying not to wince as he nudged away from the maternal contact, she smiled sadly. "That's right, a convertible. He loved that car."

"I don't have a memory of saying goodbye to him. There's just then and then there's here, Aunt Gina's house."

"You don't remember your last few days there?" They had been awful days so it was probably better he'd forgotten.

"No, and how come I remember this truck I used to play with all the time? What happened to stuff like that?"

Chloe wondered if time erased those memories or repressed them. There were specific arguments she recalled Dayton witnessing. Perhaps it was time they spoke to someone as a family. She was professional enough to know she was too close to the issue to counsel him properly. She wanted her sons to be happy and whole, so if he needed to talk about this she would have to start looking for a family therapist who could help—someone who wasn't a battered wife or his mother.

"Dayton, I married your father because I loved him. However, over time, some things changed."

"Do you still love him?"

"I think when you have children with someone, you'll always love a part of them."

It was the unfortunate truth. No matter how much she hated Marcus, he gave her the boys and she couldn't imagine a life without her children.

"Then why can't we all live together like a family again? Why do you have to go out with that guy?"

"Is... Help me out, Dayton. Is this about your father or about me going out with Mr. Cole?"

"I dunno. Both, I guess. If this guy's your boyfriend, it's like daddy's never coming back. Mr. Cole shouldn't do that if we can all be a family again."

"Dayton, your father and I are not going to live together again. Ever. I told you that long before Mr. Cole came around." Hoping for such an outcome would only lead her son to more disappointment.

"Why?" he snapped vehemently, clearly placing the blame on her.

The little similarities between Marcus and Dayton frightened her most. And when he snapped at her, she heard his father's voice. "Because we didn't get along."

"But when me and Mattie fight you tell us 'too bad'. We have to get along because we're family."

"I tried to get along with your father, but... There's stuff you don't remember that I can't tell you."

"I remember sometimes he'd get really mad at you and yell and stuff."

She wondered exactly what 'stuff' entailed in her son's mind. "Right, and no one wants to live like that."

"You shouldn't have made him so mad. He wouldn't have yelled if you tried harder and then we wouldn't have had to leave."

His blame hit her like a punch to the stomach. She fought to hide her hurt, but it was impossible as tears rushed to her eyes.

Pinching the bridge of her nose to hide her face, she explained, "It's not that simple, honey. I..." Her thoughts scattered as his words still reverberated.

Losing her ground—and her grip on her tears—she chickened out. "Listen, I want to talk about this, but I want to think about how to explain it at a level you'll understand. It's a nice Saturday. Why don't we shelve this topic for now and we can talk about it again later?"

His eyes narrowed. "Are you gonna go out with that guy?"

"I thought you liked Mr. Cole?"

He shrugged. "He's okay. But what if you make him mad the same way you made Daddy mad?"

"Dayton, no matter how mad people make us we still have to be nice to them. That was something your father struggled to understand, something I try very hard to teach you boys."

"But ... sometimes Mattie makes me so angry I don't mean to hit him, but I do on accident."

"We have to think before we act, Dayton. It's never an accident when you hit someone out of anger."

Her son sighed. "Mr. Cole's really big, Mom. He could hurt you."

She sighed. Anyone could hurt her if they wanted to, size rarely made a difference when cruelty was burned into someone's bones. "He is big, but I don't think Mr. Cole gets angry easily. And if he does, he seems to take the time to work through his emotions before acting on them."

"Why do you like him?"

"He's nice and he makes me happy. Don't I deserve to be a little bit happy?" She playfully nudged his shoulder.

"I guess."

Chloe placed her hand over her heart and wobbled. She flopped back on the bed and gasped. "To think, after all my hard work, making close to two thousand sandwiches with the crust cut off, and reading over four thousand bedtime stories, my son thinks I may deserve *a little* happiness."

Dayton laughed, quickly covering his grin with the steely expression that was his current norm. "You're a dork, Mom." He tossed a pillow at her face.

He could call her any silly thing he wanted if it meant her sweet boy smiled for a change.

# Thirteen

TRENT WIPED his palms on his jeans—damn he was nervous—and fussed with the collar of his shirt. He, as promised, had called the day after he left her sleeping on the couch. She seemed to be having a rough morning but didn't want to go into detail about it. They only spoke briefly, but he made sure to make plans for the following Friday.

That night she called him back and said that Adam and Tommy could watch the kids. They talked for a little bit and Trent was glad whatever had her bummed appeared to pass.

On Monday she called him after she finished work. It was hard being home while she was working. He had too much time on his hands and considered taking another job, but worried it would send him out of town and away from Chloe.

They spoke on the phone while she prepared dinner. When dinner was ready, he promised to call her the next day. However, when nine o'clock rolled around, he missed her something fierce. Wanting to hear her voice one last time before bed, so he called again.

He wasn't sure why or how she'd managed to captivate him. Perhaps it was the passive way she slipped back into his life, not pushing for his attention but stealing it all the same. Or maybe it was her gentleness that attracted him. He knew there was a warrior inside of her, a woman who would fight armies to protect her children. Her backbone lured him in, testified she was a decent woman and one he shouldn't let slip through his hands.

He wanted to unleash her passion, didn't want anyone else knowing the secrets she hid. In a way, she was his secret, all the thoughts over the years compiling into deep wanting. Nothing short of having her would satisfy his desires. They ended up talking on the phone for an hour.

Tuesday they talked some more and Wednesday they broke their record and chatted for over four hours. They were learning a lot about one another. For instance, he now knew that her favorite color was yellow and her favorite flowers were sunflowers. She used to collect Teddy Bears. She only recently learned to like avocados. And she won the Religion Award in eighth grade, which she claimed was a prestigious honor not to be made light of.

Every detail was a tiny treasure, a puzzle piece that helped him gain a full picture of the woman she was. On Thursday she actually called him in between patients because she claimed she missed him. He tried not to make too big of a deal out of the warm fuzzy feelings her confession brought. To keep his manhood intact, he headed over to Jeremy's for a beer.

That night, she called him after she put the kids to bed. They talked on the phone until they ran out of words. After that, they lay in bed listening to each other breathe, as they each watched reruns of old sitcoms.

He'd never had this sort of connection with a woman. Things didn't have to be sexual for him to enjoy her time. Every minute she gave him fulfilled something inside of him. She made him ... smile. He loved hearing her laugh.

This morning, Trent awoke and called the florist first thing. He gave her work address and ordered a dozen sunflowers to be delivered to her office at lunch. On the card, he had the clerk write, *Can't wait to see you tonight. Xo, Trent.*

He received her call around twelve fifteen. She made such a big deal of the gesture, he made a mental note to send her flowers often. After that, he ran to the mall to find something suitable to wear on a date. He was taking her to a place in Upper New Castle called *Antonio's*, a small family style restaurant his sister suggested.

He bought a pair of dark blue jeans with faded crease marks by the pockets, a new belt, and a deep blue button-down shirt that had some goofy design on the shoulder. The salesman highly recommended it, but Trent wasn't convinced until a younger woman passed by and told him how good it looked on him.

He grabbed a new pair of black dress shoes, only because they had them in his size, which was rare, and headed to the hair place in the mall to get a trim. About an hour later he looked like a new man.

As he pulled into Chloe's driveway he took one more moment to adjust his clothing and check for any missed store tags. When all was good, he headed to her front porch and lightly knocked. The click and slide of locks being flipped on the other end had him stepping back.

And there she was.

She looked amazing. A loose fitting blouse in shades of charcoal draped over her curves. The collar hung low and off to the side, exposing her shoulder. With his height, he could see the perfect peek of cleavage. *Nice.*

"Wow," they each said at the same time and laughed.

"Would you like to come in? The boys are already next door."

"I wouldn't want them to look out the window and wonder what we're doing in there. And with the way you look right now, trust me ... we'd be doing."

She blushed. "Okay, let me grab my purse." She hesitated, looking unsure. "Um ... should I bring anything else?"

He already told her he picked up the wine. Was she asking about condoms? He didn't want to make any assumptions, but he already picked up a box. "Like what?"

"Um..." She looked down and tapped her fingertips together. "I... Well, the kids are taken care of until tomorrow afternoon. I just didn't know if ... I'd be coming back here or if I should bring a bag."

His throat suddenly went very, *very* dry. "Get a bag."

She smiled and disappeared behind the door. A second later she reappeared with a small case. "Okay, let's go."

Laughing, he took it from her and fit it behind his seat of the truck. The simple weight of that bag in his hands and what it implied had his cock hardening to an uncomfortable degree.

They drove in sexually charged silence. Distracted by the way her hair picked up the last gleaming rays of the sun as it set over the horizon, he found it difficult to focus on the road.

"How far's this place?"

"It's about twenty minutes out."

She relaxed a little in her seat. Her fingers twisted her rings.

Placing his palm on her thigh, he gave a little squeeze. "You okay?"

"Yeah. Just ... anxious, I guess."

He was anxious, too. At first, he was a little nervous about impressing her but, now that he saw the bag, he wanted to say the hell with dinner and drive her right to his house.

"Your hair looks great."

His fingers went to the blunt ends. "It needed a cut."

"I like it."

"Thanks, doll." Her approval meant more to him than it probably should.

～

She'd forgotten the sweet anxiousness that was the prelude to a first date. It was a heady and potent mix of nerves, excitement, and lust. When Trenton had arrived at her door, hair cut, dress shirt pressed, and dark tapered jeans fitted to his magnificently long legs, she was once again taken aback by his good looks. Her panties had been damp ever since.

Tommy was right. It was time for her to move on. She'd been nervous about dating, unsure if she'd ever reopen that door again. But the way Trenton spoke to her, made her laugh, and seemed to have a curious interest in who she was ... it was different than past experiences. *He* was different.

She probably shouldn't trust someone she only met a handful of times, but there was something, aside from his attractiveness, that called to her. He was the man of her fantasies come to life. Like a love story, he'd reappeared in her world and—unbelievably—wanted to date her.

It wasn't until Tommy had pointed out that if she dated and actually went to bed with Trenton, Marcus would no longer be the placeholder of her experiences. He was more than a bookmark in some mental ledger. He was an anvil on her chest, marking all the horrible fears and dislikes she remembered. The idea of Trenton somehow washing those recollections away, even a little bit... If it was possible, he could save her in other ways. This man might somehow open up new worlds to her and save her from herself.

She liked the way he made her feel, even when he made her nervous. Her confidence had bolstered over the last five days and he had to be responsible.

What if dating a good man, having a healthy relationship, could actually repair the damage of marrying a monster?

He neatly tucked his truck along the curb across the street and pulled the key. "You ready, gorgeous?"

*Gorgeous?* Well, that was an endearment she certainly hadn't heard before. She smiled and grabbed her purse. "Ready."

She was ready for this new chapter. It had been almost a decade, but tonight she would be attempting to trust again. Every time she considered what might happen after dinner, her stomach did a little flip.

The family-owned restaurant was perfect. As their dinner was prepared in the kitchen, they chatted about their day. Conversation never lagged. Their words carried each other's thoughts as fluidly as the wind carried the clouds. Chloe didn't remember a date ever being so easy or relaxed.

He wasn't concerned with putting on airs. She loved learning all of his likes and dislikes. Trenton liked his steak rare and his beer cold. He took his coffee black and could care less about what label was on his clothing. He drove his truck because it ran well and never let him down. He took an open interest in things that caught his attention and didn't hold back his opinions.

There were no apologies with Trenton Cole because with him you got what you saw. And his confidence made him all the more attractive. He liked motorcycles, boobs, the NHL, porn, red meat, and rock and roll. He was— refreshingly—basic. He was also the sort of unrefined man she found herself very attracted to.

By the time they finished their meal the wine was almost gone. He slid some cash in the billfold and took her hand. "What do you say we head back to my place?"

Her stomach swooped in anticipation and her skin heated. Mouth suddenly dry, she simply nodded her agreement.

When they reached the lot it was more congested than before. She was grateful they parked across the street. He held her door and helped her climb into the truck. Once they were on their way every mile marker came with a new thrill of heady anticipation.

*I'm going to Trenton Cole's house!*

Then it sank in that she was actually going to have sex and she started to panic. Rather than recall the horrid memories of her past experiences, she focused on mentally recounting all the subtle ways she'd prepared herself. She'd painstakingly shaved areas she hadn't shaved in years and applied raspberry lotion to every square inch of her body. Her undergarments matched and she even bought something sexy to wear to bed. This was new ground for her and, despite her anxiety, she was excited.

*You got this. Be brave.*

They took an exit for a town called Neshannock and Trenton steered them onto an expansive road where familiar landmarks faded into nothing but space. Farm after farm passed by, houses sprinkled here and there with huge gaps of land in between.

They'd literally gone from the city to the middle of nowhere in a matter of minutes.

Her heart sped up as he navigated through a labyrinth of back roads, taking her deeper into this rural area where streetlights didn't exist and churches were more common than commercialization.

Turning onto a gravel drive, she spotted a bead of light in the distance and he glanced at her with a smile. Was this it? Were they there?

"I have sensor lights. They'll go on in a second."

Just as he said the words the structure in front of them illuminated, not at all what she'd been expecting. "It's a barn."

"Yeah. It belonged to the farm next door, but they wanted to downsize their acreage. I got it at a great price and, other than winterizing it and adding a few modern amenities, it required minimal work."

"It's beautiful."

He smiled and parked by a large wooden door. "Shall we?"

Taking her bag and her hand he led her to the barn. When he flipped on a few lights she gasped.

Wide wooden planks buttressed by heavy mortise and tenon beams created a gaping space made from raw material. A floor to ceiling stone chimney spotlighted a cavernous fireplace. Mounted antlers gave the open house a woodsy feel, unmistakably masculine. His furniture was minimalistic, a threadbare rug, two leather couches, and two utilitarian chairs made of exposed pine.

Her gaze panned to the open back staircase. He

hung by the front door, watching her. "Take a look around."

Her feet carried her to see what hid in that loft. She froze when she reached the top. There, independent of walls stood Trenton's bed.

There was a soft thud behind her as he placed her overnight bag by the steps. They were in his room, with his big bed, all alone. Every muscle in her body tingle with awareness as he stepped closer.

"You okay, doll? You still want to stay?"

She swallowed and slowly nodded. They were definitely doing this.

Walking to the lone dresser on the far side of the room, she removed her earrings. Taking a deep breath, she faced the bed. He took a slow predatory step toward her, then another, pausing only a few inches from where she stood, and her breath caught.

Tucking a piece of hair behind her ear, his knuckle skimmed a line of her jaw. "I want you, Chloe. Say I can have you."

She shut her eyes, his words reminding how different this was going to be from everything she'd known. He wanted *her*. Her mouth trembled into a smiled. She very much wanted him, too. "You ... can have me."

"So beautiful." His mouth gently kissed her neck as his fingers traced down her arms to her wrists. She shivered as his touch coasted over the swell of her hips to her ribs. "Look at me, Chloe."

Trembling with anticipation, she lifted her lashes and his smoky blue stare sliced through her. He kept his gaze on her as he teased the low neckline of her blouse, drawing her nipples to attention.

"I'm not always a gentleman, Chloe, but I won't hurt you. I'll never hurt you."

Staring at him, she saw the truth in his eyes. He was a massive man, carved of hard muscle, woven of tight sinew, but he was a gentle giant. "I believe you." If she didn't believe that she wouldn't be standing here.

As if he'd been holding his breath and she'd finally given him the password he needed, he reached for her in a rush. The kiss was explosive. His grip tightened around her waist as he yanked her close. Their tongues fought for deeper penetration. Her fingers ran through his hair, as his hands slid low and firmly gripped her, pulling her body flush against his.

She blindly sought out the top button of his shirt, kicking her shoes away. Two buttons. His mouth slid to her ear, the sound of his breath tickling her sensitized skin and sending shivers down her legs. Three buttons.

He nibbled her earlobe and she moaned, her fingers tripping over the fourth button. When he kissed her she didn't have to contemplate what they were doing. There was no time for worry or doubt because her wanting grew to an immediate need every time his lips touched hers. His mouth burned a trail of heat along her throat. Another button.

Aroused beyond measure, she forgot about the buttons and spread the collar of his shirt wide, pressing her lips to his chest. She kissed his scar, trailing her tongue to his nipple, where she teased the dark tip.

Groaning, he fisted her hair and tipped up her

face. "I have a feeling there's a lot of wild woman hiding under that sweet smile."

Standing on her toes she kissed his throat as they fought for closeness, exposing any bit of flesh they could reach. Never in her life had she experienced such a mad rush to get a man naked. Her stark curiosity fueled her desire and blurred her inhibitions. She finally got his shirt off. "I love your body."

"Your turn." He grasped the hem of her blouse and—

"Wait!"

He stilled and raised his brow in question.

Catching her breath, she glanced around the room. "Maybe we should shut off some lights."

His dark brow lowered. "Chloe, doll, I'm gonna tell you right now, there's no way I'm letting this happen without seeing every square inch of your body. You're gorgeous and I want to look at you."

"But—"

"Let's get a few things straight right now. All insecurities go out the window when we're alone. I don't want boundaries between us. I'm a greedy man and I like it good, old-fashioned, and hard. I got no patience for any prissy modern day doubts. You're all woman and I want all of you. Understand?"

His words were tempting but she couldn't forget who she was and the things he'd see once the shield of her clothing was removed. Marcus made sure she knew how far from perfect she was, frequently listing her flaws and telling her how disgusting men found certain blemishes like pudgy curves, oversized breasts, and freckled skin.

She wanted to please Trenton but worried he'd be disappointed regardless. "I'm just not very comfortable with my clothes off."

"I'll make you comfortable. But you gotta give me the chance. Let me take the lead. You can decide anything you want about the rest of our relationship, but in here, let me be the boss."

*Whoa.* She took a step away from the bed. That was a stiff spoonful of testosterone to swallow.

Her experience and common sense told her she should pack it up and get the hell out of there, but something held her still. Men who needed control were never satisfied. Or was that just Marcus?

As if reading her thoughts, he caught her chin. "I'm greedy, Chloe, but I'm not selfish and I'm never mean. I promise it'll be better than anything you ever had. Trust me to take care of every gorgeous inch of you. Give me my way, doll. No boundaries, just us."

She let out a fast breath. Could she do that? Old vulnerabilities begged her not to be so naive, but she pushed the nagging, untrusting voices away.

"What if I can't?"

"All I'm asking is that you try. If anything's too much, you say the word and we stop." His large hand rested over the scar covering his heart. "I swear you're safe with me."

She could be strong. She could do this. Tucking all cynicism away, she reached for the hem of her shirt and lifted it over her head. As the material fluttered to the floor his smile slowly curved.

"Don't stop."

Reaching behind her back with shaky fingers,

she unlatched the clasp of her bra. He dragged the straps from her arms and tossed the undergarment aside, stepping back to look at her. Her naked breasts hung between them, tipped in peach. As his gaze bore into her flesh, her nipples budded into tight peaks.

"Dear God." His breathing accelerated as he licked his lips.

A trail of pink worked down her chest as he ran his thumbs over the rigid tips of her nipples. Bowing his head, he sucked a tip into his warm mouth and she drew a sharp breath.

Corralling her toward the bed, her knees met the mattress and he eased her to her back. Rising to his full height, his hands dropped to his waist as he slowly unlatched the clasp of his belt and slid the leather through the loops. Her mind careened into a darker place, a scary place at that familiar sound triggering her anxiety. The belt fell to the floor with a punctuated clack and her fear instantly waned as he continued to watch her, dark blue eyes heavy with promise.

Thick anticipation chugged through her veins, hot and arousing. Each metal tooth of his lowering zipper punctuated what was coming with a slow *tick, tick, tick.* As the blunt head of his cock peeked out the V of his pants she inhaled, her lips parting as she gazed up at him.

Shoving his pants to the floor, he only gave her a moment to look at his generous form before climbing onto the bed. He settled over her and gave her a slow, wolfish grin.

"You're mine."

His mouth took hers with fast aggression, seemingly everywhere at one time. He kissed her breasts, her throat, and even her ears. She fell into a tailspin of sensation as his fingers tweaked her nipples, sending shockwaves to her core.

Her pants peeled away as he worked his mouth down her body. She sucked in a sharp gasp as his lips pressed into the damp silk covering her sex. "Oh, God."

His fingers plucked the material from her hips and he growled in satisfaction, nudging her knees apart. Tilting her head back, she closed her eyes as his hot tongue blazed a trail of heat. Her back bowed and she let out a moan of ecstasy.

How long had it been since a man touched her tenderly like this? Her eyes stung at the fleeting thought and she pushed it away.

He tasted her with abandon, plunged his tongue deep, licking and nibbling her clit, tracing her folds. Her breath escaped in needy pleas, speaking out of her own shock, hardly able to comprehend that this was happening, that she was actually enjoying a man's hands on her.

He was relentless, sucking and pulling, ringing every last drop of pleasure from her. He gripped her bottom so tightly she was sure she'd wear his handprints tomorrow.

"Let go, baby. I'll catch you."

Her hands fisted the blankets as her back arched, her sex grinding against his wicked mouth as he took her to the edge of ecstasy where worries disappeared. Pleasure knifed through her, hot and greedy, demanding she hold nothing back.

Never had an orgasm been so all-encompassing or soul shattering. Drunk with passion, she wasn't sure if she blacked out for a second. Breath soughed in and out of her lungs as she quivered with tiny aftershocks that tickled her body.

He collapsed next to her. "You, doll, are amazing."

She rested a hand on her stampeding heart, wondering if anything in her life even slightly compared to what he just did. One thought tripped into the next. This moment, lying next to Trenton Cole —her long-lost hero—without a stitch of clothing... This had somehow become her reality and the absurdity of that thought shook her to the core.

There were no words for how beautiful he was. She tilted her head away and shyly smiled. "Thank you ... for that."

He grinned. "Believe me, it was my pleasure."

She loved how sexual he was, how he didn't try to hide his enthusiasm. Sex had never been ... fun with Marcus. Even before the abuse started.

Trenton was showing her how freeing it could be and she wanted to embrace the theory. She rolled to her side. "Your turn."

He pulled her in for a deep kiss and she could taste herself on his tongue. As her thigh brushed against his rigid length she shivered.

Scooting down his body, she knelt between his legs. He tipped his chin and smiled at her as his cock bobbed proudly above his muscled abs. He was definitely large *everywhere*.

Slowly gliding her palm up his length, his warm flesh teased her fingers like heated steel encased in silky hot skin. Leaning closer, she brushed her cheek along his length, gently cupping him, and he tilted his head back and groaned.

At the small seam of his engorged crown rested a tiny pearl of dew. With a quick swipe of her tongue, she licked it away.

"Fuck..."

She laughed and ran her tongue under the smooth rim and he hissed in a deep breath as she took him fully into her mouth. His hand sifted through her hair and held her tight, but never forced her lower or forbade her to rise. As she worked her mouth up and down, the hand in her hair started turning her on rather than frightening her. Again, he'd proven how different he was from her prior experiences and that reminder urged her on.

He was not only long but thick. Her lips stretched over him as her rhythm increased. The more she worked him, the more *her* arousal grew, which had never happened before during a blowjob.

As she took him deep, he gave a long satisfied moan. Suddenly, he nudged her to her back. "*Now*, Chloe. I need you *now*."

She caught the flash of a condom just before he tore the foil with his teeth. Sliding it over his hard length, he grabbed her knees. With a quick tug, he slid her to the center of the bed.

Her thighs spread wide as his weight settled over her. "You ready, doll?"

"Yes." Her mind celebrated the moment, knowing it would forever erase Marcus as her last lover but also transcend every fantasy she had of this man into irrevocable reality.

He pushed the broad, blunt tip of his cock against her sex and a chill of unexpected panic set in. What if there was pain? What if she couldn't? *Oh, God...*

"Chloe, look at me."

She opened her eyes.

"You're here with me, Chloe. Stay with me."

He slowly worked himself inside, shallow dips going deeper with each stroke. Her thoughts jumbled, an irrational sense of fear threatening, and her body clenched. The sudden tightness of her sex amplified her worry. She didn't want it to hurt. So great was her fear that her eyes closed against a startling wash of tears she didn't want him to see. She wished the lights were off. Maybe they should stop. God, she was too tight and—

Soft lips brushed hers. "Tell me who's got you."

She sensed him holding back and willed her eyes to open. He nudged deeper, hitting a nerve. Her body wasn't cooperating, one moment inviting him in, the next moment fighting to keep him out. He obviously felt her tension.

She blinked and more frustrating tears threatened to fall, threatened to spoil the night with embarrassing excuses of how she was so broken all these years later she still couldn't find normal.

"Who, Chloe? Don't shut your eyes. Tell me who has you."

Breathing hard, she stared up at him, her body cinched tight and her mind spiraled into old regrets as it sliced open fresh wounds. Why was this happening? She was ready. She wanted to be ready.

"Shh..." His arms drew her to his chest as he

held her close. His breath teased her lips as he traced the softest kiss over her cheek. "I know. I know you're scared. But you're here with me. No reason to be afraid, Chloe."

His words brought a delicate peace to her chaotic mind, enough that she could separate the past from the present and see herself in the now. "Trenton."

"That's right. I've got you."

Her body relaxed and her tears abated as she recognized the soft fringe of his lashes, the gentle laugh lines surrounding his kind eyes. The fear faded and she drew in a deep breath.

"There's my girl. I missed you. Try to stay with me."

It was as if he knew more than he possibly could. His patience and understanding undid her. His acceptance that she still carried baggage from her past tripped the beat of her heart and her vision blurred again, but now for a different reason.

"I'm ready now."

He pressed a tender kiss to her lips, his fingers touching her arousal and gently bringing her body back to life. "Look into my eyes," he whispered and slid home.

They simultaneously exhaled. He held himself there for a moment and she was so overwhelmed by the fullness, not just physical fullness, but the weight of emotion she felt, that she couldn't stop the escape of a lone tear.

"You okay, baby?"

She smiled. Although she was on the verge of weeping, she was happy. She'd been brave and he'd been patient. The combination was intoxicating. "I'm okay."

He grinned. "I'm glad because it's about to get real good."

Excitement bloomed in her chest as he thrust. The bed creaked with his every advance. It felt good, better than good. And she couldn't silence her sounds of pleasure.

His speed increased, his mouth kissing anywhere it could reach, showing her a level of affection she'd forgotten could accompany sex. The sound of their bodies colliding filled the air. A gasp escaped on the tail of each thrust. For as enormous as he was, his motions stayed gentle.

His palm coasted over her hair, his thumb tracing the arch of her cheek. His mouth kissed and teased her lips, ears, and shoulders. But what affected her most, what made this a moment she'd never forget, was the way his gaze bore into her, never leaving, like an anchor that held her in the present but gave her enough space to let go.

There was such warmth tucked within his gaze, she could easily slip out words of love, words she had no right to say. But the emotion was there —tempting.

She wanted to love him for the simple fact that he made her feel like a woman again, looked at her with honest affection. The tattered ends of her frayed soul slowly stitched back together with every compliment, caress, and kindness he showed her.

He slowed his movements as his mouth found hers, drawing her mind back to the forefront. "Holy fuck, you feel incredible. I knew it would be like this. Perfect."

*Perfect.*

If only he knew how dangerously close she was to wrapping her entire heart around his sweet words. He shouldn't say such things if he didn't want more than just a night with her. But maybe he wanted more. She was falling too fast.

His tongue swept over the arch of her collarbone and he rested his forehead in the curve of her shoulder, rocking slowly, savoring each deep glide.

"I can't believe I found you again," he rasped, and the tears she worked so hard to hide slid past her lashes.

He kissed the moisture on her face. Their bodies shuddered as they finished together. She held onto him, never wanting to let go as they trembled under the intensity of the moment. If only he knew how limited her experiences had been, how harsh and cruel, he'd know how much his gentleness meant to her.

She didn't want to lose this closeness. She didn't want to lose *him*, and her desire to have him, for longer than a night, scared her in a new way. "Don't let go yet."

He thought she was only speaking about their bodies, but she was making a plea for more. She wanted his patience to last because she knew things wouldn't always be this easy. But most of all she wanted him.

His thumb swiped gently under her eyes as he stared down at her with renewed intensity. "This isn't over, Chloe. Not tonight or the next. I don't know if I'll ever get my fill of you."

# Fourteen

**TRENTON RETURNED** from the bathroom and climbed into bed. Chloe lay with her beautiful breasts peeking past the covers and a well-loved, dazed expression on her face. He kissed her cheek and nestled into her side.

"How you doin', doll?"

"Oh, I'd say I'm pretty good."

He chuckled and tucked her hips more firmly against his front. It was almost midnight and he was wiped. However, the idea of parting company with his lovely Chloe in less than twelve hours had him fighting sleep. "Tired?"

"Mm-hm," she mumbled, but when he glanced over her shoulder at her eyes they were still open.

He settled his head on the pillow. "What are you thinking about?"

"How crazy it is that we're here like this. Who would have thought we'd ever see each other again?"

Certainly not him. He gave her an affectionate squeeze.

"If you didn't stop to offer me help, do you think we would've ended up meeting anyway?"

He cleared his throat, guilt nipping with the reminder that he still had some secrets to share with her. He needed to tread lightly and didn't want to spoil an otherwise perfect moment with a conversation that deserved full attention and probably clothing. "Maybe. I've been friends with Jeremy since Okinawa and seeing as you know Jade, I guess we would've met eventually."

"But you probably never would've noticed me if I hadn't remembered you and stopped you at the party that night."

If only she knew how immediate his recognition came that night they bumped into each other. "Oh, I think I'd notice you no matter what."

She was quiet for a minute. "What were you doing in Maryland the day you picked me up?"

He took a deep breath. *Stick with the truth.* "I was working."

"Oh."

She'd given him the perfect opportunity to come clean, but this wasn't the time. He needed to tell her the truth and soon. He didn't want secrets between them and the longer he hid his association with her ex the more he felt unworthy of her trust, trust he'd been trying damn hard to earn.

"Let's try to get some sleep, doll."

~

Chloe awoke to the scratching of Trenton's jaw moving over her soft flesh as his mouth closed over the tip of her breast, sucking softly. She moaned and arched into his touch.

"I was wondering when you would wake up."

Without opening her eyes she smiled. "What time is it?"

"Four a.m."

His mouth trailed over her silky flesh and she lazily ran her fingers through his hair. "Have you been up long?"

"About thirty minutes. I tried to let you sleep. It was a losing battle."

She giggled silently as he softly kissed his way to her neck. His body settled over hers, heavy enough to let her know she wasn't dreaming. His mouth worked over her shoulder and her toes curled as he whispered, "I want inside of you, Chloe. Spread those beautiful thighs for me."

She parted her legs and he reached for a condom. Pressing in slow, finding his way deep, her body welcomed him as he stroked slowly. His mouth returned to her breast. He took his time, cradling her to him, languidly fulfilling her. She was in heaven.

Eventually, she'd have to talk to her boys about him again. Dayton would be the hardest sell, but she'd figure out how to handle him later.

She never had choices as a wife and since leaving Marcus, her sole purpose had been caring for her boys. After what felt like a lifetime of fulfilling the needs of others, she wanted to take something for herself. And she wanted Trenton Cole.

He pressed deep, bringing her back to the present. The way he made love to her was so sensuous, not climbing toward an explosive end, but rather maintaining a steady thrum of slow building pleasure. It was wonderful.

Time fell away, no ticking clocks or pressing responsibilities. Just them. They made love until the black sky faded to gray. The gentle chirping of birds whispered from outside the walls, making their hidden sanctuary all the more secret.

This was different from the night before. Softer. He made sure she came and it didn't take much. Simply having him inside of her put her dangerously close to the edge. A few tender traces of his fingers and she was done.

She loved watching him. That fragile moment when his gaze held hers, his eyes darkening under thick lashes as he trembled, fingers tightening on her skin, breath panting quickly past his lips, as he found his release. He was so ... honest in those moments, she found them fascinating and telling of the man he was.

His arm draped below her breasts and she traced circles in the dark hair covering his thick muscles, his head sweetly resting on her chest as they lay replete. She liked this part, too. Marcus had never held her afterward. But Trenton was a cuddler.

He sighed. "Do you want to shower with me? I'd offer you a bath, but I don't have a tub."

"A shower's fine." Suddenly she remembered something and tsked.

"What?" He lifted his head.

"I bought something for last night and I forgot to wear it."

He raised an eyebrow. "What did you buy?"

"It's nothing. I picked up a little nightie, that's all."

"A nightie?" He gave a wicked grin. "I'd like to see that. What do you say we grab a shower, then I'll make us some breakfast and you can model it for me? After that, we'll come back to bed and I can find the most creative way to take it off of you."

It was surreal having a man so interested in seeing her body. "Okay."

They played in the shower, soaping each other's skin and washing each other's hair. When she wrapped her body in a towel, Trenton simply buffed off the drops clinging to his body and walked bare-assed out of the room—and into the kitchen.

"Aren't you afraid someone will see you? You don't have curtains."

"No one's around for miles. Don't worry, we have complete privacy here."

She dug her blow dryer out of her overnight bag. Naked was one thing. Naked with frizzy bedhead was a totally different story.

Once her hair was dry, she put on lotion and some lipstick, and then slipped into the nightie. Turning to examine herself in the mirror, she scrunched her nose. It didn't look quite like it did on the mannequin.

The cobalt silk reminded her of Trenton's eyes. The slip was opaque and reached to her mid-thigh, where lace trimmed the hem. Spaghetti straps delicately draped her shoulders, and revealing lace covered her breasts.

"You all right in there, doll?"

Quickly stuffing her items back in her bag, she

walked to the bathroom door, took a deep breath, and opened it wide. "I hope you weren't expecting much."

His mouth slightly opened and snapped shut. His Adam's apple bobbed as he swallowed. "*That* is a vision prettier and anything I can imagine."

It was a novelty, being able to tease a man like this. Smiling, she nibbled her lower lip. "Is breakfast ready?"

He pulled his gaze away from her breasts. "What?"

"Breakfast. You said we were going to eat after our shower."

His gaze kept returning to her chest, sometimes traveling all the way down to her legs. She playfully patted his shoulder. "Come on."

Sashaying down the steps and into the kitchen, she hid a smirk. He dogged her steps like a starved cartoon character following the fumes of a feast. He'd made eggs and bacon. She took a seat and Trenton continued to watch her.

"Aren't you going to eat?"

Making no comment, nor taking his gaze off of her, he reached for a strip of bacon and bit off the end. She took a sip of coffee and realized she wasn't that hungry. He'd thrown on loose fitting sweats while she was in the bathroom, but they did little to hide the effect she was having on him.

Placing her cup on the table she gave the tented material between his thighs a pointed look. He followed her gaze and raised an eyebrow as if silently telling her *this is your fault*. He was so adorable, so unapologetically captivated by her. She'd never had that sort of effect on a man before.

Wanting to tease him, she stood and sauntered to the sitting area. "Did you kill whatever that is hanging above the mantle there?"

"It's an elk." His voice startled her. She hadn't heard him follow, but he was directly behind her.

The soft crinkle of a condom wrapper had her glancing over her shoulder as he removed one from his pocket. "How many of them do you carry around at a time?"

"Enough to have you every way possible until next Sunday. Hands on the couch, doll." He leaned her forward and gently nudged her feet apart.

His touch coasted over her ass, his right palm tracing the line of her spine and shifting the nightie out of the way. His fingers grazed her damp sex and he chuckled.

"I see you like teasing me." He spread her wet folds, feeding the blunt tip of his cock between her slit. "I've decided I like it, too."

He sank into her in one steady thrust and she rose on her toes. Withdrawing, almost leaving her completely, he slammed deep again. Her hands clutched the back of the couch as he pumped with long measured strokes.

He tugged the lace cups down, freeing her breasts, and reached for her nipples, plucking and pulling on the sensitive tips. His other hand drifted over her soft belly, parting her folds as his cock tunneled in and out of her. As he rubbed her clit, she moaned, sagging into his possessive hold.

His cock pressed deep and her body tightened,

their position so tenuous she wasn't sure she could stay this way much longer.

"Come for me, Chloe. Come all over my cock." His words were the catalyst, thrusting her over the edge into ecstasy.

Her strength gave out as her entire body quaked with the sudden force of her release. She trembled from head to toe as he held her tight, not letting her fall, working her orgasm, refusing to let the pleasure wane.

She cried out, overwhelmed by the sensations tingling through her. When she could take no more, he bent over her, folding her body to the back of the couch and thrust hard and deep, rapid strokes teasing her nerves into another storm of pleasure.

His hands clamped tight on her hips and he panted with each forceful plunge. His moans echoed in the open space, rough and thunderous, countering her softer sighs. Stiffening, his hard flesh pulsed steadily inside of her.

Slowly, his grip slackened. He pressed a kiss to her back, his breathing labored, and rested his cheek on her shoulder. "Was that too rough?"

She glanced over her shoulder from her awkward position, eyes heavy with satisfied lust, and laughed. "Not. At. All."

He chuckled. "Give me ten minutes and I'll do it again."

# Fifteen

CHLOE WATCHED Trenton's truck pull away and sighed. Drifting in a daydream to her room, she stowed her overnight bag on the side of her bed to unpack later. The empty driveway next door told her the boys were still at breakfast.

Gathering the clothes off the floor of her sons' rooms, she passed the time straightening up. A hamper was a useless item in a boy's room, but for once she was in too good of a mood to stress over such things.

She started a load of laundry and took a chicken out to defrost. At the desk in the living room, she sorted through her bills and logged online to check her bank account. After writing out the utilities, she reached for the payment book for her car and frowned.

It wasn't where she normally kept it beside the envelopes. Sorting through the basket of paperwork, she searched for the book but didn't find it.

Growing frustrated, she pulled open drawers

and rummaged through items she hardly touched. Thankfully, she found it wedged in the back of a small compartment, unsure how it wound up there.

She neatly stamped each envelope and walked them to the mailbox just as Adam's SUV pulled in the driveway. The boys jumped out of the car chatting a mile a minute and full of sugar from breakfast.

"Thanks for taking them."

Tommy scoffed. "Isn't she cute the way she acts like she's going to blow us off without giving us any details?"

"Seriously." Adam crossed his arms over his chest and raised a brow. "You're inviting us in."

She laughed and they followed her to her house where the boys were already playing in their rooms.

"So?"

She pulled a laundry basket in front of her, smiled, and whispered, "Amazing."

Tommy clapped. "So I guess you're going out with him again?"

Her face heated over her sore cheeks. It was tiring, holding a smile for so many hours straight. "Try and stop me."

"Maybe we should move game night to Sundays," Adam teased. "We're not used to you having a social life."

They chatted as Chloe folded clothes. She couldn't hide how happy she was. "I'm going to have to talk to Day and Mattie about my relationship. Any suggestions?"

Tommy gave her a look that said she was asking the wrong guy. Adam, who had been present for

Dayton's previous outburst, took the question a little more seriously. "Did he tell you why he reacted so badly at first?"

"He said he's forgetting what Marcus looks like."

"I guess you don't want any pictures of him around."

"I don't have any pictures of him. Day thinks if I go out with Trenton there's no chance of Marcus and I reconciling."

Tommy made a disgusted sound. "Like that would ever happen."

"I told him that, basically. I tried to explain to him that Marcus and I simply didn't get along, but he thinks his father only acted that way because I somehow provoked him."

Adam squeezed her hand. "Honey, you know that's not true. Abusers don't need provocation. You were never to blame. He's too young to understand."

"I know, but I don't know how to explain something so ugly to my nine-year-old."

"Well," Tommy said, keeping his tone light. "You can't shelve your social life because your children don't understand that their father is an asshole. They're just going to have to realize their mother has a life outside of being mom."

"How are they around Trent?" Adam asked a little more realistically.

"Fine. I mean, they only met him twice."

"Do they know he's the one who rescued you?"

"No, because that would entail sharing details about how I left their father without actually saying goodbye." Something she hoped time would blur for both her children. "Dayton remembers us arguing, but I don't know how much of the violence he actually recalls. You should have heard him tell me if I had been a better wife Marcus wouldn't have been so angry all the time. He thinks I'm to blame for our separation, which I am because I left, but I won't take the blame for Marcus being a monster."

"Of course not."

Tommy scoffed. "What does he know? He's nine."

"Exactly." Adam tossed him a pointed look. "You can't judge a child for what they're too young to understand."

Tommy waved away his words. "Honey, I'm gay. I judge."

"Yeah, well, he's nine. He doesn't know any better." Turning back to her, he suggested, "Maybe you should have Trent over for dinner so the kids can *get* to know him better."

That seemed the best solution, so she invited Trenton over for supper that Wednesday. She wanted to make something everyone would like, so she went with a traditional feast of corn, mashed potatoes, salad, and red meat.

"Can I help?" Mattie asked.

"Did you finish your spelling words?"

"Yes."

"Okay, then why don't you set the table?"

Mattie was her little helper, always there to pitch in where he could. Dayton said he only had a few math problems for homework but had yet to emerge from his room. He was her procrastinator.

"What's your brother doing?"

Mattie shrugged. "Playing video games I guess."

A few minutes later the potatoes were boiling, the salad was waiting to be dressed, and the corn heated on the stove. Chloe called for Dayton and turned to her youngest. "Mattie, I have to go start the grill. When your brother gets out here ask him to straighten up the living room."

When she returned from outside the pillows on the couches were still not tidied and comic books littered the coffee table. She frowned. "Did you tell your brother what I said?"

The table was set and Mattie now perused a word game website on her laptop at the counter. "Yeah."

She hoped Dayton wasn't going to make this evening difficult. While Mattie's back was turned she quickly switched the forks to the proper sides of the plates and straightened the napkins.

"Dayton?" She moved to stir the corn.

"What?"

"Why didn't you straighten the living room like I asked?"

Without a word, he skulked to the den and shoved his comic books into a basket. He pushed the pillows where they were supposed to go but didn't bother fluffing them. "Mattie, get your crap out of here."

She took a deep breath. "Dayton, can you please use nicer words?"

He huffed. "Well, I'm not picking up his shoes."

"Mattie, could you please put your shoes in your bedroom?"

Mattie paused his game and did as she asked.

She regarded her eldest. "Are you planning on being grumpy all night?"

He shrugged.

"Dayton, I told you, I just want you to get to know Mr. Cole. No one is replacing anyone."

"Whatever."

"If you can't find your manners you'll find yourself eating dinner alone in your room. Now, put ice in the glasses—please." She really hoped he wasn't going to be rude. Sending him to his room would defeat the purpose of the evening—getting to know Trenton.

He muttered something under his breath and she blocked his grumbling out with the sound of the mixer as she whipped the milk and butter into the soft potatoes.

"Who wants to lick the whisks?"

It was a decent olive branch as both came running. As Dayton tossed his in the sink she brushed her hand over his shaggy hair. "This is getting so long."

He shouldered off her touch and her heart pinched. Every day there seemed a new wall between them. Not letting him escape that easily, she pulled him to her.

"Hey. I love you, Dayton. Whether you realize it or not, there isn't one thing in my life that means more to me than you or your brother."

The tension in his shoulders eased as he stared at her, his eyes still stormy, but softening enough to let her know he understood.

She hugged him. Then, she teasingly asked, "How about this weekend we get this rug clipped?"

He gasped and shoved away. "You said I could grow it as long as I didn't fight with Mattie."

She smiled. "I know. I was joking. I appreciate you being nicer to your brother. I'm sure he appreciates it, too. Remember that next time you yell at him to pick up his 'crap', and maybe use a nicer word, okay?"

Realizing she was reminding him of their agreement, he nodded. "Okay. Sorry."

Chloe was flipping the steaks on the grill when Mattie came outside. "Mom, Mr. Cole just pulled up."

All at once, her chest, stomach, and sex tightened as she went to greet him at the front door.

As he walked up the steps he smiled. He was wearing jeans and a white t-shirt and carried a white bakery box tied with a red string.

"Hey, beautiful." He kissed her on the cheek and her heart did a little somersault.

"Hi." Already breathless, she welcomed him into the house.

"Can I do anything?"

"Everything's about ready." She carried the side dishes to the table.

"This looks great."

"Thanks. I just need to get the steaks off the grill and then we can eat. Mattie, go wash your hands and tell Dayton it's time to eat."

"Oh, hey buddy. I didn't see you there." Trenton turned back to her and smiled. "You made steak?"

She blushed and smiled back at him, knowing it was his favorite. Grabbing a large plate she headed to the grill. Trenton, she noticed, took the time to fill everyone's glasses with iced tea. He was very thoughtful of others and not one of those men who considered dinner prep below him. She supposed growing up in a family of seven would teach a man to be helpful.

They sat down and she dished out food on the boy's plates. "Trenton, you'll probably want this one. The others aren't as rare."

"Thank you, Chloe."

They ate in silence for a bit. Chloe nervously watched the boys as she took small bites of her food. "How was school today?"

"Good."

"Fine."

Mattie perked up. "Sister Gertrude farted in social studies."

Dayton snorted into his iced tea and Chloe's eyes widened, heat rushing to her face.

"You boys go to Catholic school?" Trenton asked, not flinching at the fart comment.

Both Dayton and Mattie nodded.

"I used to go to Catholic school. Of course, back then it was a little different."

"How come?" Mattie asked.

"Well..." Trenton smiled. "Back then if you laughed at a farting nun they'd whack you on the knuckles with a ruler."

Dayton chuckled and Mattie's eyes widened. "They used to hit you?"

"Only if we were rude."

"Well, when Sister Gertrude let it rip everyone laughed. She didn't say anything though."

Chloe clucked her tongue. "She was probably embarrassed."

"Did you ever get hit?" Dayton asked Trenton.

He chewed a piece of his steak, his mouth twisting into a somewhat proud smirk. "A few times."

"What'd you do?"

"Well, one time it was for talking back. Another time it was for taking an extra cake off the snack cart. But the worst time was for repeatedly writing my cursive letters wrong."

Dayton gaped. "They hit you for bad handwriting?"

Trenton laughed. "Yeah, but that was the norm back then. If you were a good student you usually didn't have any trouble. I bet your mom never got the ruler. She earned the Religion Award. Did you boys know that?"

She rolled her eyes and pointed her fork at him. "You hush." To her sons, she said, "You two, eat. That's enough talk about farts and angry nuns for one dinner."

Trenton took a large bite of mashed potatoes and grinned around his fork.

After dinner, the boys asked if they could go outside for a little bit and she agreed but told them to stay in the yard. Trenton helped her clear the table.

"That was delicious, doll."

"Thank you." She started a pot of coffee. As she filled the sink with suds and wet her sponge he approached from behind, pulling her hips against his as he kissed her neck. Shivers scattered down her spine.

"I've missed you," he whispered as he wrapped his arms around her.

The boys' voices echoed in the backyard as they chased a soccer ball over the grass. Trenton's fingers flicked open the button of her pants and she gripped the lip of the sink. She drew in a shaky breath, wondering if she should be concerned about how easily he turned her on.

"I missed you, too."

"When can you come over again?" His hand pressed into the front of her panties, teasing her clit. His voice lowered as he whispered in her ear, "I wish I could put my mouth here." His finger slid inside of her and she sucked in a breath.

She let out a disappointed sigh. "Friday's Adam's mother's birthday, so that's out."

He nibbled her ear. "Saturday?"

"I don't know if Saturday's going to work. Tommy's trying to get tickets to some event."

"I don't think I can make it to Monday." His touch intensified and her eyes closed.

"We could probably get together during the day, but I'm not sure if a sleepover's doable this weekend."

He nibbled her shoulder. "I could ask Phoenix if the boys could have a sleepover with Austin." The bulge of his erection pressed into her as he wedged a finger between her folds. "I want you to come."

"Trenton..."

"Do it for me, Chloe." His fingers thrust in and out, his palm running over her clit with each push. "You're soaked. You know you want to." His wet fingers traced over her, rubbing quickly as his hips rocked. "Give in."

Her head fell back on a silent cry as her muscles spasmed and her knees softened. "Trenton."

He kissed her throat. "Mmm, I love when you say my name like that." He slowly adjusted her pants. "Let my sister watch the boys for you, Chloe. She's great with kids."

Even with her head in an orgasmic fog, her gut said no. "That seems like a lot to ask."

"I could also ask Georgia and Amanda to babysit. They could come here."

There was nothing wrong with his sisters and she appreciated the offer, but her boys were comfortable with Adam and Tommy. *She* was comfortable with them. Turning to face him, she wreathed her arms over his shoulders and kissed his lips.

"You know I like your family, but the boys hardly know them and we need to move at their pace, not ours. Can you understand that?"

His smile was empathetic. "Yes, I can understand that."

"Thank you."

When they finished the dishes she poured coffee, hers with cream and sugar, his black, just the way he liked it. She took pride in remembering such details and saw that he appreciated her attention.

They settled in at the table, her eyes drifting to the box he'd brought. "So, what's in the box?"

"Cannoli."

She groaned. "I *love* them!"

He untied the string, lifting the lid and turned the box to her. Lined up like little snowy soldiers were a dozen Cannoli, each one sitting on its own ruffled doily. Her mouth watered.

Plucking a powdered shell from the wrapper, he held it out to her. The white creamy filling seeped from the edges, freckled with mini chocolate chips.

"Taste."

Leaning forward, she closed her mouth over the creamy tip and they each moaned.

"God, I love that mouth. Taste it again."

She smirked and stole another dollop. This time he leaned in and replaced the dessert with his mouth, chasing the sweetness and stealing her breath. Easing back, he sighed. They each wore the same regretful expression that they couldn't take things further.

A few minutes and two Cannoli later, Dayton and Mattie returned, devouring several of the Italian treats. She and Trenton finished their coffee and he washed out his mug, preparing to leave.

It was frustrating being an adult, owning her own practice, and taking accountability for two children, a home and all the responsibilities in between, yet not being able to have her boyfriend sleep over. She wanted to pout but kept herself in check.

She told the boys to go get into their pajamas and walked Trenton to his truck. Along the side of the house, where her boys wouldn't see, they kissed goodbye. She wound up kicking herself for it, because he'd once again stirred up her hormones, and it would be days before she saw him again.

When he finally pulled away an emptiness settled in her chest so deep it ached. She tossed and turned that night as she tried to fall asleep. As if on cue, just after eleven, her phone rang from her nightstand.

She smiled when she read the display. "Hello?"

"Hey, gorgeous. Did I wake you?"

"Hardly."

He made a low tsking sound. "What's the matter, doll? Can't sleep?"

She breathed into the phone. "Nope. I'm wide awake."

"What are you wearing?"

She laughed. "Honestly?"

"Honestly."

Looking down, she considered lying but opted for the truth. "An old t-shirt and a pair of sweats."

He groaned as if she said *Frederick's of Hollywood.* "Mmm. Do you have those cute little ankle socks on?"

She laughed. "Yes."

"Dear God..." He moaned. "Tell me it's the shirt that smells like rotten eggs and I may just come right now."

She snorted. "No, I burned that shirt."

"Where are the kids?"

"Sleeping."

"What are you watching?"

"Reruns."

"Should have known." He chuckled. "Turn the volume up and go lock the door."

She stilled.

"You there, doll?"

"Why am I locking the door?"

"Because in about two minutes your fingers are

going to be buried between your thighs. Now, do as I said."

Swallowing, she reached for the remote and turned up the volume a few notches, and then climbed out from under the covers and went to lock the door. "What now?"

"Take off the sweats. Panties too."

Pinching the phone between her shoulder and ear, she slid down her pants, accidentally hitting a button on the keypad. "Sorry."

"Are you sitting on the bed?"

She moved back under the covers. "Yes."

"Are you wet, doll?"

Her face heated. "I don't know."

"Touch yourself and check."

She didn't have to. She knew she was. Her hand slid between her thighs anyway. "A little."

"Good. I want you to get your fingers wet. I can still smell you on mine from earlier."

Her breath echoed into the phone as she extended her touch.

"Now I want you to touch your nipples with your wet fingers." He waited a moment. "Are you doing it?"

Her eyes closed as she imagined her hands as his. "Yes."

"How does it feel? How do those beautiful breasts feel?"

"Heavy." She pulled at her nipples and breathed deeply. "They ache."

"Are your nipples hard, Chloe? Get them nice and hard for me."

She moaned softly.

"Are you imagining my hands on you?"

"Yes." Her toes pointed and she pressed her thighs together.

"Good girl. Now, keep playing with your breasts, they deserve lots of attention, but take your other hand and slide it lower, nice and slow. Can you do that for me, doll?"

"Okay." She heard movement on the other end and wondered if he was touching himself as well. "Trenton?"

"Yes, baby."

"Are you naked?"

"As the day I was born. Now, where's that hand?"

"There."

"And how does *there* feel?"

"Warm. Wet."

"Good. I want you to take one finger and slide it inside."

She moaned and did as he told her.

"Just one, Chloe. Savor it. You haven't forgotten about those beautiful nipples, I hope."

"I haven't."

"Good. Tell me how it feels."

"Soft. Hot."

"Do you wish I was there with you?"

"Yes."

"Well, if I was, you'd see how hard I am for you right now. I'd be right there with you, kissing your neck, nibblin' your ear, spreading your thighs open. Then I'd kiss my way to your nipples and spend some time sucking those peach tips until they turned dark pink. After that, I'd work my way past your soft belly to your sweet pussy. How does your pussy feel now, doll?"

Her throat was dry. "Soaking wet."

"Can you feel my lips on you?"

"Yes."

"Good. Tell me how good you taste."

She froze. "Wh—what?"

"I want you to take that finger and taste how sweet you are."

She slowly withdrew her finger and touched it to her lips.

"How do you taste?"

"Light. Sort of like berries."

"Delicious," he modified. "Now, would you like me to put my mouth back where it was?"

"Mmm... Yes."

"That's my girl. Go ahead and put your finger between your legs again. Listen carefully as I tell you what I'd do. You do it for me with those pretty little fingers of yours. First, I'd tease your lips, kissing your soft flesh. I'd really want to suck your sweet little clit, but I wouldn't because I know it'll make you come harder if I make you wait for it. I'd press your thighs wide, needing to have a taste, and bury my tongue deep inside of you. Do you feel my tongue in you now?"

"Yes." She breathed, her finger stroking soft and deep.

"Do you want to come?"

"Yes, please."

"Aw, listen to those manners. So pretty. I'll give you permission to touch your clit, but first I want you to push more fingers deep inside and pretend it's my cock. Do you feel my cock?"

She breathed into the phone and moaned, no longer able to form words as her fingers filled her, and her other hand rubbed in tight circles over her sensitized clit.

"I feel it too, doll. I feel your soft, wet pussy gripping me. You feel so good. Do I feel good to you?"

"God, yes."

"I'm moving faster now. Tight, quick strokes. I wanna come, but I'm waiting for you. Are you close, baby?"

"Yes, yes, yes, yes..." She arched and came, moaning out his name. Her body pulsed as she exhaled on a trembling breath.

As her heart slowed from a rapping drumbeat to a gentle throb, she realized she'd dropped the phone. Rolling to her side, she searched through her pillows. When she found it, she heard Trenton's heavy breathing on the other end. "Trenton?"

His voice was hoarse. "Yeah."

She smiled and lay back down, pressing her smile into the pillows. "I came."

"Me too, doll. Me too. You think you'll be able to sleep now?"

She shut her eyes and snuggled deeper under the covers. "Mmm-hmm."

"Good. Sweet dreams, baby. I'll call you tomorrow."

"Sweet dreams, Trenton."

CHLOE WAS SITTING at the kitchen table going over flash cards with Mattie while Dayton studied his spelling words when the front door crashed open and Tommy came running inside screaming.

*"Guess what, guess what, guess what!"*

All at once she and her boys asked, "What?"

"I got Lady Gaga tickets!" He waved two tickets in the air. "You can't tell Adam though. It's a surprise."

"He'll love that, Tommy." She hid her disappointment that this meant they wouldn't be able to watch the boys Saturday.

"I know! I would've gotten you a ticket, too, but they were like a bazillion dollars and I didn't think Paul Bunion would be too gaga for Gaga."

"No, it's fine. I wouldn't have a sitter anyway."

"Oh, right." Tommy pursed his lips. "I forgot about that. Are you going to be able to go out with him this weekend?"

"She doesn't have to be with him all the time," Dayton snapped.

Tommy put his hands on his hips. "Your mom likes him. Cut her some slack, Dayton. There's nothing wrong with her spending time with a nice guy."

She cringed as Dayton slapped his notebook shut and left the room. A second later his door slammed.

"Sorry," Tommy apologized.

He meant well, but sometimes she wished Tommy would just shut up. Adam understood. He often complained to her about his husband not having a filter. She loved Tommy and typically trusted him with her children, but in terms of her delicate situation with introducing her sons, he was pushing for too much too soon.

"It's okay. Just do me a favor and don't bring up Trenton around him for now."

After he left, she finished studying with Mattie. Dinner was uneventful. Dayton didn't crack a smile until he was zoned out on the couch eating a bowl of ice cream. At least television made him laugh.

There was a light knock at the door and Adam walked in, his eyes serious. They went to the kitchen for privacy and he whispered, "Hey, honey. You okay? Tommy told me what he did."

She took a deep breath and pointed to the kitchen door. "Back porch?"

"Yeah."

They sat at the patio table as she collected her thoughts. "I know he doesn't mean any harm, but

I'd appreciate it if he didn't poke at an already angry beehive. I feel bad even saying that because you guys do so much for me and the boys."

Adam leaned forward and grabbed her hands. "Look at me, love. Those boys in there are *your* children. Nobody on this earth knows them better or loves them more than *you*. We love them too, but we're not the ones who have to raise them. At the end of the day, you're the parent. Tommy doesn't always know what's best."

"I know, and I want your opinions, just not always in front of the boys. Sometimes I don't know how to tell him he crossed a line."

"We'll always be there for you and the boys, but it's okay to have boundaries. We enjoy the kids and we love you guys. You aren't going to lose us because you tell Tommy to shut up once in a while." He laughed. "I tell him almost every day."

Chloe leaned back in her chair and moaned. "Am I asking for too much with Dayton? Is this moving too fast?"

He sighed. "Honey, that's a call only you can make. You've been single for six years and even when you were married you were mostly alone. None of us want to see you miss out on something that could be great, but it's not always going to be easy. You're ready, I think, but the boys are young and they might not be. Dayton's got a lot of emotion trapped inside of him right now."

She gave a humorless laugh. "I studied plenty of cases and journals about kids going through the same things as my son, but as a mother, I can't think of a single useful theory. And for the record, Adam, if this was something Dayton truly couldn't deal with, I…"

Wow, she didn't expect saying the words would be so difficult. She tried again. "I would let Trenton go."

Adam looked genuinely sad. "Oh, sweetie, I think it's just new and boys tend not to handle change well. So don't get yourself all worked up for nothing. Dayton will come around. He just needs a little time. There's no need to rush things. I'll talk to Tommy and tell him to back off. Everything will work out. You'll see."

"I hope you're right."

He smiled then looked serious again. "Chloe?"

"Yeah."

"Do you love him?"

She groaned. "Why do you always have to ask the difficult questions?"

"It's not a difficult question. You either love him or you don't."

She sighed. "I don't know, Adam. He's nothing like Marcus. He's gentle and sweet, and he likes *me,* not just pieces of me. He likes *all* of me. He makes me … happy."

"Okay, well, first of all, Marcus is a terrible measuring stick. The guy was a brute and a creep. Second, there's nothing about you that's not to like. You're sweet, generous, caring, and always trying to help others. You're fun and silly and great for flashing people at parties."

She laughed.

"But, Chloe, most of all, you're perfect just the

way you are because you're Chloe. If people expect you to change, that's their problem, not yours."

She smiled at him. "I love you, Adam."

"I love you, too. And don't worry about putting a label on what you feel for Trent. You'll realize it when it's time."

"Thanks." She took a deep breath. "So, you're going gaga this weekend?"

He laughed. "That's me. Do you think I'll be the only forty-year-old there?"

"No, I'm sure some parents will be there with their kids," she teased and he swatted her knee.

"Bitch."

~

Saturday morning Trenton came over for brunch. Chloe made French toast with homemade whipped cream and fresh cut strawberries. After breakfast, the kids played and she finally told him a little bit about what was going on with Dayton.

"Is it me?" he asked, his brow creased and his eyes worried.

"No. I think he would be this way with anyone. He feels like his dad's being replaced and I think he's confused about a lot of things."

"But there was the episode over at Ty's. Do you think my part in that made him dislike me?"

She hated the look in his eyes, knowing he regretted that day. "Trenton, I told you I was wrong to fly off the handle at Tyson's. I saw your hands on my son and I just reacted without thinking. I know you were only trying to protect the kids."

He glanced away, carefully choosing his words. "With Marcus, did he ever ... hurt the boys?"

She swallowed hard. "No. I worried if I stayed he would've started with Dayton, or worse, Mattie, who was still just a baby."

"I guess it's for the best he has no interest in seeing his boys."

Chloe let the false assumption lie. Truth was, six years down the line, she didn't know if Marcus thought about her and the boys at all anymore. He might've moved on to be with someone else, possibly have another family to worry about. She'd always believed if he wanted to find them he would have by now.

She understood Trenton's misconception. Like many people, he assumed she had a tidy little court-approved arrangement, maybe even one where Marcus's support checks came twice a month and he could visit his sons upon request. But it could never be like that.

She considered clearing up the misconception but feared another man would try to tell her how to handle her life. Not that Trenton typically did that, but at the moment, after the disagreement with Tommy, she was tapped out on other people's advice about how she should raise her children.

"I told Dayton there's no chance of his father and I ever living together again."

"How did he react to that?"

"He blames me."

He gave her a sympathetic smile. "He's still young, doll. He doesn't understand."

"I know. It doesn't make it hurt any less though."

"I'm sorry." He pulled her into his side and kissed her head. "I don't know much of the details of your marriage, you'll tell me about it when you're ready, but I'm pretty sure your marriage fell apart because of Marcus, not you."

After Trenton left, the day continued under a shadow of melancholy. She wasn't up for anything. The guys were excited about their concert and she tried to listen to their cheerful plans, but her heart wasn't in it. She ordered pizza for dinner and decided to catch up on the novel she was currently reading.

"Mom?" Dayton stood hesitantly in the doorway of her bedroom.

"Hey." She closed her book.

"Are you okay?" he asked, taking a small step in the room.

She scooted up and patted the mattress beside her. "I'm fine. What's up? Something you want to talk about?"

He slowly walked into the room and lay on the other side of the bed in silence for several minutes until he finally said, "Mr. Cole's nice to you."

She smiled. "I think so."

"He holds out chairs for you and always brings you stuff."

She thought about the gallon of orange juice he'd brought that morning. "He's very thoughtful."

"Did Dad used to do that kind of stuff for you?"

Her son, despite his rigid walls, was very fragile lately, so she treaded carefully. "Your father would buy me flowers on holidays sometimes."

"Did he used to hold doors for you?"

"Sometimes. In the beginning."

"Why did he stop doing that stuff?"

"I don't know, Dayton." And that was the truth. "Your father was a tricky man to figure out. He could be having a perfectly average day then, out of the blue, he would be in a rage. It would happen so fast I had a hard time figuring out what triggered it. Eventually, he just seemed angry more than he seemed happy."

"What would you do if I saw Daddy again?"

Her blood ran cold. She'd prayed she'd never have to face such a situation. "I... I don't know, sweetie."

"I'm sorry I gave you a hard time about Mr. Cole."

She blinked in surprise. "Thank you, Dayton. It's very mature of you to try to see the situation from my angle."

"I like that he does nice things for you. If I... I mean, when I'm a grownup and girls aren't gross anymore, I would want to treat them like Mr. Cole treats you."

Pride overflowed her heart. She was so afraid of the ways Dayton resembled his father. With his fairly new moodiness, her concern had doubled. To hear him make a statement like that... It was an immeasurable relief. "That would make me very proud, honey."

"I think—" Chloe's phone rang on her nightstand. "Are you going to get that?"

She picked up the phone and silenced it. "No, you go ahead, honey."

"Was it Mr. Cole?"

"Yes."

"Don't you want to talk to him?"

"Right now I want to talk to you. Go ahead."

He seemed a little surprised. His grin trembled. "I was just gonna say I think Mr. Cole would make a good boyfriend for you."

They lay there for a while longer and the conversation turned to school, video games, and who they thought should be the next winner on a reality show they watched. Eventually, they grew quiet and her son fell asleep with his head on her shoulder. Just before she shut her eyes, she smiled, thinking how nice it was to finally have her Dayton back.

# Seventeen

TWO WEEKS HAD PASSED since her conversation with Dayton and it seemed her son meant what he said. Whenever Trenton was around, Dayton was polite and courteous. Trenton also noticed the improvement.

The four of them had gone to the movies, shared several meals, and the boys even invited Trenton to game night. She was thrilled with the way things were going. Her only complaint was she had yet to spend the night with him again.

They spent several nights on the phone talking and touching until the wee hours of morning, but it was no substitute for the real thing, so she was more than grateful when Tommy and Adam offered to keep the boys overnight that Saturday.

Trenton was making her dinner at his place. She had her overnight bag packed, dyed her hair, and painted a fresh coat of nail polish on her nails. It was a pain dying her hair every few weeks, but since returning to Pennsylvania she'd maintained a dark auburn and she wasn't ready to drop that veil yet. Maybe soon.

After her shower she carefully selected her outfit, wanting something sexy, but not inappropriate for dinner. The May weather had arrived and she was enjoying the return of her spring wardrobe.

At four o'clock Adam arrived to walk the kids over to his house. "Wow, Chloe. You look prettier than sunshine."

She blushed, glancing down at her white eyelet dress. "Thanks, Adam. You sure these shoes look okay?"

"I love it. Just don't let Tommy see you. You know how he feels about white before Memorial Day."

She rolled her eyes. "Like he's the least bit southern."

"I know." He laughed.

After everyone was gone, she made sure all the lights were off and candles blown out. She walked her bag to the door and waited anxiously by the window. At five o'clock on the dot, Trenton's truck pulled into the driveway. She locked the door and met him on the walkway.

"Hello, beautiful." He kissed her cheek, and once inside the truck, he kissed her soundly.

As they approached Neshannock her nerves kicked in.

"You okay, doll?"

"I don't know why I'm suddenly nervous. We've come so far since the last time I was here, yet it feels like we're on our first date again."

"What do you think you're nervous about?"

"Honestly?" she asked, not quite sure she knew the answer.

"Of course."

"Okay." She turned toward him, shifting in her seat. "Right now, I can barely think straight for wanting you. I've been in a perpetual state of arousal since the guys agreed to watch the boys. I'm all fluttery and I can't stop picturing us naked together. You've corrupted me."

He outright laughed. "*I've* corrupted you? Babe, at least you can fake it. I feel like a fifteen-year-old boy. I've had a steady hard-on for weeks. Every time I think of you I get an erection and there's not always something around to hide it."

"You do not."

"It's the truth. I think *you've* corrupted *me*."

She leaned back in her seat and thought on that for a minute. "What are you making for dinner?"

"Pasta with homemade gravy."

"How long does that take?"

He laughed again. "How about we worry about dinner after we address our other appetites? I could give a shit what we eat if it's a choice between sophisticated dining and spending an evening naked with you. I mean, don't get me wrong, I want to cook for you, but you already have me well past half mast."

"So ... postpone dinner?"

"Definitely."

She needed him to drive faster.

Arm stretched to the wheel, he glanced at her. "I like that dress. That should save us some time. You wearing panties under there?"

She smiled. "Yes."

"Why don't you do us both a favor and slide them off."

Toeing off her flip-flops, she unbuckled her seatbelt and lifted her hips to slide her hands under her skirt and hitch the underwear down her legs, shimmying them off her body. She tucked them in the center console and buckled her seatbelt again.

He smiled at her, taking his eyes briefly off the road. "Good. Were they wet?"

Her lips pursed around a smile. "Maybe."

He sped up along the back road. "And how about you? How do you feel?"

"Like I'll burst the second you lay a hand on me."

He slowed the truck and adjusted his position in his seat. "Pull your skirt up."

"We're in the car."

"There isn't a house for another two miles and I'll tell you if I see a car coming."

Hesitating—*Oh, for Pete's sake, just do it*!—she hitched up her skirt.

"Let me see." His focus shifted between her and the road. "Show me how wet you are."

She licked her lips. "Trenton..."

"You heard me."

Face burning, she traced a finger down the seam of her sex and held out her damp fingers, glistening with arousal. "There. See?"

The truck swerved as leaned across the seat and his mouth closed over her fingers, sucking them clean. "I love the way you fucking taste."

. . .

He sped down the dirt road, each passing yard driving her pulse's tempo. The truck skidded to a stop in front of the barn and he was out of the cab a second later. The passenger door wrenched open and Trenton blocked her escape.

Formidable hunger rolled into one dark, sexy gaze. His mouth crashed to hers, his tongue plunging deep as his beard scraped against her jaw. He had her hips pulled to the edge of the seat and his fingers deep inside of her in two seconds flat.

His mouth burned a trail of fire down her throat to her cleavage. "Lie back."

He dropped to his haunches and pulled her knees over his shoulders, wasting no time. He gripped her thighs, pushed his fingers deep, and sucked her clit hard. Her body coiled and sprang with enough force to topple the Richter scale. She shouted his name as she came hard against his tongue.

He wrung every last drop of pleasure from her, not letting her come down until he was satisfied and his grip finally eased. His fingers slipped from her pulsing sex and he placed one final kiss on her swollen clit. Even that was too much. He stood and flashed a cocky male grin.

She stared at him—sure he was some sort of carnal God. Never—never in her *entire* life—had she ever experienced something so all-encompassing. She wasn't even sure she could return a favor of such magnitude, but she'd be willing to try.

He reached for her hand and pulled her upright. She slid out of the truck on wobbly legs, her skirt falling back into place. He caught her weight and kissed her soundly.

Unbelievable. One kiss and she wanted him all over again. She playfully teased him, her tongue licking at his mouth, biting his lower lip and releasing it with a quiet snap.

"Your turn, Mr. Cole."

His eyes blazed with liquid blue heat. "Inside. Now."

Reaching for her lost shoe she skipped over to the door. He hastily unlocked it and they rushed inside.

Light filtered in through the large windows as he tossed his keys on the table by the door. He pulled off his boots and unclasped his belt buckle, tugging it through the loops of his jeans with a slither and snap that echoed through the quiet home. She flinched at the recognizable sound but didn't let it break her focus as the belt dropped to the floor.

He stalked her through the den like a predator eyeing its prey. Her heart raced as he stepped onto the plush carpet in the center of the room and removed his shirt, flinging it carelessly onto the chair. She stood in front of him, practically panting with anticipation as he undid the snap of his jeans and rolled down the zipper.

Yanking her close, he kissed her, teasing her, tempting her. She melted in his arms and ran her tongue over the dark stubble of his throat. His body reflexively rocked forward, his hips bucking into hers.

Licking a trail of soft wet kisses down his tight

stomach, tracing each delicious indent and muscular bulge, she flirtatiously nipped his flesh. Finally, she dropped to her knees and spread the V of his pants wide, tugging the material down his hips.

His cock sprang free, looking even larger than she remembered. She swiped the moisture at the tip away with her tongue. He groaned and she fisted him at the root. He pressed his hips forward, following her motions. Giving a cheeky smile, she licked the underside of his shaft.

His rumble of pleasure filled the room. She could tell he held his control by a fine thread. Tracing her tongue around the tip, she decided they'd endured enough and took him into her mouth.

His hand cupped the back of her hair as he sank deep and lifted on his toes. "Jesus fucking Christ…"

She moved up and down, working her tongue and lips over his sensitive flesh, his hips working in tandem with her mouth. Fingers brushed the hair away from her face while his other hand held tight to the back of her head.

Chloe wanted to give him something mildly close to what he'd given her. She shut her eyes and relaxed her throat and took him as deep as physically possible.

He let out a roar of pleasure and pumped himself in and out of her mouth. She surrendered all control to him, loving the way he growled her name in between moans of satisfaction, always seeming on the cusp of losing control, but never getting too rough or greedy.

Gripping her hair tightly, his cock throbbed over her tongue. "Fuck, Chloe, I'm gonna come."

He tried to extricate himself from her grip, but she was having none of that. Holding onto him the same as he'd held onto her in the car, she dragged out his pleasure. He grunted and threw himself into the moment.

The first spurt of his release splashed the back of her throat and she swallowed. With another growl, his spine stiffened and his ass tightened under her grip. She milked every last drop from him, soothing him with gentle kisses and soft caresses as his legs trembled.

When she shyly looked up, he stared at her with an astonished expression. She didn't know what to make of the look in his eyes until he dropped to his knees and kissed her with nothing less than pure affection.

When they broke the kiss he whispered, "You're the most amazing woman I have ever met in my entire life. I'm never letting you go."

# Eighteen

**THEY DIDN'T SIT** down to actually eat dinner until well after ten. Following their explosive homecoming, they rested on the floor for a while, simply holding each other. Eventually, their comforting caresses escalated into heavy petting. Without making it to the couch they made love on the carpet in front of the fireplace.

As the sun set, Chloe began to shiver. Trent threw some wood in the fire, got the blaze going, and pulled a blanket over them as they lay watching the flames and talking for hours.

When both their stomachs started growling he got up to put a pot of water on to boil. Grateful he made the sauce the day before, he set it on the stove to warm and returned to the floor with a few extra pillows and a bottle of wine.

They shared a glass of wine and almost made it to round three until he heard the water boiling and figured he'd better drop the pasta in. One more time on the floor and he'd be sending Chloe home with permanent rug burn.

As he mixed the salad and stirred the sauce he watched her meander around his home, wrapped in a blanket, cradling a glass of wine to her chest, touching his things, adding something that had always been missing to his home. He loved her. There was no doubt about it.

He loved the way she blushed, he loved the way she smelled, he loved that he could convince her to be daring, yet she always remained just a little bit cautious—sometimes even fragile. He loved the way she was with her children, the way she escaped a horrible situation and started over again when most people would've just settled for the hand they'd been dealt. He loved how she talked about her patients with such affection, yet kept the details of their private life private.

There wasn't a single thing he disliked about her. He wanted to tell her all of this but wasn't sure how or if it was too soon. Probably.

Never interested in sustaining a long-term relationship with a girl, it seemed odd he suddenly wanted long-term with Chloe. Rainbows and unicorns. His biggest fear was that she would find out his connection to Marcus and turn her back on him forever. The longer he waited the more his secret felt like a betrayal.

He couldn't let that happen, so he decided to tell her the truth tomorrow at breakfast when they were both sober and wearing clothes. If they went out to eat, she'd have to listen to him, and by the time he explained how he'd done the right thing and told her ex to get fucked, she'd understand he was still a good guy.

After dinner, she helped him do the dishes and wrap the leftovers. Not seeing the point in replacing their clothes, he offered her his robe. He liked seeing her in his things, his robe, his home, his kitchen, his bed. He treasured these moments alone with her. Here, he saw a side he didn't see when she was Chloe the mother, or Chloe the neighbor, or Chloe the doctor or friend. Here she was just Chloe, beautiful and his.

They showered and she fell asleep in his arms. Sleep wasn't so easy for him that night. He desperately wanted to confess his feelings. He didn't need to hear the words back. He just wanted her to know how he loved her. But until he confessed all, he couldn't put that on her shoulders.

There wasn't much in his neck of the woods as far as fine dining went, so the following morning he took her to a small diner on the outskirts of town. The drive wasn't long, only ten minutes, but he was anxious and dreading the moment he'd make his confession.

On the way there she called Adam and Tommy to check on the boys.

"Everything good?" he asked as he parked the truck and she slipped her phone back into her purse.

"Yup. The boys are just getting up now."

"Good." Damn, he was nervous.

She pulled her purse off of the center seat and blushed when she spotted her panties from the day before. "Oh, my God, what if someone walked by and saw these?" She laughed. "I'll tuck them in here for now."

His smile died as she reached for the glove compartment. "Chloe, wait—"

*"Jesus Christ!"* She pressed her body firmly into her seat and stared into the glove compartment in horror. "Is that real? Why do you have a gun?"

He quickly shut the compartment. "I have to carry one for work."

"To install security systems? Trenton, that's not a small gun. You took Mattie to the store in this truck. Did you have a gun in here then? *With my son?"*

Clearly, she wasn't a member of the NRA. "Chloe, calm down."

"No, I'm not going to calm down. There's a fucking gun in your glove compartment!"

He never heard her curse before. This wasn't good. "Listen to me, doll. I have a gun because my job requires it. I'm licensed to carry it and I know how to use it. It isn't loaded. I keep the bullets under my seat."

"I don't understand why you need a weapon like that."

He took a deep breath. "Remember how I rescued that minor a few months ago?"

"What minor? Like a coal miner?"

"No, a *minor,* as in underaged girl."

She frowned. "What are you talking about? What girl?"

"Remember, Georgia told you all about it that night at Adam's..." His words faded away. "Right. You were drunk."

"I don't remember any of this."

"I know. Okay." He took another deep breath. "There was an underage girl who ran away. Her parents wanted to find her. The cops were looking into it, but her folks wanted to use every resource. Pete got a call, asked me if I was interested, it was good money, so I said yes. I found her, returned her to her parents, and then the cops followed up with any legal issues."

"I thought you did security and taught self-defense on the side?"

This was going to bite him in the ass if she jumped to conclusions before he had a chance to sit down with her and rationally address their first meeting. "I do, but sometimes I also do stuff like ... find people."

His chest tightened as he held his breath. Was this going to be it? Was she going to realize how he came to be in Maryland that day many years ago? He couldn't screw this up.

"Chloe, listen to me. I'm in security. We all are, me, Pete, and Jeremy."

"Jeremy works with computers," she snapped.

"Right. He works with computers, breaking and rewriting codes at every level from the small business to larger government agencies. But he also knows how to tap into private lines and track devices."

"You lied to me."

Fuck. He hadn't even gotten to the dishonest part yet. "I didn't lie about my job. I told you I'm in security and I am."

"People ... hire you? Just to find kids or is it anybody? And do you work for the police or Pete?"

"I work for myself, but anyone can hire me for the right price. Can we go inside and talk? I swear I'll give you nothing but honesty and you can ask me anything. Let's just go in and get some coffee first." He needed other people around to ensure she would give him the chance to explain everything before freaking out and possibly making a scene.

She frowned, her gaze locked on the glove compartment as her head shook in some sort of denial. Why was it so difficult for him to accept he kept the weapon for work? "Chloe, it's just a handgun—"

"Exactly. It's not for hunting and it's not in a safe. It's here in your car while we're on a date." Her eyes glazed with tears. "I want to go home."

"Chloe—"

"Take me home, Trenton. Now."

He stared at her for a moment, knowing this was the time to come completely clean with her or forever hold his peace. "Chloe, I'm not a bad guy. I help people when they have nowhere else—"

"I want to go home," she shouted, tears spiking her lashes. "You don't understand how guns scare me."

"It's unloaded—"

"Don't patronize me! You have no idea what I've been through. Have you ever had a gun held to your head, Trenton? Put in your *mouth*? *Have you?*"

His voice lowered, his stomach twisting at the thought of where this was going. "No."

"Well, I have." She wiped her eyes and clutched her purse like a shield to her chest. "I want to go home."

His heart broke at the sight of her tears, the

frantic way terror showed in her eyes as if she was seeing something he'd never be able to see for himself. "Chloe, we can talk about it—"

"Please just do as I asked." She sniffled and drew in a jagged breath, her upset getting the better of her and turning her words choppy. "I don't need to rehash my past to know where I stand on weapons. I need to get out of this truck and right now I want to go home."

"Okay. I'm sorry." His heart raced. He'd never seen a woman go from laughing to inconsolable in such a short span of time, but the last thing he wanted to do was make her more upset. "I'll take you home."

He reluctantly turned on the truck and backed out of the parking lot. She sniffled and wouldn't look at him, her gaze completely focused out the window. He needed to fix this.

"Chloe," he said softly, pulling onto the highway. "I only have the gun for protection. I've never had an accident or even a close call. I've been practicing at shooting ranges since I was eighteen. That's over twenty years' experience with handling weapons. I swear—"

"Please stop," she begged, as she wiped her eyes. "I understand why people have them. It's their right. But I don't like them in my life. I spent years living in a house with guns and it... The more you say the more upset I'm getting. I shouldn't have to explain why they scare me."

He could imagine why, knowing what he did about her ex. "I'll take it out of the truck. From now on I'll make sure it's nowhere near you or your boys."

She hastily wiped away another tear. "I can't..." Her words broke as she fought a sob. "I'm sorry. I want to accept this and be okay with it, but I can't, not after what he put me through. You aren't some stranger to me, Trenton. You're in my life. You're personal. You're around my children. I can't be with someone who keeps guns. They just ... terrify me."

Jesus. What had that fucking scum bag done to her? "Chloe, I swear on my life I'd never misuse a lethal weapon. Don't do this. I didn't know."

She used her shirt to blot her eyes. "Why do you need it in your truck?"

"Because my job's dangerous and sometimes it's necessary. Sometimes a gun's the difference between saving an innocent person and watching them die. I like be prepared. Guns can save lives, too."

"Have you ever shot at a living person?"

He swallowed, his fingers curling tight around the wheel. No more lies. "Yes."

"On purpose?"

Out of context, there was no way to pretty it up. He had blood on his hands. He'd taken lives. But he didn't usually beat himself up over it, because he also saved lives—saved innocent victims and helped those who couldn't help themselves. "Yes, but—"

"Then you can stop talking and take me home." Her lips trembled.

She was clearly too upset to see the whole picture, so he gave up trying to persuade her and hoped she'd calm down. Once she did, he'd have better luck reasoning with her.

When he pulled up to her house he tried to reason with her one last time. "Please don't let this mess up everything we have."

She stood outside his truck looking up at him. "How many guns are in your house right now?"

"They're all locked up."

"How many, Trenton?"

He swallowed. "Nine." Plus the one in the glove compartment and the ones he kept at his sister's.

Her head lowered. "I won't go back there until it's zero. I'm sorry. I just can't." She shut the door and didn't look back as she entered her house.

*"Fuck!"*

# Nineteen

"I JUST DON'T UNDERSTAND why he's suddenly so clingy. I tell him I'm fine and he goes away for a few minutes then he's back as if I never said a word. I mean, I know they say pregnancy gives you hemorrhoids, but I never knew they meant your husband turns into one. I want him off my ass! And I swear if he pushes one more glass of milk in my direction I'm going to scream!"

Chloe half listened as Jade sat across from her, bordering on almost a full hour of prenatal complaints. She should have called out today, but she didn't want to be home alone. She also didn't know what to do about Trent. She shut off her cell phone and told her secretary to hold all her calls.

She overreacted about the gun and wished she was strong enough to let go of old fears, but the thought of being anywhere near a gun filled her with this paralyzing pain. She could still taste the metal, hear the click, feel the terror she suffered every time Marcus played with his.

Disappointed in herself, ashamed of her lingering weakness, she tried to talk herself into seeing reason. The rational part of her brain told her every gun owner wasn't crazy and Trenton would never do the things her husband had done. She could almost convince herself she could get over her fear, but the second she pictured Trenton's gun, imagined it in their presence, a cold sweat broke across her shaking palms and her chest constricted with panic.

Marcus had simply tortured her too much over the years with his belts and guns and basically anything he could use to make her life hell. But he never actually shot someone. Trenton had.

Her response yesterday had humiliated her on a level she wasn't ready to explain. The times Marcus used a gun... She shivered at the thought. Over the years she'd worked through many of her triggers, but this was a big one she didn't think she'd ever get over. Marcus had held his gun to her temple too many times and done too much damage for her apprehension to ever go away.

"Chloe? Chloeeee? Hello? Earth to Dr. Wolfe."

She looked at Jade and suddenly burst into tears.

"Oh my God, Chloe, what's wrong?" Jade stood, her slightly protruding belly pressing against her shirt, her voice stricken with panic, as she pulled her into her arms. "Honey, what's the matter?"

"It's Trenton," she sobbed, hating herself for acting so unprofessional.

"What about Trent?"

"He—he isn't who I thought he was." Reaching for a tissue, she tried to pull herself together.

"What are you talking about? Who did you think he was? I never knew Trent to be anything but genuine."

"God, I'm sorry." This was completely unprofessional. She was breaking rules, not just hers, but the ones that kept her practice to a standard she'd worked damn hard to achieve. What was wrong with her?

"Oh, please. After everything I've been through... You go ahead and unleash."

She wiped her eyes and blew her nose. "I didn't mean to just explode into tears like that."

"It's fine. I do it all the time. Tell me what happened with Trent?"

Debating if she wanted to cross that line, she thought to first clarify a few things. "Jade, what does Jeremy do?"

She frowned. "He works with Trent and Pete. They all work in security together. Sometimes they do installations, but Jeremy mostly works from home doing IT stuff. Why?"

"I thought you said that Trent taught self-defense."

"He does. He also does alarms and acts as a bodyguard and even retrieves fugitives who violate their bail sometimes. Didn't he tell you that?"

She dropped her face into her hands. "God, I am such an idiot."

"Chloe, there's nothing wrong with what he does. It's legitimate, honest work. He's a hero."

"He has a gun."

"Of course he has a gun. Trent always carries one."

She looked at her friend as if she were crazy. "Always?" She thought of all the times they'd been together. Mia's birthday party, brunch, game night. "And you think that's normal?"

"Normal or not, I for one am grateful he always keeps it with him."

"Grateful? Guns kill people!"

Jade looked at her sternly. "Right, Chloe, guns can kill people—mostly when in the hands of idiots. Trent's a highly trained professional who'd never be careless with his weapons. He knows how to use a gun and has excellent aim. If it wasn't for him, I could be dead right now."

"What are you talking about?"

"What am *I* talking about? Chloe, what are *you* talking about? You know what happened to me the night of the party. Trent was there."

"I know he was there." They'd kissed. Her chest tightened another degree, but she forced the tears to stay inside.

"Trent saved me, Chloe."

Her brow tightened, true misunderstanding setting in. "What?"

"He followed me there. To that house. That fucker had me in a headlock with a pistol pointed in my face, ready to take me God knows where and do God knows what to me, and he would have if it wasn't for Trent showing up."

"You said the police came."

"*After* Trent showed up. By the time the cops got there the guy was dead. Trent shot him and saved *me*. Why do you think he was the one who had to file all the paperwork?"

Chloe pinched the bridge of her nose, trying to piece all of this together. "I thought…"

"Chloe, I love you, but there is no way Trent will ever be a bad guy in my eyes—gun or no gun. He saved my life. He's saved lots of lives. That's what he does. His job's dangerous and he needs to be armed for his own protection."

Did that mean he had a gun with him the night he drove her to Pennsylvania and she got in the car with him—a perfect stranger? As much as she trusted him now, she'd been crazy to trust him then. Another terrible decision—or was it? He brought her to her kids. He saved her. But had he been anyone else, he could have killed her before ever reaching her children.

Her stomach rolled like unsettled mush. Her back and forth debate was making her seasick. She wanted to accept this part of him, but the more she tried the more she realized how incredibly fucked up she still was from Marcus.

Her hand closed over her mouth. "I'm going to be sick."

"Look, maybe you should go home. It isn't like you were even listening to me today. Get some rest. Think about what I said and maybe call Trent. I'm sure he would be willing to explain everything. I know he really cares about you."

Jade was right. She was no use to anyone in this state. And now, after hearing Trenton had killed the sick monster who had attacked her friend, she didn't know what to think. "He had that gun in his truck when Mattie was with him."

Jade shook her head. "Maybe we have different perspectives on the Second Amendment, but your son was safe with him, no matter what was in his truck. I'd never second guess Mia's safety around him—if anything, I'd feel more secure knowing he's there."

She understood she was overly sensitive when it came to weapons, but most people weren't threatened with a pistol in their face by the one person who promised to always love, honor, and cherish them. She couldn't expect others to understand what made her this way. Even she struggled to understand the things she'd been through.

"You're right. I need to go home."

"If you need to talk later after you've gotten some rest, call me. God knows by tonight I'll need another break from Jeremy."

She tried to laugh but failed. After Jade left it only took Chloe a matter of minutes to gather her things.

"Jennifer, I'm going home for the day. Cancel my last two appointments and you can head home yourself unless you want to stay. Either way, I'll pay you for a full day."

She walked to the door and ignored her secretary's look of surprise. "But Dr. Wolfe, you have messages."

"Just leave them until tomorrow."

She walked to the parking garage in a daze and climbed into her car. She still had a few hours until the boys got off the bus and a nap sounded ... necessary.

The hazy sky thickened with clouds and the air smelled of rain. With the sun tucked away, the day felt later than it actually was. She cried most of the way home, afraid she'd screwed up the best possible thing in her life because after all this time her past still haunted her. After all of these years, despite her training, there were still crippling issues she couldn't get over.

She parked her car and grabbed her purse from her backseat, tipping it by accident in haste but catching it before everything dumped on the floor. As she headed up the walk the first spits of rain moistened her cheeks, followed by a loud crash of thunder.

Before she even had the door unlocked the rain turned to big fat drops pelting her clothing and destroying her hair. She rushed over the threshold and quickly shut the door, flipping the lock back in place.

"Hello, Chloe."

Her heart lodged in her throat at the dreadfully familiar voice and she spun around, certain she was hearing things. But he was there. In her home. "*Marcus.*"

"You've been a very bad wife."

# Twenty

A SCREAM RIPPED from her lungs as she pivoted, clawing at the door and jerking the knob, making no progress due to the locks. Her head smacked against the door as he spun her around and shoved her into the wood so hard her teeth clacked.

"What's the hurry, *wife*? We have some catching up to do."

Her heartbeat roared in her ears, as familiar hazel eyes narrowed, so full of venom and hate. She needed to call the cops. She needed to stop Dayton and Mattie from taking the bus home, figure out somewhere to send them, and find a way to get a message to the school. There wasn't enough time!

She shoved past him only to get dragged back to the door and slammed into the wood again. "Marcus, don't..." His smirk twisted as his hand closed around her throat.

In her nightmares, he never aged, but now his hair had faded from brown peppered with gray to silver peppered with ash. This was no dream.

His thumb dug painfully into her throat and she wheezed, "Marcus, please..." Tears blurred her vision.

Disgust hissed out of him like noxious gas. "Chloe, Chloe, Chloe... How you've played a game with me. Did you think I'd never find you? That you could take my sons and never pay the consequence?"

Her eyes watered. The more she tried to pry open his fingers the tighter they closed around her throat. Her phone was off and in her purse by her feet. So close yet too far.

"Marcus," she begged, pulling at his tightening fingers.

"Let's hear what you've got to say for yourself." His fingers loosened and she gulped in a breath only to have them tighten again.

"It doesn't have to be like this. I was scared. If you want to see the boys we could arrange some sort of legal visitation."

"*Legal?*" She flinched, covering her face as he slammed his fist on the wall beside her head. "What kind of fucking fantasy world are you living in? They're *my* sons! I have every legal right in the world to see them. *I'm their fucking father!*"

"I know. I'm sorry—"

The back of his hand knocked her head to the side as pain exploded in her cheek. "*Shut up!*"

She sobbed in terror, struggling to get past him, but he blocked her.

His saliva dotted his lips as he shouted in her face, making her flinch as he raised his fist again. "You're the one who'll need legal counsel. What you did was *kidnapping*! I could send you to rot in prison for what you put me through over the past six years. Then you wouldn't have to concern yourself with your family anymore, you *selfish bitch*! You've kept them from me all this time—*in my aunt's fucking home!*"

Spit mixed with the lingering drops of rain on her face. His words spread through her like poison. Sweat broke on her skin as her stomach knotted painfully and her heart stampeded in her chest. Pressure mounted as she tried to calculate a way to escape and find help. She was going to vomit.

"Look at what you're doing, Marcus. This is why I left."

"You left because you're a *selfish cunt*!" His fist slammed into her stomach, radiating pain through her kidneys. She wheezed and he jerked her away from the door, shoving her toward the couch.

"No! *No!*"

"*Shut up!*" The back of his hand collided with her head, sending her sprawling onto the floor.

Coughing, she wobbled to her hands and knees. "Please. The kids will be—"

Nausea cut off her begging. Her eyes watered and she dry heaved, the fear of what was actually taking place too much.

"Get up." He wrenched her arm behind her back, twisting her off balance and her face hit the floor. He dragged her to the couch.

She screamed in pain and tugged the coffee table, desperately trying to stop him. If he got on top of her she'd never get him off. *"Get off of me you sick fuck!"*

Pain exploded in her side as he drew back his designer shoe and kicked her. She collapsed, gasping for air. The carpet pressed into her cheek as she blinked through blurred vision and retched. Her labored breathing burned her lungs as she struggled to find her bearings and settle her stomach.

*Where is he?*

Wiping her eyes, she turned her head and stilled. He stood over her, a satisfied glint in his malicious eyes. "You always were pathetic."

Her gaze went to the door and her panic surged when she didn't see her purse or keys. She needed to call the police. Call the school and tell them not to release her sons.

He pulled an envelope from the front pocket of his shirt and dropped it to the floor. The white square fluttered and fell to the carpet with a foreboding tick. Her heart stopped beating when she recognized not only Dayton's handwriting on the front but the return address stamp with her aunt's name and information in the top corner.

"Do you know how much trouble and money you've cost me? How many professionals I've hired over the years? Thousands of dollars! You stole that from me, and time I'll never get back with my sons!"

What was in that envelope? *Oh, God, Dayton, what have you done?*

"...the first man I hired found you, but lost you around the border of Mexico."

*Mexico?* She tried to follow his words, but her thoughts were chaos.

"You've led me on a merry chase and to think, this entire time, you've been right under my nose in my relative's home. You're a criminal, Chloe. Even your children hold your crimes against you. Go ahead…" He toed the envelope closer to her with his loafer, his every subtle move making her flinch. "Read what our son thinks of his dear old mom."

"Marcus—"

"*I said, read it!*"

With shaking hands she reached for the envelope, afraid he would kick her again. The torn edges showed the same pale pink lining of the envelopes she kept in the basket on her desk. This was her envelope. It had been her son rummaging through her desk not long ago. That was why her things were out of place.

"*Read it!*"

Tears flooded her eyes as her hands shook violently, pulling the paper free. Dayton's youthful script marked the page on both sides.

*Dear Dad,*

*How are you? I am good. By the way, this is Dayton, your son. I am in 3 third grade now and go to a school called St. Ignatius. I miss you. Do you miss us? I love you. I was wondering if you could come visit us. We can show you our house and you can see my room. Maybe I can* even show you some of my video games.

Do you still live in Virginia? We live in Aunt Gina's house, but she died. Sometimes I miss her. Mattie is good. I was wondering how come you do not visit. Mommy says you will never live with us again, but I think if we all talk and try real hard we can be a family like we used to be.

We have nice neighbors and friends here. You would like our home. You could sleep over. Mommy has a big bed like at the old house. You can sleep there. I do not want to have a different dad. Last week I found a letter from a man Mommy says is her friend. Please visit soon so Mommy remembers that she is married to you. I just want us to be a family again.

Are you lonely all by yourself? I think about you at nighttime and in my prayers. Mommy told me she still loves you. Do you still love her? I told her if she tried real hard maybe you would be happy. She works every day when we are at school. We have an extra chair at the table where you could sit. Who makes dinner for you? Do you still have a red car? Our car is yellow.

If you get this maybe you can send me a letter back with a picture of you. I do not know if this is the right address. It was the only one for Virginia I could find. I am putting a picture from last year of me and Mattie in this envelope so you remember what we look like. It is from soccer camp. I scored 13 goals in one season. That is pretty good. Do you like soccer? Maybe you, Mattie and me could play one day when the weather gets warm. Do you get a lot of snow in Virginia? I have to go to bed. I am sorry my *writing is sloppy. I should have used a pencil. I hope you get this letter. I miss you.*

*Love,*

*Dayton Maxwell Hunt Wolfe*

Chloe folded the letter and placed it on top of the envelope with shaking hands. She wiped her tears and looked at Marcus with pleading eyes. "He doesn't—"

"*You think I give a shit about your excuses?*" he roared. "*They think I abandoned them!*"

She sobbed, terrified that he might punish her boys as well. "They're good boys, Marcus. Please don't hurt them."

"Here is what's going to happen. You're going to get your fat ass up and use the bathroom and then walk with me to the car. You will not run or scream or fight me in any way, or so help me God, Chloe, I will drag you right to the police and have you arrested for kidnapping. We're driving back to Virginia, where you *will be* a dutiful and obedient wife—"

"But the boys—"

"The children are already on their way there."

Terror lanced bluntly through her heart as it momentarily stopped beating. "*What?*"

He glanced at his watch. "We need to get moving. They left hours ago."

"I don't believe you."

"Saint Ignatius Elementary on Welsh Road."

Shock settled over her so heavy, she began hyperventilating, her entire body trembling. "Marcus," she pleaded, gasping for breath as the pressure in her chest became unbearable. "They won't understand—"

"*Whose fault is that?*" He drew back his hand and she covered her face, cowering in silence.

It had been six years since someone struck her. She couldn't go back to that. Nothing would break her faster than falling into her old position as his whipping post. She needed to get her boys and then she'd go to the police.

"Where are they? Who has them?"

"They're halfway home. If you want to see them, get up and do exactly as I say."

She panted, flinching at the slightest motion and holding her hands protectively above her face. Dear God, he stole her children, her babies. What were they thinking? "Can I call them?"

He laughed. "Do I look like I'm in the mood to do you any favors? You're lucky I don't choke the life out of you. Then it would be just me and Dayton and Matthew. An adjustment for them I'm sure, but they'd adapt—"

"I'll go with you." She couldn't listen to anymore. The more he spoke the more time her boys spent alone with whatever lunatic was helping him.

He let out a cold laugh. "You act like I gave you a choice." He lunged at her.

She screamed as he grabbed her jaw with

bruising force. His fingers wedged between her lips, forcing her teeth apart.

*"Open your fucking mouth!"*

Choking, unsure what he was doing, she gagged. Gripping her by the face his fingers shoved between her lips to the back of her throat. His palm covered her mouth and nose. "Swallow."

She gagged and fought him, but he jabbed a knee into her chest.

"Swallow it," he growled.

Her eyes watered and she panicked, the taste of some sort of pill leaving a bitter trail on her tongue as it dissolved.

He let her go and she gasped, dry heaving as she faced the carpet on all fours. Her concentration zeroed in on the sensation of the capsule moving its way lower. Silently, she worked her throat, trying to regurgitate whatever he'd given her, but it was no use.

"Puke and I will *kill* you," he whispered, close enough that his breath blew over her sweaty skin.

She shut her eyes and wept. Her happy life was over. She was going back to hell.

"We'll be leaving shortly." He casually adjusted the cuffs of his shirt. "You'll need to piss before we go."

# Twenty-One

CHLOE AWOKE, assaulted by the need to vomit. Before even opening her eyes she mumbled, "Oh, God, I'm going to be sick."

Her body slid to the left as her world pulled to the right. Dried tears sealed her lashes, which grotesquely pulled apart. The brief, blurred impression of highway markers flashed by, tail lights, and pine trees. Her body sagged forward, restrained by something holding her in place. Her sluggish hand moved to her chest. A seatbelt. She moaned as nausea caused her mouth to water.

Something pressed into her side and she winced as it grazed a particularly sore spot. The car door opened and though they were no longer moving, she couldn't escape the sensation of swaying. Warm fresh air hit her face and the whooshing sound of speeding traffic met her ears. Her eyes squeezed shut trying to fight the tumultuous waves sloshing around in her stomach.

The seatbelt clicked and she was yanked forward, folded over into a suffocating position. Her motor skills were non-existent. Her eyes watered with fresh tears as her hair pulled at her scalp and she was shoved low, her hands scrambling for purchase and catching on the car door.

Peeking through her crusty lashes she spotted a decomposing cigarette butt, gravel, and sun-scorched grass illuminated by the interior lights spilling from the vehicle. This had to be a nightmare.

Her vision flickered under the strobe of passing cars and inky night, as the sound of speeding vehicles hissed by. The smell of exhaust caused the shallow contents of her stomach to curdle. The hand forcing her down tightened in her hair.

"Puke."

Marcus's voice was all her stomach needed to uncap the storm in her belly. Mouth open, the contents rushed onto the gravel, drowning the old cigarette in bile.

After a few minutes of spitting and catching her breath, she was yanked upright. He pushed a tissue in her face and returned the seatbelt over her chest. "Clean yourself up."

Her head was throbbing, her neck too weak to offer any real support. Licking her lips, she tried to expel the bitter taste coating her tongue as her body sagged into the seat of the car.

"Do you have any water?"

He didn't answer, now back in the driver's seat. She blinked nervously as he pulled into oncoming traffic, tensing as they almost got rear-ended by a minivan. Her limbs were too heavy to move and she wilted in her seat as the car accelerated.

Her wavering gaze scanned for landmarks. After a few minutes, she found one for Moorefield. They were in Virginia. How long had she been out? She needed to stay awake and get to her boys.

"Marcus," Her throat was raw and speaking was painful. "Who has the boys?"

"Don't worry about them. They're my concern now."

Swallowing, she carefully formed syllables into words, the sticky saliva in her mouth enough to make her vomit again. "They must be terrified—confused. Please ... let me call them."

He gave a bitter, humorless laugh, leering at her. "How stupid do you think I am, Chloe? You will not get your fingers within a foot of my phone. I've checked in with them. They're home, settling into their rooms for the night."

She hated every word that left his mouth, making her more frightened and hopeless, but she needed to keep him talking. She was on the brink of passing out again and needed to keep herself alert.

They were only another hour or so from her old home and she needed to know as much as possible about the situation she was returning to before they got there. The more Marcus could catch her off guard, the more dangerous he was.

"Where will they sleep, Marcus? Dayton's out-grown his toddler bed and Mattie's room only had a crib."

"Their bedrooms have been prepared. I've been busy since getting the letter from Dayton. Our home's ready for all of us to start living as a family again."

She wondered what kind of preparations he'd made for her. She wanted to see her boys, to make sure they were unharmed. So help her God, if Marcus damaged a single hair on either of their bodies, she'd stab him to death with a butter knife.

Breathing deeply, in and out through her nose, her insides churned as she repeatedly swallowed to lessen the taste of bile. Whatever was in her system, she wanted it out.

"I need to use a bathroom."

He looked at her skeptically.

"Marcus, I haven't peed since we left. Please?" She actually did have to use the bathroom. They'd been in the car for hours.

He turned his attention back to the road and ignored her. She thought he was just going to let her wet herself until he finally said, "I have my gun, Chloe. You try to run from me and I'll shoot you in the back of the head before you get two feet."

It was too familiar, too recognizable as the demon she'd buried long ago, back from the grave and full of vengeance. Her chin quivered as she juggled old subservience and new independence, forgetting how to reason with a sociopath.

"Why are you doing this? You would shoot me? Why, Marcus? It doesn't have to be like this." Her words slurred, but she forced them out anyway. "It's been *six* years. Your life had to move on in some degree. If this is about the boys, we can get a lawyer. You don't care about me. I'll give you a divorce so you can find a wife that makes you happy. You can have your life and I can have mine and we'll work out something with the children."

She would spend her life figuring ways to keep him away from her boys if she had to, but lying seemed her best option at the moment.

"I'm sure you'd just love that, so you could run off with your *friend*."

"There's no one else, Marcus," she lied—or maybe it was the truth. She couldn't think beyond her children at the moment. "It's just me. Let's not do this. There are better ways to handle things, better for the children."

"You're right, Chloe. Once we get home, I'll let you have your divorce, but the children are staying with me. I want full custody. You stole them from me for six years. No court will grant you custody over me. You. Are. A. Criminal."

She wasn't a criminal. She was married to a monster and had no choice but to run to protect her babies. "The boys would never forgive you—"

"Don't presume to tell me what my sons would feel. You think you have them brainwashed, but you've always been weaker than me. You'll see. Now, you have three choices, so be grateful and decide wisely. You can either sign over custody and live your life *without* the boys, or agree to my terms in this marriage. Or I press charges and force you out. Which will it be?"

He was delusional, so much so, his threat of taking full custody wasn't even an option. It would never happen. She squirmed in her seat, her bladder unbearably full and her kidneys starting to ache.

Marcus reached behind her and she flinched,

already returning to the wife who cowered at her husband's slightest move. The car swerved as he returned his gaze to the road and rested his hand on the leather console between them. Under his palm rested a familiar, steel handgun and she quietly panted, frozen in place.

His eyes darted to the right of the road as he abruptly veered onto the shoulder and skidded to a stop. Moving the gun to his other hand he shut off the car, pocketing the keys.

"Don't move."

Was he going to walk her into the woods and shoot her? He said she had choices, but that would be just like him to decide for her anyway. How easy it would be for him to leave her there, bleeding to death, so he could have back his sons.

He left the car and she considered locking herself inside, but he had the keys and a weapon. She had nothing. Her face began to sweat as her pulse jackhammered in her throat.

He jerked opened her door. "Get out."

Paralyzed by fear, she didn't move. She needed to make it to her children. Once she had them she'd contact the proper authorities and get a restraining order and press charges. From there she'd file for divorce. She'd hire the best lawyer and try to expunge his parental rights as a father.

*"I said, get out of the fucking car!"*

She jumped and scrambled out of her seat. Her legs were weak and as she stood she was again assaulted with the need to vomit.

"Over there." He motioned toward the trees with the gun.

When she didn't move he grabbed at her neck, yanking her in the direction he wanted her to go. She cried, her tears a useless release of terror.

They walked about twenty feet into the woods, the whoosh of the cars on the highway muffled by the trees. The crunch of pine needles under their shoes and her heavy breathing now a deafening roar in her ears.

"That's far enough."

She quietly sobbed, her tears blurring her vision as she tracked the glint of the gun by passing lights of oncoming traffic. There would be no sympathy for her.

"Do you have to piss or not?"

Her bodily functions forgotten, she looked at him, and again at their surroundings. How was she here? How far would she get if she ran? Would anyone hear her if she screamed? Was the gun loaded?

"*Move it!* Either piss or hold it until we get there. But if you piss in my car you'll be pissing blood for weeks."

Pacifying him any way she could, she held up her hands and nodded. "O—okay. Could you turn—"

He laughed. "You really think I'm dumb. Let me clear something up for you right now. Privacy is a privilege you no longer have. Thirty seconds."

Her hands went to the snap of her pants and she quickly bunched them around her knees. She held the fabric away from her bottom as she squatted close to the ground. She lost her balance and almost toppled over, but steadied herself on the trunk of a tree.

"Ten seconds."

"I can't go," she cried, too panicked to relax her bladder.

The gun clicked as he leveled it at her face. "How about now?"

Her body went numb. The sound of liquid hitting the soft ground filled the silence. She forced herself to release her urine as quickly as possible. Her muscles grew weak and she was still going. She let out a breath and pushed some more.

"Time's up."

Her efforts doubled, a flood trickling over the dried underbrush and wetting the soles of her shoes. "I need paper."

"Not my problem. Get up."

She pressed the last of the liquid out and tried to shake off any excess. She lost her balance. Lightheaded, her eyes fluttered as the blood returned to her weak limbs. Her head felt as if it were stuffed with cotton. She fumbled with her pants, pulling them up, but not getting them buttoned before Marcus dragged her back to the car.

Once inside, he activated the locks, stowed the gun in the panel on his door, and instructed her to buckle her seat belt. The road was busy but not swamped. A car passed about every two seconds. She could flag someone down, use their cell phone to call 911 or scream for them to make the call and report Marcus's vehicle. The cops could reach their boys before he did.

The shoddy plan formulated in a split second

and as he slid the keys back in the ignition, her fingers snatched the handle, jerking the door as her eyes went to the lock. She reached for the buttons, but he was faster, shoving the back of her skull and smacking her head into the window.

*"Disobedient bitch!"*

She gripped her head and his fist smashed into her windpipe. A hideous sound came from her throat as she gasped for air. The metallic taste of blood tickled her esophagus as her lungs burned.

"You *will* learn to listen."

She sobbed painfully as he pulled onto the highway.

"Know this, *wife,* it would be my pleasure to give back the pain you caused me. One little reason is all the incentive I need and you'll get a glimpse of how furious I actually am. If I were you, I'd be a dutiful wife and follow directions for a change."

# Twenty-Two

CHLOE RECOGNIZED FAMILIAR, yet changed landmarks when the clock on the dash read 8:04. A mixture of anxiety and dread filled her tender stomach as they neared their destination. She wanted to see Dayton and Mattie, but she wasn't sure if things would get immeasurably worse once she saw them. She didn't know what they'd been through to get all the way to Virginia. Marcus had total leverage as long as he had her boys.

They coasted through their old town that seemed for the most part unchanged. Cars were newer, street lamps were updated, establishments looked a little more worn in places, but it was the same overall. Chloe adjusted her clothing and sat up a bit in her seat, every swallow a painful reminder of what happened when she broke his rules.

Her heart pounded as they approached the turn. Just as she was looking in the direction of their old street, Marcus drove past the turn and continued on the main road.

"Where are you going?" Her voice was a mere wheeze of sound that abraded painfully.

He didn't answer.

The car pulled into a shabby shopping strip under ill repair, same as it had been six years ago. Most of the stores were closed at this hour and the lot was vacant. They drove toward the back of the buildings and circled the property.

Crates and pallets piled alongside dumpsters. A hose spigot leaked from a cement wall, forming a puddle that spread across the rutted pavement like oil.

Suddenly, like two blinking eyes, a car flashed its lights in the distance. Marcus slowed and pulled alongside the other vehicle. The glass lowered and he waited for the other driver to speak.

"Everything's set," the driver said, his face hidden in the darkness of the other vehicle.

"Any issues?" Marcus asked.

"No, the little one was pretty upset. We gave them some nighttime remedy to help them sleep. The older one cooperated."

"Good."

Chloe's heart thundered as worry turned crippling. She strained to see the driver's face, but it remained hidden by the shadows. Marcus handed him an envelope that looked to be filled with cash.

This was the man who abducted her babies. She needed to see his face. Reaching to unbuckle her seat belt, she stilled as Marcus dug his fingers into her leg without even glancing in her direction. He told the other driver they were finished and removed his foot from the brake, their car once again in motion.

"Remember what happens when you disobey."

They pulled out of the shopping center and onto the main road. Marcus reached in his pocket and removed something that looked like a piece of gum, folded in silver paper. He held it out to her.

"Take this."

She took the item in her hand, too light and small to be gum. She unfolded the foil. "It's a pill."

"Swallow it."

Did he plan to keep her drugged? Whatever he gave her before made her incredibly sick and she needed to stay alert. "I'll do—"

The car swerved without warning and skidded to the shoulder. He got within an inch of her face and snarled, "It grows tedious, don't you think? Swallow the fucking pill or I'll make you swallow it. If I think you didn't ingest it I'll force another one down your throat with my fingers holding it there until it dissolves."

Sheer impotence had her eyes tearing. "Can I at least see the boys first?"

"You will not be seeing *my* boys tonight. They don't know you're coming. They've had a rough day, thanks to you, and I won't have you getting them worked up. Now, swallow the fucking pill before I jam it down your fucking throat. One. Two—"

She whimpered and placed the pill on her tongue and forced it down her ravaged throat while her mind reflexively tried to regurgitate the drug. Common sense and her need to survive were lost against her instincts to reach her children. She needed to be strong to do that, not battered. The tiny capsule disappeared.

She breathed and waited. Marcus looked at his watch then pulled down the visor mirror and ran his fingers through his hair.

"I wonder," he said quietly to himself. "How much have you lied to our boys about me?"

Chloe didn't answer.

"Six years is a long time." He continued to groom himself and she wondered what he was waiting for. "It's a shame they had to leave their friends without even a goodbye."

She tilted her head and frowned at his ear. It looked wrong, too curly and flat. Did he always have ears like that?

"I suppose I should give them time to adjust, but you and I have some catching up to do and that requires privacy. I've already enrolled *hem in theirrrr new spoolll...*" His words slurred and garbled as she swayed in her seat.

Why did his voice sound so far away, his words coming out slow and long? And what was he saying? She focused on his mouth. It moved slowly, sound coming out, but only a few words recognizable.

She sagged in the seat, suddenly very relaxed as the tension left her shoulders. As if in slow motion his hand reached past her and opened the glove compartment.

She rested her head on her shoulder and watched the man with the silly ear pull out a rolled up scarf and shut the compartment. The bundle un-raveled and she saw it was a necktie.

*But Trenton doesn't wear ties.*

She tried to count his fingers as they moved like octopus tentacles. He either had seven or twelve. She wasn't sure. He slid the knot up to his throat and said something she couldn't understand. A buzzing hum filled her head.

"Wellllllllllllll," he said with big eyes, too many eyes. Slow and echoing, his voice filled the air. "Thaaaaaat should doooooo."

Her belly danced as the car moved, the soft motion rocking her to sleep.

# Twenty-Three

A DOOR SLAMMED and Chloe opened her eyes. Parched. She licked her cracked lips but even her tongue was dry. Gazing around the empty room her breath stuttered. She didn't recognize the room. Like a bad dream, she wanted to shut her eyes and wish it away, but she needed to see her boys. They were near. She could sense them close by.

It was morning. Rolling into a seated position, she winced at how weak her arms and legs were. She'd been put on a mattress resting on a blue-carpeted floor. Folding to her knees she hoisted herself halfway up but had to move slowly to stand.

The windows were without curtains. Looking out the glass she tried to place the house across the street. She was in Mattie's old nursery on the second floor.

The latch on the window had a lock that required a key. Chloe moved to the other window and saw the same lock. Not that it mattered. From this room, there was no latticework or any way to shimmy down even if she managed to open or break a window. She'd end up breaking her neck. And if she tried and failed Marcus would surely break it for her.

Lurching to the door she tried the knob. Locked. Her fingers pressed over the painted surface. It was an exterior door. Metal. There'd be no kicking it down and the hinges were on the outside.

The room connected to a shared bathroom that led to Dayton's old room. She rushed to the bathroom. Where the door should have been, was nothing but wall. Pressing her hand along the flat surface, feeling for seams in the sheetrock, she whimpered, unable to detect any telltale sign of how the room used to be.

The tub was bare, not even a shower curtain liner hanging over the opening. Next to the sink was a bar of soap still wrapped in paper, a travel sized tube of toothpaste, and a toothbrush still in its package.

*Was* she in Mattie's old room? She pressed her ear to the cool wall and tried to hear something but heard nothing beyond her beating heart.

She opened the medicine cabinet, found it empty, and closed it, purposely averting her eyes from her reflection. No need to upset herself more.

She opened the cabinets under the sink that still had the child safety lock she'd installed when she was pregnant with Dayton. The space smelled of bleach, but there was nothing but plumbing underneath. Cupping her hand under the faucet, she guzzled water.

While using the toilet she smelled her clothing.

She didn't want to frighten the boys by her disheveled appearance and she was determined to see them. Every move she made was motivated by her need to protect them, both physically and emotionally from their father. She should clean herself up before Marcus brought her to them.

Her fingernails looked dirty, the polish chipped. She mechanically stood and removed her jewelry. She was missing an earring. Her numb hands adjusted the shower faucet to warm, hoping the hot water would steady her trembling body and focus her foggy mind.

Marcus was her worry. It was imperative she not make him theirs.

Forgetting herself, she gasped when she caught a glimpse of her naked reflection. Parts of her skin were discolored and starting to bruise. Her makeup was smeared and her hair was flat and matted.

As the room filled with steam, she unwrapped the soap but didn't see a trash can, so she left the paper crumpled by the side of the sink. She gingerly climbed over the lip of the tub, her muscles stiff and sore, and adjusted the shower head so the floor didn't get wet. She would *not* cry.

She worked the soap between her hands and used her palms to wash over her tender places. Her stomach ached from retching. With no other option, she washed the soap through her hair. When she was ready to get out it occurred to her that she didn't have a towel and she, again, fought the overwhelming urge to cry.

Shutting off the water, she shivered. She shook her arms and legs and squeezed off any excess water from her hair. Holding the side of the wall she carefully stepped out of the tub. Shivering, she blotted the drops off her skin with her panties.

By now someone had to realize they were missing. Adam and Tommy would be the first to notice. But how fast would they lead the police here? She was so private about her past the little they knew might not be enough to help her and the boys. And after years of guarded truths slipping out, Tommy and Adam might not know this was the time to confess all and get them the hell out of this nightmare.

Her worry blinded her as she dressed, her body cold and shivering. She would knock at the hall door until someone let her out. Stepping onto the carpet she turned and gasped, her feet staggering back until she caught herself against the wall. "*Marcus.*"

Adam's secretary buzzed the intercom. "Tommy's on line one."

Adam sighed, once again interrupted, and took the call. "Yes, Tommy?"

"She's not answering the door."

Adam held his phone between his chin and shoulder as he copied a line of numbers into a neat column. "What do you mean she isn't answering the door? Is her car still there?" He had a full schedule, and clients arriving in an hour, not really the day for Tommy's dramatics.

"Yes, and I don't hear anything inside. I know she's upset, but this isn't like her. I didn't see the boys leave for school this morning either. Something isn't right."

"Did you try her phone?" Adam pivoted in his office chair, as he searched his cell for Chloe's work number. She was never this difficult to reach.

"Yes, it's still going straight to voicemail."

"I'll call her office and see if she's there. Maybe she had car trouble and got a ride."

"Why wouldn't she ask me for a lift? Call her office and call me right back."

Adam hung up and dialed from his cell. Her secretary answered on the first ring.

"Hi, Jennifer. This is Adam Peters, Dr. Wolfe's neighbor. Is she in?"

"I'm sorry, she hasn't been in since yesterday morning."

He frowned. "What time did she leave yesterday?"

"Just before lunch. She looked like she might be coming down with something. I hope she's feeling better today. It isn't like her not to call and let me know she won't be in."

No, that certainly wasn't like Chloe. "Okay, thank you."

He hung up and quickly dialed Tommy. "Hey, get the key and go make sure everything's all right. She isn't at work and her secretary said she left early yesterday and seemed sick."

"Okay. Maybe they're all sick."

"I don't know. Go check."

Adam tried to focus on his work but found himself distracted and continuously checking his phone. A few minutes later he got a text.

· · ·

*Come home NOW!*

Adam stared at the text for a moment, unable to think, and then jolted into motion, collecting his things and calling Tommy back. "What is it?"

"They're not here," Tommy said in a panicked voice. "Something isn't right, Adam. The house is a mess and Dayton's project that was due today is still sitting on the counter."

"Fuck." Adam didn't want to think the worst scenario, but he always knew Chloe's situation wasn't bulletproof. "Call the cops. I'm leaving now."

"Jesus, Adam, this doesn't feel right. What if he found them?"

"Call the cops, Tommy. *Now*. I'll be there in a few minutes." He hung up the phone and yelled to his boss that he had a family emergency and had to go.

He didn't try to call Tommy until he was in his car and speeding home. The call went right to voicemail. Tommy never shut off his phone. That could only mean he was on the other line. He waited a minute and dialed again.

Adam was still trying to get through to him when he pulled onto their street twenty minutes later. His heart plummeted when he saw a police car at the curb and the front door of Chloe's house wide open. Dashing out of his SUV and up the front steps, he found Tommy sitting at the kitchen table crying.

"What happened?"

"They're not here. The kids aren't in school and she didn't call them out."

A uniformed officer paced on the back porch talking into a walkie-talkie on his shoulder. Adam tried to reason this out. Chloe wouldn't just take off without telling them.

"Adam... Her purse was on Mattie's bed. Her cell phone's gone."

"Fuck." Adam glanced at the officer on the porch. Spotting Tommy's socked feet he frowned. "Why are your shoes off?"

"I stepped in vomit."

"What?"

"By the door. There was a pile of puke on the carpet. I stepped in it."

The glass door opened and the officer walked in. Adam's heart raced.

~

Trent gripped his cellphone as he once again got her voicemail. It had been two days and she still wasn't picking up.

Phoenix slid a cup of coffee in front of him. "Give it time."

After catching his sister up, she took sympathy on him. Phoenix was a tough woman with guns of her own but understood where Chloe might be coming from.

She said if a person terrorized someone enough, truly made them fear for their life and safety, she could understand how that could leave permanent damage. And if Chloe's ex terrorized her with a gun, she'd likely never get over her fear of weapons. It wasn't about him. It was about her ex and the things he put her through.

Trent understood that, and he was willing to accommodate her fears to some degree, but he couldn't figure anything out until she answered the phone. "I should go to her office, insist she hear me out."

"No, you should give her time to think. She'll contact you when she's ready. It's only been two days."

If they somehow resolve the whole gun issue, there was still a bigger problem to address. He still needed to confess his link to her ex. He gripped his temples as another headache pounded in his skull. "God, I'm going to lose her. I love her and I'm going to fucking lose her."

"No, you're not. You need to stay positive."

"Oh, good, you're still here," Pete said as he walked into the kitchen. "I want you to look at this."

Distracted, Trent only half glanced at his brother-in-law, still hoping his sister would give him some magical fix for his love life. "I can't go any-where right now, Pete. I'm teaching self-defense at the community college on Wednesday night and I have some things I need to deal with."

"Well, I think you should read this."

Pete slid the form across the table. It was the standard Missing Person Report fax they received whenever someone was reported missing. Flipping the pages, he skimmed to the MP's description.

. . .

38, Caucasian, female, height 5'8, weight 195 lbs, auburn hair-medium length, brown eyes.

What the hell? He turned to the next page.

Holding Amber Alert until further investigation... 9, Caucasian, male, height 4'7.

"What the fuck is this?" Trent muttered as he flipped through the rest of the fax.

Second minor, age 7, light brown hair, hazel eyes.

Trent fumbled to find the first page again, his heart suddenly encased in ice.

Information given by Adam Peters and Thomas Stanley; MP's full name - Chloe Anne Hunt. Alias - Chloe Anne Wolfe.

"Mother fucker!" He was on his feet, frantically turning pages, looking for the 'Details of Loss' page. He found it and quickly skimmed.

· · ·

Missing from home, emesis found by front door, MP may be ill, possible struggle, PLACE LAST SEEN- leaving office Monday 11:45 pm—LAST SEEN by secretary Jennifer Blair.

Trenton gathered up the papers, his hands shaking. "I gotta go."

"What's going on?" Phoenix yelled as Trent rushed out of the kitchen.

"Chloe and the kids are missing. I think he found her!"

# Twenty-Four

CHLOE WOKE up on the floor and moaned. She winced as pain assaulted her. Her stomach was so empty and abused it felt as if it were turning inside out. Marcus made it clear she was far from forgiven and she'd been a fool for coming with him, unsure if her children were even here, but certain she wouldn't be seeing them anytime soon. Not after what he'd just put her through.

Rolling to her side, her breath hissed out of her in a rush. Too weak to rise. She had no idea how long she lay unconscious on the floor. Staring at the wall, tears clouding her eyes she tried not to let the fear consume her.

She'd never survive this.

How quickly she forgot what it felt like to live in a constant state of defense, anticipating anything but prepared for nothing. She couldn't allow him that advantage again.

*"Mattie wallows around like a fucking pansy*

*looking for his mother. What have you done to him? How is he supposed to become a man? And Dayton's in some serious need of manners. You're a disgusting failure of a mother!"*

There was nothing wrong with her boys. There was something wrong with their father. He'd degraded her, blamed her for the boys' introverted behavior. How quickly he returned her to a sense of nothingness. The punches, the screaming, the undignified way she pleaded with him to stop, it did nothing to sway his hatred.

This time was different. She wasn't sure if he'd ever be satisfied until he killed her.

She had to get out of this god-forsaken room. The longer he held her here the more proof she had that he was the unstable one. The bruises, the locks... He was manipulating her by withholding her children and the threat of kidnapping charges, but she was the prisoner.

After forcing another pill down her throat, he'd left her on the floor and relocked the door, leaving her alone with only her chaotic thoughts and what she was certain were a few cracked ribs. She lost track of time. Her mind repeatedly wondered where her children were.

Were they scared? Were they wondering where she was? Did they know she was in the house? Had they heard her screams? How many times had Marcus already lied to them? Was he being kind to them?

God, she hoped so. Let him unleash his rage on her, but please, God, save her children from ever seeing that side of him.

Her stomach curdled at the thought of him physically injuring her babies and she pushed the thought away, her mind rejecting it out of fear. She'd take the brunt of anything he dished out and be his easiest target if it held his temper at bay and protected the boys.

After beating her, he towered over her gasping, crumpled form and promised, "There will be more of that. An eye for an eye, Chloe. You sentenced me to six years. I wonder if that will be enough time for me to forgive your sins."

Then he calmly brushed a hand down his shirt and straightened his posture, a serene mask sliding over the face of a monster. But so long as he wore that mask in front of Mattie and Dayton they would be safe. Let him exorcise his demons here, with her. She'd bear the pain and degradation to save her boys and eventually, if she let him break her down the way he wanted, he'd let her out of this godforsaken room and she could save herself and her children.

The thought of spending one hour in this place made her claw at her skin. She'd never last six years, let alone six minutes, and intended to get out by the end of the day. She could barely stomach six minutes in this place. But she only needed to get through that door, convince him to let her out. Then she'd get through the next door and the next until she was free.

Hungry, thirsty, sore, and weak, she fought the urge to vomit as she rolled to her back. Heaving would only hurt. Her eyes watered as shallow, labored breaths escaped and she formulated a plan.

She would endure. For her children, she would do anything and everything to get out of this room. And then she would get them the hell out of this house.

# Twenty-Five

ALTHOUGH TRENT KNEW what to expect, nothing prepared him for the sheer terror and rage that overtook him when he got to Chloe's house. Her car, parked in its usual place, now held a sense of abandonment. The dark windows of the home, absent of any signs of light, were like soulless eyes staring back at him.

She'd only been missing for a little over twenty-four hours, but—knowing the statistics in cases such as hers—he feared the worst. The gaping void in his chest left his heart anchored to the pit of his stomach.

Where was she? Back in Virginia? Her ex was unlisted so that didn't make him the easiest person to find. Luckily, Pete had all the records from years ago. Trent just hoped the man hadn't moved. The number on file was disconnected, so getting there was the first priority.

He climbed out of his truck and grabbed the

notepad he used for jobs. He carefully examined the front door frame. No signs of forced entry.

He reached above the porch light and felt around for a key. Nothing. He lifted a flowerpot, checked in the window box, and finally found what he was looking for under the welcome mat. There, in a dusting of pollen and grit, was the outline of her missing house key.

"God, Chloe, you let him walk right in."

He checked the knob. Locked. Moving around the back of the house, he looked for any evidence that she might have been watched. There were no objects moved close to the exterior of the house. He examined each screen, searching for tears, but why bother when the key was waiting right under the mat? Chances were this wasn't the first time he'd been in her home.

As he worked his way back to the front of the house he stopped at her car. The door was un-locked. Under the seats, he found a tube of lipstick and slipped it in his pocket. The registration and insurance cards were insured to a Regina E. Wolfe. How was she managing to keep her aunt's death a secret?

"The cops already searched her car."

He turned and found Adam standing a few feet away studying him. Trent leaned back in the seat and looked up at the house, running his fingers over the wheel. "Did she say anything to you?"

"She says lots of things to me. If you're asking if she told me about the gun, then yes."

"She hates me."

"No, she hates anything having to do with violence."

This wasn't the time to focus on his insecurities, so he got to the important matters. "When was the last time you saw her?"

"Sunday, when we dropped the kids off. She was upset and wanted to be alone. Tommy took the boys to the skate park and I stayed and talked to her for a while."

He looked up as the other man's voice cracked. Adam seemed to be fighting back tears. "You didn't see her on Monday?"

"Tommy saw the boys get on the bus Monday morning. Then... Well, it was dark by the time we both got home. Her car was here. We didn't think anything of the dim house. It wasn't until this morning that things seemed too quiet and Chloe's car still hadn't moved."

His fingers played with a gash in the seat beside him. "It's been twenty-four-hours." It was time to face reality. "How badly would he hurt her?"

Adam's face tightened. "You think it's him, too?"

"The kids were signed out of school. Only a parent has the authority to do that."

"The police haven't—"

"Only a parent. They wouldn't go with anyone else and they're too innocent to see him as a danger."

Tommy stepped outside holding a cell phone. "Adam, it's the police." He handed over the phone.

Adam took the phone, covered his ear and walked closer to their home. "This is Adam Peters."

"So..." Tommy said, seemingly at a loss and lacking the energy to be his normal upbeat self. "You're gonna go after them, right? That's what you do, isn't it? Find people?"

Trent followed Adam with his stare as he ended the call.

Adam came back to the car. "That was Officer Striker. He signed the kids out."

Just as Trent suspected. "Do they have an exact time?"

"Ten fifty-three, Monday morning."

"Fuck." Trent walked to the grass and shut his eyes, pinching the bridge of his nose. "Tell me what you know about Marcus Hunt."

"We know he was abusive, lived somewhere in Virginia six years ago, and that Chloe's still terrified of him."

Trent's stomach knotted. Usually, he was the calm one on a job, but this was personal. "What about you, Tommy?"

"I know he was a brute. He abused Chloe in every way possible, not drawing lines from the kitchen to the bedroom. He never hit the kids, but toward the end, she feared that might change. She always intercepted, taking more of his shit if it meant possibly protecting Dayton and Mattie."

Trent ground his teeth as he swallowed hard. "Why this sudden interest? They're divorced. It's been six years." It was as if saying it out loud changed everything. He was a fucking idiot. She ran. Hunt was nuts. How had he convinced himself she somehow managed to get a divorce without some sort of consequence?

Because she let you believe that. Whenever her ex came up in conversation, he assumed the marriage was done. He was certain he referred to the man as her ex-husband, and she never corrected him.

Tommy and Adam were quiet and Trent knew the truth. "She's still married to him."

Adam's mouth opened, but no words came. Tommy frowned. "Honey, we thought you knew. Nothing's in her name and none of this is legally hers. It's all a lie. He stayed away because he couldn't find her."

"I thought..." His body shivered. "She changed her name. The house is—"

"Regina's. Before her aunt passed she moved everything into an LLC under the alias Chloe Wolfe. Her name's still legally Hunt and she's still married to him. He didn't give her custody of the boys. She—"

"Stole them." Jesus. Trent forked his fingers through his hair and paced. "All this time... Why wouldn't she—"

"Because he was that terrifying. And if he ever found her, he'd never forgive her."

His eyes closed. Shit just got a lot more complicated. Chloe had kidnapped her children. It was a second-degree offense and, due to the longevity and the fact that she'd crossed state lines, possibly a federal one. Hunt was no doubt using that information to threaten her.

Visions of Chloe trapped with her vengeful husband flooded his mind. He shook with rage as fear twisted his gut. "The guy's fucking nuts. He's a spoiled brat who can afford very dangerous toys and has no experience using such things. He doesn't like being told no and thinks he's entitled to anything he wants."

Hazy memories dusted off in his mind. The day he'd told Hunt he'd lost his wife somewhere along the border he'd gone ballistic. The man who hired him had fed him a load of bullshit, calling his wife unstable when he'd seen first-hand how terrified she was of her husband. He'd never seen a grown man in such a fit, throwing a tantrum like a spoiled child who lost his favorite toy. And he'd never forget the threats that spewed from his mouth as he promised to make her pay when he found her.

Fisting his hands in his hair, Trent growled. "Rather than fearing guns, she should have taught herself to use one."

He would've shown her how to arm and protect herself had he known that fucker was still a threat. His breathing was jagged and he needed to calm down.

Tommy looked as if he had seen a ghost and Adam was scowling.

"Why are you looking at me like that?"

Adam's voice held an edge of hostility. "Have you met him?"

Trent shut his eyes and sighed. *Fuck.* "I ... yes."

Both men glared at him, their distrusting eyes demanding answers.

"I'm not on his side, so stop looking at me like that! He hired me to find his wife and I did, but in the end, I made sure he never would. I brought her here and told him I lost her somewhere near Mexico."

Tommy gasped and covered his mouth. "But you were her hero."

"I..." In the end, maybe that's what he'd been, but that wasn't how it started. "It was just a job. In the end, I quit and it cost me a lot of money and stress, but I didn't betray her."

"I think it's time for you to leave," Adam growled.

"I planned to tell her everything—"

"When? Before or after you got her into bed a few more times?"

"Oh, my God. This is bad," Tommy mumbled, massaging his temples.

"It was six years ago, Adam, and I didn't—"

"*You've been seeing her for weeks!* How are we supposed to trust you when you've kept this a secret? For all we know, you led him here!"

He lunged forward and growled, "I would risk my life to protect her!"

"But you'd lie to her! You lied to all of us."

He glared at both of them. "I'm only going to say this once, so listen carefully. I love that woman. I want a life with her. But even before I knew her, I wanted to ensure she had a life for herself, the kind she deserved. You can twist the facts any way you like, but I didn't finish the job and I would *never* help a monster like Marcus Hunt. I'm going to get her and the boys home and make it so he can never threaten her again. If saving her means I lose her in the process..." An ache knotted in his chest. "I just want to get her away from him."

With that, he pivoted and marched to his truck. Enough wasting time. He was going to bring his girl home.

# Twenty-Six

CHLOE SAT IN THE DARK, only a triangle of light seeping from the bathroom. She spent most of the afternoon lying on the mattress, adapting to the hunger pains and massaging her sore body.

Sometimes she sat by the door, listening for sounds within the house. Doors opened and closed, water ran through the pipes, but there wasn't even a whisper of Dayton or Mattie's voices.

After his visit that morning he hadn't returned. She feared he'd leave her there for days, but also feared his return.

Paranoia struck and she wondered if her children were even there. Maybe he'd lied and they were back in Pennsylvania worrying about where their mother had gone, fearing she abandoned them.

She tried to remember the day before, but it felt like years ago. Jennifer would've canceled all of her appointments at some time today—was it still today? Yes, today. And what about Trenton?

What if Marcus was texting her friends from her

phone, pretending to be her? She had no idea where her purse had gone.

She stiffened as a key turned in the knob, the scrape of metal abrading her frayed nerves and sending her scurrying back to the nearest wall. She wanted to stand so she wasn't in such a vulnerable position, but she lacked the strength and time. Marcus stepped into the room and her body tensed painfully with fear.

He shut the door with his foot and locked it with a key before slipping it back into his pocket. She needed that key.

He carried a bowl to the center of the floor and produced a sleeve of crackers from his back pocket, dropping them next to the bowl. "Eat."

He returned to the door, casually leaning against the wall with his arms crossed over his chest, waiting for her to move. Fearful it was a trick, she hugged the perimeter of the room until she was close enough to snatch the crackers, her hunger beating at her.

The buttery saltiness crumbled on her tongue and tasted like heaven. Her throat swallowed repetitively as she watched him.

"Don't you want the soup?"

She dragged the bowl closer. It was cold and there wasn't a spoon. She brought it to her mouth and sipped the broth, trying her best to avoid the slimy noodles and cold chicken bits.

He enjoyed humiliating her and probably loved the idea of making her drink her supper like a dog on the floor. She ignored her stomach's revulsion, hoping any form of sustenance would build back her strength.

Within minutes, her belly was uncomfortably full and cramping. She twisted the crackers closed and placed them behind her, afraid he'd take what she didn't finish.

"I suppose you've had time to think."

She studied him, never sure of his intentions.

"The boys are beginning to ask about you."

She needed proof they were here. "Can I see them?"

"I could easily tell them you abandoned them."

Her teeth locked, but she remained silent. She'd never abandon her children and he knew that.

"Or I could tell them their mother is a criminal who needs to be punished for her crimes."

Anger festered and bloomed like pus inside of her. She wasn't a kidnapper. They were her children and she'd protected them. He'd made her life unbearable and she had no choice but to run. But Marcus had plenty of powerful friends who might see it differently. She wasn't sure what the laws were, so she couldn't call his bluff.

"I want to see them."

"The other option... We can show them we've reconciled. Which do you think would be the least detrimental for them?"

Reconciling was out of the question, and a life with Marcus was never the best option, yet, he gave her little choice. If she could fool him, convince him she was sorry and willing to make this work, he might let her out of this room. But first, she needed proof.

"Are the boys even here, Marcus? I haven't seen or heard them since we arrived." Her voice was nothing more than a dry rasp. Her lips hurt at the corners and she'd had a steady throb in her skull since he'd shown up in her life.

"Oh, they're here."

"Why should I believe you?"

"Because what other options do you have?" He laughed, taunting her.

"I want to see my sons."

"Then we need to reconcile our differences. Show me you're sorry and I'll let you see them. But you better be convincing, Chloe. If you intend to convince them, you first have to convince me."

"I'll do anything, just let me see that they're all right and—"

"Anything's an awfully big word."

The contents of her stomach clotted. Marcus had a way of making everything a negotiation without ever compromising. She understood what he was after. She'd done it before and if it got her out of this room she could do it again. She had no room to second-guess her objectives. Marcus meant nothing. He was a disgusting, rotting soul blocking her escape. She'd get through him by any means necessary. Any.

Looking up at him, she repeated, "I'll do anything. Just let me see Dayton and Mattie."

"Very well." He pressed off of the wall and her stomach lurched. His hands folded behind his back and he stared at her expectantly. "Well?"

She frowned, confused. "I don't know what you want."

"Of course you do. I want you to show me how sorry you are."

A jagged breath filled her lungs as her heart hammered in her chest. Rage and disgust became an ugliness inside of her not easily disguised. "If you want something, Marcus, just take it. My objections never stopped you before."

His calm terrified her more than his anger. His laugh held the merriment of a deranged sadist.

"Dear, sweet, Chloe. I'm not going to *rape* my wife. What kind of man would that make me? Irreconcilable differences it is then. I'll make some calls and you should find yourself in a new cell by morning. Pity. The boys will be devastated when I tell them *my* version." He turned to the door.

"*Wait!*" Her panic doubled. What if he wasn't bluffing? What if he did the research and honestly believed she could go to prison for her crimes?

The glint of the key flashed in his fingers. "I can tell you're thinking hard with that tiny brain of yours. The penalty for parental kidnapping in the state of Virginia is a class six felony punishable by up to ten years in a state penitentiary."

Her chin quivered as a sharp pain cinched around her heart. "I didn't..." Her eyes blinked as her vision blurred.

"But you did, Chloe. You stole my children. You stole my aunt's identity. You falsified documents and lied for over half a decade. I would have to do very little to see you punished for your crimes."

Her head was fuzzy and she couldn't think. He wouldn't hesitate to tell the boys she'd abandoned them. He'd twist the truth. If she was prosecuted, even withheld for a short period of time, she'd be unable to keep him away from them, unable to keep him from spewing his lies. The smallest thing might set him off and if she wasn't here for him to target, he'd find someone else. She couldn't let that happen.

Yet, if she could get to the police, even if it meant being taken into custody, she might be able to explain the situation, possibly have Dayton and Mattie moved somewhere safe until the details were worked out and—

He sighed. "This is where Mattie gets his indecisiveness from. I intend to start getting on him about that tomorrow. You know how impatient I can be."

She thought of her little baby, her sweet, vulnerable Matthew. Dayton was a fighter, but the moment he challenged Marcus he'd see first-hand why her only choice was to run. "No. If you let me talk to them they'll be better."

"I told you, the only way that can happen is if you convince me you're sorry."

She wanted to scream and lunge at him. *Get me the fuck out of this place!*

She was losing her mind and it had only been one since she arrived. There was no getting out of this room without giving him exactly what he wanted. Her mind rapidly compartmentalized, as if hiding away all thoughts of her normal life could abate the humiliation of the inevitable.

She swallowed, fighting the urge to scream. "I'm sorry."

A reptilian smile crawled over his face to match his immoral eyes. "Show me."

The key returned to his pocket. And her eyes closed. The clink of his belt buckle brought an unsteady shiver. Warm leather traced down her cheek and she grit her teeth.

"You remember this." He pressed the leather of the belt under her chin and her eyes opened. "Clothes off."

Her mind twitched as she grudgingly forced her will to surrender. It would be painful, humiliating, and, once again, leave scars where no one else could see. And like every other time, he'd given her options, but little choice.

She mechanically pulled off her clothes, keeping her gaze on the floor.

"You're still fat."

His criticism of her body was the least of her pain. She moved to the mattress, recalling all too well the way he wanted her, the way he preferred to use his belt. A tear rolled down her cheek as she silently lowered to her stomach. No matter how much that leather would cut into her skin and leave welts for days, it was the unwanted surrender of her will, the hatred he created for him and for herself that caused her to tremble.

She knew, without a doubt, by the time he dropped that belt he'd be aroused and fueled by the marks as much as he'd be excited by her cries. And that would be when the true punishment came, when he'd expect her to prove how sorry she was.

# Twenty-Seven

TRENTON WATCHED THE DARK HOUSE, unable to get within twenty feet of the sensory lights. It was almost dawn and he still hadn't been able to verify if this was where they were. All cars were tucked in the garage and there were no markings on the house that told him Hunt still owned the property. He was able to discern the home was rigged with a state of the art security system, one he couldn't fuck with unless he intended to wake the neighborhood.

No lights were on and he was riding about fifteen cups of coffee on about two hours sleep since Sunday. He prayed this was where they were. The thought that he'd come this far and possibly traveled in the wrong direction was too much for him to bear.

"I'm comin' for you, doll. I'm comin'."

Taking his truck out of *park*, he gave the house one last look before pulling away. He'd get some rest and be back once the sun was up. Then he'd get them home.

~

As the pink fingers of dawn stole the shadows of night, Chloe silently wept. Pain radiated down her back and her muscles screamed. What he'd done... It broke parts of her that couldn't be fixed.

She heard the lock jimmy and winced, too weak to sit up. Her breath held, as Marcus's silhouetted filled the door and she cringed. He'd just left. Why was he back so soon? No. She couldn't do anymore. Her mind couldn't take it.

He relocked the door, his shadowed shoulders lifting as the sound of his heavy breathing met her ears. Something was wrong.

Pocketing the key, he pivoted and stalked to the mattress. A tear rolled from her eyes as she lay defenseless at his feet. His hand went to his belt and she scrambled backward until her weight pressed into the wall. Her body couldn't take one more hit.

"Marcus, no. What's going on?"

"Not a fucking sound. You understand me?"

Sucking in a breath, she nodded, but she didn't understand. She'd done everything he'd asked. Things she thought she'd never do with him again. Keeping her mouth closed, her teeth chattered as she watched him without blinking.

What happened? The boys should still be asleep. This didn't make sense. He promised she could see them.

He moved like a shadow of death, his clothing

falling away until her eyes could bear no more. Pressing her lids shut, she swallowed a sob. Firm hands curled around her limbs as the mattress dipped. She stiffly let him shift her body, her mind going to another place as she fought the urge to fight, begging her strength not to abandon her at the same time.

"They don't even know me," he hissed. "My fucking sons, with *my* blood running through their veins, are afraid to even look at me." He jerked her to her stomach. "You disgust me. I don't want to look at *you*."

Tears moistened her lashes. The punishment, beyond his violation, rested in her shame. There was so much shame, so much vileness, and revulsion. Her flesh was so tender the slightest caress burned like a scalding blade, flaying her dignity like flesh from the bone. Her silence shattered as he brutally shoved into her.

"Mark my words..." He grunted and held her down, wrenching a silent cry from her with every punishing thrust. "You will *never* take from me without my permission again."

He gripped her wrist, dragging it to the base of her spine, forcing her to bear the brunt of his assault on her shoulders. Blurring the fine line between carnality and violence, he twisted her arm higher, ensuring she couldn't draw enough breath to scream.

His name, a plea for mercy, rested on her tongue, as pain radiated through her arm, the joint nearly popping out of socket as her face distorted in a mask of agony. He'd warned her not to utter a word and made certain she wouldn't disobey.

Her mind fragmented and terror quickened, racing through her veins like a speeding bullet spinning wildly toward her soul. His nails dug into her as he shoved forward and groaned, his weight shuddering over her welted back.

Pain shot up her arm as he released her wrist and made a derisive sound. The evidence of what he'd done—what she'd allowed him to do—smeared between her thighs. The fraying thread between her sanity and complete mental collapse seemed to burn faster than a fuse tied to a stick of dynamite.

No more. He said if she proved she was sorry she could see the boys. "Please," she rasped. "Marcus..."

He towered over her, righting his clothes. "Please what?"

"The boys..."

His lip curled. "You're going to have to beg better than that. I'm still not convinced you want to stay."

Tears spilled from her eyes as a cry choked her. Her mind unraveled, the words coming out like meaningless syllables. "I want to stay. Please. I need to see them."

"Not convincing enough."

"*Please*! I want to be here—with you—and the boys. A family. Please let me see them, Marcus."

"I'm not sure I want a fat wife."

"I'll exercise. Whatever you want me to do I'll do it, just let me see Dayton and Mattie."

He fastened his pants. "We'll see how the morning goes." He unlocked the door and left. The smooth sound of the key turning in the lock triggered a violent sob as she collapsed, broken and humiliated to a point she wasn't sure any escape could reconcile.

Sometime later, she awoke with the sense of something happening, an impending doom or perhaps a teasing glimpse of freedom approaching. Good or bad, she needed to prepare for anything.

Hobbling to the bathroom she cleaned herself up, but nothing removed the sour taste in her mouth. Her thigh had a dark black bruise and some of her veins looked overly varicose. There was a spattering of welts on her hips, thighs, and buttocks. She weakly reached for the shower and stilled as something rattled in the house.

Brow low, eyes searching, her mind worked to identify the quiet rumble. It was ... familiar, niggling at a sense of relief but also inducing a sense of dread.

Her lips parted. "The garage..."

Lurching to the window, she watched as Marcus's car, no longer red but silver pulled out of the driveway. Standing close to the wall so no one would see her undressed, she stared as the car backed onto the street and her heart clamped tight as she got a glimpse of her sons sitting in the back seat.

"*No!*" she cried, pressing her hand to the glass. The car disappeared down the road and she staggered back.

Beating at the door, she screamed, "Somebody help me! Please! Help me!"

Falling to her knees, she cried. Where was he taking her babies?

Desperate, jumbled thoughts raced through her mind as she lost touch with reality. Time fell away as the silence stretched. Her mind pranced from one memory to the next, so vivid she could smell her kitchen in Pennsylvania and feel the warmth of her couch. Her fingers traced the carpet as if touching her favorite quilt.

With no concept of time beyond the placement of the sun, she eventually moved to the window. It was still far behind the trees, telling her it couldn't be later than eight or nine a.m.

Watching the road for Marcus's car, she stared at the blacktop for an excruciating length of time until something caught her eye.

A woman in a bathrobe sat on a wicker chair across the street. She was young and Chloe didn't recognize her. She held a cup of coffee and a newspaper. Chloe's fingers tapped on the window, but the woman made no movement. "Up here... Look up..."

She banged harder, her hand aching within a few minutes. Finally, the woman frowned and lifted her head, looking around curiously. When she glanced in the direction of the house Chloe frantically pounded on the window.

"I'm up here! Help me! *Please!*"

The woman walked to her mailbox, placed a hand above her brow, and angled her head in Chloe's direction. Tears of happiness spilled from Chloe's eyes as she waved at the woman until something caught her eye.

Marcus's car turned onto the street and the automatic garage door rattled. Chloe panicked, her breath laboring as she backed away from the window. Marcus slowed and the neighbor approached his car, pointing to the house. Chloe gasped as she noted the empty back seat. The neighbor smiled and turned away.

Stumbling back from the window, she trembled uncontrollably. Staring at the door, she staggered her body to the far wall. Time moved too fast and too slow as her panic seeped from her pores.

Waiting.

Waiting.

Waiting.

It took everything she had to remain standing when the snick of the key finally came. The knob slowly turned and he stepped into the room carrying a brown paper bag by a handle.

"Are you having fun?" He appeared calm, but that meant nothing.

"Where are the boys? Where did you take them?" She couldn't hide the accusation in her voice.

"The boys are spending the day visiting their new school. I see you've found some ways to entertain yourself while I've been gone."

New school? No, they had a school. Her mind scrambled, too focused on her children to follow his words.

She edged toward the bathroom door and he arched a brow, sick amusement playing in his eyes. "Are you planning on running from me, sweet wife? Where will you go? And to think, I was going to let you see the children today. I even brought you some fresh clothes."

Her palms pressed into the wall, her heart racing. "Promise me I'll see Dayton and Mattie *today*. I need your word."

"Matthew," he corrected tersely. "And you don't make the rules. I do. If you behave, I'll let you see Matthew, but Dayton's being punished."

Protective fury swept through her. *"Punished? For what?"*

He took a sharp step forward and snarled, *"You don't question me!"* Drawing in a calming breath, he righted his posture and said, "I took him to get his hair cut and he was disrespectful."

Only trying to defend her son, she said, "All his friends have long hair."

"My son doesn't." The bag dropped to the floor. "Now, these are your options. You'll be punished for playing with the neighbor, of course. After that, you can either sit here and sulk until tomorrow when we'll try again, or you can prove you're committed to our marriage. The longer you wait, the longer you don't get to see my sons. Choose."

It didn't go unnoticed how he'd started calling them *his* sons. "I want to see the boys."

"Go shower."

# Twenty-Eight

**TRENT CURSED** himself for sleeping longer than he wanted. Loading his gun, he appraised the house once more.

He thought about barging in but decided to do things on the up and up. Marcus Hunt might be a cocksucker, but the man had more money than him and with money came connections. Chances were he knew the local cops and kept them on his side over the years. That, and he didn't know what he'd be walking in to or if the house was still even his.

He looked at the clock. 11:59. Go time.

Climbing out of his truck, he wedged his gun in the back of his jeans and took the manicured path to the front door. Everything was the picture of suburban bliss here on 100 Happy Street. Even the doorbell gave the message that this was a safe and happy home. He gritted his teeth and rang twice.

The soft echo of movement inside had him stepping back and casually leaning his shoulder against the siding. The door opened and he masked his immediate relief. The motherfucker looked as harmless as Mr. Rodgers.

"Can I help you?"

Pleased he hadn't immediately recognized him, Trent's eyes narrowed and his head cocked to the side. "Is Chloe home?"

Hunt frowned but held his cool façade. "And who shall I say is calling?"

"You can tell her her ride's here. I won't take it personally that you forgot my name. By the way, it's Trenton Cole."

Marcus did a double take and his eyes lit with anger. Trent suffered a pinch of satisfaction at catching the bastard off guard. But his satisfaction vanished as the other man's scowl twisted into a mealy grin.

"Ah, Mr. Cole. Do come in."

Not the welcome he expected, but okay. Trent stepped into the house. His hand brushing over the butt of his gun.

Hunt led him to a typical, upper-class living room. "Have a seat. I'll go get my *wife*."

His jaw tightened. "I'll stand."

"Suit yourself."

The second he was alone, he scanned the room, spotting a few outdated pictures of Chloe. Her hair was blonde back then, her eyes lifeless, a smile that wasn't genuine. He took a quick glance into the hall to get a better layout of the inside of the house and turned at the sound of approaching footsteps. Any earlier relief withered at the sight of her.

The moment she saw him she gasped. "Trenton?"

Her lip trembled and she wasn't blinking. The stiff way she held herself told him she was *not* okay, but he'd be an idiot to expect otherwise.

"I'm taking you home."

"How is it you know this man, Chloe?"

Trenton ignored whatever game he was playing and kept his focus on Chloe. "We're leaving. Where are Dayton and Mattie?"

Marcus settled into a chair as if he hadn't a concern in the world. He didn't interrupt or even so much as look at Chloe, who only stared unblinking.

"Doll, did you hear me? Where are the boys?"

Her chest lifted with quickened breath.

Marcus grinned, brow raised, confidence seeping from his pores. "Did you want to go with this man, darling?"

Her lips parted as her brow pinched. Her head twitched as if it was a difficult decision to make.

"Chloe, don't look at him. Look at me. We're going home. Where are—"

"I can't," she rasped in a hoarse voice.

He scowled. He was here. There was nothing Marcus could do to keep her against her will unless he was interested in getting the cops involved. If he tried anything, Trent would protect her. She didn't have to worry.

"Did you hear me? We're leaving. Me, you, and the boys. You don't have to stay here."

Her eyes glazed and she took a deep breath. "I ... can't go with you."

"Yes, you can. You just take my hand and walk out that door. He's not going to stop us."

A tear rolled down her cheek and he breathed

in, holding back his fury. His glare snapped to Marcus. "What did you do to her?"

Marcus tsked. "Did you have something to say to this man, Chloe?"

Her lips quivered. "I'm ... staying here. We're ... going to be a family again." Her words were too mechanical, too rehearsed. "You should leave."

He was losing patience. "What the hell's going on? Where are the boys?"

Drawing in a deep breath, she said, "Dayton and Matthew are visiting their new school. They're transferring."

This was not his Chloe. It was clear Marcus had full faith she'd not betray him, which led him to believe her last few hours had been hell. Scrutinizing her again, he searched for signs of damage. Her clothing was fresh and clean. But her eyes wore lines of tension and her lips, which always wore a shade of color, were now bone white. But she was trying to fool him. The tears he saw a second ago were gone. Why was she hiding the truth from him?

Fuck this. Stepping forward, he reached for her hand. "Chloe, he can't hurt you if you leave—"

Marcus stood with surprising speed, his cool fingers clamping around Trent's wrist. "I'm going to have to insist that you not touch my wife."

He stared at their three hands and then looked into Chloe's vacant Stepford eyes, rested on her husband. What the fuck had he done to her? Was she on drugs? "Look at me," he snapped and her gaze jerked back to him. "This isn't you. We're leaving."

"I wouldn't trust this man if I were you, darling."

Trent all but snarled when he saw the glint of satisfaction in Hunt's eyes, the smirk twisting his lips. He looked back to Chloe. "Don't listen to anything he says. He's a fucking psychopath. You're coming with me."

"Did you know he was hired to find you?" Marcus's question whispered through the air like the blade of a guillotine.

*That motherfucker.* Trent's eyes closed as Chloe's shocked face turned to him in horror. He was going to murder the man.

"That's right. One hundred thousand dollars— although I think you likely paid him enough in a different form of currency, but we'll discuss that later."

Her hand jerked out of his and Marcus grinned triumphantly. "As much as we've enjoyed your visit, Mr. Cole, I believe it's time for you to go."

"Chloe, don't listen to him. He's full of shit."

Her head shook in disbelief.

"Maybe if she saw the contract you signed she'd have an easier time deciding who to trust. Should I go get it for her, Mr. Cole?"

She blinked up at him, hurt shimmering through the tears now filling her eyes. "Tell me he's lying, Trenton. You didn't work for him..."

Her gaze pleaded, begging him to say it wasn't true. His shoulders lowered. "I love you, Chloe. I'd never hurt you."

"Did you *work* for him?" she choked.

Hunt sighed. "Oh, now you've upset my wife. I'm afraid it's true. And now it's time to go."

Ignoring him, he frantically tried to clarify.

"Chloe, listen to me. Yes, I was hired to find you, but—"

Her brow pinched as she turned away, covering her ears. "Get out."

"Chloe, don't listen to him! It was before I knew you. He wants you to hate me so you won't come with me. I'm not leaving without you and the boys—"

She spun and slapped her palms into his chest. *"Get. Out!"*

So shocked she actually shoved him, he staggered back a step. "Doll—"

*"I trusted you!"*

Hunt caught her shoulders and pulled her back. The sob that ripped from her throat cut right through his chest. "Shh," Hunt whispered, turning her toward the stairs. "Go lie down like you were. I'll take care of this."

"Chloe, *don't* go up those stairs!"

In a calmer voice, Hunt said, "Do as I said."

Trent panted as she glanced back at him one last time and then took the stairs. "You son of a bitch—"

"Careful." He held up his cellphone, 911 already showing as the next contact.

Seeing red, he grabbed Marcus by the front of the shirt and slammed him against the wall. "You think you're amusing? Everything you do to her I'm gonna do back to you, but worse," he snarled.

"Nine-one-one, what's your emergency?" The small voice played from his phone and Marcus smiled.

"Send an officer to my house immediately. A

man by the name of Trenton Cole just assaulted me and tried to abduct my wife. I believe he has a gun." He ended the call. "They'll be here in two minutes."

Trent drew back his fist and hesitated, knowing any proof of assault would only work against him. Releasing his hold of his shirt, he shoved away.

"You make her cry, I'll make you scream and beg we never met. You hurt her, I'll fucking slaughter you. This isn't over, you fucking psychopath. This isn't over." He slammed his fist into the wall beside Hunt's head, driving his point home. "We clear?"

"Oh, crystal."

Seething, he pointed in his face. "One mark on her and you're a dead man. One. Fucking. Mark."

# Twenty-Nine

SHE COULDN'T BREATHE. The gaping wound in her heart was turning her inside out. Trenton worked for Marcus?

*No.*

A sob pushed past the suffocating lump in her throat and she gasped for air. His betrayal was a living thing she couldn't escape, choking and crippling her flagging grasp of reality.

When she first saw him she wanted to cry. Her hero had once again come for her. Then reality weighed in, reminding her of the consequences. She couldn't leave without the boys and Marcus would have her arrested the moment they crossed state lines again.

Telling Trenton to leave had been one of the hardest things she ever had to do. She couldn't leave without knowing where her sons were. She couldn't risk Marcus getting to them first. But then the pain of hearing he was somehow associated with Marcus... She couldn't bear the truth, couldn't stomach it. For all Trenton's wonderful traits, he'd kept this from her.

Deep down, she believed, whatever Trenton's ties were to her husband, he'd never betray her. Marcus *wanted* her to think he would, but she knew Trenton and he cared about her and her boys. The contract—if there actually was one—had to be old.

*Oh, my God, Maryland.*

That was why he was there in the train station. He'd followed her. But why get her in his truck and...

She frowned. He took her to her boys. He didn't even stick around long enough for her to thank him. Why, if Marcus had hired him, paid him all that money, had he not finished the job?

*Because he's a good man.*

She needed answers, but Marcus would only toy with her curiosity, corrupting the truth in the cruelest way possible. The thought that Trenton might think she believed he had somehow played a role in her being here now...

*Oh, God. It hurts.*

She wanted to run after him and scream for him to go find her boys and call the police. She had to stop him from leaving. Rushing to the door she reached forward and gasped as it suddenly swung open, Marcus wearing a smug grin on the other side.

"Well, that was interesting."

She jumped, too lost in her unsettling thoughts. "He—"

"Not now." He adjusted his cuffs. "The police are on their way."

"What?" Hope rose only to be slashed down by uncertainty and fear.

"I won't be assaulted in my own home. What trash. I hope he used you like a common whore. Maybe that will teach you."

"Stop it." Her molars locked. This was what he did. He took something she loved and stole it away, used it to punish her and make her feel inferior. "You don't know what you're talking about."

"When will it sink in? No one wants a fat, lazy woman like you. He only took interest in you because I paid him to. Without my money, you're worthless to him."

He was lying. Trenton's truck was old and his home, though beautiful, was modest. He never finished the job and Marcus never rewarded anyone for failure. On the contrary, he cursed them and held grudges and sought vengeance. He was twisting the truth to hurt not only her but Trenton.

Her mind settled into a foreign, quiet place, pushing away his lies. Like sand sifting through a pan for gold, she only saw the solid facts, discarding everything else as worthless.

"You're worthless, Chloe..."

No. She couldn't let him do this to her. She couldn't fall back into that hopeless creature she'd left behind years ago. She had to keep fighting.

It was this house. This godforsaken house. She twitched and shivered.

Police. She needed to talk to the cops. If she could somehow get an officer to the house she could insist the kids get moved into protective custody and explain that she was being blackmailed and held against her will.

She winced as he suddenly gripped her jaw and forced her eyes on him. "Listen carefully. You're going to get yourself off the floor and wash your face. Then we're going to go downstairs and wait for the police to arrive. They'll be here any minute. You will agree with *everything* I say. One wrong word and I'll have them take you away for kidnapping and who knows when you'll see Matthew and Dayton again. Understand?"

She wordlessly blinked at him. She was going to tell the cops. She had to. She needed somebody on her side—

Her breath hissed out of her as his fingers dug like talons into her stomach. "I know that look," he seethed. "Don't test me, Chloe. You think they'll get you out of here safely? Maybe. But not before I get to the boys. You don't want to send me off to our sons in a temper, do you?"

There was a debilitating reality that came with being a woman. She'd read stories of women, mothers, who possessed superhuman strength in times of crisis, lifting vehicles to save their children from certain death. She wanted that strength now. She wanted to tackle him to the ground and rip out his eyes for even making such a threat.

But he was bigger and stronger and would always be more powerful. When she fought him, she lost. When she screamed, she was punished. If she wanted to get to her boys, she needed to cooperate. And maybe that was where her superhuman strength came into play because it was physically painful to agree to his terms and surrender to the fact that she wasn't escaping today.

No matter how badly she wanted to tell the police, she couldn't risk the consequence, couldn't jeopardize her boys' safety. She'd have to endure and follow whatever lie he decided. At least until she got her sons somewhere safe.

"I understand."

# Thirty

SHE FAILED. She failed herself and her children and that realization paralyzed her with defeat. As Marcus thanked the officer while walking him to the front door, she sat stunned. What was wrong with her? Help had arrived, first Trenton, then a police officer and her fear decapitated her chance of escape.

She twitched with uncertainty, wanting to scream and call the cop back as the door closed behind him, Marcus's fingers twisting the locks. If she'd known where her children were, had a guarantee she could reach them before Marcus, she would have gone with the devil himself, but he would beat her to them and then he would likely beat her—maybe the kids as well.

She had no choice but to follow his lead, agree with his ludicrous statement that Trenton Cole had barged into their home—a jealous ex-lover intent on getting her back after she'd made her choice clear. Marcus was a horrible person who didn't have a single good bone in his body, but he was the best liar she'd ever met. He even showed the cop where Trenton had apparently punched the wall, threatening him.

Only a monster could convince the world he was the victim. And she'd nodded along with every despicable lie for fear that he'd punish her through her children if she so much as blinked wrong.

And now her hope was gone. Vanished, because she'd said nothing when she could have told them everything. She felt like a balloon cut away from its string, floating to places unknown. Once the two officers took their statement and left, Marcus made her a sandwich.

"You did very well. After you're finished eating, we have some calls to make."

Her stomach was so sore and so upset she could only eat half. Her boys would be home in an hour and her excitement at seeing them also hindered her appetite. "Calls?"

"We're going to call anyone who know about us. You'll call them and tell them the same thing you told the police—that we've reconciled."

Her rage was no longer debilitating. It was now a seething animal caged inside of her, pacing until the opportunity of freedom arrived. "What about my practice?"

"You'll notify your secretary that you'll be taking an undetermined leave of absence. We can work out the details later."

He withdrew her cellphone from her pocket and her breath caught.

"Let's start with the A's. Who's Adam?"

Lying to the police was one thing, but lying to her friends... It almost gave her hope. "He's my neighbor."

"Does he know you're married?"

She kept her expression blank. "No."

"Are you close to him?"

"No. I only have his number because I get his mail when he travels for business. I think he's an accountant."

"Fine. Alison?"

She cursed herself for not realizing if *he* didn't exist to someone *they* didn't exist. She should have said she knew Adam. He might be able to argue her case to the police. But it was too late. "Alison's a patient."

"Jade?"

No, Jade had been through too much and was pregnant. "Another patient."

He narrowed his eyes. "Are you lying to me?"

Her heart beat out of sync. "She's also a friend."

"Does she know you're married?"

Her jaw trembled as she tried to recall the things she'd confided in Jade. "No. If I tried to explain this she'd be confused." That was the truth.

"Jeremy?"

She slowed her breathing. "He's a friend."

He lifted a brow. "Quite a few male friends in your life. Did you fuck him?"

"No."

"Does he know you're married?"

Considering that he worked with Trenton who now figured out where she was, they likely all knew about Marcus at this point. And if Trenton was truly hired by Marcus to find her, they might have always known. "Yes, he knows I'm married."

"You know what to say to him. Keep it short and sweet." He pressed a button and placed the phone on the table, activating the speakerphone.

"Hello?"

She glanced at Marcus and he nodded to the phone. "Jeremy, it's Chloe."

"Chloe—"

"I'm calling to tell you I've gotten back with Marcus." She cut him off before he could say anything, alerting Marcus to his association with Trenton. "I'm in Virginia in case you were looking for me."

There was a long pause. "That's ... good. The boys must be happy."

The mention of her sons put a lump in her throat, but she picked up on his carefully selected words and kept her expression blank. Dear God this had to work. "We're all very happy with the situation. They've started a new school."

"You're staying out of town?"

She swallowed. "Yes. Indefinitely. I wanted to let you know so you didn't worry. The boys will miss playing with your son ... Tyson."

Another long pause. "My ... *son* will miss playing with them. I'm sorry to hear this but I'm happy you've worked out your marriage. We were planning a trip and were hoping they might be able to come."

"Oh, I'm afraid that wouldn't work for us right now. Are you finally visiting *Phoenix*? Or is this the trip to *Georgia* you mentioned?"

"We're definitely heading to Phoenix."

Marcus made a gesture for her to wrap it up. "Well, I hope you get to Phoenix soon."

"We're leaving *tomorrow*. I hope ... he treats you well, Chloe."

"Thank you. Goodbye, Jeremy."

"Goodbye."

He ended the call. "Keep it a little shorter next time."

Her lips twitched as a new hope formed. Jeremy was smart and he seemed to understand everything she'd implied without actually saying the words. Go to Phoenix. Talk to Pete. The moment she referred to Tyson as his son he would have known she was trying to convey something in secret because Marcus was there.

Marcus glanced at his watch. "Time to go back upstairs."

Startled that he was sending her back to that horrible room she hesitated. "I thought..."

"You didn't think I'd let you roam the house while I got the boys, did you? You're far from deserving that kind of trust. I'll tell the boys you arrived this morning—after I get them home and see you've behaved."

There was always a condition. Always a consequence.

He walked her to the second floor and closed her in the empty bedroom, locking the door tight. She watched from the window as his car pulled away. Her boys... She was going to see her boys.

So as not to worry them that anything was amiss, she tried her best to fix her hair, but all she had to work with was her fingers. She straightened her clothing and washed her face, but looked nothing like herself without makeup to cover the bruising.

Sometime later, the garage door rumbled and her stomach flipped. They were home.

She stood in front of the locked bedroom door for what felt like hours as she waited for it to open. Was he dragging this out on purpose? What was he telling her children? Six years ago, when she'd been running for her life and separated from them, she'd found a way to still call them every day—even when it required the last cent to her name. They'd known something was up then and they were only babies. They would absolutely suspect something now.

When the door finally opened, Marcus said nothing but led her down the stairs. Tears of relief blurred her vision the moment she spotted Dayton and Mattie sitting on the sofa.

Mattie gasped when he saw her and ran into her arms. She tried not to flinch at the force of his hug, telling herself his arms around her were worth the pain, but an ache started in her chest at the realization that she was back to hiding bruises from those closest to her.

Dayton wouldn't meet her gaze. His hair was trimmed and neatly swept to the side. Her big man suddenly seemed such a small, fragile boy. As much as the last few months had challenged her as a parent, she wanted her audacious son back.

She walked over to him and knelt, turning his face and looking into his eyes. "Day?"

He slowly raised his lashes and gazed at her. Insecurity and guilt flashed in his eyes and her heart cinched. This chaos was too much for a little boy to bear.

She brushed the backs of her fingers down his porcelain cheek. "Sweetie, everything's okay. I'm not upset with you."

His eyes filled with unshed tears as he fought to keep them from trickling past his lashes. She hated seeing him confused and upset. He didn't say it, but she saw it in his pinched brow and trembling lips. He blamed himself for pressing *go* on this roller coaster. But she couldn't blame him. This was her mess she'd never properly cleaned up. Never his.

Pressing her lips to his forehead, she pulled him into her arms and whispered, "Everything's going to be fine. You're not in any trouble."

Throwing his arms around her neck, he squeezed her tighter than he had in years.

That night she had a chance to see the rest of the house. It was very much the same and now somewhat out of date. The boys' rooms were changed, smelling of fresh paint and new furniture. Dayton's room no longer had access to a bathroom and Mattie was sleeping in what used to be Marcus's home office.

Marcus had ordered pizza that evening and informed her she'd have a salad. She didn't care, as long as she was sharing the meal with her sons. Mattie did most of the talking while Dayton listened quietly, his eyes turned down. He was old enough to know this artificial normal was nothing but fake playacting meant to cover up something very bad.

They seemed to have questions but hesitated to ask about their situation, which was unexpected but wise. Dayton watched his father carefully, as if somewhat disappointed in the man he'd found, a glorified hero embellished over time and almost forgotten with each passing year. She wished he had a better father, someone he could look up to and respect. But she wished for a lot of things that would never be.

At seven-thirty, Marcus announced it was time for the boys to go to bed. Chloe frowned. They were nine and seven. She usually let them stay up until at least eight-thirty. She was sure they'd object to such an early bedtime, but they didn't. They dutifully stood and kissed her cheek.

"Will you read me a story, Mommy?" Mattie whispered as his little arms wreathed her neck.

Marcus, overhearing the sweet request, answered before she had the chance. "Not tonight, Matthew. Your mother's had a long day and we need to discuss some things privately."

She tried not to worry over what those 'things' might be.

After the boys were sent to bed she cleaned up the kitchen while Marcus sat at the table supervising. Odd changes had been made to their old home. Child safety locks had been replaced with key locks. She couldn't open any drawers that contained the knives or silverware. All cabinets housing cleaning products and chemicals were locked away as well. All the windows had locks and all the knobs in the house had been replaced to require a key. Their home had become a prison.

Worry over fire safety added to the sour knot in her stomach. An alarm system had been installed, the control panel located by the front door and another upstairs outside of the master bedroom.

As Marcus shut off the lights and walked her up the stairs, he blocked her view of the panel and typed in a code. There were a series of beeps.

"If anything heavier than a kitten touches that floor, the alarm will sound and the cops will arrive within six minutes."

As she turned to the empty room she now considered hers, he caught her arm and she shivered. "We're going to try something different tonight."

He waved a hand toward the master bedroom and her old cell suddenly called to her like a sanctuary. Being locked in that hollow vault was better than sharing a bed with him. So many horrible memories.

Marcus nudged her into the room and she slowly stepped to what was once her side of the bed, the knot in her stomach tightening painfully. The door shut and locked with an unsettling click.

"Remove your clothes."

Shutting her eyes, she comforted herself with the fact that she saw her boys today. He'd kept his word and if she kept up her agreeable act, she might see them again tomorrow, so she did as he said. She endured once more, every forced surrender stealing a bit of her dignity she'd never get back.

She cringed as his fingers tripped over her flesh with cool, placid entitlement. His calm unsettled her and her muscles jerked with every caress, her instinct to pull away enough to make her whole body tremble.

He made her feel dead, like a frog pinned to a sheet of wax in a high school science lab, prostrate to his poking, prodding, and mental dissection. She'd bear it. Build up her strength and get the fuck out of this place eventually.

She tried to escape twice before. Once she failed and he'd broken her hand. The second time she wasn't so careless. This time she'd have to be even more cautious.

Her mind slipped away as he entered her. It hurt, but she did little more than gasp and wheeze as his weight settled on top of her, rutting into her with punishing thrusts and grunts. Arms going numb under his weight, she shut her eyes and waited for it to be over.

She hurt from places she couldn't name. She hurt in her heart. She hurt from hunger and thirst. She hurt from thinking too hard. She hurt on the outside and even worse on the inside. She hurt so much she didn't know if she'd ever not hurt again.

When he finished she felt more like a receptacle than a human being. She lay there, staring blindly at the wall, as he caught his breath beside her. How many more times could she survive that? If he didn't beat her to death, he'd kill her in other ways. Her mind was already fragmenting, her usual thought patterns forgotten and replaced with a sort of cognitive gibberish.

Standing, he wrapped a robe around himself and handed her a nightgown. She slipped it over her body.

"Come with me."

Hopeful that he might be returning her to her cell, she did as he said. Walls between them—locked doors or not—were always better than suffering next to him.

He unlocked the door to the empty bedroom and held out a hand. "Take this."

Another pill, this one small and blue. All the drugs he forced on her over the past two days probably weren't helping her stomach, but the thought of mental oblivion was tempting. Only... She had to remain coherent in case anything happened with her boys. It was better not to take it.

"I'm already exhausted, Marcus. I promise I'll sleep. I'm—"

"It's not a sleeping pill. It's birth control."

This might be the nicest thing he'd offered her in years. She took the pill and willingly swallowed it. "I'll be back in a few hours." He shut the door and locked it.

Her body sagged. Finally, she was alone. She walked into the bathroom and filled the tub, wanting every last trace of him off her.

# Thirty-One

IF SHE BELIEVED she'd get a night of undisturbed sleep, she was wrong. Perhaps it was the boy's presence that brought him through the door each night. It was as if he waited for those pre-dawn hours when the children were sleeping, biding his time to catch her off guard and inflict his rage.

There was no preparing for a monster in your bed. No way to protect oneself when said monster woke you from a dead sleep. Ripped from her slumber, gasping and choking on her pain, he never gave much of a chance to assimilate. Catching her off guard was, what she believed, his favorite part of hurting her, perhaps retribution for having his world pulled out from under him six years ago.

Chloe wasn't sure if he'd ever forgive her. She didn't need or want his forgiveness. She'd never be sorry for those peaceful years she stole for herself and her children. The only thing she needed was a way out. She vowed with every thought that she would escape again.

When he drove the kids to school she was a shell of the person she had been the day before. Her hope was of the thinnest ice, fragile and tenuous, and she feared any more pressure might leave her drowning in an abyss of broken dreams and pain. All of her hope that Jeremy understood her clues enough to get her the fuck out of here seemed a universe away.

He was a monster, a broken mind that drew thrills from her agony. When she cried, he twisted harder. When her knees buckled, he laughed and kicked her. When she refused to stand up and walk to him, he came to her and stomped on her foot until the bones popped.

As her body cried for relief, her mind battled to make sense of such injustice, and her heart broke under the weight of uncertainty. Was she protecting her children by adapting or was she failing them?

Days felt like years. Minutes passed like weeks. Two days? Three? She hadn't been here long, but he'd broken her so fast she'd somehow misplaced her logic. There was pain, cruel verbal lashings, rape, endless taunting and threats, and no escape in sight. Perhaps it would be weeks before she regained her strength and found a way out. But she knew she only had days before losing her mind completely.

Every minute, her perception became more skewed, the unbearable reality of her existence erasing memories as if they were written in something as removable as chalk. Normal was so far away from this place, so unreachable, her surrender became less of a choice and more of a condition, borne of insufficient strength, exhaustion, and an inability to suffer anymore.

*Mercy...*

The word fluttered through her mind several times that morning, yet she didn't breathe a sound. It was as useless in her head as it would be to his ears. He had a merciless, evil soul, and the thread of survival instinct she still held was slipping away. The mind was a scary place when wishes of death intercepted the necessity to save her children.

That's what Marcus did. He made life so miserable, so unbearable, her will to live became a flicker of light that grew too dim to find in the dark.

Her thoughts were sporadic and disjointed. Every time he laid a hand on her another piece of her died. Memories of the past collided with the present, and the in-between seemed just a dream.

When he returned he marched her downstairs and demanded she make him breakfast. Why wasn't he at work? The thought had been weighing on her more and more.

Her body was as off as her mind and her motor skills were severely suffering. When she delicately tried to flip the second-attempted egg, Marcus hovered at her shoulder. She whimpered as the yolk bled onto the whites.

"Get out of my way." He shoved her aside, throwing the copper pan into the sink. "Is it that fucking hard? It's easier to teach a dog tricks!"

When he reached for her, she cowered. He grabbed her arm and she screamed, terrified, as he dragged her up the stairs. Tumbling to her knees, she pleaded and begged, apologizing for things outside of her control. The anticipation of the unknown sent her into a spiraling hysteria.

Her cries silenced on a startled sob as he slapped her. "Shut up!" He shoved her into the empty room. "You're useless."

The door slammed and locked. A few seconds later the garage door rumbled and his car sped down the street. Falling to her knees, she covered her face and cried. She couldn't take any more. Her body collapsed to the carpet as she pulled her knees to her chest and wept.

She no longer wasted the energy on trying to track time. And she couldn't sleep for fear of leaving herself unprotected again. Her stomach cramped painfully, knots of tension tightening around her hollow gut.

The hum of Marcus's Mercedes had her sucking in a breath. No more.

Her wild thoughts quieted as she awaited the rumble of the garage door that didn't come. A car door slammed and then another door. Footsteps pounded up the steps and her heartbeat shook through her in utter pandemonium.

"*Chloe!*" At Marcus's shout, she wrapped her arms around her head and braced for whatever was coming for her. The key hit the lock and the door flung open.

He stalked toward her and she recoiled, bracing for a strike. Her eyes opened at the sound of a click.

"Damn it." He cursed when the bathroom light didn't turn on. "The power's out. Take a shower. I'll be back in five minutes."

The door slammed and locked. She blinked at the empty room as her heart struggled to slow. The power had gone out? Would he blame her for that, too?

As she rinsed off in the shower the lights flickered. Marcus returned saying something about a blown breaker and told her to get dressed.

"The kitchen floor needs mopping."

She was filling up the bucket in the sink, Marcus resetting the oven clock after the power outage when the doorbell rang and they both stilled.

"Don't forget to clean under the burners when you do the counters. Do that before you do the floor," Marcus instructed before leaving the room to answer the door.

She grabbed her rag and lifted the burner, her ears never losing track of his proximity.

"Yes? Can I help you?" His voice carried from the hall.

"...from PDW Alarm. We were notified of an interruption in your service. I just need to check the main panels then I can be on my way—make sure everything's running properly."

The rag fell from her trembling hands as the stranger's voice struck a familiar chord. Keeping her head down, she wiped her way closer to the edge of the counter as Marcus showed the man where the two control panels were.

"It's just these two key panels in the house?" the man asked.

"Yes. Is this going to take long? I'm in the middle of something."

"I should only be a minute."

She finished at the stove and moved to wipe the kitchen chairs, keeping her eyes hidden by her lashes as she seesawed her gaze between the chair and the hall. The man's voice was deep. The recognizable way he dropped his vowels made her neck prickle. At the sound of footsteps, she lowered her eyes to her work.

"Make sure you get in between the rungs," Marcus said as he placed his coffee cup in the sink and walked back into the hall.

"This is a nice home you got here, sir. Everything should be running fine now. I checked the sensors in each bedroom. It's just the four, correct?"

"Yes."

The man came into view and Chloe's gaze traveled over his shoes. Yellow work boots tucked under blue slacks led her eyes up to a trim waist and a PDW Contractors shirt. He was taller than Marcus and her breath sucked in when her gaze lifted to his face.

Bright green eyes and wavy blond hair. "That should be all then, sir. Just sign here." As Marcus bent over the clipboard to sign, Trenton's brother-in-law looked over his shoulder, right into her eyes and winked. "Thank you very much." He tucked the clipboard under his arm and handed Marcus a card. "You let us know if you have any more issues."

"Thanks. I will."

As the man left, the alarm system let out a short beep, announcing that the door was closed tightly. Marcus clicked the locks. "Those chairs aren't going to clean themselves."

Her focus staggered as she wiped down the rest of the chairs. Marcus sat, observing her.

"Do the floors now."

As she pushed the mop over the tile floor, which hid layers of grime in the corners, her thoughts spun. Pete was here. Was it Pete or someone who remarkably resembled him? No, he winked. It had to be him. Was he here with Trenton? Were they coming back for her? The boys?

It became difficult to breathe as she tried to understand what this meant. Did they know the boys weren't here? She had no idea what school Marcus had enrolled them in.

She carefully rinsed the mop in the bucket. "The... The boys seem to like their new school."

He glanced up from his paper. "I'll be enrolling Matthew in Martial Arts this week. He needs to toughen up. No son of mine will be bullied."

She didn't reply. He wasn't asking her permission.

After finishing the floor he instructed her to make lunch. Marcus would enjoy a turkey sandwich with torn lettuce and soup, while she was permitted only the lettuce. Though she had no access to sharp utensils, she was able to stir the soup with a rubber spatula.

As she placed his plate on the table the doorbell rang again pulling an irritated huff from Marcus. Her stomach clenched. Marcus leaned back in his chair so he could see the door and wiped his mouth, tossing his napkin on the table.

"Fucking bible beaters."

Hovering by the table, she glanced at the front door. A narrow-framed male in black pants and a short-sleeved dress shirt waited on the other side of the glass panel.

"No matter how many times I send them away they keep coming back. Worse than fucking locusts." He stood and went to the door.

Chloe watched, unblinking as he unlocked the door.

"Hello. My name's Ben. I'm from Holy Calvary."

Chloe's heart stopped beating as *Tommy* handed a brochure to Marcus. What was happening? First Pete, now Tommy. Where were they hiding?

"We're visiting the area today to spread the word of the Holy Spirit and invite friends to share in the message of our savior Jesus Christ. Do you feel the Spirit speaking to you? We believe everyone can be *saved.*"

She stared, unable to process what he was saying. This was Tommy, her silly, funny, never serious, flamboyant, *agnostic* neighbor. Yet it wasn't. He was speaking in a southern lilt—wearing clothing Tommy wouldn't be caught dead wearing.

Numb, her breath coming fast, she wanted to cry out, demand that he get her out of there.

"We belong to the Catholic Church." Marcus began to shut the door.

"That's wonderful. We'll be celebrating our savior today at one. We'd like to invite your family to join us down at the park. At *one. Today.*"

"No, thank you. We don't need to be saved."

"Sir, *everyone* can be saved."

"I said we're not interested." The door closed.

The pot of soup hissed on the stove and she moved to stir in the rice. Marcus returned to the kitchen and tossed the brochures on the counter. It appeared to be legitimate church flyers. But the bold print on the front caught her eye.

**_ALL CHILDREN will be saved TODAY._**
   *1:00 pm*

Her gaze darted to the oven clock. 12:43. What was happening in seventeen minutes? How would they save her boys? That had to be what this message meant. *All children...* They were going to save her babies and then—hopefully—come for her.

## Thirty-Two

THERESA ST. John gathered the last of the attendance records and stood, pausing as a woman stepped to the counter. "May I help you?"

"Hi. I'm Chloe Hunt, Dayton and Mattie's mom. I forgot the boys have a dentist appointment this afternoon." She slid an appointment card across the counter with the local dentist's name on it. "I've been so busy with moving and unpacking since we returned, it completely slipped my mind. I really need to find my day planner. I swear a mother's lost without one."

Theresa grinned, identifying. She had children and knew how overwhelming managing all the day-to-day appointments of a family could be. "I completely understand. Would you like me to have their teachers send them down?"

"Thank you. I hate interrupting their second day, but this appointment was made a month ago. I'm hoping to have them back before the end of the day." She chuckled. "I guess it depends on how well the boys have been brushing. Can you believe Dayton had two cavities at his last check-up?"

Theresa laughed. "I'm constantly harassing my youngest to brush his teeth. I swear he just runs his toothbrush under water and puts it back. Sign here and I'll need to see your ID."

Mrs. Hunt withdrew her wallet and placed her driver's license on the counter. Theresa searched the small card catalog and found the blue card under H, matching the name of the woman to the name of Dayton and Matthew's mother. Yes, Chloe Hunt. She paged the boys' teachers, asking the children be sent down to the office with their things.

Mrs. Hunt sat patiently in one of the chairs along the wall, her long, slender form at ease as she made small talk. "Counting down the days until summer yet?"

Theresa picked up her mug. "And sleeps. June can't come soon enough. They should be down in a couple minutes."

"If we don't make it back before the end of the day, should I have the dentist sign a note saying that they were there?"

"Yes, that way it'll be filed as an excused absence."

"I expect we shouldn't be too long."

Theresa waved a hand. "Don't trouble yourself if it's close to dismissal. Avoid the traffic."

The boys entered the office, hesitated, and then grinned widely the moment they spotted their mother. Mrs. Hunt stood. "There are my beautiful sons. I forgot we scheduled your dentist appointments for today, boys. This move has me so scattered. Come along."

"Wh—where's Dad... Mom?"

"At work, silly. Come on, we don't want to be late."

"Have a nice day." Theresa finished her coffee before lifting the blue card from the counter to return it to the file box. Only then did she noticed the note written on the back.

*Mr. Hunt will make all pick-ups and drop-offs. Please contact him directly before allowing anyone else to sign out Dayton or Matthew Hunt.*

She frowned and read over the number provided. Surely that didn't include the boys' mother. To be safe she'd call to make sure he was aware the children left early for an appointment.

# Thirty-Three

CHLOE CAUGHT HER BREATH, her weight resting generously on the counter as she stirred the soup, her heart beating erratically as she watched another minute pass on the clock.

"What's taking so long with that soup?"

Her eyes closed as she wished a thousand painful deaths on him. "It's almost ready."

"It's lunch, not dinner."

"Did you want saltines?" Her hands shook as she stirred the steaming pot.

Marcus's chair scraped along the freshly polished floor. She tensed as he approached. "It's done. Let's go. I swear you're like a sloth."

"The rice needs another min—"

"Are you fucking deaf? I said it's done."

Her gaze shifted to the clock. 12:52. What was happening in eight minutes?

He slammed the cabinet and pushed a bowl on the counter. *Six minutes.* Her eyes scanned the obstacles keeping her here. *The door. The locks. Trying to outrun him. Failure. Pain.*

Her stomach lurched and she cupped a hand over her mouth, bile rushing up her throat at the thought of so many complications. Saliva built in her mouth but her stomach only locked painfully.

"Problem?"

Her head shook as she swallowed against her jangling nerves, but the nausea remained. That ache in her side was getting worse, pinching every time she took a breath and stabbing whenever she stood. *If someone doesn't save them I'm going to die here.*

Sluggishly reaching for the bowl, she flinched as his cell phone rang. *Four minutes.*

"Hello... Speaking..."

She hesitated, her attention focused on him as his posture stiffened.

"*What?* My *wife* is standing right next to me. What did she look like?"

She flinched as his hand closed around her forearm and squeezed painfully. He glared at her.

"*I'm calling the police. And you can clean out your desk, you fucking idiot!* As soon as I figure out who has my sons I'll be ensuring you never have a job around other people's children again!"

Chloe froze. Someone had her boys?

Marcus gripped his phone, ending the call and already dialing 911. "*Don't fucking move!*" He brought the phone to his ear and paced. "I need to report a kidnapping. I was just notified that a woman with dark brown hair, blue eyes, approximately five foot nine, signed my children out of school using a fake ID with my wife's name."

Her mind raced trying to think of anyone fitting that description who would be able to pass for her. But the school didn't know her, so they had no basis for comparison.

The keys he kept in his pocket rattled as he flipped through the ring. He unlocked a drawer and Chloe panicked at the sight of his gun. Breathing unsteadily, backing into the oven away from the gun, she looked at his hand then looked at the clock. 12:59. He checked the cylinder and she saw it was loaded.

"The secretary, a Mrs. St. John, signed them out, to a woman I don't know, without contacting me first. I want the secretary detained until I find my sons. I intend to press charges."

As if in slow motion the numbers switched to one-zero-zero and something clicked inside of her.

*All children will be saved...*

Marcus's phone slammed on the counter and her body was shoved into the cabinets. *"What did you do? If I find out you had something to do with this I'll fucking kill you!"*

Her hands went protectively to her face. "Marcus, I don't know what's happening."

"I know you did this!" The blurred image of his body lunged and she screamed. Past her breaking point, she reached to the stove and hurled the pot of boiling soup at his face.

*"Don't touch me!"*

*"Ah! Fucking bitch!"*

The gun fell to the floor as he covered his face, screaming in pain as he jerked back and pivoted, bending, screeching.

*"Fucking cunt!"* He roared in agony as the steaming broth scalded, blisters rising upon contact.

She bolted out of the kitchen and raced to the front door.

*"You fucking bitch! I'll kill you!"* He stumbled after her, slipping in the spill on the floor.

She ran as fast as she could, ignoring her body's protests. Her palms slapped into the door, her hand fumbling over the knob. Footsteps pounded after her.

She jerked at the door, scrambled to twist the lock, yanking, but the door wouldn't budge. *The deadbolt!* Her shuddering fingers flipped the lock and the door pulled away from the frame, the alarm screeching, as he crashed into her with the full force of his weight.

She screamed, plummeting into the door and falling to the foyer floor as he tackled her. Something smacked into her eye as the flash of metal waved in her face. Her vision blurred under the flood of warm blood as he wrestled her to her back.

*"You think you're getting away?"* His fist tangled in her hair, wrenching back her head as cold metal pressed into her cheek. *"Where are my sons?"*

Her nails clawed down his face. She scratched at his raw flesh, drawing blood as he roared and jerked back.

*"Get off me!"* She twisted, scurrying on her belly to the door.

He dragged her, punched the back of her head, and thrust her to her back. *"Bitch!"*

He shook her, jerking the breath from her lungs as his fingers closed around her throat. The gun pressed into her eye as he strangled her. She tore at his hands, unable to draw in a breath. The gun clicked, their bodies jostling with his aim as she frantically tried to move.

Her lungs burned, her strength sapping as she silently begged for mercy. Her arms grappled, shoving him to no avail. Her hand pushed the gun away and he shoved it back to her face. Air cut off as her windpipe closed under the pressure. Arms flailing, eyes watering, her fingers clawed as the lack of oxygen burned her chest. Her legs thumped against the floor as he grunted in her ear.

Rapid flashes of her children and their home in Pennsylvania rushed through her mind. Her freedom. Faces of those she loved. Tommy and Adam. Her boys. Jade. Her Aunt Gina. *Trenton.*

Her sight winked out of color, the edges of her peripheral vision fading to black. *Dayton's sweet face... Mattie's tender hugs... Her boys.*

She couldn't leave them. Bringing up her knee, she shoved it into his groin and a shot exploded. Particles of shattered tile stung her face as her eyes burned and all sound disappeared in a piercing hum, whooshing back as if her ears were now stuffed with cotton.

She gasped and choked for breath, attacking the arm holding the gun and biting down on his hand until she tasted blood. He screamed and she jerked it out of his grip, falling to her back. Barely able to see, she raised the weapon and pointed it at him. "They're *my* fucking sons."

Her fingers pinched as her hands jerked, another deafening blow cracking through the air. The force of the shot stole her balance. A dark stain bloomed under his shirt. He careened forward, grabbing into the air and she pulled the trigger again, blasting a hole in the sheetrock.

Tripping over his feet, he sagged into the wall, his body leaving a smear of blood as he fell. Gurgled breaths wheezed as he strained to grab her.

Her arms shook violently as she leveled the gun as best she could and pulled the trigger again, landing a bullet in his throat. She gasped in shock as blood spurted like black oil as his lax body collapsed.

Horrified she stumbled back as he twitched and the world went silent. Motionless. Marcus's eyes faded to milky white as they stared at her.

Her fast breath sounded like a siren to her ears. The gun clattered to the floor. She exhaled with a sickening wheeze, coughing blood into her hand and struggling to breathe as she collapsed. No more.

*No more.*

*No ... more...*

# *Thirty-Four*

THE ALERT CAME through the radio just as Trent's sister's text hit his phone. "Phoenix has the boys. She and Tommy are heading back now. We don't have much time."

"Let's move." Pete threw the van into drive and floored it. "We have to move fast if the police were already notified. That means he knows they're missing."

Trent didn't waste time on comments. He gripped his gun and opened the door before the van stopped. An alarm squealed and his blood turned to ice as a shot rent the air. "Fuck!"

The van rammed into the curb and he stumbled onto the grass, his legs pumping as he raced over the lawns, his eyes on Hunt's house, his finger on the trigger.

Leaping over a low row of hedges, he spotted Hunt's car in the driveway. Another shot blasted from within the house. *"Chloe!"*

His heart burst with fear as another shot exploded. His feet slid out from under him as he skidded around the car. *"Chloe!"*

The piercing shrill of the alarm was deafening. He shoved into the door, grunting with effort as it grudgingly gave. On the floor, a bloody hand, tipped with chipped polish, came into view and his heart stuttered.

"No." He pointed his gun through the opening and carefully shoved his way in, his gaze torn between the heap on the floor and Chloe's wilted form behind the door.

"Baby." He crouched, quickly placing a finger on her pulse and shoving away the gun by her side. He panted, rushing to the body filling the hall and using the toe of his boot to get a better look. Hunt's cold, lifeless eyes stared back at him.

*Jesus Christ...* Turning, he holstered his gun and dropped to his knees. Blood speckled her knuckles and covered her face. "Chloe, I'm here."

A ravaged cough, painful to his ears, preceded a moan. The wind knocked out of him as he took in her battered face, her throat a mass of purple bruising, blood seeping from a cut above her eye.

"Chloe, baby, open your eyes." Tears blurred his vision as he carefully pulled her wilted body onto his lap. "We got the boys. They're safe." Sirens whined in the distance. "The police are on their way."

She lay, unconscious, her face, hair, and eyes smeared with blood. The gash by her eye continued gushing slick crimson. He pressed his fingers over the wound to slow the bleeding as he cradled her face in his arms. The air filled with the metallic scent.

"He can't hurt you anymore. You're safe now..." He rocked, fighting to catch his breath and stop the bleeding.

His jaw quivered as he carefully examined the laceration marks around her delicate neck. A strangled sob left his throat. Her pulse remained light, the slightest ripple of a butterfly wing. "You're gonna be all right. Everything's going to be all right." He needed to hear the promise out loud.

"Jesus." Pete stood in the doorway, his eyes wide at the sight of so much violence.

"She's gonna be all right," Trent told him in a hoarse voice he barely recognized.

Pete assessed the other body with a quick once over and nodded. "Let's get her out of here."

Cradling her flaccid body in his arms, he rose to his knees as Pete held the door. The alarm coming from inside the house blended with the nearing sirens. He collapsed on the lawn, rocking her body with his. Pete's shadow fell over them.

"Don't let the boys see her like th—this. Tell Phoenix to get them out of here."

Pete's voice whispered behind him as a rush of lights flashed. Squad cars and an ambulance crowded the curb as people neared and voices spoke to him. He couldn't make sense of their words and panicked as a gloved set of hands tried to pull her out of his arms. "She's hurt."

"We're going to help her, sir. You need to give us space."

He let go and swallowed back a gasp. His heart

filled his throat as they laid her body out on the lawn. He reached for her curled fingers, delicately holding them in his. "You're gonna be all right, baby. You're safe now."

Random thoughts rushed through his head. Her smile. The sound of her laugh. Making love. The sight of her blush. The fear in her eyes the first time she looked at him in that subway six years ago. The way she looked at him the other day when Hunt told her the truth of his betrayal. The way she looked now.

He dragged the back of his hand under her eyes. "I'm so sorry, Chloe."

Marcus Hunt was dead and that should bring him some level of satisfaction, but seeing what it had cost her... No one deserved this.

He could have prevented this if they'd moved faster. When the cops warned him to keep away, he should have argued harder. He told them Hunt was lying, but Chloe had given a statement confirming Hunt's accusations. How terrified she must have been to lie for that animal.

His lips trembled as they lifted her onto a stretcher. He hovered, never letting go of her hand. "Be careful with her."

Pete's hand closed over his shoulder. "The cops need—"

"They can wait. I'm not leaving her side."

His brother in law nodded. "We'll be right behind you."

# Thirty-Five

CHLOE'S MIND came awake and she grimaced, her throat raw, each jagged breath scraping painfully along her larynx. She needed water. She tried to open her eyes, but they seemed sewn shut. Panic pressed down on her chest.

*Where am I?*

A faint chirp beeped, the speed increasing as her lungs tightened, incredible pressure bearing down on her chest.

"Help," she wheezed in a soundless whisper.

Her fingers twitched, closing over air until they tripped over wires. Then a soft hand grasped hers. "Shh, shh, shh. You're safe, dear. You're at Walter Reed Hospital. Just relax," a female voice soothed.

"My boys?" she mouthed.

"Your boys are safe. I was just about to clean you up. There's a handsome man who's been very eager to see you."

What man? Marcus? Her head shook and she winced as pain lanced down her shoulder.

"Easy. You don't want to move too much just yet."

Why couldn't she see? "Don't let ... him near ... my boys..." She forced her voice out, her body trembling at the effort and pain.

"Is she awake?" another female voice asked.

"Just coming out of it. Why don't you get the man waiting—"

Her breath came faster. "No..."

"Easy, hon. I'm fixing your IV to help with the pain."

*No more drugs.* "No..."

"I'll get the doctor."

Chloe's mind spun, her memory a jigsaw of images that made no sense. She needed to find Dayton and Mattie. "Please..."

"Shh... The doctor will be here in a minute."

She couldn't hold on. Her mind fought to stay awake, but she was too weak.

~

Trenton watched as Chloe slept. The nurse said she'd woken up briefly during a sponge bath, but was disoriented and upset. She'd fallen back to sleep by the time he was permitted back in the room. He'd never forgive himself for letting Marcus do this to her.

She was hardly recognizable. Her eyes were swollen holes of black. Her nose was puffy. Her lips were split, her throat black and blue. Even her hands and arms showed bruises. He had thought that was the extent of her injuries, but he was wrong. So. Very. Wrong.

Her injuries ran from her face all the way to her ankle that showed a hairline fracture in the x-rays. Fresh welts and bruises layered over other marks, some days old, others only just forming. She had three broken ribs, welts up the backs of her legs, and her hip looked as if it were wrapped in a storm cloud.

Then there were internal injuries. He hadn't been able to hear any more after they discussed the damage done to her cervix and the long-term issues she might face. It seemed impossible one man could do so much damage in a matter of days. If he wasn't strong enough to hear it, how the hell had she been strong enough to endure it?

This was his fault. He could have somehow stopped it from getting to this point. He'd been there, knew she was being manipulated and kept against her will, and he fucking left.

There wouldn't be a trial. The evidence was plain to see. So plain, he struggled to keep himself in check each time he looked at her. And yet, the true extent of the damage was still to come. She might never be the same again.

A soft moan drew his focus to her face. Her lashes twitched. He sat forward, carefully cradled her hand, but it remained slack. "Doll? Can you hear me?"

Her lips twitched. "Day—Matt—"

His body shuddered at the rasp of her voice. "They're safe at my sister's. She's been calling every hour to check in. Adam and Tommy are with them."

Her brow pinched then smoothed. "Marcus?"

His mouth firmed. "He's gone."

Her lips parted as if she were releasing a breath she'd been holding for over a decade. He brushed a finger softly over her arm.

"You should rest."

Her fingers briefly tightened around his. "Hero."

His gaze lowered. He wasn't a hero. A hero would have stopped this when he had the chance. "Get some sleep. I'll be here when you wake up."

As she drifted, he kept vigil. A little after midnight she awoke and asked for water. Trenton held a straw between her lips and helped her take a sip. She coughed but tried again. Every time she woke up she asked about her sons. Each time, he assured her that they were safe and sound.

Adam called his cell the following morning. He tried to speak softly but the ring must have woken her.

"My boys?"

He held the phone away from his face and reached for her hand. "No, sweetheart. It's Adam. The boys are still sleeping."

She squeezed his hand weakly. "Let me talk."

Her voice was little more than a pained rasp, but he couldn't tell her no. Holding the phone to her ear, he waited as she caught her breath.

"Adam," she sighed and smiled weakly. Words were said on the other end that he couldn't make out. "Love you, too." She turned her head away and Trenton knew she was finished.

He offered Adam a quick goodbye and returned his phone to his pocket.

Her left eye had a broken blood vessel that filled the white with murky red. Seeing her look up at him with those familiar brown eyes so battered broke him in two.

Pressing his brow to their entwined fingers, he hid his tears. "I'm so sorry, Chloe. I'm so fucking sorry."

"Don't cry..." Her whisper crawled into him, so calming and heartbreaking. "You saved me. You saved my boys."

But he hadn't. She saved herself at a terrible cost because he was too late. He'd let a stupid warning from the police slow him down when his gut told him there wasn't time. A restraining order never would have stopped an animal like Marcus Hunt, so why had he let it slow him?

He'd been on the phone non-stop, reaching out to child services, coordinating with Pete and Jeremy to work out a plan. But he knew she'd never leave until her children were safe. And his theory they were in danger wasn't enough to spur a response from children's services. Not until this morning had someone from CPS returned his call. He told them it was handled, but really he wanted to tell them to get fucked.

Thankfully, after everything that went down, Dayton and Mattie hadn't seen the extent of the damage their mother suffered. There were some big talks happening and he trusted his sister to handle the situation with care. The boys knew something was wrong the day their father took them out of school. Trenton's heart broke for them as much as it did for Chloe.

He sniffed and tried to get his emotions in check.

"Don't be sad," she whispered.

All he'd wanted a week ago was her trust, but now it slayed him. He didn't deserve her affection or her forgiveness. "This is my fault."

"No. It's Marcus's."

He lifted his head, looking into her battered eyes. "I would have stopped him from finding you and the boys if I knew he was close. Please believe that. I *love* you, baby."

A tear slid down her cheek. "Saved me twice."

He wouldn't argue with her, but he knew it was a lie. She saved herself.

They tried to keep anything with a reflection away from her for as long as possible, but once the nurse removed her catheter there was nothing to be done. She was expected to keep her ankle rested, iced, and elevated as much as possible over the next two weeks. With her foot in a boot the way it was and her other injuries still tender, she had a long road of recovery ahead, but she insisted to see her reflection, demanding to know what her boys would see when they saw her.

Reluctantly, Trent brought her a mirror. Her head tilted as she studied herself, her fingers ghosting over the injuries she could see.

"You'll heal, doll."

She began to cry. "They can't see me like this."

His heart broke again, knowing how badly she wanted to reunite with her children, but agreeing with her all the same. They couldn't see how bad her injuries were. "You'll heal fast."

She lowered the mirror and shut her eyes. "He..." A tear rolled down her cheek. "He used to be so careful not to hit my face."

His molars locked, thinking of the damage he'd inflicted beneath her gown. "You scared him. He wasn't thinking in the end because he knew he was going to lose. You won, Chloe."

"I feel like I lost."

He swallowed against the lump in his throat. "No. You won."

Once she was discharged nothing could stop him from getting her out of this god-forsaken town. Chloe agreed to let the boys stay with Pete and Phoenix a while longer. Her voice had a long way to recover, so she used his phone to text them hourly. They had lots of questions and the conversations quickly exhausted her.

He filled his truck with pillows and blankets so she wouldn't jostle too much on the ride. The pain pills seemed to help her sleep. A nurse was scheduled to visit the house once they got settled and he was determined to make sure she got there safely.

He'd thought she'd been asleep as they crossed through Maryland, but she surprised him by reaching for his hand and whispering, "We've been here before."

He glanced at her and tried to smile. How was she taking this so much better than him? "It's where we first met."

She smiled, her eyes tired. "Trenton ... Get me home."

His hand closed tighter around hers. "Always."

He'd called ahead for Adam to unlock the house. When they arrived in New Castle it was four in the morning. As he pulled into her driveway he spotted her neighbors waiting by her front door.

He carefully carried Chloe up the front steps. "She's asleep," he whispered as Adam held the door.

Tommy anxiously waited inside, his eyes wide as Trent carried her to her room. He tucked her into bed and the three of them stood over her, silently wiping their eyes.

"I never imagined..." Adam breathed. Tommy totally broke down, sobbing into his hands, and exiting the room.

Trent stood stoically, awaiting their blame, but it never came. When Adam's hand touched his back, attempting to comfort, Trent lowered his head.

Adam looked at him, his mouth compressed in a sad smile. "Don't do that."

"Do what?"

"This is happening to all of us. And none of us are to blame."

"I should have saved her."

"You did."

"I should have saved her sooner."

"See if telling yourself that makes this easier on anyone, Trenton. We can't go backward. This is where we are and we can only move forward from here."

# Thirty-Six

CHLOE AWOKE to the sound of whispering. She was home. She felt it in her tired bones before she even opened her eyes. *Home.*

Blinking at the familiar yellow ceiling of her bedroom, she focused on what was being said, but her head was foggy from all the painkillers. Trenton whispered and a woman's voice she didn't recognize answered him softly.

"Good morning, beautiful."

She grimaced, knowing she wasn't even passing for attractive. Swallowing, she winced, the movement still a little painful.

"Here, have some water." Trenton held a glass with a straw to her lips.

His eyes had dark shadows and his jaw needed a shave. She sipped, scrutinizing him. "Did you ... sleep?"

"I'm fine. Do you need anything? Are you in pain?"

"Bathroom." Her throat was unbelievably sore.

The woman at the door stepped forward. "Chloe, my name's Sue. I'm your nurse for the next week. I'm here to check on your injuries, show you some physical therapy exercises, and help in any way I can. What do you say I help you to the bathroom and from there we get you cleaned up? How does a bath sound?"

Her eyes closed on a long blink. "Divine."

Trent reached to lift her, but Sue placed a staying hand on his shoulder. Chloe almost laughed at the threatening look he shot the nurse.

"Mr. Cole, she needs to use her muscles in order to heal. Let's give Chloe a chance to sit up and try to walk on her own?"

"She has a fracture—"

"Yes, and she also has a crutch. Chloe, do you think you can pull yourself up?" She held out an arm and Chloe struggled to rise but made it. "Good. Want to try walking to the bathroom?"

Nodding stiffly, she slid her legs to the side of the bed. Trenton gently adjusted the crutch under her arm as Sue helped her find her balance.

"Careful of your ribs," he warned.

He followed as she slowly hobbled to the bathroom. At the doorway, she avoided her reflection, awkwardly shuffling the crutch out of the way as Sue helped her lower herself onto the toilet seat. By the time she was seated she was sweating and out of breath.

Trenton closed the door, giving them privacy and Sue started the tub. "Would you like me to add some of this?" She held up a bottle of sun ripened raspberry bubble bath.

Chloe frowned, unsure of where the bottle came from. "That's not mine."

Sue uncapped the bottle and shrugged. "It smells nice." She dumped the pink liquid into the bath and the room filled with a familiar scent of berries.

Once the tub was full, the nurse helped her undress. Still sitting on the toilet, Chloe's gaze dropped to her legs. Her skin was hideous. Her face was a mess. Her ankle was fractured, as were her ribs, and her limbs were incredibly weak. It was all suddenly too much to bear and she shook as tears fell down her face.

"Shh, it's okay. We'll take it slow." The nurse wrapped a clear plastic bag around her foot. After Sue helped to lower her into the warm water and made a pillow of soft towels for her foot, she shut her eyes and let the heat soothe her aching body.

Sue filled a pitcher with warm water. The gentle cascade trickled down her back, wetting her hair, as the nurse carefully protected her eyes, massaging shampoo into her sore scalp. "You're doing great."

Sue repeated the process with conditioner. It had been so long since she'd bathed properly and felt clean. She lathered up a soft brush, the kind the hospital gave new mothers for their newborns, and gently washed her skin.

"You'll be back to feeling like your regular self again in no time."

"I don't know if that'll ever happen."

"Sure, it will. Your friends told me how strong you are. They all believe in you. What do you say we take this old nail polish off while you soak?"

She looked at her chipped nails and grimaced. She was a disaster.

Sue stood and opened the medicine cabinet. "Exactly where I keep mine. Let me guess, the cotton balls are under the sink." She bent and retrieved the cotton balls with a smile.

Chloe silently watched as the woman swabbed away her old nail polish, and cleaned the grit from under her nails. Using a file, she smoothed out the jagged edges. By the time the water had chilled, she felt like a new woman. She was clean, shampooed, and ready for a painkiller and a nap.

Requesting Trenton wait in the other room, Sue helped her slip into a nightgown and tucked her into bed. "Is there anything else I can do before I go?"

The woman was such an angel Chloe found herself searching for wings and a halo. "You know that big man hovering around here?"

"Mr. Cole?"

"Please tell him to get some sleep."

"I'll try, but I'm not sure he'll listen to me. He seems set on keeping an eye on you. Why don't you ask him to come take a nap with you?"

The thought chilled her blood and she looked away. "I..."

"I'm sorry. I'll give him your message before I go. Try to rest and keep that foot elevated."

"Thank you."

∽

After the nurse left, Trenton went to check on Chloe. Her entire room smelled like raspberries. He was glad she'd found the bubble bath he'd asked Tommy to pick up for her.

She was sound asleep so he quietly refilled her glass with fresh water, pausing when her eyes opened.

"Sleep," she whispered.

"I didn't mean to wake you."

"No. *You* sleep."

"I'm okay. I was going to heat up some oatmeal or would you rather wait until after your nap?"

"Not hungry."

He wanted to lay with her but wasn't sure he was invited. "I'll let you rest."

"Trenton..."

He paused at the door, his heart flipping at the hope that she'd let him stay. "Yeah?"

"Leave the door open."

Nodding, he pushed the door and quietly left.

~

Trent smelled popcorn as he awoke on the couch.

*"That was the summer of 1963 - when everybody called me Baby, and it didn't occur to me to mind..."*

Someone sighed. "I love this movie."

"Me too." Chloe rasped. "I can't believe he died."

"I know. Tragic. Jennifer Grey should've never changed her nose. Also tragic."

At the sound of Chloe's laugh, Trent's eyes

opened. How long had she been awake? He shoved off the couch and headed to her room.

Tommy, propped up in the bed beside Chloe, glanced at him and smiled. "Morning, poodle. You snore."

He scowled. "You're getting popcorn on the bed."

"Ooh, and grumpy when you wake up." Tommy turned back to Chloe and said, "Remember in the eighties when they had the TV series *Dirty Dancing*?"

She laughed again. "Do you? You were, what, five?"

"Six. I remember it. I thought Charlie Stratton was *hawt*. I think that was the first time it occurred to me that I was gay. Well, that and how much I enjoyed decorating my Nana's dollhouse with miniatures."

She was sitting up, snuggled close to Tommy, another bowl of popcorn on her lap. *He* was supposed to make her something to eat—something that passed for nutrition. He would've given her actual food, not junk.

"Did you have lunch?" The sun was fading outside the window.

"I wasn't hungry."

"You should try to eat something more than popcorn."

Her eyes focused on the television as she nibbled a kernel. "This is fine."

"Chloe, you have to eat if you want your strength—"

"I said this is fine." The room chilled and she

gasped and covered her mouth. "I'm sorry, Trenton. I don't know why I snapped."

Maybe he was making too much out of nothing. "It's okay." Ignoring the tightness in his chest, he said, "You guys enjoy your movie." He should be happy she was enjoying herself at all, even if he wasn't included.

No one objected as he left the room.

~

"Your face looks a hundred times better today. Pretty soon you'll be able to cover up the last of the marks with just a dab of concealer." Sue stretched and flexed Chloe's wrist as they chatted on her bed.

"I miss makeup."

"So wear some."

"What's the point? I'd like to wear my lipstick, but I can't find it."

"I'll look for it when we're done here. If I can't find it I'll stop at the store on the way over tomorrow and pick some up for you. What brand do you like?"

Trent stepped away from the door, envy burning a hole in the pit of his stomach. Chloe was doing great. She often smiled and sometimes laughed, but never with him. She seemed happiest with Tommy or Sue or when speaking on the phone with her sons.

Adam didn't seem to mind that they were the odd men out. Maybe Adam didn't feel left out. But Trent did. He wanted to make her smile. He wanted to sit close to her. It had been days since she let him touch her. When he reached for her hand, she tensed and he always drew back. He didn't understand why she seemed to be avoiding his contact when she didn't seem to mind anyone else's.

When Sue arrived the next day Chloe immediately perked up. "Look what I got," the nurse cheered as she walked into Chloe's room, holding a bag from the drug store. She pulled out a small black tube.

"My lipstick!" Chloe smiled.

His hand went to his pocket, his fingers brushing the tube he'd been carrying for days. He should've given it back to her, but he'd grown so used to touching it in his pocket, he couldn't bear to let it go.

After Sue left, he brought Chloe lunch. She wasn't in bed. The bathroom door was cracked, light showing from the inside. The clatter of her crutch hitting the tile floor brought him rushing to the door. "Chloe—"

*"Get out!"*

She was sitting on the toilet, but not indecent. Her nightgown covered her thighs. He quickly bent for the crutch. "You should have—"

"I said, get out!"

Startled by her self-consciousness, he shut the door. Adam stood behind him holding a basket of laundry.

"Is she all right?"

Trent shook his head. "Tell her I'm running to the store. Text me if she needs anything."

~

Trent was selfishly relieved it was Sue's last day. He knew the nurse did a wonderful job restoring Chloe's confidence, but he wanted to be the one to do that. He wanted to take care of her. When she finally left, Chloe cried, and he felt terrible for wanting the nurse to go.

Trent went to comfort her, but, again, she shouldered away his touch. He tried not to panic at the gaping distance building between them. Now that she was more lucid, taking her pain meds less and less, she probably resented him for not being the hero she'd thought he was—if she even remembered saying such things.

Entering Dayton's room, he shut the door. He'd been sleeping in the small bed, finding it slightly more comfortable than the couch. But tomorrow the boys were coming home and that left him wondering if it was back to the couch or back to his empty home. He didn't like the thought of leaving her when things still felt awkward between them.

He'd been there for days but never found the right time to address his worries. The last thing he wanted to do was put more on her shoulders, so he kept his mouth shut and tried to be there when she needed something. But she definitely didn't seem to need *him*.

Needing some air, he headed out back and walked to face the trees at the edge of the property. He gripped his temples, palm over the bridge of his nose as tears of frustration burned his eyes.

"Hey."

Sucking back his emotions, he quickly blotted his eyes and turned to find Adam. "Hey."

"You okay?"

"Sure."

The man studied him. "No one's going to judge you for falling apart, Trenton."

He swallowed. He needed to stay strong for her. "I'm good."

"Wanna talk about it?"

"What's there to say?"

"Plenty."

Trent's shoulders sagged. "I feel like I can't reach her. Every time I try to comfort her, she pulls away."

Adam took a few steps closer. "You know, when we first moved here, Chloe never let anyone touch her other than the boys. It took years for her to actually hug us. At first, we thought it was because we were gay, but then we sort of figured it out."

"I can't make it years without being able to hold her hand. She lets Tommy sit with her and—"

"Tommy only wants to *sit* with her. Maybe she's afraid that won't be enough for you."

His gaze met Adam's. "I just want to be there for her."

"Then be patient. She'll come around."

He nodded, knowing the man was right. "She has nightmares."

"I'm not surprised."

Last night he'd heard her crying. She'd been sleeping with the lights on and he brought her a glass of water and a pill for the pain, but she didn't want the medicine. "She hasn't talked about what happened."

"And she might never talk about it. We can't force her."

"I'm not even sure she wants me here." Adam was silent and he worried he knew something Trent didn't. "Has she said anything to you?"

"She misses the boys. She won't be herself until they get here. Even then it might take a while for her to find normal again."

The question was, was he a part of that normal?

The day the boys returned home, Trenton understood how deeply she'd missed them. Chloe gathered them into her arms, kissing their heads as she cried. Her love for her children was so pure and profound it moved him in ways nothing else could. As an outsider looking in, it became a palpable truth how much she would endure to save them from the slightest danger, and his heart ached for the lengths she must have gone to see they were, for the most part, unharmed by Marcus Hunt.

As their young voices filled the house, so did tons of other visitors. People were constantly coming and going, wishing Chloe a fast recovery.

Some discoloration remained around her eyes and she still had her foot in a boot, but Trenton had no clue how the rest of her body was faring. He made sure she was eating three square meals a day, drinking plenty of fluids, taking her antibiotics, and resting. If she needed anything from the store he was her go-to guy. Adam kept the house tidy and Tommy was there to entertain her with the boys.

Once she started getting around easier, she

moved from her bedroom to the living room where she'd sit with visitors throughout the day. Eventually, she began attempting more of her regular tasks, getting frustrated whenever he offered to do something for her.

She wanted to be the one to make Mattie his peanut butter and jelly sandwiches so she could cut the crust just right. She also wanted to play video games with Dayton and sit outside in the sun, watching the boys while they kicked the soccer ball around.

She savored her time with her sons and decided they wouldn't be returning to school that year, as there were only a handful of days left. Trenton visited their teachers and collected work for the summer so they didn't start the following year behind. The school was very understanding of the family's circumstances.

As the days passed, the distance between them continued to grow. She no longer looked him in the eye and was often short and snippy when she spoke to him at all. They rarely talked, and when he asked her a question her answers were always matter of fact.

He frequently caught himself massaging his chest where an ache had formed. He never thought a breaking heart could actually cause physical pain, but he believed different now. The more he accepted he'd worn out his welcome, the harder the ache was to ignore.

He would always love her. He loved her then. He loved her now. Hell, he might have even loved her six years ago when he watched her straighten her shoulders and use her last dollar to call her boys. But he wasn't sure if she'd ever love him.

She knew the words and said them often to others, but never once uttered them to him. He tried not to let it bother him. He had said from the beginning, if she was home safe that was all that mattered. He just never expected her shutting him out to hurt this bad.

It became apparent she no longer needed him there when she had so many other people by her side. Any one of the guys could run to the store or cut her grass. Although she couldn't carry laundry down to the basement, she still did the folding. She couldn't vacuum, but she swept. Her determination to find her independence again was remarkable, but the more she recovered the less reason he had to stay. Perhaps she was waiting for him to leave.

He began searching the house for things to fix so he could keep himself busy when she had visitors. Wrapping up the fix he was making to Mattie's door, he collected his tools and followed the sound of voices into the den, for once grateful to see a recognizable face smiling back at him.

Jade grinned and held out her arms. "Trenton!" She gave him a hug and he sighed, needing it more than anyone realized.

"Hey, scrappy."

The man with her turned and Trent did a double take. Apparently, Nathan Lithe was the lawyer handling the paperwork for Marcus's estate, Jade explained. Another decision he hadn't been a part of.

He shook the man's hand. "Good to see you again."

"Once again I wish it was under better circumstances." The conversation halted and Nathan glanced expectantly at Chloe. When no one said anything, Lithe asked, "Is there a private place we can talk, Dr. Wolfe?"

Trent frowned when she glanced up at him and quickly looked away. "I guess I'll just put my tools in the truck."

He walked out and let the screen door snap shut behind him. Apparently, he wasn't welcome to sit in on such private matters. Rather than go back inside he sat on the porch steps.

The door opened and Jade shuffled out. Leaning her hand on his shoulder, she plopped down beside him and sighed. Her short legs stretched and a flip-flop fell off.

"That's gonna be a bitch picking that back up."

Trent reached down and retrieved the tiny sandal, handing it to her.

"Thanks. You okay, big guy?"

"As good as can be expected."

"Hmm. That good?"

"*That* good."

She gave him a shoulder bump. "Wanna talk about it?"

Everyone kept asking him to talk, but he had no idea what to say, so he sighed. "I think Chloe wants me to leave."

"Why do you think that?"

"Everything's different now. I can't figure out where my place is in all this."

"Where do you want your place to be?"

"I love her. I wanna be with her. I'm doing my best to fix this."

"Some things can't be fixed, Trent."

That's what he was afraid of. He had a reoccurring nightmare where he was back at that house and Chloe was by the door, but he was too late. She's already gone when he got there. How was it he'd returned her home and still somehow felt like he lost her?

"Tell me it gets better over time, Jade. I need something to hold onto."

Her hands rested on her belly, smoothing down the fabric of her sundress. "It gets..." She tipped her head as if trying to find the right word. "There's no universal definition of normal, but eventually you find balance again. Trauma affects everyone differently. I can't remember who I was before last August. I mean, I remember what I did, but I can't remember how my mind processed things. I may look the same, but I'm totally different on the inside."

He looked down at her belly, an affectionate smile curving his lips. "You look a little different with that bean in the belly."

She smiled. "*Two* beans."

He raised a brow. "No shit?"

"I shit you not."

He wrapped his arm around her shoulders and gave her a brotherly hug. "Two beans. God love ya."

"She'll come around, Trent. One thing Chloe taught me was that everything's a process. It just takes time."

His mom used to say to him a watched pot never boiled. "Maybe I'll take a job."

"That might be a good idea. She's not going anywhere. It'll be a good distraction to get away."

Since January, he'd spent almost every waking minute thinking about Chloe. Distance wasn't going to stop that. The ache in his chest tightened. "What if we're over?"

Jade looked up at him and gave a sad smile. "I wish I could make you promises."

"I know you can't. No one can."

"I don't think she'd resent you for leaving. The space might do both of you good. Sometimes we need a little distance to see the whole picture."

He nodded, already mentally collecting his belongings and trying to picture that goodbye. "Just promise me... If she asks for me..."

"I promise I'll let you know."

"Thanks."

Thirty-Seven

"WHAT DO WE TELL HER?" Mattie asked as Chloe walked the boys to a small office located just behind the local mall.

"You tell her whatever you want, whatever you feel." Though she'd yet to start therapy herself, she insisted her boys sit down and speak to someone. Their father had died, and though they didn't have a long history with him or all the gory details of his death, grief counseling seemed a necessary step in the search for normal. Her appointment was tomorrow, but she wasn't thinking about that.

Dayton held the door to the office and Chloe signed them in. The pen hovered over the clipboard, her mind picturing tomorrow when she'd be signing her own name. She placed the pen on the counter with an unsteady hand and sat beside Dayton.

A few minutes later he was invited back. She sat with Mattie while his brother had his session and when that was over she sat with Dayton while Mattie had his.

On the way home, Mattie asked, "Do we have to go back?"

"Didn't you like talking to Dr. Shields'?" Her eyes watched through the rearview mirror as he shrugged.

"I dunno."

Her gaze shifted to Dayton. "How about you?"

Her eldest shrugged as well. "Dad was a jerk."

Unanswered questions rushed through her head, but she worried she might not be able to handle the truth. "It's okay to be sad."

"I don't care," Dayton said, his attention focused on the window as they drove. "He can't yell at you anymore and that's what I care about."

Had he been able to hear them fighting? Hear her screaming? "I think we should visit Dr. Shields a few more times before you decide whether or not to go anymore." Because she would never be able to properly counsel them about Marcus. Too many demons of her own clouding her judgment.

The next day when she returned to Dr. Shields's office, she stared down at the clipboard, gripping the pen, her hand hovering and shaking violently. She silently placed it on the counter and left the office. She couldn't do this.

She was a hypocrite, knowing if she were the therapist in this situation she'd do everything she could to help a client in her shoes. But in all her experience, no one else ever came to her with the same situation. And as much as she would want to help, she couldn't see how an outsider might do so. It was a paralyzing and lonesome realization that stole any hope. She was on her own and until she figured out her own thinking, she didn't have the energy to voice her thoughts to someone else.

She missed walking without crutches and couldn't get far without getting winded. But she made it to the mall and sat on a bench, watching people stroll by. There were mostly women, hardly looking up from their shopping missions and finding some sort of satisfaction in the act Chloe could no longer conjure.

When couples passed her brow tightened, her eyes studying the way the men positioned themselves protectively at the women's sides, or perhaps flirtatiously. The women seemed to hold all the power. They were the lure and the men were the hungry fish. Didn't some of them feel slightly hunted?

The smiles and laughter she sometimes saw made her chest ache. Sitting in the mall, surrounded by dozens of people, filled her with a sense of loneliness almost too painful to bear. When would someone hold her hand like that again? The thought made her shoulders hunch inward. How many therapy session would she skip before she accepted that she might never heal?

She'd lost her faith in herself and the profession she'd built her life around. What a hypocrite. For all the coaxing she'd done, trying to get clients to open up and bare their deepest scars, she couldn't even face her own. Festering wounds too ugly to show, too shameful to name, too many to count.

Of course, therapy would probably help with some of these concerns, but she couldn't speak of the things that happened. Most days she could hardly make sense of it in her head. If she couldn't understand, how could anyone else?

She refused to force herself into another vulnerable spot, too raw to risk the scrape of criticism or some outsider pointing out a way things could have gone differently. She had her own cruel conscience for that.

They'd rush her back to normal when she still needed time to heal, deciphering her longing for companionship and making suggestions that she follow those yearnings. She couldn't. It would feel forced and she'd been forced into enough.

The things companionship entailed... The closeness, the touching, the exposure... No. Her mind shuddered at the thought of anyone trespassing into those private territories, yet her heart continued to yearn for that nearly forgotten bond she'd lost with Trenton.

Her inadequacies frustrated her to no end. This wasn't a *throw yourself back on the horse after a fall* situation. This was anger. Eventually, there might be acceptance, but right now she was too pissed off about the husk of a woman Marcus had left in his wake to predict when those other stages might show, when she might—if ever—find normal again.

Using her crutches, she slowly walked back to her car. Another day, the same redundant epiphany. No matter how much she envied couples and the closeness they shared, she'd likely be alone for the rest of her life.

Trenton was gone, off on some job, and she was here, not healing, not coping. Just ... existing. Whenever he returned, he'd find the same broken woman he left behind. And no matter how much she wished things could be different, how she wished she could be the woman he used to know, she knew she'd never be that person again.

His attention and affection would wane the more he realized that truth. And eventually, he'd wise up and move on for good. She was better off letting him go first. She'd be better off doing a lot of things, but that didn't mean she could force herself to do them.

At the end of every day, he was one of her last thoughts. She was losing him because, after everything she'd been through, she'd lost herself. She didn't much care for the woman she'd become. Chances were Trenton wouldn't like her either. Being in love had never hurt so badly.

## Thirty-Eight

ON THE FOURTH OF JULY, Chloe and the kids went to Kat and Tyson's Independence Day cookout. It was a sweltering one hundred degrees, the air so thick with humidity it seemed drinkable rather than breathable.

Her boot was driving her nuts and she couldn't wait until her appointment the following Monday to have it removed. Between the heat and the way the gnats kept swarming her head, she wanted to scream. Luckily, she wasn't the only miserable one in attendance.

Kat had been having contractions all day but insisted on having the picnic anyway. Chloe sipped a slushy margarita while Kat and Jade enjoyed virgin ones, their swollen feet submerged in a kiddy pool.

The children were having fun in the sun, playing under a sprinkler, and the men seemed to be hiding from the women at the grill. Trenton wasn't there.

It had been two weeks since he'd left her home

to take a job. Chloe wasn't sure if he was back in town yet or not. He hadn't called and it hurt too much to mention his name to the others.

She understood his absence was probably for the best. Once she had permission to take the boot off, she'd be, outwardly, healed. Trenton probably had better things to do than wait around for the internal damage to fade—if it ever would.

She couldn't be what he needed, so they should at least be honest about the future. The thought of anyone touching her made her break into a cold sweat. She had nightmares every night and couldn't bear the thought of sleeping next to someone, letting herself ever be that vulnerable again.

Trenton liked to call the shots and the way he used to touch her body... Her mind shut down. If anyone grabbed her from behind she feared she'd scream and freak out. She couldn't hold it against him for pulling away when he did.

Their spark had disappeared. When he'd been staying at her house, he no longer looked at her with lust, but with sympathy.

Deep down, she was angry about her sexuality. Being a woman made her feel like a walking orifice any man could violate. Although Trent had only been trying to help, when he would tell her to eat or go to bed she resented him for assuming she needed to be told how to take care of herself. Then she hated herself because she knew he was only trying to take care of her and his suggestions were nothing like the orders Marcus would issue.

Whenever anyone presumed to tell her what she

should be doing she got snitty. She was bitter and had every right to be. None of them knew what it was like to have their free will stripped, to have every decision made for them, to bear the humiliation she endured, the fear, the... No one knew and she didn't have the strength to explain it to them. That was probably why she hadn't kept her appointments to speak to a therapist.

Despite being one herself, her faith in the practice was shaken. No one had been in that room with her aside from Marcus. He was dead and she wanted every memory of him to die with him. Who cared if she was compartmentalizing to separate her thoughts from her feelings? Marcus had stolen so much from her. She didn't want to give him one more second of her life.

She would trade a million pleasures to never have to think about the misery he put her through ever again. She had books and experience. When she was ready, she'd heal herself. But even her limited foresight told her she'd never be the same. The woman Trenton expected her to be was gone.

"I can't eat this."

Chloe looked at Kat as she pushed aside her burger, shoving away her thoughts for another time. "You okay?"

"Yeah, just uncomfortable."

"It's this damn heat. I can't stand it." Jade fanned herself with a paper plate.

Kat took a deep breath and held it for a long moment. Was that another contraction?

"Do you want me to get Ty?"

"No, I'm fine." She shut her eyes and exhaled,

making a small tight O with her lips.

"Katherine, I have to get going—" Kat's father frowned. "Are you feeling all right, sweetheart?"

"I'm fine, Daddy. Thanks for coming. I'll see you this Sunday at dinner."

"Maybe I should take Mia with me in case you go to the hospital tonight."

"No, I'll be fine. Thanks, though."

She didn't look fine, Chloe thought. "Kat, maybe you should go inside to the air conditioning for a little bit."

"It'll pass. This is just a long one."

"I would go inside if I could get my fat ass out of this beach chair," Jade griped. "Why do I keep sitting in low chairs?"

Kat moaned and Chloe scanned the yard to Tyson.

Gloria walked over, her braids tied tight to her head, a wet handkerchief draped across the back of her neck. Her long orange nails wrapped around a margarita. "God, it's hot. You girls need anything?" Gloria's eyes bulged when she looked at Kat, "Girl, you all right?"

"I'm—I'm fine." Kat breathed and pressed her hands to her sides.

"You don't look fine. Looks like you about to have a baby!"

"My contractions aren't close enough yet, please don't get everyone all worked up for nothing."

Jade removed her sunglasses and studied Kat. "How many have you had in the past twenty minutes? You sound like you're having sex."

"Oh, it doesn't feel like sex." Kat breathed.

Jade paled. "Oh, God. It hurts, doesn't it? How bad is it?"

"I think I'm going to get Tyson," Chloe said, but Kat placed a staying hand on her arm as she moved to get up.

"Please don't. It'll be over in a minute."

Gloria put her fist on her hips and scowled. "Honey, whether you admit it or not, you're in labor and we're at a picnic. Now, I don't know what you think's gonna happen, but in the words of Prissy, '*I don't know nothing 'bout birthin' no babies*' so you best get yourself out of that chair because you're goin' to the hospital. *Darrel!* Get Ty! Kat's in labor."

As if a fire alarm sounded, everyone flew into motion. Tyson rushed to Kat's side, still wearing his grill apron that said *I leave it smokin' and well done.* He ushered her to the car, his mother following with Kat's hospital bag.

Mia ran over as Jeremy hoisted Jade out of her chair. "Is Momma having the baby?"

Chloe didn't know what to do so she stayed out of the way.

"What's going on?" Mattie asked beside her.

"Kat's having the baby."

"Cool!" He was quiet for a minute then asked. "How do they get it out?"

Chloe's mouth opened then snapped shut. "Go find your brother."

Five minutes after Gloria's announcement the yard was empty. The Four Tops played on the radio as paper plates and checkered tablecloths fluttered in the hot breeze. The sprinkler waved in the empty space and even a few chairs lay tipped on their sides.

It was a ghost town. Everyone was gone.

"Boys, let's clean some of this up."

Chloe gathered up trash so it didn't blow all over the yard. She folded tablecloths and instructed the boys to bring the food inside. Sitting at a picnic table, because she couldn't stand without her crutches, she covered the leftovers with foil as Mattie carried them to the fridge.

"Dayton, if you drag over some of those chairs I'll collapse them."

She was fighting with a chair when her skin suddenly prickled and the hair on her neck lifted with a chill.

"Need a hand with that, doll?"

She slowly turned to find Trenton standing at the gate of the picket fence. His hair was tied back and his jaw wore the stubble of a few days. His long, tapered legs filled out a pair of well-worn blue jeans and his shirt was nothing special. So why did her stomach feel like it was doing summersaults? "Trenton."

"Hi." He pushed through the gate and scanned the vacant yard. "Where is everyone?"

"The hospital. Kat's having the baby."

"No shit? That's great." He laughed and then frowned. "They left you here to clean up?"

"No, they all just sort of left, so I figured..."

"Do you need help?"

"We're about done."

"Oh." He took the chair she'd been trying to fold and closed it.

He looked much more rested since the last time she saw him. "Are you just getting back into town?"

"I got back on Wednesday."

She lowered her gaze. "Oh." He'd been back for days and not contacted her. Rather than acknowledge her confusing disappointment, she changed the subject. "This weather's horrible."

When she glanced up at him he was frowning. "How are you feeling?"

She lowered her eyes again. She understood people were concerned, but she didn't like the attention or the reminder. "Better. I go to the doctor again on Monday. Hopefully, I'll be done with this boot."

"Do you need a ride to the doctor's or anything?"

"No, I've been driving. It's my left foot."

"Oh. Right." He glanced at the house. "Are the boys here?"

"They're inside playing Tetris with the fridge and leftovers."

He chuckled and she smiled. She missed his laugh.

"You look good, Chloe."

Her smile faltered. "Thanks. So do you." He always looked good.

The screen door opened and Dayton came out. "Mom, everything's off." He stilled when he saw Trenton.

"Hey, bud."

Dayton's head tipped back as he looked up at Trenton. "You're back."

"For now."

Chloe's gaze turned to him, wondering at his

response. Was he leaving to take another job again? So soon?

Mattie came out and smiled up at Trenton. "Mia's mom's having her baby!"

"I heard." Trent smiled, brushing a hand over Mattie's sweaty hair. "Did you grow?"

"I dunno. Do you know how the baby gets out?"

Trent flushed and looked to her. She smiled. "Mattie, go find the toys you brought. Dayton, you too."

When they scampered off he laughed. "That was a loaded question."

"Dayton will explain it to him."

"Does he know?"

"About storks? Of course." The joke wasn't made out of lazy parenting. It was made from a desire to give her boys some of their innocence back—at least for a little while.

The boys came back with their action figures in hand. "Are you coming to our house?" Dayton asked, tipping his head back to look at Trenton.

He glanced down at her and back to the boys. "Not today."

More unwelcome disappointment. She forced a smile. "We should probably get going."

"I'll walk you out." He escorted them to the car, holding her door but never attempting to touch her, not even in the friendly way he sometimes brushed a hand over the boys. As he hovered by her car door it became more difficult to hold a smile.

"Thanks for walking us out."

He hesitated, his hand still on the door.

"Chloe... If there's ever anything you need ... or want..."

She blinked away and fumbled with her seatbelt. "We're doing okay. You've done enough."

Something flashed in his eyes and she'd sensed she'd somehow wounded him when that wasn't her intention.

"I just mean that you've already done so much, Trenton. I know you have other things going on."

His thick lashes lowered and his hand released the door. "Sure." He stepped back and tilted to see in the back windows. "You boys be good for your mother."

"Bye, Trenton," they called and Chloe hesitated as she watched through the mirror as he walked away.

She sighed. "Who feels like ice cream?"

The boys let out an enthusiastic cheer.

That evening, Tyson Adams, Junior was born. No matter how devastated Chloe was on the inside, the outside world continued to progress. Days passed, and milestones were marked all around her.

While excited for these small markers in time and what they meant for her friends, everything in her personal life seemed frozen. She marked days off on her calendar as if she was counting down to something important, but she didn't know what.

Summer passed in a hot blur of nothingness and by early September the boys were back in school and Chloe was feeling emptier than ever. She wondered if she'd ever go back to work. Her mind frequently touched on her patients, but she worried how useful she'd be in her state. The last session she'd had was with Jade, the day Chloe humiliated herself in front of a client and Marcus showed up.

Late September, Nathan Lithe contacted her with the news that Marcus's house had sold. She was given a lump sum, which she intended to move into a trust for the boys. She'd forgotten how wealthy they were. The house in Virginia alone sold for three hundred and fifty thousand. But all the money he'd left behind failed to bring any sense of vindication.

Life would be so simple if dollar bills could heal human souls, but domestic abuse left scars no amount of time or money could mend. She knew what she was up against, and for all of her training, she didn't know how to fix her disjointed heart.

Shame was as slippery as envy and as intangible as her rage. The only emotion she could fully grasp was guilt. She was happy, but discontent.

She hadn't spoken to Trenton in months, not since running into him at Kat and Tysons. What they shared was clearly over. She missed the sound of his voice, his presence in her life, and knowing how his days were going. But no matter how often she wondered about him, she knew he'd be better off with someone else, so she resisted the urge to contact him.

Every now and then she drank her coffee black, shutting her eyes and recalling how his kisses tasted early in the morning. That was as far as her mind could go. Memories of their evenings and the things they did at night in his bed... Those things didn't fill her with the same warmth the thought of his kisses did.

That autumn, for her thirty-ninth birthday, Chloe bought herself something special. Rather than try to find another office to lease, she invested in a building in New Castle and hired Adams Construction to handle the renovations. She wanted to return to work but intended to do things a little differently this time.

It was the first time she didn't have to fear putting property in her name would lead to trouble. Signing the mortgage with her now legal name felt like signing away a weight she'd carried for years. There was no consequence and no fear, only hope that she was moving in the right direction.

"So tell me what you envision?" Tyson asked as they walked through the open space.

Chloe's chest warmed as she understood this could be anything she wanted and with her recent inheritance, the sky seemed the limit. "I want it painted in a welcoming color, a soft yellow I think, with cheery white accents. We'll need state of the art washers and dryers installed in the basement, at least two of each. I'm buying a large donation bin to keep out back, so there will be a lot of items to clean."

"We'll make sure you have the right amp service for that." Tyson made a note on his clipboard.

"In the front, I'll need those planked walls they have in stores to display the clothing. Some shelving, too. We're going to stocked everything from hair dye, to spray tan and wigs. And a fully equipped bathroom where women can shower and literally *change*."

"Definitely going to have to upgrade the plumbing."

"The bathroom doesn't have to be on the first floor."

He grinned. "Chloe, this is your renovation. We'll put the bathroom wherever you want. What's going in that big room back there?"

"I have a plan for it, but I'm... I was thinking we could just leave that alone for now."

"You don't want us to touch it?"

"I want to keep the rafters exposed and only finish off the floors and paint the walls." When he looked confused she explained, "I'm thinking of making it a gym, but I need to talk to a self-defense instructor to figure out the best way to set it up."

Understanding registered in his eyes. "Gotchya. We'll clean it up for you and leave it until you're ready to ask him."

She flushed, assuming they both realized she was hoping to ask Trenton.

"So where do you envision your office?"

Her office was going on the second floor beside rooms that would be devoted to legal matters, medical exams, and a private area with cots and blankets for temporary residents. "Upstairs near the residents' quarters. Security is a major concern."

"Not a problem." He made another note. "We'll get Jeremy to order a top of the line system and install monitors at all the doors. We can even build a panic room if that's something you want."

"Really?"

Tyson grinned. "I told you, Chloe, this is your design."

She smiled, unable to recall a time she ever had so much freedom of choice. It seemed ironic that the money Marcus left was paying for it. In a long line of nasty Hunt men, this was the most meaningful legacy they would leave behind. She only wished Aunt Gina could have lived to see it.

Though she hadn't done much since spring, this was shaping up to be the project of a lifetime. She planned to call it *BASE, Breaking Abuse and Securing an Escape*.

The safe house would offer sanctuary to any women and children in need of one. Her finances allowed her to operate on a non-profit level and so she contacted a number of physicians and gynecologists who might be willing to work with her, pro-bono and on call. Nathan Lithe, when he found out what she wanted to do with her inheritance, agreed to volunteer his services, free of charge, for women seeking legal advice.

Everything was coming together so easily it was as if her plan was somehow meant to be. Once the renovations started, every day was a new adventure. Within a month they were stocking the shelves and pantries with supplies.

Jennifer returned to Chloe's payroll and Tommy applied to manage the clothing area. BASE needed to offer complete anonymity to residents—no names or money required to stay. She wanted women to know the resources offered, but discretion was key.

She started with a web page and a story about a woman who hid her pennies in a canister of flour. Jeremy set up the site to scramble the search history, so no visitor's computer could be traced back to BASE. Brochures where left where women visited, ladies rooms, women's dressing rooms, gynecologists' offices, and libraries. Once the site was live, questions slowly followed. Every answer was posted on the FAQ page, another way to boost confidentiality and keep any inquiries untraceable.

Sometimes pennies in a jar took too long, and she'd learned first-hand how a few days could be the difference between life and death. Domestic abuse was a lonesome and sometimes deadly war. The goal was to let women know they didn't have to fight for survival alone. And with every rescue came a tinge of pride, a thread that seemed to reinforce this new foundation she was building and mend some invisible part of herself.

One week after their doors opened they had residents arrive. Packets were mass-produced to educate women about safety precautions, including everything from hotlines to helpful tips like keeping a can of wasp spray by the bed. Wasp spray had a reach of twenty feet and could debilitate an attacker for an hour, much more powerful than pepper spray.

"When do you intend to talk to him about the big room?" Tommy asked as Chloe sifted through receipts.

She shut her receipt ledger and sighed. "I haven't seen or heard from him in months, but I plan to call him eventually—when I'm ready."

"You know he'd do anything for you, Chloe."

She wasn't so sure. Before, when they were dating, maybe. But now... All she could offer him was a minimal paycheck and a space to teach self-defense if he was interested.

"We'll see. I'm sure Jeremy could recommend someone else if he's not interested."

"You can say his name."

She frowned. "I know." Of course, she could say his name. It just seemed healthier not to. "When I'm ready, I'll call. This is about BASE, nothing else."

His gaze dropped and he offered a sad smile. "I know, sweet. I didn't mean to push." He glanced at his watch. "You better go. Trick or treating starts soon."

She looked at the clock. "Crap." Gathering her things, she said, "You know how to enter those last receipts?"

"I'm on it. Go. And do me a favor and make sure Adam isn't handing out toothbrushes or apples. I bought good candy and I expect him to use it."

"You got it."

That evening, after a long night of knocking on doors, the boys dragged their pillowcases full of candy through the door and the phone rang. Another milestone.

Jade finally gave birth to the twins, Jason and Julia. Mom and babies were healthy and doing well. Dad was still recovering.

She was happy for her friend and promised to pay a visit tomorrow. Another sign that time was moving on. Another reminder, aside from the changes at BASE, she was still broken and still the same.

Thirty-Nine

"THEY'RE BEAUTIFUL." Trent brushed a delicate finger down the velvet cheek. "Which one is this?"

Jade laughed. "That's Julia."

"Julia," he repeated, a vicarious sort of pride mixing with his envy. Her little face was so small and perfect. "Can I hold her?"

"Of course." Jade carefully passed him the precious bundle and he smiled, cradling the baby's slight weight in his arms.

Jeremy stepped to his side, holding Jason. "They're perfect, aren't they?"

He smiled at his friend. "Absolutely perfect."

The door creaked and Trent's heart punched hard against the wall of his chest. Chloe looked at him, expression blank, arms holding a basket of flowers attached to two large balloons, one announcing a boy, the other announcing a girl. She took his breath away.

"Chloe," Jade said, interrupting their eye contact and leaving Trent's heart racing.

"Congratulations." She placed the basket on the table and kissed Jade's cheek.

He silently watched as she congratulated their friends. Her hair was longer and lighter as if she were trying to get back to her natural blonde. She looked so ... different and still so beautiful.

Jeremy passed Chloe the baby and her face lit with an expression he'd never seen before. Her smile lit the room and he added little Jason to list of those he envied most in this world when she pressed a kiss on the baby's head.

Her gaze lifted and collided with his. He shouldn't stare, but he couldn't pull his gaze away. Her chest lifted as she stared back, an invisible thread seeming to anchor them in that special moment.

"Since you're both here," Jeremy said and glanced at Jade. His wife nodded. "We have a question for you two."

Chloe's focus turned to Jade and Trent's gaze followed. Jade smiled. "We were hoping you two would be godparents."

Chloe gasped. "Are you sure that's what you want?"

"We love you guys. Of course, it's what we want."

Trent beamed. Not only was it an incredible honor, it somehow made him feel closer to Chloe. "Yes. Definitely. I'm honored."

Jeremy clapped a hand on his back. "Thanks."

"Thank *you*. I don't know what to say."

They all turned to Chloe and she quickly nodded. "I'd be honored."

He and Jeremy broke into conversation, his ears catching on every other word Chloe said as she quietly chatted with Jade. After a while, Chloe announced she had to go. His chest knotted at the unbearable thought of watching her walk away.

"I should get going too." He passed Jeremy the baby and stood.

Chloe was already through her goodbyes and slipping out the door. He rushed into the hall just as she turned the far corner. He raced after her.

"Chloe, wait..." Coming around the bend, she turned and looked up at him. He caught his breath. "How've you been?"

"I've been ... good. You?"

He was happy she considered herself doing good, but part of him regretted she'd gotten to that good place without him. It had been months and he'd not heard from her. Every time he picked up the phone to call, he told himself not to push. Each day without her was more excruciating than the last.

He wasn't just lonely. He was incomplete without her. "I've been ... okay. I miss you."

Her gaze darted to the ground as her cheeks flushed. "I've been meaning to call."

His heart soared. "Why didn't you?"

"I..." She glanced up at him, biting down on her lip. "I don't know."

"I wanted to call you a thousand times. How are the boys?"

"They're doing wonderfully."

"And you? Jeremy and Ty tell me you have quite the operation running in Upper New Castle."

Her smile radiated with pride. "It's pretty amazing what you can do when you finally have money."

Money wasn't responsible for what she'd created. Her good heart was the culprit. "I'd say it's more passion than finances. From what I hear, you've created a one of a kind facility."

"A necessary facility," she corrected. "It's not finished yet, but it's getting there."

"Can I come see it?"

"I... I actually wanted to talk to you about what we would need to turn one room into a gym for self-defense classes."

His eyes lit, a full smile curling his lips. "Anything you need. I'm your man." How badly he wished that was true.

"We're non-profit, so the pay isn't much, but I'd love to have you teach classes if you're—"

"Yes. I'll do it."

She laughed. "What about your other job."

He shook his head. He'd saw off his leg for an excuse to be close to her again. His other job could wait. "It'll all work out."

"Well ... thank you. I'm usually there between nine and two. You can stop by whenever—"

"I'm free now."

"Oh ... okay. That works, too."

Relieved he wouldn't have to say goodbye just yet, he waved a hand toward the elevators. "I'll walk you to your car."

~

When they arrived at BASE, Chloe gave Trent a tour of the space, her heart beating a mile a minute as her belly flipped every time he looked at her. It seemed as impossible to hold his stare as it would be to hold her hand over a flame, so she kept her gaze mostly focused on their surroundings.

He appeared impressed with everything she'd showed him so far. When she took him through the back room, he pulled out a small notepad and made a list of equipment they would need.

"I can price out all this stuff and work out all the installation details with Ty for you. It'll only take me a few days to get you an estimate."

"That would be great. Whatever you need. I have money put aside for the improvements. I want it equipped with anything that'll help our residents."

He smiled and a shiver raced up her spine, her focus falling to his shoes.

"This is amazing, what you've done here, doll. I've been in security for almost fifteen years and I've never seen a facility this thought out for the purpose you're serving. You should be incredibly proud of yourself."

Heat rushed up the back of her neck. For some reason, his praise was more valuable than others'. "I am."

"What's new with the boys?" His tone was cautious.

Discussing her sons was always easier than discussing herself. "Dayton's making straight A's and Mattie finally started piano lessons. He's a natural. I don't know where he gets his talent."

His eyes softened, creasing at the corners as his smile gentled. "I miss you."

It was the second time he said so and twice as impactful. She missed him too, painfully so. But her situation was still the same. No matter how badly she wished she could go back to the way things were, she couldn't get past the thought of sharing herself intimately with someone else. It was a painful realization no matter how many times the thought occurred to her.

"I've missed you, too. But..." And it was even more painful to admit out loud.

"Hey." He gently touched her cheek and her breath held. "No tears."

She blinked, mentally demanding she not do this in front of him. "Sorry."

"Don't apologize. If you cry, I cry."

She nodded tightly, stuffing down her emotions. "I wish things could be different."

"They are different, Chloe. I see that."

But he didn't fully understand. "I don't want to lead you on."

"I'm a big boy. Why don't you let me take you out to dinner this week? We can discuss everything that needs to be done for the gym and classes. I can help you set up a schedule and write an ad description so the girls know what to expect."

"Trenton..."

"Just dinner, Chloe. Think of it as business."

His words relieved and worried her. "Okay. A business dinner."

When he smiled she wondered if she was making a mistake. Those sapphire eyes were her undoing. She couldn't mess this up. If they could somehow figure a way to be friends, if that could somehow be enough for him, she'd be the luckiest woman in the world.

No... Her mind objected. *The luckiest woman would be able to have all of him.*

# Forty

SHE MET Trenton at a restaurant called The Honey Pot. It wasn't a date, but it still filled her with the same jitters—maybe even some new ones. When she parked her car he was waiting at the front of the establishment. The sight of sunflowers in his handmade her second guess his words from the other day.

Her gaze remained nailed to the flowers as she approached. "I thought this wasn't a date."

"It's not. It's business." Pulling open the door, he handed her the bouquet. "Congratulations on opening your new business."

She pursed her lips and hid a smile. Sunflowers were her favorite and these were especially beautiful in shades of burgundy and orange. "Thank you. They're lovely."

"So are you." He turned and addressed the hostess, giving her no chance to reply. Once they were seated, he flipped his menu open and scanned the options. "What are you in the mood for, doll?"

Her hand trembled as she opened her own menu. "Probably just a salad."

He scoffed. "Get more than that. It's my treat. Look, they have cannoli."

Her mind instantly flew to the morning he fed her at her kitchen table, the way he kissed her and touched her. "I'm trying to lose weight."

"You don't need to lose weight. Indulge a little."

The waitress took their orders and Chloe fiddled with the silverware, her eyes on the table. *Not a date.* "So, what have you been up to for the past few months?"

"This, that, and the other thing. You lightened your hair."

Her fingers nervously touched a strand. "I... Yes, I'm trying to get it back to my natural color. Although, by the time I get there it might be gray."

"You don't have gray hair."

"After this year, who knows? I'm lucky I'm not bald." She surprised herself with her attempt at humor, but Trenton didn't laugh so she shut up.

"Is that a new ring?"

She glanced at her fingers and touched the stone. "Yes. Adam and Tommy got it for me for my birthday."

"I missed your birthday?" He frowned, drawing back in his seat a little. "I'm sorry, doll. I didn't know."

"You didn't miss anything. We just stayed home and ordered pizza. At my age, it's no big deal."

"What's this new obsession with your age?"

"I don't know. I'm almost forty. I just feel ... done."

"So am I. I'd hate to think I shouldn't live anymore. I still feel fairly young."

"Milestones seem bigger now. Maybe it's just me."

"Trust me. Your life's far from over. You just opened a business, you're financially secure, you don't have to watch your back anymore, and your kids are doing great... The world's your oyster."

She laughed nervously. For a business dinner, things were getting awfully personal. He touched her hand, stilling it from playing with the silverware. She should probably bring up the gym.

"Seriously, Chloe, you can do anything you want. Don't fool yourself into thinking time's passed you by. You're young. You're beautiful. Make as many wishes as you want. I think you're owed a few."

She slid her hand out from under his and placed it on her lap. "A wish?" When was the last time anyone acted like wishes changed anything? "I'm not sure I believe in wishes anymore. All I have are memories I wish I could forget, but no amount of wishing takes them away."

"I'm sorry." His gaze shifted away as if she'd just stabbed all his generous optimism right in the heart.

They hadn't even eaten yet and she was already spoiling the night. "Please don't apologize."

"I could have—"

This time she was the one to take his hand. "No. A lot of bad has happened to me, but you were only responsible for the good. *I'm* sorry. I shouldn't have said anything."

His blue eyes stared at her, tight at the corners

with worry and regret. "No, we can talk about it. Or we don't have to. I'm just glad we're talking."

Her lips pressed tight. "I wish I could forgive everything that happened to me." Trenton had saved her not once, but twice. She owed him some level of truth. "I hate him. He's dead, but my hatred for him is still very much alive. Even with my education and background, I can't make sense of how anyone can be so evil. He left this anger inside of me..." She sighed. "I've made a dozen appointments to talk to someone and canceled every single one. How can I sell a sort of healing I won't buy?"

"I think you need this gym more than you realize."

Of all the things he could have said... "Why do you say that?"

"You need to bang something around, get the anger out. You'd be amazed how much it can help."

Her laugh was silent and her smile unconvinced. "Sometimes I question if violence is the only way to stop violence. It's a bit hypocritical, isn't it?"

"Are you sorry he's dead?"

She met his gaze. "No."

If he only knew the demented thoughts she had, that she wished Marcus had suffered more. Her hatred was a systemic, sometimes crippling weight she never put down.

"I think you're handling it well."

She broke eye contact. "I've had years of practice hiding the pain on the inside."

"You've never been able to hide that much from me, Chloe. I'm trained to sniff out the truth. You think I'd judge you for wanting him to suffer more than he did? Never. You're human and he was an animal that needed to be put down. My biggest regret is that I didn't kill him years ago when I had the chance."

Her head lifted and she saw something dark and unforgiving flash in his eyes. "You're a good guy. Killing isn't your style."

He leaned closer, lowering his voice. "He hurt you. Good guy or not, it would have been my fucking pleasure to make him suffer."

His words should have terrified her, but they brought a twisted sense of satisfaction. Her lips quivered as she fought the urge to cry. What kind of woman thought like that? "Don't let the ugliness from my life change the sort of man you are, Trenton."

"What sort of man am I?"

She shut her eyes, her lashes growing damp. "You're the sort who never deserved the things I said to you that morning I found your gun. I realize that now and I should have realized it then. You could never be the bad guy because you're too good at being the hero. You're strong yet gentle. You're always there for the people you care about."

She shut her eyes, a hollow ache forming in her chest. "You deserve a girlfriend who isn't … broken. I know we had a lot of fun before everything got messed up, but the truth is everything *did* get messed up. You need to find someone who can give you everything you deserve and want."

"What I want is you."

She dashed away a tear. "Trenton—"

"Chloe, I know what happened changed you.

I'd think something was wrong with you if it didn't. There's nothing you could say to me that would change my mind. You're who I want. Because without you, I'm just as broken."

"He haunts me. I can't talk about it because I don't want to remember any of it. I just want to forget and I'm afraid if I let myself ... get close to someone else, it'll make me remember the worst parts. I..."

He pressed a napkin into her hand and she blotted her eyes. "It's killing me not to be able to hold you right now, Chloe. But I get it and that's why I'm sitting over here and not over there. Yes, I want to touch you and hold you, but I also don't want to scare you. I know what you're afraid of. I'm not asking for that. I'm just asking for a chance at your heart."

She sniffled and a nervous chuckle slipped out. "This was supposed to be a business dinner."

He smiled. "I'll always make it my business to be sure you're all right. These last few months have been torture. I ask about you and the boys all the time. I can't think. I can't sleep. I *love* you."

Such sweet words shouldn't cause so much pain, but their situation was heartbreaking. Marcus stole her last chance at a normal life and she hated him for it. He destroyed what had taken her years to find and left her confidence more damaged than ever.

"I'm done, Trenton. Kids... I have mine. Marriage... It doesn't agree with me."

"What about love?"

Another tear slipped down her cheek. "I'm just too fragile."

"You're tougher than you realize."

"I'm not."

"Bullshit. I watched you get out of there *twice*. You're the toughest woman I know."

"I don't feel tough. I feel battered and beaten in every sense of the word."

His jaw noticeably clenched as he stared at her. "My future's with you, Chloe. I can either suffer through everything that comes after this moment, wonder every day if you're happy, or I can make sure of it. But you have to let me at least try. With all my heart, I believe I can make you happy. I did once. Let me try again."

Gathering her hands in both of his, he squeezed. "I'd be a good guy to Dayton and Mattie. I'd love them and protect them as if they were my own. I just want to love and take care of you—all of you."

Her vision blurred. "Why?"

"Who gives a shit why? I love you. I love you blonde, auburn, or gray. There hasn't been a day— in nearly seven years—that I haven't thought about you, wondered if you were all right. It doesn't take work because my heart just goes there. I'll worry about you no matter what. It's the only thing I've consistently done in my life. I don't wanna say 'this isn't perfect, let's throw it away and shop new'. This is you and me. It's what I want. I want ... us."

"Trenton, I ... you're a very sexual person."

"So are you."

"No. That's what I'm trying to tell you. I was, but I'm not anymore."

"Chloe, what do you feel when you see me?"

*So much.* "I don't know."

"Think."

Her lips pulled into a sad smile. "Happy. Nervous."

"What kind of nervous? Nervous like fear or excitement?"

"Nervous like I'm rolling down a hill in a fast car and my stomach feels like it's going to jump out of my body."

"You make me the same kind of nervous. When I see you, a fire catches in my lungs and makes it hard to breathe. My skin tingles all over. I feel breakable and impetuous, and always a little unsure because I know each time I'm with you, I'm with the kindest, most beautiful woman in the world and I don't want to mess it up."

Her brow creased. "I do that to you?"

"Yes! Will you listen to me, woman? You make me crazy. Do you know what that nervousness is, Chloe? It's desire. Circumstances might've doused it, but nothing can destroy it. You just need some kindling and that little flame will grow so big and strong, before you know it you'll be racing down those metaphorical hills remembering how fun it is to let go."

Her heart was breaking. Everything he said, she wanted to believe it could all be true. She loved him so deeply and yet she feared he'd eventually grow tired waiting for her. She could handle disappointing someone she hated, but she couldn't bear to disappoint someone she loved to the degree she loved him. "I'm scared."

"Scared how?"

"I'm scared if I try, I'll end up letting you down."

"Never."

"We have to be realistic, Trenton. You could touch me and I could lose it. I can't even be alone in an elevator with a man. You don't know how bad it is."

"We'll get there. I don't care if it takes years."

"You say that now—"

"You're getting ahead of yourself, Chloe. I mean, don't get me wrong, sex with you was off the charts, honestly, the best I ever had, but there's so much more. We'll deal with all that when the time comes. For right now, I just want to be with you, a part of your day-to-day life. Even if we never get to the sex, I'm okay with that."

"You ... can't be okay with that."

"Yes, Chloe, I can. That's how much I love you. If I can get your mind and your heart, the other parts are just a bonus."

"I don't know if I believe that." Not because of her trust issues or because she doubted his sincerity, but because she knew he'd never be satisfied with a sexless relationship—even if he wholeheartedly believed he could be.

"Chloe, I've been sniffing your clothes for almost eight months. They're running out of smell."

She froze. "What?"

"The bag you left at my house, everything in it smells like you. I'm not crazy—well, maybe it's a little crazy—but I miss *you*. Here—" He reached into his pocket, opened his hand. A black tube lay in his palm.

She gasped. "My lipstick."

"Yeah, I should've given it back. I didn't know you were looking for it until Sue bought you a new one. I found it in the car the day you went missing. I've carried it around ever since."

"You were at my house the day I went missing?"

"Yes. I came and searched your house for anything the cops might have missed. I found this under the seat of your car."

She picked up the tube. It was lighter. She lifted the cap and found it empty. "What happened to it?"

"I told you, I've been carrying it around for over six months. It was a hot summer. It melted. All of my jeans have pink stains in the pockets."

"Why didn't you throw it away?"

He moved to take it back, but she pulled it away and his eyes turned pleading. "Because it reminds me of you. It smells like your kisses."

And here she was thinking herself crazy by drinking her coffee black because they tasted like his kisses. She held the tube under her nose and inhaled the familiar scent of cosmetics. She supposed it did smell like her. She handed it back to him and relief stole over his face.

She realized in that moment that he hadn't moved on at all. Maybe neither of them had. Just like he'd thought of her all these years, she also thought of him—her hero who saved her when she needed to be saved.

He never asked her for much but he was asking for everything now. If there was any possible way she could save him from pain, she wanted to. Maybe, somehow, they could save each other.

"Okay, Trenton. We can try. But you have to be patient with me."

His blue eyes lit as a smile stretched across his face. "Doll, I'm not a fancy man, but I plan on wooing you in ways that would make the greatest poets cry. If patience is what you need that's exactly what you're going to get."

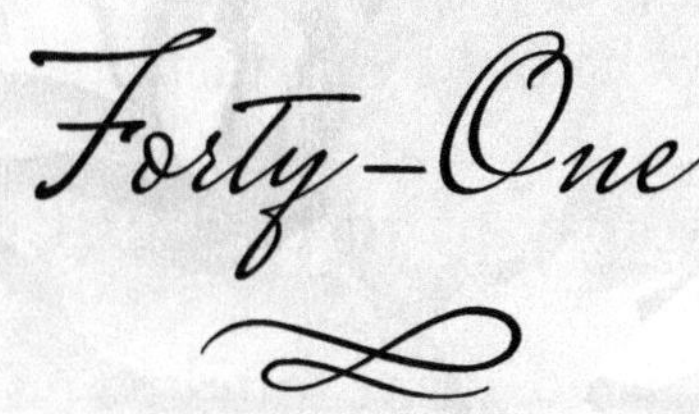

# Forty-One

CHLOE OPENED her office door and frowned at the antique teddy bear with copper button eyes sitting on the floor. She picked it up, noting the vintage style mouth and stitching.

"Tommy, do you recognize this?"

He looked up from the basket of freshly washed clothes he was hanging. "Never saw it before."

"It was outside of my office. Do you think it belongs to one of the residents?" They only had two at the moment.

"No."

Her gaze narrowed at his quick answer. "We should at least ask."

"Go ahead and ask, but it doesn't belong to anyone."

"How do you know?"

He sighed and hung a shirt on the display wrack. "Maybe Cupid left it, Chloe."

"Was Trenton here?" That had to be what he

meant. Either that or she was missing the punch line.

"I saw nothing."

He was no help. "I can just check the security cameras."

"Sure, if you want to be a brat about it." He winked.

Her lips twisted as she fought a grin. She carried it back upstairs and placed it on one of the empty shelves in her office. The gesture was sweet—*if* it had actually been Trenton who left the bear.

Within an hour she was rolling back the security feed, because, yes, she had issues. With everything she'd gone through of late and her duty to protect those staying at BASE, she couldn't rest until she was certain who had been outside of her door. Trenton had access codes now and the necessary clearances, but...

She exhaled as she watched the footage, recognizing his large form approach her door as he bent and carefully placed the antique bear on the floor. She smiled, almost wishing she hadn't needed the reassurance but feeling much more at ease now that she was certain.

The next day a small box wrapped in twine sat outside of her door. She searched the hallway but saw no one. Inside the box sat a vintage pocket watch. She placed it with the others in her collection, making sure it was in the front.

For a week straight she found little trinkets at her door, each one uniquely beautiful and showing her that he paid attention to the things she liked. She wanted to do something in return, so she took a detour on her way to work Friday morning and picked him up a stainless steel travel mug and had his initials engraved in it.

Later that day, when he was unpacking a large shipment of equipment in the gym, he looked up from sipping said mug and gave her a knowing smile. She lingered by the door.

"Where you looking for something, doll?"

"No. I just wanted to see if you needed anything."

His brow lifted. "There's plenty I need. What are you offering?"

She didn't dare step any closer. "How's the coffee?"

His smile held. "It's the best I've tasted in years."

"Good." She reached into her pocket and held out the rock that had been left by her door that morning. "Do you know what this is?"

He took a step, still leaving several feet between them. "Looks like a rock."

"I know it's a rock." But she didn't understand the meaning behind it after a week of other trinkets. "I'm trying to figure out why someone would leave it by my office."

He took three slow steps to cross the distance between them. "May I?"

She placed it in his palm and he examined it as if he'd never seen it before when she knew he was the one who left it. There had to be some meaning behind it.

"It's a sedimentary rock. See all the little granules of sand and broken shells? Look how you can see all the layers on this side. Each one's different."

She stepped closer and glanced up when she heard him inhale close to her hair. His gaze held hers. "Why would someone leave this for me?" There were several thin layers built over time.

"Hmm. I'm not sure." He placed it in her hand. "Careful, it looks fragile. In the wrong hands, it could break. I'd keep it somewhere safe. It's rare to find such a pretty stone with so many layers. I bet each one tells a different story." His thumb dragged over one beveled edge. "Each one made it stronger. Even these little broken pieces... It's all part of what makes it unique and beautiful, fragile yet resilient."

Her fingers closed protectively over the rock. "Is this rock supposed to represent me?"

Head still tipped close to hers, he smiled. "I don't think it would be as pretty if it still was just a smooth little pebble that never moved or changed. Its imperfections are what make it special. I bet you could search the world and never find a stone exactly like that one." His fingers brushed over the backs of her knuckles. "That's something I'd take care of. Something that wouldn't be able to be replaced if anything ever happened to it."

She blinked as he casually strolled back to his boxes and picked up his coffee mug, his blue eyes watching her as he took a long sip and winked.

When she returned to her office, she placed the stone on her desk, turning it so the roughest side with all the layers faced her chair. Of all the treasures he'd left her that week, this one was by far her new favorite.

Her client list was low but BASE kept her busy. They never had more than a few residents each month and the times she offered her counseling services, she was left weighted in a solemn state of mind. She was helping, but it didn't feel like enough. What worried her most were all the emails from women promising they'd get there but never showed.

Trenton made a habit of arriving in the mornings and lingering until she left to pick up the boys from school. Every day he'd walk her to her car, but he never made any move to kiss her or ask her on another date. She was selfishly satisfied with the comfortable way they interacted. He made her happy and surprised her regularly with subtle gestures like the novel he'd left by her door that week.

Missing him, she took her lunch down to the gym. He'd set up a desk in the corner and sat with his head bowed over some paperwork.

"Am I interrupting?"

His head lifted and he put down the pencil he held. "Not at all."

She took the seat across from his desk and opened her lunch, splitting her sandwich in two and handing him half. "What are you working on?"

"Schedules for the classes."

"I hope we have more residents soon or you won't have anyone to teach."

"If you build it they will come. You gotta be patient."

"I sent a few women some bus tickets today." She shipped the tickets to a public pick up point and hoped this time the women found a way to use them.

"You've been doing that a lot."

"I know. It's not the most fiscally responsible way, but I can't read their letters and do nothing."

"Can you write it off?"

"No. It comes out of my pocket."

"What happens when you start getting more letters? You can't finance every woman's journey."

She peeled away the crust of her sandwich. "I know. I've been thinking about a fundraiser, but I feel like we have to be more established to start asking private donors for contributions."

He said nothing.

"My biggest fear is not being able to help the woman who needs it most. I can't stomach the cost of a bus ticket getting in the way of someone's happiness. So many say they'll come and they never show up."

Her mind flashed to the time she tried to run away and failed. Rotating her wrist, remembering her scream as Marcus slammed it in the car door, she let out a long breath and shook away a chill.

"If you're worried about staying afloat, we could close off this section of the building and open the self-defense classes to the public. They'd never have to know what's hiding upstairs."

"That's a possibility." She crumpled up her trash and put it back in her lunch bag.

"It'll get there, doll. I have faith in your dream."

She smiled, his confidence lending itself to hers. "Thank you." She watched him as he sat back and rocked in his chair. "Trenton, would you like to come to our house for dinner tonight?"

His smile told her he'd been waiting for her to ask. "I'd love to."

The boys were happy to see Trenton. He listened to Mattie play piano and played a few video games with Dayton, who no longer brooded and seemed much happier this school year.

After dinner, they watched a movie and he held his hand open on his thigh. Her gaze continuously turned to his open palm and splayed fingers until she finally laced her fingers with his. Focused on the screen, he closed his hand around hers and smiled.

A storm unleashed in her stomach, warm and exciting. The turbulent way her nerves bounced whenever he was near put a sense of urgency inside of her she couldn't navigate. The looks, the featherlight touches, they were all pleasant and therefore confusing.

More confusing was the hollowness she suffered when they parted. The more time they spent together the more she looked for him when he wasn't there. Her thoughts turned to him at night and during her solitary moments of the day.

Her thoughts became so preoccupied with Trenton, she hardly ever thought about Marcus. Then one day out of the blue, she realized, as if she didn't already know, that Marcus was dead.

*Dead.* Never coming back. She'd pulled the trigger and finally exhaled as he drew his last breath. No sense of remorse came and perhaps her fear of guilt was what kept her from accepting the finality of her actions. She'd killed her husband.

The police, when she'd sat down with them, had done their own investigation. Everyone who knew her gave a statement and Nathan had handled the legal matters to shield her from the unsavory memories whenever possible. But not once had anyone made her feel as if her actions were not justified.

The things Marcus had done to her... They were cruel and pre-meditated, guaranteed to inflict the most harm. He'd given her no choice but survival because in those last horrific moments his intent to murder her had been painfully clear.

She fought. She defended herself. And she ... was alive.

The simple realization had her lowering into her seat and dropping her weight like an anvil. He was dead. The finality of such an epiphany struck hard and left her numb. She wanted to tell someone but that would just be stating the obvious. They all knew he was dead. They knew how and why, so how come this information was just processing in her brain now, months after the fact?

He was gone. Forever. Dead. It was an absolute that could not be undone and the realization filled her with a grotesque giddiness.

*Place your bets. I bet dead. Dead it is! I'm gonna let it ride on dead. Place your bets again... Dead! I can't lose! He's always going to be dead!*

She grinned and covered her mouth, ashamed to joke about such things but not ashamed for what she'd done. She was probably a little crazy, but who wouldn't be?

Yes, it was horrible to rejoice in the death of the father of her children, but he'd never really fathered them or taken the time to know them—even when he'd had the chance. He was too interested in cloning himself to see that her boys were already better than him.

He could never hurt her again. She was free. So why wasn't she living the life she dreamed of someday having, embracing all that was stolen away for so long? Her time with Marcus didn't represent everything she was. She was no longer borrowing happiness for a time, she was entitled to it—forever. He was the one who had stolen her entitlement away. But in the end, she took her freedom back. Permanently.

This was her life and her choice how to live. Why had she been so convinced she didn't deserve to be happy again? She wanted to be happy—*dear God, she wanted it!*

She hated his control, but that should have died with him. Was it a force of habit? Because he was gone and she was here, yet she was still letting him control her from the grave.

She bolted up from her chair and scowled. She needed to do something. She needed to do something *right now*. Something that proved she was in control.

Storming out of her office, she marched down the stairs and into the gym. Trenton was sorting equipment and looked up as she entered. "Hey, beautiful. You all right?"

The walls were covered with padding. Different kinds of punching bags hung suspended from the ceiling, and the floors sported a glossy new finish.

"No, I'm not all right. This whole time Marcus has been dead and I didn't realize he was really dead until about two minutes ago."

He raised a brow. "Come again?"

She huffed and shook her head. "I've given him

control from the grave. I knew he was dead. I saw him draw his last breath. Nathan faxed me a copy of the death certificate, I got his money, and I sold his possessions. But it never clicked. And now that all these light bulbs are flashing like crazy in my head, I feel like a fool standing in a blinding spotlight."

He grinned and shoved the box aside. Crossing the mats he wrapped his arms around her and pressed his lips into her hair. She tensed, but he held her loosely and waited for the tension in her shoulders to ease. She was too enraged by her stupidity to worry about their proximity.

"You're not a fool. You spent six years hiding from an invisible man, a man you never saw, yet existed enough for you to always fear him. Just because you couldn't see him didn't make him any less real or dangerous. It makes sense that you would continue thinking along the same lines. You didn't see him before. You don't see him now. But this time he's never coming back. Ever."

The therapist inside of her recognized this for the breakthrough it was. And Trenton had predicted something like this when they had their first "business" dinner not long ago. Someone should be paying him.

"I'm so angry at myself for wasting so much time. When I was there, I thought I'd never escape. And here I am, free to do whatever I please, and I'm not even living!"

"Sure you are, doll."

"No, not the way I want. I'm still letting him control parts of my life."

"You'll get there. Here." He turned her to one

of the bigger bags hanging from the ceiling. "Give me your rings."

"Trenton, I told you this isn't my thing."

"Have you ever tried it?"

"No."

"Then give me your rings."

She hesitantly removed her jewelry, certain this would hurt more than it would heal. He slipped them into his pocket and adjusted her shoulders.

"Punch the bag. It's the second best way to relieve tension."

"What's the first?"

"Sex."

She rolled her eyes. "Walked right into that one."

He chuckled, adjusting her arms so her hands were in front of her chest. Chills raced down her spine, but she focused on the target, hoping this might relieve some of her tension.

"Okay. Now make a fist. No, no. Put your thumbs on the outside so you don't hurt yourself." His warm breath tickled the back of her neck. "Now, spread your feet apart and sway with me, but keep your hands up."

His loose grip rested on her hips and she shut her eyes, bracing for panic that never came.

"Keep yourself relaxed. Don't tighten up." They continued to sway in a slow bobbing glide, back and forth, back and forth. "Doll, you can't aim if your eyes are shut."

"Oh, sorry."

Her breath sucked in as he pressed a kiss to her neck. "That's okay." He held her forearm. "You're going to aim for the center of the bag so you don't lose your balance. Just like this." He extended her arm, touching her knuckles to the bag just above eye level.

"I've never hit anyone before. Well, except…"

"Shh, you're not hitting someone. You're hitting a bag of sand. Don't worry, it doesn't have feelings." He stepped back. "Go ahead. Give it a try."

Straightening her shoulders, she punched. The bag didn't move. She took a deep breath and swung again, this time hitting a little harder.

"Good. Keep swinging until you find your rhythm."

She really wasn't good at this. She hit the bag, but it didn't make a loud noise like when guys landed a punch. After a few minutes, she lowered her arms and faced him.

He smiled expectantly. "Well, what do you think?"

"I think sex is more fun."

Shock lit his eyes and a smile broke over his face. His laughter filled her belly with a sort of liquid heat she hadn't felt in months. His lashes lowered over his dark blue eyes as he gradually approached, gentle fingers carefully brushing a hair away from her face.

"I concur."

Her breath caught as she stared up at him, uncertainty and courage melding into determination. He was going to kiss her and she wasn't going to stop him. She was ready. She wanted his lips on her.

Her lashes lowered as he tipped his head to the side, angling closer by small degrees. His warm breath skated over her mouth as the last inch separated them. She shut her eyes...

"Chloe?" The sound of Jennifer's voice had her eyes springing open. "Your one o'clock is waiting."

"Thank you, Jennifer." Chloe touched her burning cheeks and walked out of the gym without looking back. "We were just inspecting the new gym equipment."

Jennifer smiled and muttered, "Let me know when it's time to check the mats. I'll lock the door for you."

Trenton's laughter echoed.

# Forty-Two

OVER THE PAST WEEK, Chloe had been reading the worn copy of *Tristan and Isolde* Trenton left outside of her office. She was surprised Trenton owned such a novel, especially when she fanned through the pages and saw he not only read the classic but highlighted his favorite parts. The first highlight she read reminded her immediately of the first time she met him.

> "What is your name?"
> "Oh, I think it's better if we don't
> bother with names."

Though he had never asked her name when they first met, she could easily envision a better, more sophisticated version of herself giving such a response. Sometimes her fantasies let her be the woman she wished she were, rather than her actual self. They were, after all, *her* fantasies. So when she pictured Tristan and Isolde she soon found herself imagining herself and Trenton.

She was totally engrossed in the love story, which began with a journey. The hero escorted the heroine while facing a silent struggle. Should he honor his promise to the king and return his betrothed to Cornwall, or do what he believed was right for Isolde? Her heart broke a little when Isolde married the king, knowing her heart would always belong to Tristan.

> "I'll pretend it's you," Isolde
>     sobbed.
> "Come with me," Tristan had
>     pleaded.
> "I can't. Please go!"

It was unmistakably familiar, her mind returning that horrible day Trenton begged her to leave with him and she had no choice but to stay. She identified with every word of love and anguish. She ached for the couple and found their time apart tragic.

It was a beautiful story that she was glad to have read. It made her think of wasted time and the fleeting moments they had here on earth, emphasizing how important it was not to waste a single one.

On the last page, Trenton had scribbled his own words, one final surprise before she closed the book.

> Love is not told, but shown.
> What you don't whisper in my ears,
>     you breathe into my heart and
>     soul.
> I love you, Chloe. Only you. None
>     before and there will be no one
>     after.
> You are, forever, my heart.

Reading this book somehow took her back to the beginning, reminded her of moments she'd almost forgotten. Was that why he gave it to her, so she wouldn't forget where their journey began? How could she ever forget when his name played like a caress upon her heart? Their relationship was so long, it was impossible to recall the exact moment she fell in love with him, but he'd lived in her heart since the day he delivered her safely to her boys. He was her hero, her fantasy, and her survival.

Holding the book to her chest, she sighed. She fanned through the pages, brushing her fingers over his note and reading it again.

> Love is not told, but shown.
> What you don't whisper in my
>     ears...

. . .

Her smile fell and her mind stilled. Her eyes retraced his words as a horrible thought suddenly occurred to her.

She flipped through the pages, stopping at each highlighted section where he'd scrolled a quick *I love you* in the margin.

"Oh, God..." She lowered the book to her lap and stared wide-eyed at her bedroom door. "Oh, God!"

Her brow pinched as their interactions spun through her mind like a carousel, playing back and slowing at every smile. His sweet, unforgettable words whispering softly...

*"I love you, Chloe. I'd never hurt you."*

*"I love you, baby."*

*"I can't think. I can't sleep. I love you."*

*"Who gives a shit why? I love you. I love you blonde, auburn, or gray."*

*"That's how much I love you... If I can get your mind and your heart, the other parts are just a bonus."*

*"I love you, Chloe. Only you. None before and there will be no one after."*

Her hand went to her tight brow, massaging the creases of worry. "What's *wrong* with me?"

She must have told him. In all this time, everything he'd done for her, everything he made her feel... But as her mind scrambled, she couldn't place one memory where those words had come from *her*.

"Oh, my God!"

Reaching for her phone she quickly texted

Tommy to come over right away and bolted out of bed.

"Shoes. I need shoes."

"Chloe?" Tommy came racing into the bedroom and she raced past him into the den, shoving her feet into her sneakers.

"Can you watch the kids? I have to go."

"Where? What the hell's going on?"

"To Trenton's. I have to go tell him I love him!" She fisted her car keys and flung her purse over her arm.

"Finally!"

She grabbed the knob and stilled, confused. Turning back to him she said, "Wait. What do you mean *finally?*"

"Honey, we all know you haven't told him you love him. Poor poodle's been suffering for months. The torture has to end. Go! Go!"

She was the worst girlfriend ever. "But *I do* love him."

"Well, duh. We all know he's owned your heart for years. But *he* doesn't. Please, go tell him how you feel."

She swung open the door. "I'm going! Lock up behind me."

It took her twenty minutes to get to Neshannock and another ten to get to Trenton's property. She bounced in her seat as her little car barreled down the gravel drive and skidded to a stop only inches from the back of his truck.

"Please be awake."

The sensor lights kicked on and he stepped outside in a pair of jeans and nothing else. She scrambled out of her car and froze, struck dumb by the magnificent sight of him.

"Chloe? What's wrong?"

"I'm an idiot," she yelled.

He scanned the yard and scowled. "What happened? Why are you here?"

Realizing she was worrying him, she quickly reassured, "I'm fine. Everything is fine."

"I don't understand."

She took a deep breath that shook her insides. Moving to the front of her car, she faced him, the length of his truck separating them. "I *love* you, Trenton. Please tell me you know that."

His expression blanked and his head lowered, his hands pushing into his pockets. That wasn't the response she'd been expecting.

"Trenton?"

~

Trenton's heart lost its rhythm at the sound of her words and he needed a second to compose himself.

"Trenton?"

Breathing what felt like the first breath of the rest of his life, he smiled and lifted his head. She was beautifully undone, standing at his door in her mismatched clothes with those little ankle socks peeking out from her shoes.

"Say it again."

She took a small step forward. "I love you."

His heart punched inside his chest as he crossed the distance and pulled her into his arms. His face went to her shoulder, breathing her in. "I've waited an eternity to hear you say that."

Her fingers tunneled through his hair, turning his face so that he looked into her eyes. "I feel like I've loved you for an eternity."

His body shook as he studied her. The sincerity rested in those wide brown eyes. Her smile wobbled as she slowly brought her face closer to his, the innocent curiosity in her gaze tightening him in knots.

"Kiss me, Trenton."

He lifted her to him, closing the remaining distance and sealed his lips to hers. Her arms tightened around his neck as he tasted heaven. Her surrender was the most real sensation he'd ever known. She kissed him in a way that could only be love. She kissed him with passion and trust. She kissed him with promise.

"Chloe..." Her name whispered from his lips as he trailed them over her jaw to her rapid pulse. She blinked up at him, a calmness settling over him, centering him.

Her smile was fragile. "You don't have to wait anymore."

He drew back. "W—what does that mean?"

In the silver moonlight, her blush gave her an angelic glow. An adorable smile tied her full lips into a bow as she looked into his eyes. "I don't want to wait anymore. I want our future to start now."

"Does this mean...?"

"Yes. You're the only man I've ever wanted, Trenton Cole. Before you there was none and there will be no one after. Will you please make love to me?"

"You're sure?"

"I've never been more certain of anything in my life."

His mouth crashed to hers as her legs locked around his hips, lifting her higher as he pivoted toward the house. "God, I fucking love you."

He didn't put her down until he reached his bed. The sense of relief, of indescribable euphoria tunneling through him was so immense he battled to keep his emotions in check.

"Chloe," he whispered, peppering kisses along her neck and nibbling her ear.

His lips teased her throat and her pulse jumped under the swipe of his tongue. She arched into him. A whirlwind of passion tunneled through him and he reminded himself to take it slow. Her needy hands groped him, and he edged back.

"Easy..."

"It's okay," she rasped, her breasts lifting with each panted breath. "I'm okay. When I'm with you, I'm always okay."

He'd never let himself imagine the moment they'd actually be together again. He wanted to, but he'd also meant what he'd said. He only needed her mind and her heart to survive. Anything more would just be a bonus. "I can't believe you're actually here."

She cupped his face, staring into his eyes. "Thank you for waiting for me, for being so patient..."

He shut his eyes, a thousand emotions rushing to the surface. "Do you want to take the lead?" The fears she mentioned weren't ungrounded and he wanted to do this right.

Her fingers traced along the scar on his jaw and she smiled. "I trust you, Trenton. No matter what, I know I'm always safe in your arms."

His heart pinched at the sincerity in her voice, felt the truth of that trust. His mouth lowered to hers and she came alive in his arms. Every kiss was a missed opportunity coming back to them, a priceless secret the two of them shared.

Their clothes fell away as their hands became reacquainted with each other's body. Every caress radiated to his soul.

When she kissed the quivering muscles of his stomach, working her way lower, he felt as though he was being touched this way for the first time. Anyone who came before no longer mattered. And there would be no one after. She'd come back to him and they were finally here.

He sucked in a sharp breath as her mouth closed over him. His hands were gentle as he watched her, his need to touch her enough to pull her to his chest and roll her to her back.

"I want a turn."

Careful not to overwhelm her, he kept his weight off of her as he took her nipple into his mouth. He teased her slowly, licking, kissing, pinching, and sucking. Her breathing turned shallow as her legs wrapped around his waist, pulling him closer. The brush of her wet folds along his cock had him trembling with anticipation.

He shimmied down her body, stopping to lick the sensitive curve of her hip. He traced the soft seam of her thigh, not lifting his tongue until he trailed it across her clit. His cock grew unbearably thick as he tasted her. Holding her thighs, pressing his face between her legs, he savored every sweet moan he brought to her lips.

She cried out his name, her fingers pulling in his hair as her body trembled in release. He reached for the drawer and she stilled him. Sharp concern stabbed through the haze of lust as he looked into her eyes.

"What is it, doll?"

Her smile was gentle, her gaze pulling him back. "Nothing between us this time," she whispered, lacing her fingers with his. "But I do have one request."

"Anything."

"I want to face you."

Understanding why she needed to face him this first time, his face gentled and he cupped her cheek, softly kissing her lips. "See my eyes, Chloe."

She nodded.

"They won't look away from yours." He eased her back, his gaze locking with hers as her body opened to him. Her chin trembled as he lined up their bodies. He was gentle, holding eye contact as he waited for her to give him a sign that she was ready.

Her fingers trailed down his spine and she lifted into him, her lips parting as he slowly filled her.

"You okay?"

She nodded, her gaze still locked with his. "Yes."

He pushed deeper, his hands surrounding her face as he looked into her eyes. "I love you, Chloe."

"I love you too, Trenton." She blinked and he understood her tears were not made of fear or sadness.

He softly kissed them away. "You'll always be safe with me."

She smiled up at him and sniffled. "I know."

# Forty-Three

SHE'D FINALLY DONE IT. Maybe it was her revelation that she wanted to be happy. Or maybe it was realizing she loved a man who actually loved her back. The reason wasn't as important as the result. Whatever the catalyst, she'd successfully sat through her first hour of therapy that morning.

It was her first time acting as the client rather than the therapist. But she liked Dr. Shields and intended to keep her weekly appointments from now on—at least until she worked through her remaining scars and came to see them as badges of courage rather than marks of shame.

Trenton was helping in ways he probably didn't even realize. Every time he smiled at her or complimented her, it hit like a dose of confidence. She was working on communicating her own feelings as well. After years of guarding every word and being punished when the slightest sound slipped out, she'd built a habit of keeping her emotions to herself. But seeing how happy Trenton was when she shared her feelings with him helped her understand love should always be a reciprocal thing.

Imagine that, loving someone and knowing, without a doubt, they loved her back. She smiled, feeling more centered than she had in months.

It was Friday. Trenton told her not to make plans because he'd be whisking her away right after work. Adam was picking up the boys from school and she was free until tomorrow afternoon. She took a minute to appreciate her happiness. After all was said and done, she was truly happy.

There was a light knock at her office door and Trenton stepped in, a nervous set to his brow. It wasn't like him to be the worrier and whenever she sensed his concern, hers doubled. "What is it?"

His hand brushed the back of his head, another telltale sign of nerves. "I—I have something for you."

"Okay." She didn't understand his expression. For so long he'd been her compass in the dark. And whatever he was about to give her was more serious than the surprises he usually left by her door.

"Before I give it to you, I want you to know that it means nothing more than I love you, so don't read too much into it."

Now she was getting nervous. "Okay…" That was rather cryptic.

He reached into his pocket and slid an envelope in front of her.

She stared at it, not sure she wanted to know what was inside. "You know, there was an episode of *Sex in the City* when Carrie was dumped via Post-it. We women frown upon stuff like that."

He laughed but his eyes still pinched with apprehension. "Definitely not breaking up with you. Go ahead and open it."

She broke the seal and removed a slip of paper, her eyes widening at the sight of a check made out to BASE for five thousand dollars, and thirty dollars in cash. "Oh, my God, Trenton, what is this?"

"You see, seven years ago I took this job. I wound up not getting paid because I had ethical issues with the case. I did end up meeting this woman though. She was amazing—scared, yet incredibly brave. She left some things in my car, a large diamond ring, two diamond earrings and some cash I gave her to help her get back on her feet. I figured, since she was escaping a bad situation like the women you help here at BASE, she'd be happy if I sold her old ring and donated the money to help other women in similar situations."

Chloe's hands trembled as her eyes blurred with tears. "You ... kept my ring? All this time?"

"I never forgot you, Chloe. Those things weren't mine to keep. They were yours, something borrowed I'd always hoped I'd be able to return. I always hoped you found the happiness you were after. Being able to see you every day, knowing that you have, that's worth more than any diamond in the world."

She blinked rapidly, a smile contradicting her tears. "I found happiness." She laughed. "This is going to buy a lot of bus tickets."

He kneeled down in front of her and kissed her cheek. "It's yours. Do whatever you want with it." He held out his palm, two familiar studs flashing in the light. "She also gave me these, but I could tell they meant more to her than the ring, so I didn't have the heart to sell them."

She gasped. Her mother's earrings. "Oh, Trenton."

"I didn't know if—"

"They weren't from him. They belonged to my mother."

He placed them in her hand, folding her fingers over the diamond studs. "Well, I'm sure she'd want you to hold onto them."

Her lips trembled as a watery laugh escaped. "Thank you for keeping them safe for me."

He kissed her and she slid out of her chair to hug him. Pulling back, he brushed a tear from her cheek. "Now, don't get too emotional. I have big plans for tonight. How long until you're finished up here?"

She glanced at the papers sitting on her desk. "I just need five minutes."

"Perfect. I'll meet you downstairs."

When he opened the door, she called, "Trenton?"

"Yeah, doll?"

She smiled at him, her hand tightening around the earrings in her palm. "I think that woman you saved would be more than proud of what you did with her ring. I also think you don't have to worry if she's okay anymore. I have a feeling she's happier than she ever imagined possible."

His smile softened, the worry she spotted earlier replaced by a knowing look in his deep blue eyes. "I hope so."

He pulled the door closed and she opened her hand. He was incredible.

A few minutes later she put on her coat and walked downstairs, wearing her mother's earrings. Buttoning the last button on her jacket, she called for Trenton. They didn't have any residents at the moment so the facility was quiet.

"In the gym."

She loved having him so close during the days. They started their first self-defense class that week and already had a full roster for this session and the next.

She dug in her purse for her lipstick, looked up, and froze. Trenton stood in front of her, surrounded by a group of unexpected faces. She frowned in confusion when she saw Adam there with her sons, standing just in front of Jade and the babies.

"What's going on?"

Trenton stepped forward. "Chloe, you told me you were mine, always and forever. And I'd like to collect on that promise. I've asked your boys' permission and they agreed, so long as I always treat you nice, buy you cards and flowers once in a while, and extend their bedtime to ten-thirty on the weekends, they said I have their blessing. Now, I just need an answer from you." He dropped to his knee. "Chloe, doll, I want to be with you always. Make an honest man out of me and be my wife."

The faces watching her swirled as she stared through a wall of unshed tears. This was so unexpected and everyone who mattered to her was here.

How had he planned all of this without her realizing?

Overwhelmed, she covered her mouth and smiled. "You asked my boys?"

"Of course. We're all in this together."

She glanced at Dayton and Mattie. "You bribed him?"

Mattie flushed and Dayton shrugged.

She glanced at Adam and Tommy, Jade and Jeremy, Kat and Tyson. They were all there. "You all knew about this?"

"Yes, we all knew," Tommy squealed. "For the love of God, answer him!"

She looked down at Trenton, still on one knee. Twin tears tumbled past her lashes. "Of course I'll marry you. You're the love of my life."

She flinched as a loud cheer burst from their friends. Trenton stood, wrapped her in his arms, and kissed her soundly.

"Gross!" Dayton and Mattie said at the same time.

Tipped back in Trenton's hold, she stared into the sweetest blue eyes she'd ever seen and let out a shaky laugh. "I can't believe you planned all this without me knowing."

"Tommy helped."

"And my boys, you let them in on it too."

"They were so cute when I told them. Chloe ... I always wanted kids and you've got two great ones."

Another wave of emotion struck and she smiled. "I always wanted them to have a good father, someone they could count on."

"A family." He kissed her again and quickly

pulled back. "I almost forgot." He removed a small velvet box from his pocket. "Now, before you open it, if you don't like it we can pick a different one."

She laughed, certain she'd love it because it was from him. He opened the box and she gasped. It was stunning. The center stone was round and set in a ring of smaller diamonds surrounded between twin sapphire baguettes. It was bold, yet incredibly delicate and feminine.

"Trenton... It's beautiful."

He slid it onto her finger. "Don't go giving this one away."

She smiled. "Never." She wrapped her arms around him and rose to kiss him. Everyone cheered again and she whispered, "I'll wear it forever."

His happiness added to hers. There was so much love in that room that day, her soul felt at peace. Her boys laughed as Trenton teased them. Jade and Kat gushed over her ring. Tommy and Adam rattled on about wedding plans as Tyson and Jeremy toasted the future bride and groom.

Chloe took a moment to take it all in. Her future husband leaned over an iPad as Dayton showed him something on the screen, his eyes lighting up every time Trenton shared his enthusiasm. Mattie raced over with a bag of tennis balls and asked if he could play with them. Trenton promised they'd play catch.

Her hand rested over her heart and she sighed. All those layers, all the broken pieces had somehow melded back together with time and formed this beautiful foundation in front of her. It didn't matter what the outside world saw.

Inside—*in her heart*—she was whole and happy. Trenton's gaze found hers from across the room and he winked, silently mouthing *love you*. She smiled and mouthed it back. She had loved him for a long time and would love him forever more.

## THE END

**Want more edgy romance from Lydia Michaels? Read *CRUSH* next!**

**Claim your FREE book when you subscribe to Lydia's newsletter!**
Click here to sign up for Lydia Michaels' Newsletter.

Are you follow Lydia Michaels?
Stalk her on TikTok, Instagram, Facebook, Goodreads, and BookBub!
TikTok @LydiaMichaels
Instagram @lydia_michaels_books
Facebook @LydiaMichaels
Goodreads
BookBub

**Show Your LOVE**
*If you enjoyed this book, please don't forget to leave a review.*

**LYDIA MICHAELS' READING ORDER**

**MCCULLOUGH MOUNTAIN**
Almost Priest

## ADDICTED TO YOU
Crush
Bang
Throb

## THE ORDER OF VAMPIRES
Original Sin
Dark Exodus
Prodigal Son

## THE SURRENDER TRILOGY
Falling In
Breaking Out
Coming Home

## STAND ALONES
La Vie en Rose
Simple Man
Sugar
Breaking Perfect
Hurt
Protege

## About Lydia Michaels

Lydia Michaels is the award winning and bestselling author of more than forty titles, a certified life coach, and transformational speaker. She is the consecutive winner of the 2018 & 2019 *Author of the Year Award* from *Happenings Media*, as well as the recipient of the 2014 *Best Author Award* from the *Courier Times*. She has been featured in *USA Today, Romantic Times Magazine, Love & Lace,* and more. As the host and founder of the *East Coast Author Convention*, the *Behind the Keys Author Retreat*, and *Read Between the Wines*, she continues to celebrate her growing love for readers and romance novels around the world.

In 2021, Michaels released the groundbreaking, non-fiction series, ***Write 10K in a Day,*** to commemorate her career in the publishing industry. She looks forward to many more years of exploring both fiction and non-fiction writing, teaching about the craft, and learning from the others in the author community.

Lydia is happily married to her childhood sweetheart. Some of her favorite things include the scent of paperback books, listening to her husband play piano, escaping to her coastal home at the Jersey Shore, cheap wine, *Game of Thrones*, coffee, and kilts. She hopes to meet you soon at one of her many upcoming events.

You can follow Lydia at www.Facebook.-

<u>com/LydiaMichaels</u> or on Instagram
@<u>lydia_michaels_books</u>

## <u>Read By Mood</u>
### *Billionaire Romance*
<u>Falling In</u> | <u>Sacrifice Of The Pawn</u> | <u>Calamity Rayne</u> | <u>Blind</u>

### *Contemporary Romance*
<u>Wake My Heart</u> | <u>The Best Man</u> | <u>Love Me Nots</u> | <u>Pining For You</u> |<u>Almost Priest</u>| <u>My Funny Valentine</u> | <u>Side Squeeze</u> | <u>Almost Priest</u> | <u>Beautiful Distraction</u> | <u>Irish Rogue</u> | <u>British Professor</u> | <u>Broken Man</u> (LGBTQ) | <u>Controlled Chaos</u> | <u>Hard Fix</u>|<u>Intentional Risk</u>

### *Emotional Favorites*
<u>La Vie en Rose</u> | <u>Simple Man</u> | <u>Wake My Heart</u> | <u>Sacrifice of the Pawn</u> | <u>Crush</u>
### *Romantic Comedy*
<u>Calamity Rayne</u>

### *Erotic Romance*
<u>Breaking Perfect</u> | <u>Protégé</u> | <u>Falling In</u> | <u>Sugar</u>

### *First in Series*
<u>Almost Priest</u> | <u>Falling In</u> | <u>First Comes Love</u> | <u>Wake My Heart</u> | <u>Crush</u> | <u>Original Sin</u>

### *Paranormal Vampire Romance*
<u>Original Sin</u> | <u>Dark Exodus</u> | <u>Prodigal Son</u>

### *LGBTQ+ & Menage Romance*
<u>Broken Man</u> (MM) | <u>Breaking Perfect</u> (MMF) | <u>Crush</u> (MMF) | <u>Hurt</u> (Non-Consensual) | <u>Protege</u>

***Sexy Nerds & Second Chances***
Blind | Untied
***Teacher Student, Workplace, and Age-Gap
Love Affairs... Oh my!***
British Professor | Pining For You | Breaking Perfect |
Falling In | Sacrifice of the Pawn

***Single Dads & Single Moms***
Simple Man | Pining For You | First Comes Love |
Controlled Chaos | Intentional Risk

***Dark Tortured Hero Romance***
Hurt

***Non-Fiction Books for Writers***
Write 10K in a Day: Avoid Burnout

# Domestic Abuse

Domestic abuse is a pattern of behaviors used by one partner to maintain power and control over another partner in an intimate relationship. It does not discriminate by race, age, sexual orientation, religion or gender. It affects people of all socioeconomic backgrounds and educational levels.

In the United States, 24 people per minute are victims of rape, physical violence or stalking by an intimate partner. 1 in 3 adult women (35.6%) living in the United States have experienced rape, severe violence and/or stalking by an intimate partner. 30 to 60% of perpetrators of intimate partner violence leads to child abuse in the household and psychological damage to children.

If you are in an abusive situation and need a way out, the National Domestic Violence Hotline can help you develop a safety plan to escape and provide legal counsel.

DOMESTIC ABUSE

www.thehotline.org
1-800-799-7233